IN SATAN'S POWER

Without warning, the door burst in and the room was inundated with a freezing cold. Her eyes, bulging from their sockets, watched as the heavy bedspread was torn from its place and the sheets billowed upward to the ceiling. Unseen, rough hands grasped Bobbe and lifted her high above the bed before hurling her unceremoniously to the mattress.

Her lids clamped over fright-filled eyes and she yielded to an unseen weight pressing down on her, forcing her nude body deep into the mattress.

"The only thing you will be allowed to do is what you are commanded!" The voice seemed to fill the room and press in on her as much as the weight holding her to the bed. *"You will be normal when you are with people and act the holy slut necessary to be accepted!"*

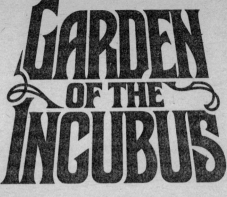

GARDEN OF THE INCUBUS

JOHN TIGGES

*The
sleep of reason
produces monsters.*

—Goya

LEISURE BOOKS NEW YORK CITY

For Kathy,
naturally

A LEISURE BOOK

Published by

Dorchester Publishing Co., Inc.
6 East 39th Street
New York, NY 10016

Printed in the United States of America

PROLOGUE

SEPTEMBER 1936

Golden shafts of September sunlight filtered through the leaves of the elm trees lining Melby Avenue, casting miniature spotlights in complete disarray on the sidewalk and well-manicured lawns. Birds, concealed within the leafy boughs, offered their songs from offstage. The unorchestrated cries of children at play, notably absent because of the reconvening of school, would miraculously reappear with the dismissal of the first day's classes. Kindergarten, the new adventure for neophyte students, always let out its small charges early, allowing new habits and routines to be learned in easy stages.

Bobbe Moore, nonchalant in her reluctant gait, paused at each new discovery she made on her way home from St. Paul's kindergarten. Why did school have to end so quickly? Just when she had gained control of the sandbox, too. No, it was a sandtable, the Sister had said. No matter. Hanging back as the rest of the children filed out of the brightly colored room, Bobbe had made Sister Evangaline promise four times that school would be held again the next day. Then the young nun had bent down and hugged the small girl before sending her on her way home.

Now, secure with the promise of more fun tomorrow, Bobbe walked slowly and lightheartedly toward her house. Proud because her mother had trusted her to make her way home alone, the six-year-old decided to enjoy her new, albeit short-lived independence. She knew the way from St. Paul's to her house on Sycamore Street by heart. Didn't she walk to church with her parents almost every Sunday? Unhappy she had not found anything of worth to explore since leaving school, she picked up her pace, trying desperately to avoid stepping on the cracks between the bricks that made up the sidewalk. After all, she certainly didn't want to break her mother's back.

The whirring clack of lawn mower blades slicing through the quiet afternoon brought Bobbe to a halt. Searching for the source of the sound, she located it in the front yard of that old man, Mr. Dudley. Somehow, she didn't like him. He was dirty and had a funny smell she didn't like at all. The well-being of her mother's spine forgotten, Bobbe moved forward carefully and quietly. Perhaps she would be able to walk right by without being seen. Just as she reached the corner of the front yard, which was surrounded by a cast-iron fence, she froze. Had he seen her? Pressing in tightly to the fence, Bobbe held her breath.

The lawn mower stopped and Edgar Dudley stared at the corner of his yard. Something had moved there. His eyes weren't as good as they had been when he was young but he swore he had seen something or someone standing beyond the fence, using the bridal wreath bush, which cowered in the corner, for camouflage. An almost toothless grin spread across his face when he realized the splotches of bright red were really a dress and a small girl was standing motionless trying not to be seen.

"Come here, honey," Dudley cooed. "Don't be afraid. I won't hurt you. I *like* little girls."

Wide eyed, Bobbe peered through her leafy protective wall. *He liked little girls?* All this time she had thought— Deciding she had been wrong, she stepped closer to the fence.

"Did you go to school today?"

"Yes," Bobbe answered in a tiny voice.

"What? I didn't hear you. You'll have to speak up. I don't hear so well. Why don't you come out in the open where I can see you?"

"Yes," she said, raising her voice slightly. "I went to school."

Don't talk to strangers, her mommy had warned as she walked out the front door when she left for school. But this man wasn't really a stranger. She had seen him many times before.

"Are you hungry, little girl? I'll bet you are. Going to school and learning all those things can make you awfully hungry, can't it?"

Bobbe stared at him through the leafy barrier but didn't move toward him. She *was* hungry and it seemed like a long way to walk home. He was right. She had gotten hungry today. Her first day of school had been exciting—new friends; Sister Evangaline, who was much younger than her mother; and now this man, whom she had always thought was a nasty old man, was really nice and concerned about her. The lunch her mother had given her had not been enough and a little snack would certainly taste good. Besides, she felt she knew this man.

"I've got some nice candy and cake in the house—just for you." His voice whispered peculiarly.

Candy and cake? Why that would taste *so* good. She was certain her mother would not let her have either one for a lunch. Stepping from behind the shield of the bush, she walked toward the gate where she hesitated. Should she go in?

"That's a good girl," Dudley encouraged. "Just push it in and—" His eyes darted back and forth in his bony head as he surveyed the immediate neighborhood. There was little if any traffic on Melby Avenue at this hour and from what he could see, his nosy neighbors were minding their own business for once. "Just follow me into the house." He smiled evilly and turned to shuffle toward the screened porch.

Her appetite whetted by the promise of candy and cake, Bobbe followed at a short distance, her mother's words forgotten.

Dudley closed his eyes, anticipating his plans for the small girl. Now that his mother was dead, he would be able to do the things that had been denied him. For years, while she had been ill and bedridden, he had been with her almost every minute. Money had not been a problem since the railroad had paid her a pension for his father's accidental death. But his life had been wasted by being a nurse to her—a mean, vindictive old woman whom he had grown to hate. Life and its rewards and pleasures had eluded him, but now—*now* he would

7

make up for them.

Fully aware of what the years and bitterness had done to him physically, he was equally aware there wasn't a woman who would have him under any circumstances. Even the small town's two prostitutes had rejected him. At fifty-eight, Edgar Dudley's gray, unruly hair projected at right angles from his angular head. The dominant feature of his narrow face was the bulbous nose separating his closely set eyes. Bloated from inactivity most of his life, Dudley knew what would happen if he asked any woman out for an evening on the town. If whores rejected him, there was no hope for any type of relation with women. He licked his thick lips when he thought of the things he had dreamed of doing with a woman—any woman.

But a little girl would be a different matter. He had watched them going to and from school for years when they had passed his house and feral fantasies had brought wild sensations to his groin, causing him to slobber drool down his chin and shirt front. How many times had he mentally rehearsed holding and caressing one of the schoolchildren? His dreams were full of girls who openly allowed him to fondle them, and when the pain in his groin would reach its epitome of frustration, he would awaken, sobbing and crying. That had been when his mother was still alive. Now, the time was right. She had been dead for three years and the fantasy he had experienced so long had suddenly presented itself in the form of Bobbe Moore, age six, and he was about to fulfill his dreams. Rubbing the bulge he felt growing in his pants, he held the screen door of the porch open for the approaching child.

"Go right on in, honey," Dudley purred breathlessly when Bobbe was on the porch.

The small girl walked hesitantly toward the open door that led to the interior of the large house. With two quick, catlike strides, he followed her in, leaving the heavy door ajar.

Standing in the dark hallway, Bobbe allowed her eyes to adjust to the gloom before turning to face the old man. "My name is Bobbe," she said cheerfully, "and today was my first day in school. I like it. I like my Sister and all of the children, too." Puzzled when Dudley didn't return her smile, she wondered why he wasn't cheerful or as kindly appearing as he had been in the yard. "Where is my candy, please?"

Dudley coughed and pointed to the living room off the hall. "In here," he said thickly, pushing the girl ahead of him. Anticipating the sensations he was about to experience for the first time in his life, he gasped uncontrollably. He crossed the room and collapsed in an overstuffed chair next to an end table. "Come here," he whispered hoarsely and picked up a glass dish containing lemon drops. "Come here and I'll give you some candy."

Bobbe edged closer to reach the candy dish the man had placed on his lap. When she touched the candy in the precariously tipped dish, his hand lashed out and roughly grabbed her by the shoulder. Struggling fitfully as he pulled her to him, she was unable to break his hold.

"Here," he said soothingly, "here's some candy. Isn't that what you came in for?" He held the dish, which had half emptied in the brief struggle, in his free hand.

Frightened by the man's sudden movement, Bobbe sobbed and wiped her eyes with the back of her right hand and took some of the yellow candy in the other.

Any thoughts of the consequences of his act were shoved from his mind as the all-possessing obsession for the child controlled him. Effortlessly, he picked her up and placed her on his lap, moaning, "There now, isn't that much better, sitting here on my knee?" He relaxed his grip to stroke her long black hair with his calloused hand.

Quieted by the realization of the promised candy, Bobbe sucked on a lemon drop and looked around the shade-darkened room. She didn't mind sitting near him although his body odor brought wrinkles to her nose. There's too much furniture, she thought and called to mind her own living room. The mental image of her mother suddenly appeared and she cast an apprehensive eye toward the door through which she and the man had just entered. She didn't like this house or this room or—well, maybe the man was all right. He had given her the candy he had promised. After having more of the lemon drops and talking with him, she would be able to decide if she really liked him.

Shifting as if to get off his lap, she cried out in pain when he tightened his grip around her waist. Placing the candy dish on the table, Dudley ran his free hand up and down her arm before dropping it to her leg. Bobbe froze and sat statuelike. Her daddy often caressed her but not like this. A tear formed in one eye to perch indecisively on the edge of her lower lid.

Without warning, he pushed the frightened child from his lap and held her with one hand while he tried to undo his belt with the other. Unable to release the buckle, he glared at her and growled, "You stay right there now, you hear me? You move and I'll spank your bottom good."

Slowly releasing his grip, he watched her for indications of disobedience to his order. Convinced she would remain standing there, he moved his hands to the stubborn belt buckle.

Bobbe watched wide eyed as the old man undid his pants and dropped them, revealing his long underwear, stained a brownish-yellow near the bottom of the row of buttons. Suddenly galvanized into action, the child darted for the door, grabbing a handful of lemon drops as she passed the candy dish, and threw them at the pants-hobbled man now struggling to maintain his balance.

"Goddamnsonofabitch!" Dudley cursed in a high-pitched scream as he saw his intended prey dashing for and through the door to the porch. "Goddamnit!" he cried again before taking up the pursuit only to fall headlong to the floor, tethered by his trousers. Rolling over, he pulled them up and, clutching his pants at the waist, stood to chase his fleeing quarry. Dudley stopped short of dashing out the screen door when he realized the girl could cry out for help if he followed her and then he would be in trouble. Just as he aborted his pursuance, he could see Bobbe racing along the outside of his cast-iron fence.

"Damn you!" he yelled, shaking his fist. "Goddamn you, anyhow! Aw, shit! Let the devil take you. Yeah! Take her, Satan, she's all yours! I don't need the little bitch! There's plenty more like her around." With tears of frustration and anger picking their way through the stubble of his beard, he turned and reentered the house, mumbling to himself.

Realizing she was not being followed, Bobbe slowed her pace and examined two pieces of sticky candy clinging to her sweaty hand that had remained when she threw the lemon drops at Dudley. Directing her footsteps toward the curb, she shook the yellow pieces loose and wiped her dirty palms on her dress. With a smile, she began skipping toward home. Several minutes later she turned the corner and was on Sycamore Street. When she was able to see her house, the tardy kindergarten child broke into a run and dashed up the front walk.

"I'm home," she cried out when the front door swung open easily.

"Well, young lady," her mother scolded, "you're late and on your very first day at school. I thought you were a big girl, Bobbe, and could be trusted to hurry right home when Sister let you out. Where have you been? Mommy's been worried sick."

Bobbe looked up at her mother, realizing she was not angry but frightened. Crossing the room, the girl put her arms around her mother's neck when the woman crouched to be nearer her prodigal daughter. "Don't cry, Mommy, I'm here now. Everything's all right."

"Where were you, Bobbe?" Clare Moore asked and held her daughter at arm's length.

"I—" Bobbe began and was ready to tell about the mean man who tried to act nice and give her candy, but the image of the incident as she remembered it slowly dissolved into nothingness only to be replaced by a small white puppy with black patches, romping across her mind's eye. "I—I saw a puppy and played with it for a while, Mommy. I'm sorry. Really, I am. I won't do it again," she whispered apologetically.

"Well, all right." Trying to remain stern, Clare hoped she was not betraying her feeling of relief at seeing her daughter home nor the amusement she was experiencing at the serious attitude of her only child. "Now, get your clothes changed and clean yourself up. Your hands are sticky and dirty."

With surrogate thoughts of the puppy milling about in her mind, Bobbe hoped her parents would get her one just like it. She had had so much fun with it. She just knew she'd love it to pieces.

Running up the stairs to her room, Bobbe hummed a tune

she had learned in school, the incident with Edgar Dudley erased from her mind forever.

PART ONE

BOBBE

**July 18, 1951
to
November 22, 1951**

CHAPTER ONE

A gentle breath of night air ruffled silver crusted leaves, sending a soft whispering through the quiet, almost deserted town park in Springfield. Overhead, stars vainly attempted to be seen only to be lost in the glow of the July full moon. Two figures embraced, kissing tenderly, before separating to look deeply into each other's eyes.

"I love you, Bobbe," Jay Livingston said softly.

"I know, Jay. I love you very much, too."

"I'm glad we went to a movie before coming out here."

"Why?" she asked, smiling as though she knew his reason.

"We're alone. I thought everyone would be gone by eleven or so and I was right."

"Why is it so important that we be alone?"

Jay looked past Bobbe Moore's head into the darkness. He didn't have to see her face to be encouraged. Every inch had been memorized years before when they first started going together in high school. The dark blue, almost violet eyes seemed to be transparent enough to view her innermost thoughts. Her finely chiseled nose, a full mouth, which was prone to break into a smile at the slightest provocation, were constantly in his memory whenever he was not with her. Shoulder length blue-black hair framed her perfectly shaped oval face—a face he loved to touch and kiss gently for fear it would shatter and he would awaken from a glorious dream.

"I think you know, Bobbe."

Her lips parted in a smile, revealing even, white teeth. "I guess you want to satisfy everyone in town by marrying me. Right?"

14

"Wrong! I don't care what anyone thinks about you and me. I do want to marry you and I can now that I'm almost finished with college."

"What do you want to talk about then, Jay?" Her forehead furrowed in puzzlement.

"I want to make plans for the future, including marriage. I'll be taking over the lumber yard when Dad retires and—well—" His voice trailed off.

"What's the matter, Jay?" she asked with an impish smile playing at the corners of her mouth. "You haven't changed your mind, have you?"

"Shhhhhh," he hissed and held up a hand for quiet.

Bobbe turned her head to look in the direction where Livingston was staring. "Do you see something or—" she began, but stopped when he motioned for her to be silent again.

"I thought I saw something move over there in those bushes," he whispered. "Yeah, there it is again. There's someone over there, watching us."

A sudden movement in the undergrowth caused Bobbe to step behind Jay and, as the shadowed greenery parted, a large black dog stepped into the moonlight.

"Is that Midnight?" Bobbe asked.

"I—I think so. It looks like him." Jay sighed with relief.

"What's the matter? You're not frightened, are you?" A smile flashed and her eyes sparkled when she teased him.

"No. But hell, you never know if someone might be trying to scare us."

"Come here, Midnight," Bobbe called to the animal. "Come on, boy. That's a good dog."

The huge canine hesitantly approached the couple. Midnight, everyone's name for the mystery dog, had just appeared one day and adopted the entire town. Few if any were able to approach the seemingly wild animal without being warned off with deep-chested growls and bared fangs.

"Hey, don't call him, Bobbe," Jay warned.

"Don't be silly, Jay. He and I are old friends. He always lets me pet him."

"You're kidding?" Jay said incredulously. How many times had he seen people try to approach the dog only to be

15

snapped at when a kind hand was offered?

Midnight stopped five feet away from Bobbe and Jay, glaring at them.

"Don't move, Bobbe," Jay said softly.

"I'm not afraid of him, Jay," she said firmly and stepped forward.

The dog's tail began wagging and he licked Bobbe's hand when she tried to pet him.

"Well, I'll be—" Jay sighed with relief. "I wouldn't have believed it." Stepping to Bobbe's side, he stopped short when the animal growled, baring his fangs.

"I don't think he likes you, darling," Bobbe said.

"Let's see if we can walk away from him." Jay held his hand out to her.

Standing, Bobbe moved to his side and they slowly left the clearing with the dog standing in the middle of the sidewalk.

"I think he got the hint," Jay said when he realized the canine was not following them. "How long have you had the ability to overcome wild animals?"

"Oh, really, Jay. He's not wild."

"Ask anyone in town and they'll tell you it's next to impossible to get close to him."

After strolling through the moonlit park for several minutes the dog soon was replaced in their minds with thoughts of their future. Choosing a picnic table swathed in moonlight, Jay helped Bobbe sit on it. Placing her feet on the seat, she leaned back resting on her thrust out arms.

"Now where were we?" he asked in mock forgetfulness. "Oh, yes. Now I remember. We were talking about getting married. Does the thought appeal to you?"

"What do you think?" she asked simply. "We've been going together since our junior year in high school. I've dated no one else while you went to college. I assume you dated no one."

"I led a really full social life—women pounding on my doors at State the whole time. Finishing three years of business in two really didn't allow any time to horse around."

"I know, Jay," she said taking his hands in hers.

"Just a minute." He pulled free of her gentle grasp and fumbled in his jacket pocket before withdrawing a small box.

After he had opened it, the diamond gathered in as much moonlight as possible and threw it back into the night.

"I know I'm being presumptuous when I take for granted you'll marry me, Bobbe, but you will, won't you?"

A sound like muffled voices suddenly approached and the dashing figure of Midnight burst into the clearing. Leaping onto the table, the animal sat next to Bobbe, his fangs bared in a silent growl.

"What the hell?" Jay blurted.

Slowly, Bobbe circled the dog's neck with her arms.

A wistful expression crossed her face settling in her eyes. "I—I'm sorry, Jay," she said quietly. "I—I can't. I can't marry you."

Her tone of voice brought a sudden expression of surprise mixed with disbelief to Jay's face when he realized she was deadly sober. "Are—are you—serious, Bobbe?" he managed after several minutes of silence that seemed to crush in on him.

"I've never been more serious in my life, Jay."

"Why, Bobbe? Why can't you marry me?" His voice reflected his thoughts plaintively as he felt the hurt of the words impressing their meaning on his numbed senses. "Why, Bobbe?" Looking at the diamond ring he held in his hand, it now seemed as drab and dull as his future would be without Bobbe Moore. When she spoke he looked up and studied her face—her beautiful face—that was now drained of all emotion.

"I can't marry, Jay. I can't ever marry you." Raising her eyes to meet his, she said quietly, "I—I've decided to enter a convent."

Stunned, his mind reeled for several minutes before he was able to muster his voice again. "You've what?" His voice was sharp as it pierced the quiet. Any minute he expected her to break into a smile to show she was trying to make his proposal memorable by refusing before accepting.

"You heard me, Jay. I've thought about the convent for a long time and—" The words, monotonous in the droning tone she had adopted since he had asked her to be his wife, grew softer until they were inaudible.

Reaching out, Livingston stopped as Midnight glowered at

him. When the animal did nothing to prevent his touching Bobbe, Jay tenderly caressed her bare arm. "You're cold. Are you all right? Bobbe, what's wrong? You're not sick or anything, are you?"

Stroking Midnight's nose, Bobbe stared hollowly at Livingston. "I'm not ill. I'm perfectly fine."

"Then tell me you're joking. My God, you really had me going there for a minute."

"I'm not joking, Jay," she insisted flatly.

"You can't be serious." Irritated, he refused to believe her. Now, feeling his anger rise, he fought to control the intruding emotion and added weakly, "I—I love you." As he studied her in the moonlight, watching and hoping for some reaction, he noted the pale, translucent quality her skin had assumed. Somehow, she seemed more like an unreal stranger than the girl he had loved for almost four years.

"It's over between us, Jay. I'm sorry if you're hurt but I feel my life belongs to someone else now," she said softly and hugged Midnight's neck. "There's no place for you or marriage in it anymore."

"My God! The convent! That's for dried-up old maids and women who can't get a man!" The words were blurted in frustration. This couldn't be happening. He was being cheated. Then, as though hearing his own words echoing back to him, he realized what he had said and apologized. "I'm sorry, Bobbe. I didn't mean that."

Smiling indifferently, her eyes stared through him into the night, her words giving voice to their listlessness. "Forgive me, Jay. I know you love me but you must forget me. It's right for both of us. You know as well as I do that things always work out for the best. When you hurt your leg playing football in high school, you never dreamed the injury would keep you out of the Army and Korea. Possibly, it may even have saved your life."

Livingston fell back, repulsed by the impression that her eyes were sinking into her skull. Recovering from the momentary illusion and convinced it was the half light of the moon, he stepped forward to be within a foot of Bobbe. Confused, he shook his head bewilderedly. "The convent? It doesn't make sense. Why the convent? Another guy I could understand, but the convent—"

"You know it's right for you to be working with your father at the lumber yard, don't you? Well, I know it's right for me to enter the convent." Staring deeper into the silvery gloom she whispered hollowly, "It's just right."

Livingston ran a hand through his blond crewcut. His mouth felt dry and his complexion seemed to blanch despite his well tanned skin. What should he do now?

"Will you take me home, Jay?" she asked with an air of finality. "I have many things to do."

"At this hour?"

"Of course not. But I do need a good night's sleep. I want to see Father Dolan and the Sisters at St. Paul's tomorrow."

"Come on," he said angrily and was startled by Midnight bounding off the table and into the shadows. When he looked at Bobbe he found her smiling radiantly. That smile. This was the Bobbe he had always known but somehow she seemed different. Despite the fact he had felt strange when she was telling him of her decision, he now felt at ease but held her in a different attitude than he had just a few short minutes before. How drastically his life had been altered by the few words and minutes that had passed between them.

Leaving the picnic table, they silently walked back to his car.

As the Pontiac glided through the deserted streets of Springfield, both were reticent. When they stopped in front of the Moore residence, Jay got out and helped Bobbe from the automobile. Reaching the front door, he took her hand in his. "Well, I guess this is it, Bobbe. I wish you'd think about this for a while before you bury yourself in some convent."

"I'm not burying myself, Jay. It's an exciting, fulfilling life and I know this is what I want. Won't you wish me luck?" Smiling, she withdrew her hand as though the gesture by itself would convince him of her sincerity.

"Yeah, lots of luck," he said bitterly. Turning on his heel, he hurried back to his car.

Bobbe watched him get into the front seat and spoke softly as he turned the motor over. "I'm sorry, Jay. I'm so sorry."

A tear welled and built up in one of her eyes before plummeting down her cheek. A sob burst forth from her chest as he drove away and she opened the front door of her home quietly. Easing it closed, she ran soundlessly up the stairs to her room. Throwing herself on the bed, she sobbed uncontrollably until sleep enveloped her in a dreamless void.

Across the street from the Moore residence, the large black dog, its amber eyes reflecting the moonlight, watched Jay Livingston hurry toward his car. When the vehicle turned the corner and was out of sight, Bobbe entered the house. The large animal stretched languidly while his tongue, lolling from the side of his mouth, began slaveringly to lick his chops.

Then he disappeared.

CHAPTER TWO

Rolling over on her back, Bobbe opened her eyes to stare at the ceiling. A blank expression held her oval face immobile as segmented thoughts ricocheted through her mind. Slowly sitting up and rubbing her temples, she wondered why she was still fully clothed. Unable to stop the patterns irresistibly forming in her memory, the scene she had played with Jay in the park the previous evening came together and repeated itself over and over.

She gasped when the enormity of the words she had spoken to Livingston finally registered. "Oh, my God!" Clasping a hand over her mouth, she stared wide eyed about the room. What had she done? Why had she said those things? Would Jay forgive her? She wouldn't blame him if he never spoke to her again. The idea! The convent! The whole thing was utterly preposterous.

Her mind racing with various apologies she could use, Bobbe slipped off the bed and began undressing. When her panties fell to the floor and she stood naked in the center of the room, a smile crossed her lips. The convent, indeed. "There's no way possible for that to happen," she said softly to herself and stopped, barely taking a breath. Someone was outside her bedroom door. "Mom?" she called, grabbing her chenille bathrobe from the chair beside her bed. "Is that you, Mom?"

At first, it sounded only like a gentle breeze edging around the corner of the house. But then, growing in volume, individual moaning voices slowly became distinguishable and Bobbe dropped the robe she held to stare at the door.

"Mom?"

Without warning, the door burst in and the room was inundated with a freezing cold. Her eyes, bulging from their sockets, watched as the heavy bedspread was torn from its place and the sheets billowed upward to the ceiling. Unseen, rough hands grasped Bobbe and lifted her high above the bed before hurling her unceremoniously to the mattress.

Her lids clamped over fright-filled eyes and she yielded to an unseen weight pressing down on her, forcing her nude body deep into the mattress.

"The only thing you will be allowed to do is what you are commanded!" The voice seemed to fill the room and press in on her as much as the weight holding her to the bed. *"You will be normal when you are with people and act the holy slut necessary to be accepted! You belong to the master and no one else! Do you understand?"*

Bobbe managed to nod.

"Answer me! You have a voice! Use it!" The hissing voice filled her head, hammering at her conscious mind.

Opening her mouth, Bobbe found it difficult to speak. "I—I under—stand," she managed.

"Good! Don't try anything on your own. I am with you now as I have been!"

Her naked body rose from the folds of the mattress and she lay on top, scarcely breathing. The same blank expression, which had held her face the previous night when she refused Jay's proposal of marriage, now commanded her features and she left the bed once more. Moving like an automaton, the girl went to the bathroom and showered mechanically.

The warm water felt relaxing and exhilarating at the same time when Bobbe thrust her face to the shower head. Now hidden deeply within her subconscious, the episode in her bedroom was gone from her mind and she reveled in the fact it was Saturday morning. Her weekends were precious and she welcomed the relief of not having to report to the F & C Insurance Agency where she had worked since her high school graduation.

There was something she *had* to do today and despite her efforts to recall the task, she frantically grasped at mental straws while toweling off after her shower. What? What did she have to do? There was something—something she had said to Jay last night—about—about? Nothing would formulate long enough for her to examine it. Please, God—? Please, God—? Why couldn't she finish the simple prayer? Assuming she must be sleepy yet, the idea of a heavenly supplication to straighten out her thoughts was abandoned. The missing thought would eventually come to her.

After rushing to her room, she found her robe where it had dropped when the door flew open and, picking it up, hung it in the closet before selecting an outfit to wear for her visit with Father Dolan. That's it, she thought. I've got to see Father Dolan—and the nuns at St. Paul's. Now, why couldn't I think of that in the bathroom?

As though guided by unseen hands, she chose a demure brown dress and plain shoes. Left untouched were the dozen pairs of thin, spike heels and brightly colored skirts, dresses, and blouses. I *must* impress Father Dolan and the nuns, she thought.

A quick check in the mirror of her dresser convinced her she was presentable, but she ignored the simple cosmetic accoutrements she normally used and left her room. Freshly perked coffee perfumed the air as she lightly made her way downstairs. A gentle clattering of dishes filtered to the living room through the closed kitchen door and Bobbe made her way to the back of the house.

The swinging door opened easily and she greeted her mother, Clare Moore. "G'morning, Mom."

"Good morning, honey," Clare said cheerfully. "The coffee's just about done."

Smiling, Bobbe didn't offer to carry on the conversation immediately. She and her mother were good friends and had always gotten along well. Now Bobbe wondered how her mother would take her decision to join the convent. How would her father accept the announcement? Following Bobbe's birth, the young couple had been told by the doctor they would not be able to have any more children, and as a result their only offspring was showered with all the love and affection Dan and Clare Moore were capable of providing.

Looking up to find her daughter staring at her, Clare said, "Is my other head showing this morning?"

"Huh? What?" Bobbe stammered. "Oh, no! I was just thinking how pretty you look this morning."

"Flattery will get you everywhere," she said and laughed while she poured two cups of coffee.

Bobbe smiled as she eased toward the door. She loved her mother's sense of humor as well as the fact they had been good friends from her earliest memories. Even though Bobbe could have passed as Clare's younger sister, there was a mutual respect that allowed the dual roles of mother and daughter as well as friends to exist simultaneously. The only time they had had any disagreement had been Bobbe's decision not to continue her education in college. That particular rift had been healed quickly, and the two continued sharing confidences as Bobbe matured into a beautiful young woman.

Now she didn't want to confide in her mother. Not right away at least. Everything had to be settled for her entry in the convent as much as possible before telling her parents. A question of doing things in proper order rose in her mind but she quickly dismissed it without giving it time to formulate.

Refusing the proffered cup of coffee her mother held in her hand, Bobbe turned and said as she headed for the swinging door, "I really don't have time, Mom." An overwhelming compulsion to run toward the outdoors and the buildings of St. Paul's filled her as she stopped, knowing Clare was staring at her.

Surprise etched deeply into Clare's face when she realized Bobbe was refusing her first cup of coffee. Both women had always enjoyed their Saturday morning coffee *klatches.* "Are you all right, honey?" she asked, setting the cup back on the counter.

"I'm fine, Mom. Really, I am," Bobbe said as her eyes darted to the clock above the sink. It was almost eight-forty-five. Father Dolan should be finished with eight o'clock Mass by now, she thought. "I just don't have time for coffee. I've got a nine o'clock appointment." She left the kitchen without waiting for any more comments. If she stayed with her mother too long, it would be difficult to resist telling her before seeing the priest and nuns.

"When will you be back—in case Jay calls?" Clare called

after her.

"In a couple of hours." She answered loud enough to be heard from the front porch and punctuated the response by slamming the screen door.

As Bobbe walked determinedly down Sycamore Street toward Melby Avenue, Jay's handsome face persistently flashed in her mind. A pleading, uncomprehending look creased into his youthful countenance, his lips forming one word over and over, "Why?" Bobbe shook her head trying to disperse the image, and when she turned the corner onto the busier street, the warmth of the July morning, the bustling activity of the avenue, and her own determination finally succeeded in ridding her of Jay Livingston's puzzled face.

Up ahead she could see Edgar Dudley watering his lawn, his gray shaggy hair sprouting in confused profusion from beneath his sweat-stained hat. Quickening her pace to pass him and his dark, foreboding house before he stopped her for some reason, Bobbe wondered why she felt such a revulsion for the old man. Old. He had seemed old from the very first time she had ever seen him. But the queer, uneasy feeling, which struck at her like a venomous snake whenever she saw him or walked by his house, now seemed out of control. There had been Hallowe'ens in the past when she and her friends had harassed the man and they had wound up in trouble with their parents. Nothing had ever been done to warrant involvement with the police but those few episodes had been the only times she had felt secure and at ease when he was near. Perhaps she had felt safety in numbers.

Sensations of having her wishes fulfilled when she visited with the priest and nuns swept over her, and a feeling of exuberance brought a radiant smile to her face. "Good morning, Mr. Dudley," she cried out cheerfully before she could analyze her feelings.

The old man, startled at the sound of her voice, turned to see who was greeting him so happily and inadvertently turned his squirting hose directly into an open window in his living room.

Almost as startled at the friendly outburst, Bobbe was out of hearing range when Dudley realized where the errant stream of water was going and his curses and threats

25

evaporated harmlessly in the warm air.

The remaining two blocks she had to walk were soon behind her and she directed her way toward the rectory, next door to the church. Low bushes and carefully tended flowers bordered the brick walk leading to the old frame house's front entrance. A feeling of inadequacy punched at her, sending her reeling toward the door. What would she say? How should she say whatever it was she came to say? Perhaps Father Dolan would help her. She hoped he would. Slowly, her finger came opposite the doorbell and she pressed it firmly, sending a harsh, grating noise sawing through the quiet house.

Several minutes passed while Bobbe stared blankly at the wooden barrier separating her from her goal before the door swung open.

"Yes?" the large, white haired woman looming in the doorway demanded.

Fighting the urge to turn and run from the rectory as fast as she could, Bobbe spoke timidly. "Is Father Dolan busy? I'd like to see him. It—it's very important."

"Hmph!" the housekeeper snorted as she swung the door open wider, allowing the girl to enter. It's always important, she thought. Why can't they just stop by and visit with him once in a while? Poor man. Poor, lonely man. "Whom should I say is calling?" she asked and glowered at the girl standing in the hallway.

"Roberta Moore, ma'am."

When the heavyset woman indicated a small office off the hallway in which they were standing, Bobbe obediently stepped in and sat down on a straightbacked chair. A large rolltop desk held a rigid dominance over the small room by virtue of its size. Papers and stacks of correspondence vomiting from the open cavity hinted eloquently that the top had not seen the light of day for many years. Several file cabinets lined one wall and held their overflow in unsymmetrical stacks reaching almost to the ceiling. Old, faded certificates and diplomas hung askew on the wall, which Bobbe faced, surrounding a picture of Jesus. Puckering her full lips to spit at the image of Christ, she stopped when she heard padded footsteps in the hall.

"Good morning, Roberta," the thin priest said cheerfully,

extending his hand to greet his attractive guest. "How are you this morning?"

"Good morning, Father," she said smiling as they both sat down.

"Well, there must be some reason to make you come see your pastor on a Saturday morning. What is it, child?" His eyes twinkled with good humor. He was positive he knew why Roberta Moore was calling on him. But where was young Livingston? Why wasn't he here?

"Father," Bobbe began hesitantly, "I—I've decided to—to become a Sister of the Bearer of the Divine Word." Dropping her eyes to avoid his penetrating stare, she clasped her hands tightly together until her knuckles turned white.

Dumbfounded, Dolan's face froze in the cheery smile he had displayed seconds before but his eyes no longer twinkled. With a shake of his head, he regained his composure and scrutinized the young woman sitting opposite him. Was she serious? A beautiful radiance sparkled from her lovely face and he found enthusiasm smouldering in her eyes.

"Well," the old man said, running his fingers through his snow white hair after several long minutes had crawled by. "If you had come in here and said the Pope himself was to be my next assistant, I don't think I could be more surprised. How long have you been considering the convent, Roberta?"

"I—I can't honestly say, Father. I guess—for a long time."

"What about Jay Livingston?" he asked looking at her intently. "You've been dating him for some time now, haven't you?"

Bobbe slowly nodded her head.

"I assume you've talked with him about this."

A hesitant shake of her head intensified Dolan's attention. "You haven't? I assumed, since you two were keeping such close company, that you'd come here to arrange your wedding. Had you ever talked marriage with Jay?"

Raising her face to meet his watery hazel eyes, Bobbe thought her answer through before finally speaking. "We talked about a lot of things, Father. I—guess we talked about marriage—at one time or another—but—I didn't believe it was serious. He asked me to marry him last night."

"What did you say?" he exclaimed, his eyebrows arching.

Bobbe blinked to remove Jay's countenance from her mind again. "Well—naturally I told him what I wanted to do with my life." Closing her eyes, Jay appeared instantly and was gone when she opened them to face the priest. What did she want to do with her life? Uncertain of her participation in the conversation with the priest, she felt more like an observer. Why did she have to force each answer as though it were something unpalatable she wanted out of her mouth?

"What was his reaction?" Dolan asked, unmindful of the girl's uneasiness.

"He was—upset, I guess you'd say. But really, Father, he shouldn't have been. I don't believe I ever gave him reason to think I was ready for marriage."

"You're absolutely positive of this, Roberta?"

"Yes. Yes, I am," she said quickly, suddenly aware of the fact she had all the answers to whatever questions the cleric would ask. "I have something to say about my life and what I want to do with it, don't I? I don't think it's right for people to pair off young couples and expect them to get married just because it seems it would be right. Do you, Father?"

Confident of herself now, Bobbe sat back in the chair and relaxed.

A rueful smile crossed his face as he mentally chastised himself for being guilty of the girl's encompassing charge. "I do agree with you, Roberta. Young people should have the right to pick their own partners and vocations in life—just as you apparently have. My, it's been a long time since St. Paul's has had a youngster choose a religious vocation. I assume you've visited with the nuns quite a bit?"

"No. Not yet. Outside of Jay, you're the first to know, Father. You see—"

"Not even your parents?" Dolan blurted.

"No, Father. You see, I wanted to tell them after I talked with you and the nuns. I wanted to be positive this was—was—"

"Genuine?" he finished for her when he realized she was groping for the word.

"Yes. Genuine."

"Well, Roberta, I've known you and your parents for an awfully long time and I can't think of any reason why you wouldn't make a good candidate for the convent. As far as I know, you've led a good, exemplary life and should certainly be able to contribute much to the fulfillment of Christ's work here on earth. After you finish visiting with Sister Basil, I'll be requested to write a letter of recommendation for you. Rest assured, I will recommend you most highly."

"Oh, thank you, Father," Bobbe answered with a broad smile that didn't reflect warmth but instead, seemed to be forced.

"Now, before you go," the priest said as he stood, "let me bless you, child."

Bobbe dropped to her knees before the man and bowed her head.

Spreading his arms, he began speaking in Latin, so fast it seemed to be an unintelligible mumble until he brought his hands together before making the sign of the cross over her. Then, slowing the cadence of the prayer, the priest said clearly, "*In nomine Patris, et Filius, et Spiritus Sanctus. Amen.*"

While he invoked the blessing with closed eyes, Bobbe's face tightened into a grotesque mask. When she stood, her radiant smile beamed at the older man.

"Thank you, Father," she said humbly.

"Thank you, Roberta. This makes me as happy as, I'm sure, it's made you," Dolan said escorting Bobbe to the front door where they said their good-byes.

She could hear the door close softly behind her as she retraced her steps along the brick sidewalk. Somehow she felt totally alone—as though she were the only person in the world. The door closing behind her had not sounded right— what had it reminded her of? Something—but what? It had closed but it was closing a million miles away from her. Afraid to turn for fear the house wouldn't be where it should, she shuffled mechanically toward the front walk.

The last thing Jay Livingston wanted to do was stop at Moore's Service Station but the load of lumber on the flat bed he was driving had to be delivered before noon and the International's tank was almost empty. Gingerly guiding the loaded truck into the far position opposite the outer island, he turned the ignition off and hoped one of Dan Moore's helpers would come out to fill his tank instead of Bobbe's father. If he hadn't insisted on running an open account at Moore's for their fleet of trucks, Jay wouldn't have to run the risk of facing the good-natured man this morning.

"'Morning, Jay. How you doin'?"

Livingston didn't have to look. It was Dan Moore—his weatherbeaten face wrinkled into a beaming smile when he saw his future son-in-law. "Hi, Mr. Moore," he offered sheepishly and pushed the driver's door open.

"Boy, that must have been some night, last night," Dan said as he unscrewed the gas tank cap.

"Huh? What do you mean?" Jay sputtered.

"You look like you haven't been to bed. I thought I heard Bobbe come in around midnight," Dan said pointing to Jay's puffed eyes—eyes that hadn't seen sleep the previous night. Scuffing the toe of the one shoe on the concrete apron which supported the gasoline pumps, Jay said softly, "You did. I guess it was just about midnight." Unaware his emotions were so close to the surface of his very being, Jay had lain across his bed until morning, weeping for the loss of Bobbe's love.

"When you two goin' to tie the knot?" Dan pressed as he wiped the truck's windshield.

Damnit! Damnit, damnit, damnit! Why did he have to ask? He should know there wasn't going to be any wedding. At least, not for Bobbe and him. Maybe he didn't know. Jay brought his eyes up to face Dan who was watching him and rubbing the glass clean by instinct.

Moore's love of the outdoors was etched deeply into the ten miles of bad roads he called a face. A warm spirit beamed from his eyes and the laugh lines he had developed to go with the effects of hours of harsh weather denied any temper or irrationality.

"Well?" Moore asked again when he moved to the passenger's side to clean the glass.

Shrugging his shoulders, Jay tried to speak but found himself unable. We're not getting married, Mr. Moore, he wanted to say. Your daffy daughter has decided to run off and join the convent. Sorry 'bout that. I tried. *Damnit!*

30

Another car pulling into the drive distracted Dan and when the tank was full, Jay quickly pulled the nozzle from the neck and screwed the lid on. "Just charge it, Mr. Moore," he called, putting the hose back in place.

Dan's farewell was lost as Jay revved the motor and pulled away from the island. If Dan Moore didn't know about Bobbe's plans, he'd soon find out. What the hell? He didn't care anymore, did he? Somehow he knew he'd make the adjustment and accept the fact his life would not be shared by Bobbe Moore. All he wanted was a logical explanation from her. An explanation he could understand.

Turning the truck onto Melby Avenue, he thought of all the times he had stopped at Moore's residence while out delivering for his father, to spend just a few minutes with Bobbe on the days she didn't work. Not today. She had made that painfully clear last night. She didn't want to marry him and she wanted to enter a convent. Fine by him.

A bitter sour taste filled his mouth as he drove past St. Paul's Church and rectory. None of it made sense but—did he care? He might for a while but it would pass. That was the conclusion he had drawn just as the sun had begun graying the eastern horizon. It would be hard but he'd get over it.

Wiping his damp cheeks with the back of his hand, he pressed on the accelerator, sending the truck roaring down Melby Avenue past the church property. Jay kept his eyes glued to the road and didn't see Bobbe emerge from the priest's house.

Just as she reached the walk that would take her past the church and to the nuns' house, she stopped in midstride when she heard the same deep voice she had encountered earlier in her bedroom. A quiescent expression, similar to the one she had displayed to Jay the previous evening, eased across her face.

"Keep moving!" the voice boomed within her head. *"You got by him all right! Now for the nuns!"*

Obediently, Bobbe turned from the walk that led to the rectory and headed for the Sisters' home on the other side of St. Paul's church.

High bushes surrounded the sides and back of the large frame house and only the front was completely visible from

Melby Avenue. When she had mounted the steps to the small front porch, she rang the bell. A distant muffled buzz could be heard filtering from inside, followed by hurried footsteps. The heavy door swung open and a short, older nun, Sister Isadore, stood in the entrance.

"Yes?" she inquired sweetly.

"Hello, Sister, how are you?" Bobbe said when she recognized her former sixth grade teacher.

"Should I know you?" the older woman asked, searching Bobbe's face for some clue to a name from her past.

"I'm Roberta Moore, Sister."

"Roberta? My, how you've changed. Come in, come in. How are you?" The nun stepped back to allow the visitor entry.

"Just fine, Sister," she answered blandly and slipped past the nun, into the cool, half light of the hallway.

"What have you been doing since you left St. Paul's?"

"Well, I graduated from high school in forty-nine and I've been working at the F & C Insurance Agency since then."

"Not married yet, are you?" the nun asked with a twinkle in her eyes.

"No, I'm not, Sister. Is—is Sister Basil in?"

"I believe so. Take a seat in the parlor and I'll go fetch her for you. It's been very good, seeing you again, Roberta," she called over her shoulder as she moved down the hallway.

Bobbe couldn't remember the nuns ever treating her so cordially when she had been a student at St. Paul's. Whenever she had had occasion to be in the nuns' home, she had always been instructed by one of the women to wait here, in the hall. Somehow, the hall had always reminded her of a tunnel leading to oblivion. Turning, she entered the small room and found it cool but stuffy, with its windows closed and shades drawn. She selected an overstuffed easy chair that appeared more comfortable than its lumps would allow. The peculiar feeling invaded her again. What was she doing here—here in the parish convent building? She didn't belong here—did she? Maybe she should leave—now—while she was able.

"Stay seated!" the voice ordered. *"You're going to be a nun and I'll help make you the best!"*

Bobbe felt herself being forced back into the depths of the chair, the weight of her own body being reinforced by some unnatural, unseen thing.

If I want to leave, she thought, why don't I just get up and walk out?"

Blinding sunlight gushed into the room as one of the shades suddenly flew to the top of the window with a flap, flap, flap.

The weight gone from her body, Bobbe leaped to her feet and stood quivering like a lamb frightened of its own shadow. Unable to move farther, her legs felt as if they were made of lead and would not obey her commands to move. The sound of approaching footsteps in the hallway grew louder.

"Sit down!" the voice bellowed within her. Lowering herself into the chair again, she awaited the arrival of the nun.

The figure of Sister Basil, Sister Superior of the nuns assigned to the convent at St. Paul's, appeared in the doorway where she hesitated momentarily before entering to greet her visitor.

"Roberta, how are you?" she asked crossing the room in an authoritative manner.

"Very well, Sister," Bobbe answered timidly and stood, her instincts of survival suddenly honed to the same degree of sharpness she had experienced in Sister Basil's fifth grade. For some reason Bobbe had never been able to fathom, the nun had always frightened her as a child and now the same fear gripped her. The hawk nose and sharply chiseled features wrapped in the coif gave the woman an almost ominous appearance.

"What can I do for you, Roberta?" she asked pointedly.

"I—I just came from Father Dolan and—and he said I would have to talk with you, Sister," Bobbe said apprehensively, feeling like a little girl again. Ever since she had seen *The Wizard of Oz,* Bobbe had thought Sister Basil and the wicked witch could have passed for sisters. The same feeling of terror she had experienced the first time she became aware of the resemblance now filled her.

"Well," the nun snapped impatiently, "what is it you have to see me about? My time is valuable."

"Sister," Bobbe said in a stilted manner, "I have—arrived at the decision—I—I belong to—to God and I want to serve Him by entering the—your convent." Feeling a bit more at ease now with the reason for her visit in the open, Bobbe sat on the edge of the easy chair.

After jockeying a straight-backed chair opposite Bobbe, Sister Basil sat down and smiled warmly. "That *is* wonderful news, Roberta," she began, her manner changed from that of the efficient Sister Superior to one resembling a confidential friend. "How long have you thought about this?"

"I—I guess for quite some time, Sister," Bobbe said in a soft voice.

"You guess?"

"I'm not certain when I considered it seriously."

"It was just there one day?"

"Y—yes."

"Not unusual."

"Actually, I turned Jay Livingston's proposal of marriage down last night. He was—"

"I was going to ask you about that," the nun broke in with a serious tone of voice. "I'd heard you and he were seeing quite a lot of each other. Had the two of you ever discussed marriage before last night?"

"In an offhand way, Sister. I guess he was serious while I was still trying to determine what I really wanted out of life." The words were rolling smoothly from her tongue and any signs of hesitation were now completely gone.

"Are you completely sure of this, Roberta?"

"Oh, yes, Sister. Absolutely."

"What do you know about our order? Anything?"

Bobbe could feel the blood draining from her face. What *did* she know about the order? Closing her eyes to blot the waiting nun from her vision, she suddenly knew everything about the community of nuns and its history.

"It was founded," she began in a hollow voice and opened her eyes to level her gaze at Sister Basil, "in 1521 by Sister Theodosia Hummel of Luxembourg and was established to aid priests in the missionary field. When China began opening up to trade with the west, Sisters of the Bearer of the Divine Word were among the first to visit the Orient. However, since the Communist takeover of China, the order's activities have been redirected to Africa. Is that right, Sister?"

"Correct," Sister Basil intoned as though hearing a history lesson being recited by a student, but she was unable to suppress a smile of delight.

"Your rules are quite strict, and members of the order staff schools in parishes like St. Paul's all over the United States. The mother house for the United States is located at Cedar Falls, where my life as a nun will begin," Bobbe recited unemotionally.

When the nun saw Bobbe was waiting for a comment from her, she said, "Ours is a simple order, Roberta. We are teachers and missionaries. Strict? Yes, I suppose we are by certain standards. But if you are going to give your life to God, the rules by which you live should not make any difference, should they?"

"No. Of course not," Bobbe agreed automatically.

"You understand, of course, your college courses would have to be completed before you could teach."

Bobbe nodded.

"If it is determined you should go to the foreign missions, you would have additional courses in language and history and so forth," she added, studying Bobbe who now exuded a warm innocence that had been absent during her recitation. Standing, Sister Basil began pacing the room. Could a young woman as beautiful as Roberta Moore be willing to give up her worldly pleasures for the barren existence of the convent? Why not? In God's eyes all his children were equal and beauty or the lack of it was not a criterion for the religious life.

"How long will it be before I am a full-fledged nun, Sister?" Bobbe asked as she watched the woman pace back and forth.

Stopping at the window whose shade now rested at the top, Sister Basil stared outside. Without turning, she asked, "Are you absolutely certain you would be willing to die, right now, for Christ, Roberta?"

"Wh—what do you mean, Sister?" Bobbe stammered in amazement.

"Would you be willing to give your life for Christ?" the woman asked again without facing Bobbe.

The quiet of the room pressed in on Bobbe as she mulled

the question over in her mind. "Of course I would, Sister," she said with finality. "If that is the way I can best serve him, then I would not be afraid." An evil smile crossed her face but disappeared when the nun turned and crossed the room toward the seated girl.

Certain of Roberta's vocation now, Sister Basil smiled broadly. Many girls thought they had a vocation but had never taken the aspect of dying for Christ, under any circumstances, into account. Usually, a young person, when forced to think of dying, would be repelled and attempt to change the subject. Few ever want to think of their own death. But this one sitting here, this beautiful young girl, would not be afraid to die for her God. "I'm sorry, Roberta," she apologized, "you asked a question before and I didn't answer it. What was it?"

"How long would it take to become a nun—so I could go to Africa?" Had she thought of going to Africa? Why not? The Dark Continent would be a wonderful place—no—*the* place she would have to be assigned.

"We make absolutely certain our postulants are not making a mistake by having them take general college courses for the first year. During that year you experience convent life and life as a nun. If you feel, and the Reverend Mother feels, you should continue, you become a novice. At the conclusion of your first year as a novice, you take your first vows. You continue your studies and take your final vows at the end of your third year as a novice, or fourth year at the convent."

"I'm so happy, Sister," Bobbe said enthusiastically. Despite her bubbling voice, her eyes, dull and vacant, clung to the woman, boring into her, not allowing the slightest chance for faltering on the part of the nun at this point. "I don't know when I've been happier in my life. When may I enter?"

Knitting her brows in concentration, Sister Basil turned away from Bobbe to clear her mind. "It's almost the end of July—there should be time to finalize your application so you can enter this fall. I believe the courses begin September fifteenth. I'll ask Father Dolan to write a letter of recommendation and I'll also want to interview your parents. What do they think about your joining?"

Shrugging her shoulders, Bobbe said softly, "I—I haven't

told them yet."

"You haven't told your mother and father?" the nun snapped and was instantly transformed into the wicked witch Bobbe had feared so much as a child. "Why haven't you?"

"Well, as I said," Bobbe said quietly but firmly, "I've been thinking about this for a long time but I wanted to make the decision myself before I told anyone. I just decided to talk with Father Dolan and you first."

"Well, for heaven's sake, hurry home now and tell them, child."

"I will, Sister," Bobbe said and rose to leave.

"Don't forget to tell them I want to visit with them," she added following the girl to the front door.

"I won't, Sister."

As Bobbe walked down the front steps of the convent building, the rough voice growled at her. *"You're as good as in. Behave yourself and do what the MASTER commands. Step out of line and you'll be sorry."*

Without a backward glance at St. Paul's, Bobbe walked toward her home.

CHAPTER THREE

"Coffee?" Clare asked when Bobbe sat down at the kitchen table.

"I want to talk with you, Mom," Bobbe said seriously, nodding her head in answer to her mother's question.

"About what?" Clare placed two mugs of coffee on the table and sat down opposite Bobbe.

Staring into the dark liquid, she absentmindedly stirred it, knowing she would have to pick and choose her words carefully. *Don't just blurt it out*, the voice whispered. *Be casual. Relax.*

"Mom," she began hesitantly, "do you have any idea where I went this morning?"

Clare studied her daughter's face before answering. After a several second pause, she said, "No. No, I don't. There's nothing wrong, is there? You don't have a problem of any type, do you?"

Although her face burst into its widest smile, Bobbe felt she was forcing the air of serious nonchalance that was necessary at this point. "No, Mom," she said with a little laugh, "there's nothing wrong. No problems. I went to see Father Dolan and the—"

"Father Do—" Clare exclaimed. "You're getting married, aren't you? Oh, Bobbe, I'm so happy for you. But—but—why didn't you tell me first?" A look of puzzlement replaced her happy, excited smile.

Reaching a well-manicured hand out to touch her mother's, Bobbe sobered. "No, I'm not getting married," she said simply.

Clare grasped her daughter's hand and squeezed it tightly. "You're not? You and Jay aren't getting married? Then, why did you see the priest?"

Bobbe coughed, clearing her throat. "I went to see Father Dolan because I—I'm entering the convent. I went to see the nuns, too."

Releasing Bobbe's hand, Clare could feel the blood draining from her face. "The—the what? I don't think I heard you correctly."

"You heard me all right, Mom," Bobbe said softly. "I've decided to enter the convent. The same one the nuns at St. Paul's belong to."

"You've never talked about it. Not once. Never. What made you decide this?"

With a shrug of her shoulders, Bobbe stood and walked to the sink. Turning, she leaned against the counter to stare at her mother. They had had differences of opinion so infrequently, had been such good friends, that now Bobbe was mentally grasping at words that would convince her mother with the least amount of effort. The last time, the only time before this, Bobbe had ever seen her mother with a look of anguish creasing her face, was when she had announced her decision not to continue her education.

"I just don't want to go to college, Mother," she had said over and over. "I'm perfectly equipped to get a job in an office anyplace."

"But darling," her mother persisted, "you have so much going for you with full scholarships to two different schools—"

"And both out of state and away from you and Daddy," Bobbe said, finishing Clare's statement with her own argument.

"You have to leave sometime," Clare said soothingly. "There are times when I question if we raised you right or not."

"Mother!" Bobbe said in shock. Why would her mother say something so untrue? "That's not right and you know it. You and Daddy are good—no, the best parents in the world."

"We're not, if you're totally dependent on us and can't or won't leave home," Clare said flatly.

"You're not getting anyplace," Dan interjected. "I think I might have a solution that will please both of you."

Bobbe and Clare turned to face the burly man.

"Why don't you take a year off, Bobbe?" he said and rose from his easy chair where he had been listening to the verbal tennis match. "At the end of that time if you have a job and are happy with it, your mother and I won't pressure you to go to college. If, on the other hand, you're not happy, we'll investigate those scholarships—if they're still available."

"But, Dan—" Clare began but was stopped with an upraised hand from her husband.

"That's the way it's going to be, if Bobbe agrees to the idea. Bobbe?"

"Can I sleep on it?" she said and winked at her father. Dan had always told her not to make snap decisions about anything important without sleeping on it first and certainly this was important enough to warrant at least one night's sleep.

"You're the one who has to do the deciding, honey," Dan said nodding his head in agreement.

Her decision had been to take the year off from school and find a job, which she had done the same day. Within her first, crucial year as secretary to the owner and general agent of the F & C Insurance Agency, she was promoted to office manager when her predecessor resigned to get married.

Happy with her advancement, Bobbe had made her mind up to forsake further education and had her decision reinforced shortly before the year's trial was about to expire. Approaching the kitchen one Sunday morning after Mass, she overheard her father say, "I'm just glad she's staying here."

"Dan!" Clare exclaimed. "You don't know for a fact she's not going back to school. Or has she said something to you?"

"She hasn't said anything to me. The reason I'm glad is there's no telling what would happen if she did go away to school. I'd just as soon have her living down the street from us, raising kids, and being close to us."

"Do you really mean that, Dan?" Clare asked, disbelief evident in her voice.

40

"Darn right I do. There's just too much going on in the world to shove your kid into it. Take that police action in Korea—police action, hell! It's a war and it's taking a lot of young fellas away from school and work. And you hear about girls getting into trouble with guys all the time. I'm damned glad we have a girl like Bobbe, instead of a boy."

"Why?" Clare asked, knowing Dan had on more than one occasion bemoaned the fact he had no son to take fishing and hunting.

"Because if a boy didn't want to go to college in this day and age, he'd wind up in the Army or something and probably go to Korea. Maybe get killed or maimed. Then, in order to stay out of that situation, if he went to college he'd be nothing better than a draft dodger."

Bobbe could still hear her father's voice now as she watched her mother who was seated at the kitchen table, shock and disbelief etched into her face.

"What made you decide this, Bobbe?" Clare repeated, breaking the startled silence that pressed in on the room whenever there was a lull in the conversation.

"I—I don't know. I guess these things just sort of happen. Sister Basil didn't seem to think it was out of the ordinary."

"I just don't believe it," Clare said again. "What about Jay?"

"What about him?"

"What's he think?"

"He was surprised. But he understood." Her forehead wrinkled. She thought he had understood.

"I can well imagine how surprised he was. Your father and I have been waiting for—for—well, you two to get married. I question if you really know what you're doing."

"I know all right. Marriage is just not for me."

Clare stood and walked to the kitchen window. "All my life—at least ever since you were born, I've waited for the day I could do something for you. Something I had never had done for me."

"What are you talking about?"

"You don't remember Grandmother Simms, do you?"

"Your mother?"

"My stepmother. I was always afraid of her. She was always so prim and straitlaced that I was petrified if I ever did anything wrong. The day I came home and told her and my father your dad had asked me to marry him, she pulled me out of the room and gave me her so-called advice. What to do and what not to do where—well, you know, things in the bedroom were concerned. She said, 'When you get married, you have a duty to perform for your husband. There's not much I can tell you about it, other than it will hurt terribly and is not very enjoyable. But if you desire children, you'll have to endure the hardship of your husband's carnal desires.'"

"Oh, Mom. That's awful. She really said that?"

"She was wrong," Clare said nodding. "Your father and I love each other and we've gotten along beautifully. I always thought I could tell you better than my stepmother ever told me. Now—" She spun about to shut her daughter from her sight and prevent the girl from seeing the tears flowing down her cheeks.

Bobbe crossed the room and turned Clare to face her. They embraced.

"Now," Clare said between little sobs, "I'll never have the chance to confide in you about things we would have in common if you were getting married instead of going to the convent. I still don't believe it."

"Father Dolan and Sister Basil both want to talk to you and Daddy. Then, they can make the arrangements for my admission."

"When—when would you go?"

"In September."

With an incredulous expression replacing the mask of shock and hurt, Clare said, twisting away from her daughter, "I still don't believe it. You've never been particularly religious. The convent? No! Not you."

"Why is it so difficult to believe? Aren't you happy for me?" Bobbe asked with a pout forming on her full mouth. Tears of anger and frustration began building in her eyes.

"Oh, darling." Clare recrossed the room and took her daughter's hands in hers, suddenly accepting the direction Bobbe's life would now take. "Of course, I'm happy for you. It's just that—well, it is unexpected. You have to admit that much. You've been dating Jay for over three years and never once gave any indication of what you were actually thinking."

Pulling her hands from Clare's grasp, she said, "I guess I have thought about it for a long time. The idea of marriage just doesn't appeal to me. Sister Basil told me a lot about the convent and I'm really excited. What do you think Daddy will say?"

Dan Moore sensed a tenseness in the atmosphere of his home when he entered the kitchen shortly after one-thirty that afternoon. Saturday was his favorite day, since the traffic at the station slowed to a dribble and he allowed himself the luxury of a half day off. He had a good assistant in Marty Miltonson who shouldered the responsibility of the business's operation whenever Dan was not there. On his way home he had anticipated cutting the lawn and having a few beers while listening to the broadcast of the Cubs and Giants ballgame. Lying under the willow tree with the radio playing in the garage nearby, smelling the freshly cut grass as he closed his eyes, picturing the game action as it was described was the only way Dan Moore wanted to relax on a balmy summer day.

But now, as he stood in the center of the kitchen, he knew something was amiss—something was not just right. When Clare and Bobbe joined him within seconds of his arrival, he could tell something was wrong. Clare's still surprised but drawn look reminded Dan of a customer who had been told his transmission must be replaced. In contrast to her mother's appearance, Bobbe was relaxed although Moore thought he detected a touch of unrest in his daughter.

"Give it to me in easy doses," he quipped, hoping his expansive mood would soon erase the air of apprehension he found exuding from his wife.

"You'd better tell him right now, Bobbe. I can't," Clare said evenly.

Before Dan could draw a hasty conclusion as to the cause of his wife's upset, Bobbe spoke.

"You'd better sit down, Daddy," she said, pulling a chair out from the table.

Dan fixed his eyes on his daughter and gingerly sat on the edge of the chrome-legged chair.

When she saw he was relaxed, she continued. "I saw the nuns at St. Paul's this morning and they want to talk with

43

you and Mommy."

"Why, for heaven's sake?" Dan asked, diverting his eyes to Clare who was staring into space.

"I—I've decided to enter the convent." Bobbe held her breath, not knowing how her announcement would affect her father.

The hum of the refrigerator suddenly seemed to fill the room while Dan digested the simple announcement. Standing, he moved to the window overlooking the backyard, where he stood silently.

When she realized Bobbe had told her father, Clare snapped out of her lethargy. "Are you all right, Dan?"

"I'm fine, I think. I also think I'm hearing things," he said slowly. Without moving, he continued surveying the yard, mentally calculating how long it would take to mow the lawn. Stretching his six-foot frame, he turned to face his wife and daughter.

"You're not hearing things, Daddy," Bobbe said. "I really want to join the convent."

"And I want to be president of Signal Oil," Dan snapped. "How long? How long have you thought about this, Bobbe?"

"Why—why for quite a while," she said, taken off guard by her father's gruff attitude.

"What about Jay?" he asked, recalling young Livingston's evasive manner earlier that morning when he had been at the gas station.

"We talked it all out last night. We parted friends," she said as her brows knitted together in thought. They *had* parted friends, she was almost positive. The doubtful thought had entered her mind only to be erased before it could be examined.

"Are you really serious about this?" Shaking his head, he hoped the negative motion would be contagious and she would deny the whole thing as a practical joke she had concocted to tease her parents.

"I am *really* serious, Daddy. Be *for* me, not *against* me," she said with a pleading sigh. "You were all for me not going to college and wished nothing but happiness and safety for me. Remember?"

Dan reflected at length for several moments before

nodding his head in reluctant agreement. Closing his eyes, he mentally watched the picture he had created in his mind—a picture of Bobbe, Jay, and several children—his grandchildren—dissolve into nothingness.

"Well, then," Bobbe continued her argument, "I'm very happy having made this decision and you certainly couldn't ask for a safer place than the convent." She smiled triumphantly but wondered why she felt so empty over the victory.

Clare continued studying her husband's face, knowing he was beginning to accept the choice their daughter had made.

Coughing to clear his throat of the lump he had found forming when the last grandchild had disappeared, he managed, "I suppose you've slept on this?"

Again her brows pulled together in thought. Had last night, when Jay asked her to marry him, really been the first time she had spoken of or even thought of entering the religious life? No. That would be ridiculous. She must have thought about it very much to make the announcement now. Her thoughts were too well drawn only to have this be a whim or snap decision. She felt her stomach tighten. "Many nights," she blurted. "I have thought this whole thing through, Daddy. It's what I want. It's what *He* wants."

"Well, never let it be said I tried to interfere with the Almighty's plans." Dan turned to Clare with a smile. "Although, I'll guarantee you this—it'll take a lot of getting used to. Right now, I'm going outside and cut the grass." Shaking his head, he left the house and walked to the garage.

"I've got things to do upstairs," Clare said. "Want to come up and visit?"

"I'll be up in a little while," Bobbe said. "I think I should go talk with Daddy some more."

"All right, honey." Clare wiped a piece of imaginary dust from the table and left the kitchen.

Daddy's not convinced, Bobbe thought. I'll go out and assure him this is all right for me to do.

"You'll stay right here, slut!" the voice boomed within her. *"He's bought the whole line of shit. Everything's going according to plan. Don't fuck the works up now, or you'll be sorry quicker than you should be."*

Bobbe stood rooted to the floor, unable to move. Fighting

desperately to cry out to her father, she was unable to utter a sound. One small tear formed and cascaded down her cheek before an evil smile was given life on her full lips. Then, seemingly at ease, she turned and rushed to be with her mother upstairs.

CHAPTER FOUR

Following their visits with Father Dolan and Sister Basil, Clare and Dan hesitantly accepted their daughter's sudden announcement to become a Sister of the Bearer of the Divine Word. All too quickly, the days grew into weeks during which Bobbe's apparent happiness and joy proved contagious and her parents' hesitancy became a full recognition of her vocation. At the suggestion of Sister Basil, Clare began preparations for a reception—a sort of farewell party that would enable Bobbe to see friends and relatives one final time before her departure. On more than one occasion, during the weeks before Bobbe was to leave, Clare had caught herself thinking of the party she was planning as a wedding reception for Bobbe and Jay Livingston. A quiet tear would form when the truth reared its head and she would think, "A reception without a groom—a reception without a groom." Pragmatically accepting the situation, Clare would retrace her mental footsteps to the point of full acceptance and continue her thought patterns in a more controlled way.

Then, the time evaporated and less than two days remained before the Moores would drive to Cedar Falls where their daughter would remain.

"We'd better get a good night's sleep tonight," Clare said soberly when she had finished wiping the kitchen sink dry. "The reception tomorrow and driving to Cedar Falls the next day are going to wear us out."

Bobbe forced a warm smile when she thought of the wedding dress she would wear the next day. The white dress had been an idea from Sister Basil during one of their visits to

47

the parish convent and both Bobbe and her mother decided a wedding atmosphere would be an appropriate one.

"Are you tired, Bobbe?" Clare asked when her daughter did not respond. "Do you feel all right? You're not thinking of backing out now, are you? What—?"

"Mom!" Bobbe said curtly. "Slow down. I'm perfectly fine. Really. I was just thinking about tomorrow, that's all. And no, I'm not thinking of changing my mind. I'm really going—day after tomorrow."

After hanging the dish cloth on a hook, Clare turned to study her daughter. More beautiful than ever, happiness seemed to emanate from the young woman. She was really going. There was no turning back now. The only thing Clare could see happening to stop her daughter's plans was failure to meet the rigid standards Sister Basil had outlined for them. Before a glimmer of hope could form, a kaleidoscopic summation of Bobbe's successes and achievements ran through her mind and she knew any shortcomings that developed would be dealt with and repolarized from negative to positive.

Joining Dan, who was reading the newspaper in the living room, the three made attempts at awkward conversation until ten o'clock when Clare suggested they retire. After checking the doors and finding them locked, Dan made his way upstairs with Clare following. Bobbe stopped halfway up the open staircase and surveyed the living room, now lighted only by the hall light. Her mother had cleaned the house thoroughly and tomorrow morning, while they attended the special Mass Father Dolan was offering for her, those women who were managing the reception would come in to finish the preparations.

Slowly, she walked up the stairs and went to her room. Undressing quickly she was soon in bed lying on her back, her eyes closed. Within minutes soothing sleep began cleansing her body of fatigue and weariness. The glowing face of her alarm clock watched the shadowed scene impassively for several hours, its hands obediently marking off time.

After three hours of undisturbed sleep had passed, Bobbe's eyes opened to study the blackness surrounding her. She felt alert—curiously restless. Throwing the covers back, she sat up and twisted to turn on the dressing table lamp. There was something she must do—must accomplish tonight. But what? What was it skittering through her mind, never stopping long enough for her to examine? Bobbe stood and crossed the room to face herself in the dresser mirror. There was something she had to finish—no, do— there was something she had to do before the reception tomorrow. Searching her image's eye for the answer, Bobbe's hands dropped to the cluttered dresser top. Without looking, her fingers searched through the maze of jars, tubes, and brushes. Finding the object of her search, she opened the bottle and began applying creamy liquid makeup to her naturally lovely face. Her eyes riveted to her reversed face, Bobbe's hands groped again for eye shadow and mascara, which, when applied, accented her deep blue eyes and complemented the honey-hued makeup. Once more her hands fleetingly touched the disarray on the dresser, search- ing, groping until they locked onto a tube of lipstick. Her sensuous lips were quickly outlined in deep red giving Bobbe's face a Sybaritic air.

Slipping her nightgown straps over her shoulders, she wiggled until the cotton garment slithered to the floor. A carnal smile worked its way onto her mouth as she ran her hands over her full breasts and hips. She lustfully admired the reflection of her body's left side before turning slowly, to study the right profile.

A sense of craving inched its way into her, before sweeping through her entire being. Her mouth opened in a mirthless laugh before she glided silently to the closet. Throwing demure clothing to the floor, Bobbe found a sheer blouse and tight skirt, which she hurriedly slipped over her hips. A pair of thin high heels completed her attire.

Checking herself in the mirror, Bobbe patted her un- combed hair into place and, satisfied with the wanton look she had achieved, quietly descended the stairs without making a noise. Once outside, she knew her departure had been undetected by her parents and she hurried down the walk.

Springfield's streets were dark and quiet, her footsteps

echoing hollowly in the stillness. Hurrying through the small downtown area, she came to the highway, the only place showing lights and activity. An all night service station beckoned to nonexistent travelers and Bill's Truck Stop appeared deserted with the exception of a moving van that was parked in the lot adjacent to the small restaurant. The only time Bobbe had ever been in the café was the night of her high school graduation, when the all-night party which the parents sponsored every year petered out and the need for more excitement became paramount in the minds of the revelers. Their party had poked fun at the simple decor and smell of frying grease that hung thickly in the air and, after mixing the sugar, salt, and pepper together and making confetti of most of the napkins in the booths, they had been asked to leave.

Now, Bobbe made her way to the door and entered without hesitating. She was to do something—something of which she wasn't quite positive, but she felt she would know what to do when the situation presented itself. The same heavy, oily smell coated her nostrils and she surveyed the room with a quick glance. At this hour, only one customer sat hunched over a cup of coffee at a table. Seated at the end of the counter, a waitress looked up indifferently and turned back to the movie magazine she was devouring. Confidently, Bobbe strode over to the table and the man, whom she assumed was the driver of the truck parked outside, looked up when she pulled a chair out and sat down.

"Do you mind?" Bobbe purred, her smiling lips inviting more than just conversation.

The man's head popped up at the sound of her low, throaty voice. "It's a free world," he said and refocused his surly eyes on the cup in front of him.

"Is it?" she asked and smiled seductively.

"Huh?"

"Is it?"

"Is it what?"

"A free world?"

"How the hell should I know?"

"You just said it is."

"What the hell you talkin' about?"

"Making conversation."

"Go make it someplace else."

"You invited me."

"Aw, fercrissake."

"How long are you going to be here?"

"Where?"

"Here—in the truck stop? In Springfield?"

"I just pulled my van in five minutes ago. Why?"

"I thought maybe we could do something—if you know what I mean?"

"If I know what you mean?" he mocked. "If you knew what's on my mind right now, honey, you'd get up and leave." His eyes stripped the thin blouse and skirt from her body, as though he knew she had nothing else on, to devour the smooth, firm flesh he was sure she possessed.

"That's where you're wrong," Bobbe said softly. "If you have an hour or so you'd like to spend with me, just say so and we can have one hell of a good time."

"You're kidding," the trucker said and suddenly found himself engrossed in studying the beautiful young woman sitting next to him.

"I'm not kidding," she said. "I—I do this all the time." The words echoed hollowly in her head as if someone else had said them and she was merely listening to the conversation. She didn't do this—at anytime. Still, she felt compelled, driven to seduce this man. Bobbe looked at him quickly and then diverted her eyes to the far corner of the room. He was not the least bit attractive—his thinning hair was rumpled and his pockmarked face was red from a combination of wind and whiskey but his eyes held their place in Bobbe's memory the longest. They were set too far apart—separated by a wide bridge above the misshapen nose—and seemed to burn their way into her mind even though she no longer could see them directly.

"Let's go!"

She heard the words ring in her ears when he jumped to his feet and placed a worn cap on his head. Standing automatically, Bobbe followed him from the diner into the cool early morning air. Pointing to the Wayfarer's Inn across the two-lane highway, she said, "There's a nice little motel over there.

Why don't you go register and I'll wait outside."

"Either you're drumming up business for this crummy dump," he said gesturing toward the Inn, "or you're on the level. Which is it? How come I have to go in alone?"

"They—they might recognize me," she stammered wondering what she was doing here, talking with this strange man.

"I guess I'm willing to invest the price of a room to see if you're still here when I come out," he said hurrying across the road, pulling Bobbe with him.

"I'll wait here in the shadows," she said wrenching her wrist loose from his grasp. When she saw the look of doubt cross his dark features, she added, "Go on. I'll be here when you come out."

Without a word, the trucker entered the office and banged on the desk bell.

After several minutes, Bobbe could hear the muffled voices of the man and the motel manager. She turned away. Leave. She had to leave right now. This was wrong. She felt confused—disconnected from herself. This wasn't right and she knew it. Considering what she was doing the day after tomorrow—no, tomorrow, it was already past midnight—she wondered suddenly if her purpose was proper. What was her purpose? She felt so mixed up. What was it she was doing tomorrow? Something—but what?

The turbulence raging in her mind quieted when the door of the office opened and the man reappeared. She *must* go with him. She *must.*

"Well, I'll be goddamned," he muttered when he saw her hugging the wall, blending into the grays and blacks of the shadows on the porch extending the full length of the eight-unit motel. Roughly grabbing her hand, he pulled her toward the last unit. They entered the room and the door softly closed behind them.

After he had turned the ceiling light on, the man slipped off his jacket and moved to the bed. Sitting down heavily on the edge of the thin mattress, he growled, "Hurry up and get undressed. I ain't got all night." He opened his shirt, exposing thick, matted hair that covered his sagging chest and protruding belly. When his pants were off, he lay back on the bed and wiggled ungracefully from his shorts. Naked, he sat up to find Bobbe still fully clothed. "Get a move on, willya?" he snarled.

"Come on, lover," Bobbe cooed, "we've got all the time we need." Moving in a tantalizingly slow manner, she unbuttoned her blouse.

When it fell open, exposing her bare breasts, she could hear the driver suck his breath in. "Hurry up!" he wheezed.

Without answering, she opened her skirt and smoothed it down over her hips until it fell in a neat pile around her feet.

"Just what the hell do you think you're doing? Working a burleyque job?"

"Patience, my dear," Bobbe purred.

"What the hell do you want from me, girlie?"

"What have you got to offer?" Bobbe asked, throwing her head back in a silent, mirthless laugh.

"Anything you want and then some."

Again Bobbe threw her head back in mocking laughter.

"Don't laugh at me, baby," he said coldly. "You never can tell, I just might turn you on and we can spend the rest of our days doing what we're going to do right now."

Bobbe snickered impishly and winked at the man.

"Come on over here," he coaxed. "I got something for you."

Bobbe shook her head and didn't move.

"Oh, fer crissakes! I should have known," he growled, his voice becoming rough and gravelly. "None of you good-lookin' broads ever go for a guy like me."

Bobbe stiffened as her face went blank and the turbulence in her mind began once more. What did he say? Something that should have been most important to her. Grasping at minuscule bits of thought, which maddeningly eluded her, she stared into space as she tried to fathom her dilemma. What had he said? Something to do with her imminent future. How did he know what she was going to do when she couldn't even think of it herself?

"What—what did you say?" she asked stiffly.

"I said you good-lookin' broads never go for a guy like me. I ain't that bad, am I?"

Staring at him, Bobbe decided those were *not* the words he

had said before. He had said—he had said—. She couldn't remember the exact words but whatever they had been they meant something to her. Something very important.

"I—I think you're very handsome," she finally murmured.

"Then get your sweet ass over here on the bed and I'll give you something you won't forget for a long time," he ordered gruffly.

Obediently crossing the room, Bobbe lay down beside the man who began to run his hands over her white skin, pinching and kneading her flesh. She winced at the leathery roughness of his palms and fingers but was unable to ignore the warm feeling she felt building in her thighs and lower abdomen. Reaching out she stroked his erect penis.

Encouraged, the man propped himself on one arm and kissed her indecorously and crudely on the lips, forcing his tongue into her mouth. His breath was awful and tasted like a chemical, but Bobbe could not place the peculiar sapor. Lying back, she began moaning in response to the man's expert touch.

God, what had she been missing? A tingling sensation washed over her body in fuguelike waves. She should have been doing this a long time ago. Such feelings! Such—

Lifting himself, he rolled over on top of her and pushed hard. A whimpering gasp erupted from her lips when her hymen broke and he entered her.

"Oh, God!" she screamed. His penis was huge and she was unable to understand how anything could feel so awful and yet so good at the same time. He pushed harder and when his movements became more frenzied, she opened her eyes, realizing the same state of confusion her mind had gone through before joining him on the bed was about to occur again. This time, her jumbled thoughts were different.

She detachedly studied the man who was attempting to pump his seed into her body, but found herself thinking of Jay Livingston. Slowly, the man's bloated face changed into Jay's youthful handsomeness and she encircled his neck with her arms. Raising her head, she closed her eyes to kiss him on the mouth but gagged when she recognized the same vile taste of the trucker's saliva and breath. Pulling away, she didn't see Jay any longer nor the trucker, but a totally different man: darkly handsome, his hair was combed back tight to his head and his flaming amber eyes perforated the last shred of decency and sanity within her. Her roiling thoughts mixed together, forming a solid impenetrable mass, and she moaned in ecstasy. A feeling of dizziness began forming within her as her first orgasm built to a peak but refused to reach fruition. Without climaxing, she could feel another starting deep within her.

Seemingly incapable of stopping, the strange man drove his hard member faster and faster into her body. Finally, mercifully, he shuddered and reached his own climax, exploding his semen within her. Would the torrent never stop?

She could feel the semen running out between her legs. Strangely, the thick sticky fluid felt cold to her. That was odd. She had always imagined it would be hot or at least warm.

After several minutes, the panting truck driver rolled off her aching body. "Geezus! That felt good," he moaned. "What's your name, honey?"

"Bobbe," she whispered.

"Bobbe what?"

"Just Bobbe. What's yours?"

"Howie."

"Howie what?"

"Just Howie," he said imitating her.

She smiled at the gentle insult and stood. "I'll take a shower and be on my way, Howie. If you and I ever get together again, we'll screw up a storm, won't we?"

Closing his eyes, he smiled with satisfaction and anticipation intermingling on his coarse face. "You can count on it."

When Bobbe stepped into the stall, she heard a loud snore from the bedroom and turned on the shower. Quickly soaping her frustrated body, she stood under the warm spray for ten minutes before stopping the flow of water. She dressed after toweling herself dry and could hear, off in the distance, the town clock solemnly striking the hour of four. The fourth and last note hung over the town before dying away when Bobbe opened the door and slipped from the room.

Keeping to the shadows until she was on Main Street and

close to her own neighborhood, she hurried along the still, dark streets. Pink and yellow blotches etched themselves into the scattered clouds hanging over the eastern horizon. It would be light soon and she wanted to get home before anyone saw her.

A look of questioning bewilderment crossed her face. What had she just done? More important, why had she done it? The fact she was not remorseful bothered her as well. She could not understand what had prompted her to make love with a total stranger when the very next day she would enter the convent.

The convent. The idea was suddenly funny. Doing what she had done and wanting to be a nun was very funny. She laughed to herself. What was wrong with one last fling? She would have to be pure and chaste the rest of her life. At least she wouldn't wonder what having sex would have been like later on when she would be a full-fledged nun. No, Jay had been wrong. The convent was not for dried-up old maids.

"Wait a minute," she said aloud and stopped walking. Was that what she had been trying to remember back in the motel room? The trucker, her lover—what was his name? Howie! That was it. Howie had said something about "none of you good-lookin' dames" or something like that but it had been the word "none" that she had tried to say and was unable.

"Nun!" she cried aloud. Skipping down the street toward her home she chanted, "I'm gonna be a nun and I won't get none cause I don't want none!"

CHAPTER FIVE

Although Bobbe had not made her appearance yet, the house was filled with relatives and acquaintances by two-thirty. Upstairs, Clare made last minute adjustments to her daughter's white satin wedding dress. It had been her stepmother's costume when she married her father. Clare had worn it when she and Dan had repeated their marital vows. The dress was to have been Bobbe's for her wedding. Instead, she was wearing it at a reception without a groom.

No, that wasn't quite right. Christ was the groom and she shouldn't be complaining. She suddenly felt it was very wrong to question her daughter's vocation at this point. Deep inside, she felt warm and happy. The loss of Bobbe's presence was only a surface thing that ranked with the loss of future grandchildren, future visits, future holidays spent together. A tear formed but she blinked it into oblivion.

"There," she said, standing. "I think that about does any final changes. You look absolutely beautiful, Bobbe."

Bobbe pirouetted in front of her mirror. The dress fit perfectly. "I feel strange all of a sudden, Mom."

"Strange? I don't understand. Are you ill?"

"No. Nothing like that. I mean the dress makes me feel strange. After what you told me about Grandma and how she lied to you about being married."

"She didn't lie to me, honey. She was just—well, uninformed."

"Maybe. But I can't help but feel uncomfortable in it. She must have been very unhappy."

"Don't bother yourself worrying about her. She's been

57

dead for almost twenty years and we should let her memory rest."

Picking up a comb to run through her long hair one more time, Bobbe recalled how she had cleaned her dresser off after waking at dawn. She had unceremoniously swept everything into her wastebasket, filling the metal container to the top. Then the thought she had disposed of her deodorant, shampoo, hand-cream, and other vital cosmetics crossed her mind and she quickly retrieved them. The initial act still bothered her when she thought of her feeling of repugnance and how she had stood trembling when the clatter of jars and bottles colliding finally died away. The brightly colored containers had been pushed with a vengeance as though she despised the thought of seeing them or using them in any fashion.

"I'd better get downstairs," Clare said moving toward the door. "I know there's a lot of people here already. Don't be too long, darling."

"I won't, Mom," Bobbe said without turning to face her mother, watching her in the mirror instead.

Closing the door softly, Clare made her way downstairs and was quickly swallowed up by the people milling about the living room and front entryway. Slipping through the crowd, she said hello to everyone as she inched nearer the kitchen to check on the progress of the women who were preparing the food. A smile crossed her lips when she thought of Dan and how uncomfortable he was in his suit and tie. He disliked being dressed up and felt more at ease in his coveralls or, when he wasn't working, in a sport shirt and slacks. She had caught a glimpse of him sitting on the arm of the couch, talking with his Aunt Kate. Finally, she reached the kitchen door and pushed it in.

Dan examined his fingernails. They weren't his. They were too clean. The hands weren't his either. His usually had grease caked under the nails and worked into the cracks and crevices. Running his fingers through his thinning gray hair, he sighed deeply. Sometimes he felt older then his forty-eight years. Clare looked much younger then he did and he had teased her many times that the day when someone

58

mistook him for her father was the day he would leave.

Leave. Depart. The thought of Bobbe leaving them the next day when they took her to the convent exploded in his brain. Was this really happening? Was this the right thing for his daughter? His Bobbe. Going right out of his life. Totally. No son-in-law. No grandchildren to play with, to take for walks, change diapers, and rock to sleep. No—

He shook his head. No more thoughts like that, he scolded himself. It had taken weeks for him to accept Bobbe's decision. It was wrong to resurrect his arguments at this point. Accept it. Maybe she wouldn't make the grade as a nun. Then, she would be back in his life. For all he knew—

"Danny?" his Aunt Kate said in apparent frustration. "Whatever is the matter? I've been talking to you and you haven't heard a word I've said. Are you all right?"

Dan turned and looked down at the tiny, gray-haired lady who was staring peculiarly at him. Fumbling to adjust his thought patterns to the crowded room, he said, "I'm sorry, Aunt Kate. I was just thinking. What were you saying?"

"I was saying," she began crossly, annoyed she would have to repeat the whole statement, "that you are very lucky to have Roberta going into the convent. Not all parents can rest easy, knowing their child will have no problems in life and that her eternal reward is assured."

"Oh, we'll have plenty to worry about, Aunt Kate," he said softly. "If she gets through her studies and actually becomes a nun, she may be traveling all over the world as a missionary. You've heard stories about priests and nuns being tortured and put to death by some of the pagans and heathens in the world, haven't you? That's a lot more to worry about than if she were living down the street from us, having the same kind of problems we have."

"I know, dear, but think how close she'll be to God. Why, she's a regular little saint now. So pretty and sweet and—"

Cries of "Here she comes now!" interrupted the old lady. All eyes in the room turned to fix themselves on Bobbe who was now standing on the open stairway, gazing into the living room.

It won't be long now, Bobbe thought after Clare left the

room. Tomorrow about this time, I'll be at the convent. The next day seemed so far off, so removed from this time span. She felt as though she were standing in a timeless cul-de-sac, one in which she found herself unable to turn and extricate herself. Was this a dead end for her? The words of Father Dolan came back to her as she peered into the mirror with unseeing eyes. Just as she was about to leave the communion rail, where she had been allowed to receive the Sacred Host alone, he had stayed her departure by placing his free hand on her shoulder.

"For those here gathered," he said in his soft, well modulated voice, "I beseech you to pray for Roberta. Remember her in your daily prayers, calling to mind she is on a sacred and blessed mission in this life. Hers will be a rewarding existence on this earth, doing the will of God and performing His tasks. Many think of a religious vocation as a voluntary seclusion from life's challenges. Not so!"

There had been more but, with the Host still in her mouth, she felt it best to swallow it and begin her thanksgiving to God while the priest continued his impromptu message. Then, and she had tried to decide several times since then, she either choked on the Host or began gagging from a sudden stomach cramp. The two sensations had occurred so closely together, she was unable to determine which had happened first. By the time she had returned to the pew after Dolan cut his talk short when he noticed his esteemed subject was in difficulty, the sensations had passed and she gave thanks in a normal manner.

Strengthened by the recollection of the priest's words, Bobbe was certain hers would be a fulfilling life. After one last check in the mirror and a fluff of her hair, she turned toward the door. Bobbe wondered if Jay would come to the reception? Why wouldn't he? She had called him two days before, hoping he wouldn't take time to debate the pros and cons of his appearance at the party and just come. She found it peculiar that two people who had seen each other practically every day whenever Jay was in town had not even seen each other coincidentally at church or downtown or at a dance since her announcement.

No, wait, she thought. Since telling Jay of her intentions to enter the convent, she hadn't gone to many places—except church. No matter, she felt they should have run into each other at some time.

When she and her mother sent out the invitations, she purposely did not send one to him, opting instead to call him on the phone and extend a personal invitation. Taken off guard, Jay had flustered for several minutes, groping for the right words before he reluctantly agreed to appear.

Now as she stood poised at the top of the stairs, ready to descend and greet her well-wishers, she suddenly felt apprehensive about seeing Jay. What would their reaction be to seeing each other again. Memories flooded her mind—gentle memories, tender memories of exploratory touches that had been curtailed before either's passions became too much to control. A tiny smile played at the corners of her mouth. She was glad they had never become involved physically since she would not feel pure and worthy to serve her God. No, it was best she was still a virgin.

Tentatively placing one foot on the first step, she stopped when she heard a familiar, low, coarse laugh. Staring downstairs, she tried to locate the author of the evil chuckle, but was unable to determine its source.

A chorus of cries, "Here she comes!" greeted her and the thought of the laughter was erased from her conscious mind.

For the next two hours, Bobbe circulated about the room chatting with friends and relatives whom she would not see for a long time. Her first regular home visit would not take place for five years—when she would be a nun. As she moved about, a constant turnover in faces occurred and when she and Clare suddenly were thrust face to face by the crowd, she sighed quietly.

"Would it be all right if I were to go upstairs and rest for a few minutes, Mom? I've still got almost an hour and a half to go before the reception is over."

"I'll go with you," Clare offered and took her daughter's hand to lead her through the entanglement of guests.

Promising to return in a few minutes when they were stopped at the foot of the steps by recent arrivals who had not spoken with Bobbe yet, Clare, beaming with pride, followed her daughter to the upper floor of the house.

"It's certainly hectic down there." Bobbe turned to face the mirror as her mother closed the door. "I had no idea we knew so many people. I think half of Springfield has been here today."

"I'm really tired out from all the excitement, dear," Clare said, "but I slept well last night. Did you?"

"I think I must have fallen asleep when my head hit the pillow." Bobbe immediately pursed her lips and thought for a minute. No, she hadn't gone to sleep right away. Wait—now she remembered. After going to sleep, she woke up. Around one in the morning. Had she gone someplace? Had she been dreaming? It seemed so real now. Why hadn't she remembered it sooner?

A puzzled look clouded her face as the image of Howie materialized in her thoughts. The experience of the night before refused to jell and take form, remaining instead a nebulous shadow in her memory, always there but never in clear focus. Shaking her head as if to throw the idea away, she said lightly, "I'll bet we sleep well tonight, too, Mom."

Her mother smiled while she fixed a pleat on the wedding gown. "Little Ronnie asked if this dress was your habit," Clare said and they both laughed.

"Bobbe?" Dan called softly from the hall as he knocked on the bedroom door. "Jay's downstairs. Are you coming down soon?"

"Yes, Dad. I'll be down in a few minutes." She turned to her mother, an aura of apprehensiveness about the impending confrontation replacing the tired but happy air she had displayed just seconds before. "You don't think he'll make a scene, do you, Mom? Maybe I shouldn't have invited him. I practically insisted he be here. What'll I do, Mom?"

"Jay's a pretty levelheaded young man, Bobbe. Besides, why should he make a fuss since the two of you parted friends? Haven't you seen each other since your decision?"

Shaking her head, Bobbe managed a smile. "I was just thinking before how silly it is that two people can miss each other or avoid each other in a small town like this. The last time I saw Jay was when he brought me home—the night I told him I wanted to enter the convent."

"Well, don't worry about it, dear," Clare said comfortingly.

62

"I'm sure Jay just wants to wish you the best of luck in your vocation."

Hesitantly, Bobbe nodded in agreement as they started for the door.

"I think I should see him alone," she said thoughtfully. "That way, in case he's embarrassed at being here, we'll be alone and he won't feel so self-conscious."

"All right, darling," her mother agreed. "Why don't you go to the back porch and I'll send him there."

Separating at the foot of the stairs, Bobbe made her way almost unnoticed to the kitchen and then the back porch. Clare found Jay talking with her half brother, Leo Simms, who was teasing Jay as she walked up.

"So you lost out, huh, boy?"

"Oh, Leo," she scolded. "Really!" Then, lowering her voice, she said quietly to Jay, "Bobbe wants to see you on the back porch."

After thanking her, Jay made his way to the back of the house. With his eyes cast down so he wouldn't have to greet many people, the young man felt uncomfortable. He hadn't planned to come when he heard of the reception's preparations. Thankful he hadn't received an invitation, he was unable to refuse Bobbe's personal request when she called him.

Pushing the back door open, he found Bobbe staring into the backyard. "Hi!" he said shyly.

Snapping out of her childhood reflections of games played and good times she had enjoyed in their backyard while growing up, she turned to face him. When Bobbe saw him, she had the feeling of having irrevocably lost something. "Hi," she managed weakly, forcing back tears of confusion.

As they stood confronting each other for the first time i seven weeks, their relationship spun wildly in both minds—a collage of memories—brief flashes of remembered picnics, dates, dances, and parties.

To Jay, their last meeting had been a nightmare. For the better part of four weeks he had sat in his room, leaving only to eat and go to work. Unable to concentrate, the single thought coursing through his mind like a recurring night-mare was Bobbe's refusal to marry him. As time passed the injury's intensity diminished and Jay began to accept the reality of her choice. Now, looking at her, the wound was torn open and his emotional blood was rising to the surface ready to run freely again. Biting his tongue to hold back the tears, he chose to speak—to break the awful silence that separated them now—this last time.

Just as he opened his mouth to speak, Bobbe, moved by his apparent inability to do so, said, "I'm glad—"

They burst out laughing when both began talking at one time.

"You first," Jay said and took a step toward her but stopped when he realized he was going to take her in his arms.

Clearing her throat, Bobbe said, "Please don't think too harshly of me, Jay. I'm doing what I have to do. I hope you understand that. You're the last person in the world I would ever want to hurt. I guess I'll always have a warm spot in my heart for you."

"Bobbe, sweet Bobbe," Jay murmured. "I—" His throat constricted and he coughed to clear the lump he felt forming. "I—I guess I lost out to a power greater than my love for you. I've finally accepted the fact you're no longer mine— But, I still don't really believe it, Bobbe." He smiled his little boy smile and thought perhaps he should ask if she was actually going.

Before he could voice the question she shook her head. "It's truly happening, Jay."

Watching Bobbe shake her head, Jay thought back on their four years of high school—the four years which seemed to take eons to pass but in retrospect had gone all too quickly. Jay Livingston had been no different through his first two and a half years of secondary education than his schoolmates, when it came to the opposite sex. The first year, girls were an object of ridicule and suitable objects of torment. Suddenly, on the first day of his sophomore year, the discovery was made they were no longer little girls but opening blossoms ready to burst forth in bloom. However, they were still taboo— look but don't associate or talk with them. During his third year somehow the mystique was removed, the ban lifted, and serious conversations could be carried on without any consequences to be paid. It was finally all right. Still, Jay had dated infrequently with the bulk of his time divided between sports and his school work.

The first time he dated Bobbe had been the summer between their junior and senior years during which they found a warm rapport grow with each other. Jay found her to be a comfortable companion and always felt great whenever they were together. Besides hiking and picnicking, they had gone to movies and all of the important dances at school. But the times he had enjoyed the most were the long drives they had taken in his "new" old car—riding quietly, barely speaking but communicating nevertheless. She had helped him with his trigonometry and he had shown her how to improve her backhand in tennis. They visited freely at each other's homes and on graduation night, they had exchanged class rings.

Now it was over and she would be out of his life forever. Jay could feel the familiar lump building in his throat again and coughed once more to restrain his feelings.

"I guess," he finally said, "I find it hard to believe because I love—no, I'd better make that past tense, right?—loved you so much. I might add the past tense was perfect."

The gentle pun brought a smile to her face as she recalled the problem she had had explaining to him the past perfect tense in Latin and English assignments.

"I suppose," Jay added after a several second pause, "I always will love you and I'll never forget you. The best of everything, Bobbe."

Stepping forward, she filled the void between them and kissed him lightly on the cheek. Without a word, they turned and went back to the house, entering side by side. Once they reached the living room, they were soon separated by the milling crowd which now seemed to be bigger than ever.

Jay, thankful for the chance to see Bobbe once more and even more thankful he had not broken down and made a fool of himself, worked his way through the crowded room toward the front door. As he passed the punch bowl table, he bumped into Crystal Brauerman, upsetting her glass.

"I'm sorry," he said quietly before recognizing the girl. "Crystal! How are you?" His tone relaxed when he realized she was by herself and could be someone with whom he could talk and not feel awkward.

"How are *you*, Jay?" she asked, ready to offer a sympathetic ear for any grief he might want to express. Realistically, Crystal was fully aware of the fact Jay Livingston was for the first time in his life, among the more eligible suitors in Springfield. After she poured him a glass of punch, they visited, their conversation lost in the constant hum of voices. Several minutes later, they left.

The house had assumed a quiet weariness by six-fifteen when the last of the well-wishers had departed. Only a few women, who had volunteered to help clean up, remained.

Father Dolan had arrived late and was still in the living room with Bobbe. Preparing to leave, he squeezed her hand and whispered, "May God's holy light always shine on you and guide you in your life's work, my child."

Gratefully acknowledging his good wishes, Bobbe humbly bowed her head. "How can I ever thank you for all the kind things you said about me at Mass this morning, Father?"

"You don't have to thank me, Roberta. I rejoice that God has picked you to join Him in doing His holy work. Perhaps by talking about you the way I did, some other youngster in the parish will be inspired to consider the religious life for a vocation."

"I'm really looking forward to doing *His* work," Bobbe said, her voice suddenly dull and hollow. She accompanied the priest to the front door and bade him good-bye.

By eight o'clock the house was back to a normal state of neatness and all evidence of the numbers who had visited that day were removed. When the women who had done the cleaning were gone, the house assumed the atmosphere of a morgue. Dan aimlessly roamed through the house three times before announcing he was exhausted and going to bed.

"I think that's an excellent idea," Clare echoed as she looked to Bobbe for agreement. All of them were tired but Clare noted how the strain of the day showed most clearly on her daughter. "Let's go up and I'll help you out of your dress."

Clare hadn't minded when Bobbe cleaned the ash trays and washed dishes without changing clothes. This was the last time the dress would be worn by anyone—for any occasion.

Once in her room, Bobbe undressed quickly, deciding to shower in the morning. Muscle and bone weary, she fell into bed, exhausted. Smiling up at her mother, who leaned down to kiss her good night, she said, "That's the last time you'll be kissing me good night for a while, isn't it, Mom?" Knowing her mother was about to cry, she reached up to place a hand on Clare's cheek.

Fighting back the tears, Clare forced a brave smile. "I—I know, darling. Sleep tight." When a tear escaped its flimsy prison, she turned and hurriedly left the room.

The door closed softly and Bobbe reached for the bed light plunging the room into darkness with a snap of the switch.

Once in the hallway, tears of sadness and joy freely cascaded down Clare's cheeks. Hurrying along the hall, she went to hers and Dan's bedroom. She closed the door quietly and whispered, "Dan? Are you still awake?"

A guttural snore was his only response.

Clare smiled wanly and prepared to retire. Tomorrow they would drive to the Mother House in Cedar Falls and leave their only daughter there—forever. With a deep sigh escaping into the quiet of the bedroom, she lay down. Then memories of Bobbe's childhood caressed her tired mind and she fell asleep with a smile on her face.

CHAPTER SIX

Gently braking the three-year-old Chevrolet, Dan adjusted his speed to a slower one as they approached the outskirts of Cedar Falls. To the Moores, the town, although larger, appeared to be much like Springfield. The highway divided the business district instead of bypassing it but the similarity was evident. Displays in shop windows heralded the local high school's homecoming football game. Banners proclaiming the same event, stretched from one side of the street to the other, flapping lazily in a fall breeze.

Bobbe, who had been lulled into a fitful sleep by the hum of the automobile's tires on the pavement, was now wide awake, inspecting the town. Somehow, for no reason she could identify, she felt Springfield would be her last contact with reality. More than once during the last weeks, she had tried to sort her feelings and thoughts but for some reason had been unable to concentrate. Questions such as, "Why was she doing this?" and placating thoughts of being able to leave if she discovered the convent was not for her, slithered away to hide in the deepest recesses of her mind. The consternation now forgotten, she mentally checked off stores, which would be of future necessity, should any needs arise.

A department store flashed by with a pharmacy located next to it. Then a hardware store, a men's haberdashery, and a movie theater passed her window like fleeting, random thoughts. Passing through the next intersection, a jewelry store flashed by and she thought of Jay—Jay standing with a look of dismay and shock etched into his shadowed features as he stared first at Bobbe and then at the diamond ring esting in his hand. She closed her eyes, squeezing an unordered tear into existence where it hung precariously on her lashes. Blinking quickly, she resumed her study of Cedar Falls and found another, smaller department store with a book and novelty shop nestled alongside before her father braked the car to a halt for a traffic light.

Across the street, she saw an insurance office that brought a smile to her unadorned lips as thoughts of her days at the F G C Insurance Agency surfaced. After the car was moving again, a service station, a bank, and a vacant lot were passed before they went through another intersection. In the next block, Bobbe saw a service station and restaurant combination with several trucks parked outside. Furrows wrinkled unfamiliarly across her forehead as she studied the truck stop intensely. What was there about restaurants that seemed to arouse a long forgotten memory? Or was it the gas station? Or the trucks parked outside? Turning in her seat, she watched the station diminish in size, unable to form in her mind the recollection now slipping away with the other nebulous thoughts.

Now, homes lined the streets with an occasional vacant lot breaking the pattern. A school and church interrupted the monotony as they continued through the residential district.

Approaching a side road, Dan slowed the car to make a turn onto it. A small sign humbly announced the way to the *Sisters of the Bearer of the Divine Word.* The smooth blacktop road wound through low hills, and when the car climbed to the highest mound, they saw the Mother House— Bobbe's new home.

The main building, large and old, resembled a medieval castle in its Gothic hauteur. A bell tower rose in back, two stories higher than the three-floor convent. Smaller outbuildings hovered nearby on either side, like embarrassed serfs, waiting to do the bidding of the elegant master.

Easing the car into the horseshoe-shaped driveway, Dan parked and said, "Well, here we are." The sound of his voice startled him as well as Bobbe and her mother; he realized they had hardly spoken a word since leaving Springfield.

Clare turned in her seat and smiled reassuringly at her daughter who returned the gesture. Hesitantly, they got out of

69

the automobile and stretched. Arm in arm, Bobbe in the middle, they walked up to the main door. Somewhere, far off in the distance, a bell rang when Dan pulled the knob he found off to the side of the entry. After what seemed an interminable wait, the huge, wooden door swung open on soundless hinges and an old nun greeted them before escorting the visitors to a waiting room. Once the guests were situated in a drawing room, she laboriously made her way back down the hall to summon the Reverend Mother.

"She must be a hundred and fifty if she's a day," Dan whispered.

Clare shushed him and Bobbe smiled.

Looking about the room to which the old receptionist had guided them, they found it to be large and high ceilinged with overstuffed chairs, sofas, and straight-backed chairs arranged in such a manner that more than one conversation could be carried on in private if necessary. Centered in the middle of the room and beneath a huge, baroque chandelier which dominated the parlor was a bare library table. Paintings of past Reverend Mothers were spaced evenly about the walls.

"Are you sure, Bobbe?" Dan asked suddenly, breaking their self-imposed silence again.

"Oh, Daddy," she said abruptly, almost impatiently. Studying her father for a moment, she wondered if she were proving to be a disappointment for him. She turned and walked away from her parents who had taken chairs several feet apart. He would have to accept her decision—her vocation.

Her vocation? Being a nun? What was she doing here? She didn't belong in this place. Where's Jay? She wanted Jay with her. He'd know what she should do. Did she really want to be a nun? She'd said it hundreds of times in the past weeks but now, standing here physically in this room with thirty nuns glaring at her from framed paintings, she was suddenly uncertain of everything.

The voice began building in volume as she heard it chanting within her. *"Cunt! Cunt! Cunt! Dumb cunt! Dumb cunt! Keep your fucking mind on the business at hand,"* it boomed hollowly within her, *"or I'll fix you good—right here—NOW!"*

"Wh—what?" Bobbe cried aloud, startled at the words she had heard. Who had said that? Certainly not her father whom she found slumped comfortably in a large chair when she turned.

"I didn't say anything," Dan said with a puzzled look when he saw his daughter staring at him.

Although she knew it hadn't been a woman's voice, she fixed her attention on her mother who was seated closer to the door through which they had entered.

"Mom?"

Lost in her own thoughts, Clare did not respond to the plaintive one-word question.

"Mom, did you say anything?"

"What, honey?"

"Did you just say something?"

"No, dear," she said, and went back to her own pre-occupied thoughts.

Then the voice ricocheted in Bobbe's head and body again. *"Stupid slut! You're not hearing me! You're sensing my thoughts in yours. Keep quiet and pay attention. Don't try to sort things out. It's beyond you. You're doing what has been commanded and you have nothing to say about your life. Behave and do what you have to do and say whatever has to be said to get into this stable of sows!"*

A becalmed expression crossed Bobbe's face and her parents smiled when they noticed, grateful for the relaxed attitude of their daughter. If she were benign, they would have no difficulty at this moment.

Bobbe wandered around the drawing room studying the portraits. The habits had changed little over the centuries since the order's founding and the only difference she could detect seemed to be in the mellowness of the older portraits' colors when compared to the harsh brightness of the newer, more recent paintings. A small white headband held a black veil covering the sides of the head and fell down the back. Each woman's face glared from a white coif, which was tucked in a starched equally white collar surrounding the neck. The lower collar edge spawned a stiff bib partially covering the breast and contrasting sharply with the black floor-length dress and guimpe. Looped through the white ropelike cincture girdling the waist was a full rosary, reaching to the knees. The former Reverend Mothers resembled one another in the stern, serious pose each had held for the artist. Perhaps they had only been serious on this one occasion. More likely they were like that all of the time.

No more fun and laughs for me, Bobbe thought, wandering to the far side of the room to peer out the window. A perfectly manicured parklike garden extended several hundred feet away from the building and was enclosed on three sides by a high stone wall. Evergreen trees stood haughtily in their verdure while their lesser neighbors were in the process of shedding their colored apparel. Silently standing guard a short distance from the back of the main building, a statue of Saint John the Baptist watched over the quiet sanctuary.

Nuns and white-veiled novices walked about singly and in pairs, their heads bowed in prayerful meditation, lost in private devotion. The younger women walked faster than their older, more staid companions. At a crosswalk, two nuns and a postulant almost collided but managed to miss each other as though guided by a mystical hand.

What they need there is a traffic light, Bobbe quipped mentally and smiled at the idea. And maybe a gas station or a nun stop.

Truck stop! What was she trying to remember about a truck stop? Shaking her head she decided she absolutely hated truck stops.

"No, I don't," she murmured softly to her reflection in the window. "They're nice."

"Of course they're nice," the deep bass voice cooed gently.

Knitting her brows, Bobbe silently wondered about the voice. She had not thought about it since the day she had visited Father Dolan and Sister Basil. Now, she had heard it again—twice in one day. There had been other times but they remained buried in her memory, skittering to the surface of her mind to tantalize her and then lightninglike, disappearing into the folds of her subconscious.

"Who are you?" she whispered.

This time Clare, who had moved to a chair closer to the window her daughter was standing at, heard her. "What did you say, darling?" she asked quietly, breaking out of her own private, tortured thoughts.

Spinning about, Bobbe glared at her mother for several seconds before her eyes softened and she said in a controlled voice, "Nothing, Mother. Nothing. I'm just—watching the nuns in the garden."

Clare shifted her gaze from Bobbe to her husband who had also heard her speak. Sitting up more straight in the easy chair, Dan studied his daughter outlined in the window. Shrugging his broad shoulders after several wordless minutes passed, he sat back, not knowing what to say, content with his own thoughts and reverie.

"You're really stupid," the voice hissed. *"I know what you think. You don't have to talk aloud to me for now. Understand?"*

The sounds were coarse, grating in Bobbe's head and as the growl died away, the silence of the room pressed in on her. Frightened, she nodded, unnoticed by her parents, in mute agreement. Quickly scanning the room in a furtive way, she could see there was no one else there. The window through which she had studied the garden drew her attention again and she blinked her eyes unbelievingly. Floating on the window, intermixed with her own reflection, the truck driver's face weaved back and forth, a lascivious grin baring his teeth. The garden dissolved behind him and as the Wayfarer's Inn motel room materialized, Bobbe smiled in recognition.

Now she could feel the weight of him pressing down on her and his rock-hard penis thrusting into her again and again. Her eyes closed and a low, animalistic groan began forming deep within her as she relived the act she had performed the night before her reception. Running one hand up her body to her breasts, she slowly kneaded them while her other began rubbing her lower body. Her excitement built and within minutes she felt a dampness between her legs. His frenzied pumping continued in her mind and she bit her tongue to prevent a scream of ecstasy from being born.

"This must be Roberta," a gentle voice said behind her. Instantly, Bobbe was thrust back to the parlor and turned to see a nun, who looked as though she had stepped down from one of the portraits, approaching her.

Stepping forward with outstretched hand, Bobbe accepted the nun's and the two women, one delighted at welcoming a newcomer into the realm she was responsible for and the other, confused by nebulous, erratic thoughts but serene and calm on the surface, met for the first time.

"I can't tell you how happy I am to meet you, Roberta," the nun said. "I'm Mother Job."

"How do you do, Mother," Bobbe said quietly. "These are my parents—Mr. and Mrs. Moore."

After the introductions were made, the nun indicated they should all be seated as she pulled a straight-backed chair out of formation, enabling her to be nearer them. Once they were relaxed, Mother Job began talking in generalities about life in the convent.

Bobbe watched the woman's mouth move and although the droning of her voice seemed both near and far at the same time, she was unable to distinguish the words being spoken. How could she give her undivided attention to this virtual stranger when her own thoughts needed scrutiny? Why hadn't she heard the nun enter the room? What had she been thinking about that had absorbed her so deeply? Maybe she should stop this— Stop? That was it. The sidewalk needed a traffic light at the intersection—no, that had been before.

Shifting in her seat, she realized the Reverend Mother was talking to her directly. "I'm sorry, Mother Job, my mind must have been wandering. What was it you said?" Bobbe asked, embarrassed by her daydreaming. Certainly, this was no way to impress the Mother General of the Order. Consciously aware of the dampness on the inside of her thighs, she wondered if she had wet her panties, although it somehow felt different.

Before Mother Job could repeat the question she had put to the new candidate, Clare quickly spoke up in defense of her daughter. "Forgive Roberta, Mother. We had a very big day yesterday. Bobbe's—I mean, Roberta's reception and then the long drive today have made us all a little tired."

Smiling, the Reverend Mother patted Bobbe's hand. "I can well appreciate the fact you're tired. What I had asked, Roberta, was how long have you thought about entering our order?" Her voice was well modulated and she pronounced each word distinctly.

"Actually, I can't tell you exactly when the thought first occurred to me. It seems like I've thought about it for years but—" Bobbe's voice trailed off as she gazed at the tall woman sitting so straight and prim. She appeared to be a little older than Clare. Laugh lines crinkled at the corners of her gray eyes, which were kind, yet firm, hinting she could be stern if the occasion demanded. Although the only features readily visible were her face and eyes, Bobbe dwelled on them. A thin, finely chiseled nose impassively attracted attention as did her high cheekbones. Despite attenuated lips, all components fit together like a well-designed mosaic. Bobbe quickly decided Mother Job had been and still was a most alluring woman before concentrating on what the nun was saying.

"It's most common to be unable to pinpoint exactly when one's vocation becomes apparent," she said simply, realizing the young woman opposite her was not going to answer. Turning, she faced Dan. "The Lord operates in mysterious ways, doesn't he, Mr. Moore? Tell me, how do you feel about Roberta's joining us?"

Suddenly finding himself the center of attention, Dan blurted, "I couldn't believe it, Sister. Why I ran that service station of mine in a daze for a week before it finally sunk in."

"Oh, you operate a service station, Mr. Moore?" she asked with genuine interest.

"Yes, Sister. Three islands and four bays."

"I have a brother who operates one, too."

Service station? Gas station? Truck stop! Again the trucker was fondling Bobbe's breasts and pulling her nipples roughly. Her hands flexed impatiently, unnoticed by the others. Once more she was clawing his back with her nails, while low, velar almost bestial sounds came from deep within them. Bobbe closed her eyes, relishing the memory for a brief second. Then, reluctantly, she pulled herself back to the room.

After visiting for a while longer, the Moores rose to follow the Reverend Mother on a limited tour of the convent. Leading them down a corridor with small rooms on either side, she said, "Most of the convent is off limits to outsiders but I will be able to show you the classrooms and the chapel."

"We have visiting Sunday twice a year and at those times these rooms are used for private visits with parents and family," she explained, indicating the tiny parlors as they walked down the hall. "Of course, we do have occasional visitors at other times but mostly business callers and the like."

They continued until they came to another passageway extending to their left. "Down here, we have the classrooms. Classes are from eight until noon."

"What will Roberta be studying, Mother?" Clare asked mouthing the unfamiliarity of her daughter's given name.

"General college courses such as English, history, mathematics, teaching methods, and, of course, religion. If the foreign missions are to be her calling, she'll also study first aid and some nursing, and languages such as Swahili and various other African dialects. In the past we taught Chinese but since we can't send our sisters to China anymore, it seemed senseless. Besides, Chinese is a difficult language to learn."

Bobbe smiled but not at the words of the Reverend Mother. Instead thoughts of the truck driver ricocheted through her mind. A Chinese truck driver? What had her truck driver looked like? Now faceless, the image slowly dissolved into nothingness and Bobbe reconcentrated her attention on the nun.

Continuing down the hall after inspecting several classrooms, Bobbe smiled confidently to herself. Each room had exuded a quiet dignity and sought-for excellence much like any classroom she had ever been in. She felt at home here. The friendly rooms set aside for education reeked of familiar odors—sweeping compound, furniture polish, and chalk dust. But there was a fourth scent intermingling with the known ones. The aroma of burnt incense, filtering from the chapel, subtly worked around and through the polish and dust, creating a relaxed and peaceful atmosphere. Was this mixture the smell of sanctity?

Turning a corner, Bobbe sensed a sudden change in Mother Job's attitude. There, in front of them, was the chapel entrance. Gleaming, ornately carved doors blocked their way but swung aside easily at the Reverend Mother's touch. The squeak, which did not sound, was more eloquent in its absence than if the hinges had shrieked loudly. The small, Gothic church's stained glass windows cast shafts of color in the air, ending in misshapen pools on the seats and backs of the pews. Here the smell of sanctity was heavier with incense than chalk dust but the ever-present furniture polish battled for recognition with the bland odor of candle wax. The Stations of the Cross were painted on the walls between the windows, and an elaborately carved altar of varnished wood trimmed in gold leaf completely dominated the small church.

"This is the chapel of Saint John the Baptist, our patron saint," Mother Job said softly. To the right of the altar stood a statue of Christ's herald and the convent's mystical mentor, a plaster sheepskin draped precariously over one shoulder. The figure leaned heavily on a traditional walking staff with his right arm thrust out, appearing to deliver a dissertation on the coming of God's Son. His face, radiant with the knowledge he bore, was frozen in perpetual ecstasy.

To the left of the altar was a statue of the Blessed Mother. The sad face contrasted startlingly to John's joyful expression. Outstretched hands, held slightly away from her body, implored God, her eyes gazing heavenward, to spare her Son the agonies He was to endure.

The atmosphere of calm and peace permeated every room and hall of the convent but was epitomized in the church almost to a degree of tangibility. After saying a silent prayer for Roberta, as her parents now found themselves referring to her, the Moores stood along with their daughter and the Reverend Mother to leave the chapel.

Once outside in the hall, Mother Job said, "We have Mass every morning at six o'clock, the Angelus at noon, chapel services at two in the afternoon, and Vespers at six in the evening right after dinner. We do pray a lot." A smile played on her narrow lips and her eyes beamed with good humor. "Of course, the novices and postulants are at liberty to come to the chapel any time they wish during their free hours."

"What about routine, Mother?" Clare asked taking Bobbe's hand in hers. Soon, she would not be able to reach out and touch her daughter anymore.

"Roberta will have the rules we live by, given to her tomorrow. Once she has permission to write home—"

"Permission?" Dan asked breaking into the Reverend Mother's explanation.

"It may sound harsh and difficult to one who is not a member but by having to secure permission for almost every simple thing—such as writing a letter to her parents— Roberta will understand and accept the degree of obedience she must render to God."

"What else is different?" Dan asked, narrowing his eyes suspiciously.

Reaching her office, Mother Job stopped and opened the door before answering. "Nothing uncommon since discipline is expected from all members. We are a communal organization. Permission is needed to use the sewing machine, going to the parlor, walking outside in the garden. None of us is ever allowed outside after dark alone. We must always have a companion no matter where we go. Of course, we are allowed to go into the morning darkness. An invigorating walk in the fresh air before six o'clock Mass starts the day off right."

Nodding in understanding, Dan decided to have one more go at asking Bobbe to reconsider.

"Since we are a communal group, Roberta's things will be owned by the convent, once you have shipped them here. They will be properly marked in the event they must be returned. As you know, she'll be free to leave during the first year, should she choose—or in case she doesn't make the grade, so to speak, from the convent's viewpoint. The vows she takes at the end of her first year bind her more closely to God and her decision to stay with the order will be one based on some experience. Perhaps convent life will be too difficult and different from the world she is used to. I will add, however, all of us here are very happy and I'm sure Roberta will not be an exception."

Mother Job extended her hand to Bobbe's parents. "It certainly has been a pleasure meeting you. Should you have need to communicate with us, I will always be at your disposal."

"Take good care of our little girl, Mother," Dan said softly as he shook the nun's hand carefully. "She—" He choked back a sob and the Reverend Mother placed an understanding hand on his shoulder.

Clare remained silent. She had promised herself she would not break down at the last minute and embarrass Bobbe. Regaining control as they walked back to the front of the building with their daughter, Clare said, "I'm glad we said our good-byes at home."

The scene in the kitchen played before Clare's eyes again as she and Dan tearfully hugged their daughter. That farewell had happened a thousand years ago and had nothing to do with the separation that was about to happen. Saying good-bye there had been easy. The two-hundred-fifty-mile drive was still ahead of them and Bobbe was going to be with them all the way. Now, the rehearsal was over. Tears stung her eyes. She turned her head so Bobbe wouldn't see them.

Leaving the building, they stepped into the late afternoon sunshine. "I hope you two don't plan to drive all the way back home tonight," Bobbe said huskily as they stopped by the trunk of the car. "Both of you must be as tired as I am. I really think you should stop at a motel and get a good night's sleep. Will you?"

"Only if we feel we should, honey," Dan answered and busied himself opening the trunk and pulling out Bobbe's suitcase. The best thing he could do to ease into a life without his daughter was throw himself into his work. No time for thinking about unpleasant things if you're busy was one of his mottoes. He knew Clare would have to contend with the empty house and it would be full of memories. Her adjustment would be the more difficult. And what of Bobbe? Would she be able to acclimate herself to a starkly simple life such as the Reverend Mother had outlined? Inside, he had promised to make one final try but Bobbe would have to be receptive before he pushed too hard.

Setting her suitcase on the ground, Dan turned and faced his daughter. "Just one more time, Bobbe. Are you absolutely sure you can do this? You've always had just about everything you've needed—or wanted. Your mother and I have always treated you like an adult—pretty much had your own way with everything. Would—"

Bobbe smiled as tears rolled down her cheeks. Stepping forward, she hugged her father. "Oh, yes, Daddy. I'm positive. This is what I want. I'm doing it for—for—*him,*" she sobbed.

Squeezing her tightly, Dan muttered, "Bye, baby. If you decide you don't like it here or things aren't working out for you, just call and we'll be at the front door before you hang up. Understand?" A big smile crossed his face despite the tears and he held her at arm's length.

Managing a sob and a little laugh at the same time, Bobbe said, "I understand."

Her mother, who was standing nearby, stepped closer and the three hugged tightly.

"I love you both so much," Bobbe managed between sobs. "Please be happy for me. I know it's right for me to be here, and I want you to think of it that way."

Unable to speak, Dan and Clare nodded in agreement.

"'Bye, Mommy! 'Bye, Daddy!" she whispered hoarsely. "I'll miss you both."

Without another word, her parents got in the Chevrolet and swiftly drove away. Bobbe watched until the top of the car disappeared beyond the low lying hills before picking up her suitcase. Turning, she faced her new home. Looming above her, the building seemed so large and she suddenly felt so very small.

Then an evil smile destroyed her pouting mouth and she said hollowly, *"I am here!"*

CHAPTER SEVEN

Sister Damien, Mistress of Novices, tapped on the desk to gain the attention of the girls seated before her. Although there was hardly a whisper in the room, each of the prospective candidates seemed to be holding her breath, waiting for their first indoctrination session.

"I should like to take this opportunity to welcome all of you to your new home," she began. "I'm certain each of you will find happiness and complete fulfillment of your vocation and life here. For those of you whom I have not yet met, I am Sister Damien, Mistress of Novices. It is my responsibility to guide you into the smooth flow of convent life." Her voice droned on enumerating her duties where their success and well-being were concerned.

Bobbe covertly watched the girls and young women around her with interest as she felt drawn into the confidence of the convent. Practically awestruck at the silence the building seemed to impose, she had not found it difficult at this point to accept the few rules she had been made aware of. There were periods of the day when no one spoke with the exception of the Reverend Mother and those nuns who were involved in a task or duty requiring communication. Each woman, most especially the candidates, was to execute personal assignments to the best of her ability with celerity and cheerfulness, bearing in mind at all times their effort was being done for and in the name of God, Whom they were to serve the rest of their lives.

Thoughts of her restless night eased into her mind when she recalled the difficulty she had going to sleep in the strange little room which had been assigned to her. She smiled at the aptness of the name each bedroom was called—cell. Although she hadn't actually stepped the area off, Bobbe knew it could not be much more than ten by twelve feet. Her bed proved to be uncomfortable and most of the night was spent trying to find a position that would allow her to sleep. When she finally dropped off, it seemed only minutes had passed when she heard a bell clanging off in the distance. The window was still black with night as she sleepily dressed.

Her attention was drawn back to the front of the room and Sister Damien who was concluding her dissertation. "Since this period is almost over, I want to finish by saying you will find when you go out in the world that all people, regardless of their individual faith or belief, will respect you and hold you in the highest of esteem. You young ladies must remember to accept their special courtesies as homage to God and not to yourselves personally."

On cue, the bell clanged, ending the meeting and Bobbe thought of the scene as pupils exited to hurry to another classroom. Random thoughts of the previous evening, when the nuns were introduced to the new candidates, brought a smile to her face when she recalled some of the women's chosen names. There had been easy names to remember such as Sisters John, James, Timothy, Edward, Michael, Raphael, Stephen, Damien, and naturally, Mother Job, most of whom Bobbe guessed to be under fifty years in age. The older women's names had caused more than a bit of confusion when the newcomers were introduced to them: Sisters Theophania, Theodosia, Theophilia, Seraphina, Flavia, and Linus were some she managed to recall while following the group into the hall.

"Roberta?" a voice called from behind her.

Turning, she saw Sister Damien motioning for her to come to the desk at the front of the room. "Yes, Sister?"

"During this period, while the others are at liberty to pray or meditate individually, I believe there's something we should take care of right now," the nun said adjusting her thick-lensed glasses on the bridge of her aquiline nose.

"Sister?"

"Your hair," she said simply. "Your hair must be cut. It's too long and will require too much time to care for in its present state. Perhaps you noticed. You're the only girl with her hair below her collar."

Puckering her lips in thought, Bobbe recalled the group who had just quitted the room. Her position in the last row enabled her now to mentally replay the scene in her mind's eye. It was peculiar she hadn't thought of the fact when the mental image of twenty-nine heads of bobbed hair loomed in her mind.

"Whatever you say, Sister." For some inexplicable reason she felt she would leap off the bell tower if one of her superiors were to ask her. She felt compelled to obey, no matter what the directive. If obedience counted, she knew she'd be a success.

"Follow me, Roberta," Sister Damien ordered and Bobbe fell in behind the woman as she marched from the classroom. "Hair can be such a vain thing if we allow it to become such. I'm certain you've had many compliments concerning yours but you'll find as you progress in your studies and vows that hair is not necessary for salvation."

Bobbe followed without comment and they turned into a room down the hall where they found a white-veiled nun apparently waiting for them.

"This is Sister Felicia," the Mistress of Novices said briskly. "She's a senior novice and has handled the hair-cutting chores since her arrival four years ago. Sister, take care of Roberta's hair, please."

"Yes, Sister," the young woman said as her superior departed and then turned to Bobbe. "Sit down, Roberta."

Bobbe sat on the stool, which was placed in the center of the room, and sighed.

"You have lovely hair," Sister Felicia said and began cutting it with practiced twitchings of a scissors.

"Had," Bobbe whispered to herself.

"What?" The scissors stopped.

"Nothing."

"You said something, Roberta. What was it?"

"Had."

"I don't understand."

"You said I have lovely hair. I merely corrected the tense of the verb. I had beautiful hair."

"Don't be vain about it." The scissors began harvesting her hair again.

"God gave it to me, didn't He?"

"Yes."

"All I was doing was taking care of what He gave me." Bobbe felt comfortable when she recognized a touch of rebellion in her voice.

"It's also His to take away, Roberta," Sister Felicia admonished.

Falling silent, Bobbe concentrated on the nervous sound of the scissors opening and closing as her blue black hair fell to the floor. It had been a long time since she had worn short hair and, accepting the inevitable, closed her eyes to picture what she would look like. By the time the trimming was completed, she had accepted the mental image forming in her mind and smiled inwardly. It wouldn't be so bad.

"There. I think that about does it," the novice said and brushed the last few remaining long strands from Bobbe's shoulders to the floor. "You're free to go to the chapel or you can go to the garden and pray and meditate."

Thanking the young woman, Bobbe decided to go to the small church since they were to receive their white collars and black chapel veils during the next period. Making her way through the still unfamiliar halls, she found the carved doors and entered. Selecting an empty row of seats, she was soon joined by another candidate who smiled as Bobbe slid over to allow access to the pew.

Leaning over, the newcomer whispered, "My name's Connie Devler and I preferred your hair long. Why'd you cut it?"

Bobbe's attention fixed on the red-headed girl kneeling next to her but she said nothing until she saw the humor snapping in her companion's eyes. Then, unable to restrain themselves, both girls began giggling softly.

By the end of October, Bobbe and Connie became close friends. Although their backgrounds were dissimilar, they found the differences to be the basis for their initial conversations. Learning about each other in degrees whenever they had the opportunity to visit, they grew fond of their friendship.

During the weeks following their arrival at the convent, both girls had managed to write a letter home each week, despite the heavy load of school work the teachers assigned every day. The routine of the order quickly absorbed Bobbe and Connie and by the end of their first six weeks, neither thought anything of arising each day at five o'clock to take a brisk walk outside before Mass was celebrated. Following their silent breakfast, classes dominated the morning, and after their noon prayers and lunch, the postulants managed to relax for an hour during which they talked or wrote home when permission was granted.

Having missed Bobbe at the refectory, Connie went to the garden after lunch to meditate. Large puffy clouds floated through the air against an azure sky as nuns, novices, and postulants took advantage of the Indian summer's last-minute reprieve, by praying in the garden. The trees, stripped of their leaves, waited patiently for winter's onslaught. Here and there, a missed leaf of nondescript brown, which had escaped the rake of the part-time gardener, hid against an equally lackluster lawn.

Her red hair reflecting the sun's warm rays like burnished copper, Connie walked with her head bowed, as though in prayer. Her mind wandered back to her childhood home on an Iowa farm. Visions of her four older brothers clicked through her memory when thoughts of family quarrels, picnics, and parties, as well as the hard work all of them had had to partake in to help their mother operate the two-hundred-forty acre farm were called to mind. Carl Devler, her father, had been gored to death by a frenzied bull when she was three years old. Frightened by the calamitious event and its aftermath of tears and lingering hurt, she had sought succor more than once from her brothers who happily accepted the position of surrogate father whenever they were called on to fill the role for their little sister.

After graduating from high school, the privilege of continuing her education was insisted upon by her mother and brothers. Since the farm had long become a paying business, the tuition was no problem and Connie gratefully accepted their dictum without reservation. An outstanding student, it became apparent in her junior year when her grade average slipped a full point, that some outside influence was preoccupying her mind. By the end of her junior year in college, she had decided her life belonged to God and withdrew from school to enter the Sisters of the Bearer of the Divine Word as a postulant candidate.

Now, strolling along in the warm October sunshine, her thoughts flitted from subject to subject, still somewhat amazed at her decision to become a nun. Rolling like beans from a jar, her daydreams flashed by without the courtesy of stopping long enough to be examined in detail. Slowly, her future as a religious began intruding, elbowing aside the memories of her past, interjecting images of foreign countries and people like herself, bedecked in her order's habit, as the focal point.

Sensing a presence near her, she turned to find Bobbe beside her.

"Have you cracked the books for that history test we have to take?" Bobbe asked, hoping her friend would offer to study with her. She had found it peculiar, since her arrival at the convent, that her ability to concentrate as she had in high school, seemed to have been left at home in her bedroom. Some of the more familiar courses had come naturally, by instinct. But other times she felt totally incapable of confronting a new challenge. Completely helpless. Yet her compulsion to obey the nuns was as great as the first full day she had spent at the convent. That bothered her too. Where was her spirit of rebellion? Her individuality? Her ability to think for herself?

Her own thoughts had been undisturbed by anything out of the ordinary since the day her parents had left. Why she had stood in front of the building and announced to no one in particular that she was here puzzled her at best. To her it seemed odd she had accepted so readily and without hesitation the strict discipline of the convent. Perhaps this was where she belonged. Perhaps she would make a good nun.

The rhyme began softly at first. "Nun! Nun! I'm gonna be a nun and I won't get none 'cause I don't want none! Except from—"

Then it stopped when Connie, glad her friend had interrupted her own gyrating thoughts, answered her question. "I've looked at it some but not to any great extent. Why?"

"Let's study together."

"Do you think we can get permission?"

"As long as we're not planning something devious, I think Sister Damien will allow it. If we're to be good sisters—"

"—we must apply ourselves and help each other whenever possible," Connie interrupted, finishing the Novice Mistress's oft repeated statement and both girls snickered.

"Other than the African history test, what were you thinking about just now, before I walked up?" Bobbe asked.

"Believe me, the test was the farthest thing from my mind. I guess I was thinking about a million things all at the same time. My brothers and my mom. Our farm. College. Being a nun and all that is ahead of me—us, yet."

"You want to know what I was thinking about?" Bobbe asked with an impish grin.

Connie shook her head.

"Hallowe'en. It's today and I was thinking about some of the tricks we used to play on people. Did you do anything when you were a kid?" Bobbe asked turning to her friend to wait for an answer. It was the difference in background both girls found fascinating. Bobbe had never had much to do with farm life and had on isolated occasions wondered what farm kids did for entertainment. Hallowe'en was just such a time she now found herself curious about.

"Nothing special. My brothers never wanted to take me along with them when they were old enough to drive the car and be gone from home on special occasions like dances or games at school or Hallowe'en."

"I thought you said you got along famously with your brothers?" Bobbe asked.

"I did and I still do. But they were pretty stubborn at times and I guess they figured I'd only get in the way. Once I was too old for Hallowe'en but old enough for dances and parties, they always took me along."

"Oh."

"What did you do, Bobbe?"

"Most of the time just the usual. You know— 'Tricks or

treats! Money or eats!'" she chanted softly.

An older nun, walking in the opposite direction, looked up when she heard the rhyme. Frowning for the benefit of the two postulants, she lowered her head once the girls passed her and were unable to see the smile the couplet had generated.

"Those were the good times. Even the nasty things we did are pretty funny now, although—"

"Nasty?" Connie asked. "What did you do that was nasty?"

"We'd throw dried peas or beans at people's windows who hadn't given us anything. We could always picture them sitting in their house so relaxed and comfortable when the beans would hit the window and scare the daylights out of them. Sometimes we soaped windows and hid rubbish barrels."

Connie giggled. "Too bad we can't do something like that here."

"Do you suppose Sister Damien would let us go?"

Connie shook her head and continued laughing.

"Maybe if we took her along, she'd let us," Bobbe persisted and both girls mentally placed a black mask on the Mistress of Novices behind her wire-rimmed, thick glasses.

Fighting to control their laughter when they compared notes and found they had masked their immediate superior in much the same way, they continued walking, now toward the back of the garden.

Convinced that reminiscing about past Hallowe'ens was just as good a meditation as a serious topic, Bobbe continued, "One time, we got an old man who lived a couple of blocks away really mad at us. We buried his garbage pail in his front yard and put a homemade tombstone over it. He caught us and called our parents. Boy, did we get heck. He ranted and raved at my mom and dad something terrible and said we'd all burn in hell if something wasn't done about the criminal element growing up in Springfield."

"Looks like he was wrong—where you're concerned, at least," Connie said lightly.

"Daddy thought it was awful but he laughed about it after he had spanked me. I guess I was about eleven or twelve at the time. Did you ever wonder why things that were serious enough to be spanked for were always funny enough to be laughed at afterward?"

Recognizing the truthfulness of an ironic contradiction, Connie nodded as the two postulants walked toward the convent.

The next morning, Father Grant, the convent's confessor who came every morning to celebrate Mass and again every evening for Vespers, delivered the Feast of All Saints sermon. Shortly after their arrival, the new candidates had been told by a first-year novice how Father Grant had three hundred sixty-five sermons and delivered one each day to the Sisters. The newcomers had broken into gales of laughter when the informer finished by saying any fourth year novice could stand in for him in the event the old priest became ill or lost his voice. For several years, everyone had expected the aged man to retire but methodically, Father Grant made his appearance each day. Confident his failing eyesight would soon prevent him from driving his automobile, the nuns bided their time.

Following his longer than usual sermon, the priest continued with the Mass and soon the nuns, novices, and postulants were lining up to receive communion.

"*Corpus Domine, Jesu Christe—*" he intoned before placing the blessed wafer of unleavened bread on the outstretched tongue of each woman. "The Body of our Lord, Jesus Christ—" The rest of the prayer was hidden in a rush of wheezing breath as he moved on to the next recipient. A sleepy eyed altar boy, who lived nearby and assisted the priest every morning, held a golden paten under each chin in case a Host or piece of one should fall from the mouth of the communicant—or from the unsteady hands of the old priest.

The nun to Bobbe's right received and stood to return to her pew as the priest moved to his right to deliver the next host.

"*Corpus Domine, Jesu Christe—*" he intoned again before placing the Host on Bobbe's outstretched tongue. Her head, tilted slightly back to receive the wafer, held rigid as he gave her the Body of Christ, under the appearance of bread. Immediately the Host fell to the paten as if it had taken on a life of its own and abhorred its destiny to enter the postulant's mouth. Startled, the old priest retrieved it from the metal plate and placed it on Bobbe's still outstretched tongue. Again it slipped off.

Embarrassed, Bobbe wondered what his problem was. She felt foolish with her head tipped back and her tongue jutting from her mouth.

Once more, the priest held the Host, more tightly than before and gingerly placed it on her protruding tongue.

Quickly, Bobbe drew the blessed wafer into her mouth. With a sigh of relief, the priest moved on to Connie who was kneeling next to the flushed postulant.

Standing, Bobbe turned to leave the communion railing and was instantly struck with cramping pains in her mid-section. Barely able to stand upright, she rushed from the church instead of returning to her seat and hurried toward the nearest lavatory. Retching, Bobbe ran down the hall. Her stomach felt ready to burst when she pushed the door of the rest room open. Dry heaves convulsed her body after she knelt before the stool, gagging for several minutes before vomiting the contents of her stomach into the bowl. The Host, still intact, was as black as it had been white when she received it. Staring at it unbelievingly, she watched it slowly disintegrate in the water.

"I don't think I would be upset if I were you, Roberta," Mother Job said confidently.

"But, Mother," Bobbe persisted, "the Host was black— black as coal. I had just swallowed it." Instead of waiting, she should have seen the Mistress of Novices two days before, right after the incident. But with so many prayer sessions scheduled for the holy day and individual visits to the chapel encouraged the next day, where prayers were offered for the peaceful repose of deceased souls, she had missed her superior each time she had sought her out.

Then, by accident, she had met Mother Job in the hall following her second class. The Mother Superior had greeted Bobbe, immediately detecting the anxiety in the postulant's voice, which led to the impromptu visit in Mother Job's office.

"And you were ill—ill enough to vomit. I'm certain you only had an overabundance of acid in your system, which made the Host change color," the older woman said.

"Why would I feel so sick—just from the Host?"

"Have you ever had this sort of thing happen before, Roberta?"

Pausing before she spoke, Bobbe could not recall a single instance when she had reacted so violently to anything she had ingested. "No, Mother, I haven't—at least not that I can remember," she said quietly and fixed her eyes unblinkingly on the Mother General of the order.

"Then, forget it. I'm sure there's nothing wrong with you since you obviously feel just fine now. Ahhh—you do feel all right, don't you?"

"Yes, Mother."

"Did anything happen yesterday or this morning when you received communion?"

"No, Mother."

"And you feel well now?"

"Yes, Mother. I'm fine. I guess I was concerned I wouldn't be allowed to stay in the convent if I were ill and couldn't complete the course of study or do my work here."

"Child, you must remember how the Little Flower suffered physical ills and pains before she was permitted to leave this earth and go to our Heavenly Father," Mother Job said, her voice assuming a velvety air of comfort, one Bobbe was positive reflected the true nature of the woman behind the desk.

"Very well, Mother," she said and turned to leave. "I won't concern myself with it any longer if you say so."

Reaching under her guimpe, the nun produced a small silver watch and checked it against the electric wall clock. "You'd better hurry or you'll miss the rest of your African History class," she said reassuming her air of authority.

"Yes, Mother," Bobbe said as she closed the door quietly.

Hurrying through the now familiar halls, Bobbe managed a smile. She had been completely upset by the incident and had lain in her bed for two nights, eyes wide open, afraid she would be asked to leave. Concluding she had overreacted to the whole episode, she approached the door to the classroom quietly and entered.

Slipping into a seat in the back row, she tried to pick up on the thread of the class's stream of ideas. She watched Sister

Madonna, *The Pacer,* as the nun had been dubbed by the class after several sessions, now move from one side of the room to the other as she lectured.

The nun had found it more relaxing to stand and walk about the room when she spoke to the class, than to stay seated or rooted to a lectern, reading from notes. Her sense of dedication was etched deeply into her face as she extolled the wonders and mysteries of the "Dark Continent."

A well-manicured hand was suddenly thrust heavenward in an attempt to attract the nun's attention. Bobbe strained to see who wanted to ask a question but was unable from her point of vantage.

"Yes, Joan?" Sister Madonna acquiesced in the inevitability of a question from her eager charges.

Standing, Joan White said, "I appreciate, Sister, that we are to do God's work but what if we have absolutely no success in communicating with the natives? What then? Do we move on to another tribe or area or what? What do we do?"

"You will find, Joan—all of you will discover," Sister Madonna said patiently, sweeping the room with her authoritative stare, "once you are in the field, that these poor unfortunate creatures, who have been denied the Word of God because of their birthplaces, will welcome the work you do. You will not only be teaching them about Jesus and His Works but also about improving their lot in life. You will nurse them when they are sick. Laugh with them when they are happy. Cry with them when they are sad."

"How do we get all the supplies we'll need, Sister?" another girl asked without standing.

"You learn to use the things you have to work with. There are no smooth highways in Africa where you are needed, at least not the type with which you are acquainted. No trains. No trucks."

Her voice droned on but Bobbe was no longer hearing anything she was saying. The word *truck* had triggered an all but forgotten memory as she mentally writhed on the bed with her nameless lover. No, that was wrong. He did have a name. Howard. No, Howie. That was it. He had been rough with her but she had enjoyed his crudities. His penis had been so large she wanted to scream as she recalled the fierce sense of pleasure it had given her when it entered her body, ripping through her virginity. Shuddering in erotic pleasure, she recalled with a pang of fear, how cold, almost freezing cold his member had been and thought again that it should have been warm, even hot like her own body had felt that night. Involuntarily trembling when she revived the sensation of his ice cold semen spilling into her, she managed a tortured smile as each thrust was savored.

"Roberta? Roberta!" Sister Madonna snapped angrily as all heads in front of Bobbe turned to stare at her silently. "Good heavens, girl, do your daydreaming someplace else. Not here in the classroom. It's very important you know all about Africa and its history if you are to go there one day. Now," she coughed and cleared her throat, "as I was saying, we have given up most desires and wants and the right to bear children so we can serve God to the best of our abilities. We are, in a sense, married to God and it is He, Whom we shall serve."

Bobbe, still perplexed and mentally floundering at the nun's mandate, tried to remember why she had been daydreaming. What had held her attention so tightly that all sense of time and place had been lost?

Then, a familiar sensation washed through Bobbe's body as a cramp, not unlike the one she had suffered at the communion railing All Saints Day, began heaving and contracting. Growing more intense the contractions and pain caromed from one area to another but she resisted doubling over. Abruptly, it stopped. Now she could feel a new, different phenomenon. A feeling of growing—her body seemed to be expanding. Dropping her head forward, her eyes widened in terror when she saw her abdomen swelling, billowing out- ward. Unable to comprehend, she was thankful for her tardiness and the fact she was sitting in the last row, near the door. If it became necessary to leave, she would be able to do so with the least amount of disturbance to the class.

Attempting to move a hand to her midriff to check herself, Bobbe found to her horror she was unable to shift her arm. Desperately she tried to bring the other into motion, but it too held fast in its position on the desktop. Her legs refused to budge. About to cry out for help, she gasped when the room faded as though the sun had gone down for the night and dark folds of blackness crushed in on her.

Unaware of Bobbe's plight, Sister Madonna decided it was time her lecture returned to the topic at hand. Facing the blackboard, she pulled a map of Africa from its window shade roller when a deep male voice boomed out in the room.

"Sows! God will never fuck you! But I will, if you let me!"

Whirling about, Sister Madonna saw only her students with expressions of surprise and bewilderment on their faces. The only sound in the room was the map spinning back to its resting place.

"Who said that?" she demanded, knowing no man should be in the building at this hour.

No one answered.

With an audible sigh of relief, Bobbe felt normal once more and nervously shuffled her feet under her desk just to make certain she could move them again. Surreptitiously moving her hands from the desk top so she wouldn't attract attention, she felt her abdomen and found it, too, in its natural state. Unaware she had spoken, she had heard the voice but no one had turned around quickly enough to see her mouth the lurid challenge.

CHAPTER EIGHT

Tension, folded onto itself, weighed heavily in Mother Job's office, pressing down on the three women as they watched Kathleen O'Reilly, the last postulant to be interviewed, leave. Following the obscene remark in Sister Madonna's history class, the nun had ordered her students to search the entire convent building. When nothing out of the ordinary was found, she sent her charges to the chapel and hurried to Sister Damien. After explaining what had happened, the two women, distraught at the idea that something of this nature had taken place within the confines of their home, rushed to Mother Job.

Now that all of the students had been questioned, Sister Madonna stood and began pacing the floor. "I simply don't understand it, Mother. A man's voice, very deep, very rough and hoarse, was heard by everyone in the room. Yet nothing or no one was found when we looked. I don't understand it, at all."

Her eyes, magnified by the thick lenses she wore, reflected Sister Damien's dismay at the incident. "At least the girls' stories were virtually identical," she said turning from Mother Job to Sister Madonna who nodded in agreement.

"Roberta Moore described it somewhat differently than you or the others, Sister," Mother Job said keeping track of the pacing teacher without moving her head. Her smooth complexion was unwrinkled by the laugh lines around her eyes. "Perhaps we should talk with her again, just to make sure."

Finding herself being sought out for affirmation when she

found the Reverend Mother peering at her, Sister Damien said, "By all means, Mother. I think it would be an excellent idea."

"Would you call her, Sister?" Mother Job asked of Sister Madonna.

Turning, the teacher left the room and returned several minutes later with Bobbe after having dismissed the class who were waiting in the hall. Sister Madonna took her place in a straight-backed chair next to the desk and opposite Sister Damien who was seated on Mother Job's right side.

Feeling she was being reprimanded by a board of judges, Bobbe stood in front of the desk, an apprehensive, almost frightened expression on her face. Surely, they didn't suspect her of having made the scandalous statements in the classroom since her voice was nothing like the coarse sounds they had heard. But if they didn't, why had she been singled out of the class to be called back for more questions? She had told them exactly what had happened, just like everyone else. Despite Mother Job's gentle admonition not to talk among themselves about the incident, each girl knew everyone who had been in the room had been asked the same questions. Then, why had she been called back when none of the others had? Why?

"Roberta," Mother Job began, "would you be kind enough to give us your account of this afternoon's occurrence again? We want to clear this up if we possibly can."

Her anxiety transfigured into terror when she gasped, "Mother, you don't think I had anything to do with it, do you?" Her frightened tone covered the disbelief she felt at the insinuation.

"Good Lord, no, child," Mother Job said quickly and looked to her two companions for confirmation. "But we have to solve this and we will be talking to all of the girls again. We had to start with someone. Now, go ahead."

"Well," Bobbe began slowly as she mentally reviewed the scene in the classroom again, "Sister Madonna had just finished scolding me for daydreaming and had—"

"You didn't say you had been scolded for anything before, Roberta," Mother Job said, looking quizzically first to Sister Madonna and then to the Mistress of Novices.

"Yes, I caught her daydreaming, Mother," the history teacher offered, "but I don't believe it's relevant to the matter at hand. Do either of you?"

"I feel it's immaterial," Sister Damien said quickly.

"I don't see how it could have any bearing, Sister," Mother Job agreed and nodded to Bobbe. "Go ahead, Roberta."

"Sister Madonna then turned to the—no, she said something about us being married to God and serving Him and then she turned to the blackboard to pull down the map of Africa. Just as she began, the voice—the voice—said—what it said. I—I don't have to say the words, do I, Mother?" Bobbe's eyes pleaded eloquently with the head of the convent.

"I'd rather you didn't. They're scandalous and blasphemous."

When nothing more was said and the three nuns continued perusing Bobbe's face, she felt obligated to continue. "It—they—the words seemed to be in answer to Sister Madonna's statement about being married to God, I think."

"We've come to that conclusion," Mother Job said. "How did the voice sound? Could you describe it?" The Mother General's words and facial expression conveyed to the frightened postulant that she was not suspect and could only be helpful by restating her story.

"Well, it was very deep and—rough. You know, kind of hoarse. And it sounded as if I were thinking it or hearing it inside of me."

"Inside of you?" Sister Damien said, her eyes widening thickly behind her glasses.

"As though it came from another room through the walls or something like that. I don't know, it's hard to describe. It all happened so fast."

"I know," Sister Madonna said and turned to Mother Job, nodding her head in agreement. "I have difficulty myself trying to explain how it sounded. But I must emphasize I did hear it with my ears, not inside of me. What do you mean by that, Roberta?"

"Well, maybe saying it sounded inside of me isn't exactly right. It was more like thinking it or feeling it. Kind of like—I know this will sound silly, but have you ever stood close to a big bass drum when a band marches by?"

Slowly nodding their heads, the three women exchanged disturbed glances before refixing their attention on the girl.

"Well, it was the very same feeling," she said brightly as she recalled the impression. "You know, you hear the drum but your whole body seems to vibrate along with the beat. Then, you feel the sound within yourself as well as hear it."

"I see," Mother Job said slowly and turned to Sister Madonna. "Where in the room does Roberta sit, Sister?"

"Normally toward the front but she wasn't in her regular seat."

Looking toward the Mistress of Novices Bobbe said, "I was here, in Mother Job's office. I stayed beyond the starting time of class and was late. When I got to the room, I just sat in the last row near the door."

Mother Job nodded in agreement and asked, "Was anyone else sitting close to you, Roberta?"

"Not really, Mother," Bobbe said as she pictured the seating pattern as it had been when she entered the room. "There was at least one row of empty seats between me and the others."

"That must be it, then." Mother Job's face brightened as she turned first to the woman on her right and then on her left. When she saw they were puzzled by her proclamation, she continued, "Don't you see? That's why Roberta describes the sound so differently. The voice must have come from the hall through the closed door. Ah—it was closed, wasn't it?"

"Yes, it was, Mother," Bobbe said while Sister Madonna only nodded.

"Some degenerate man," Mother Job offered, "must have gotten into the building with some device to magnify or distort his voice. He probably escaped before anyone saw him."

"That sounds logical to me," Sister Damien said and smiled broadly at her superior.

"It does make sense, Mother," Sister Madonna slowly agreed, the solution weighing heavily on her mind. "What in heaven's name is this world coming to anyway?"

"You may go now, Roberta," Sister Damien said. "It is all right, isn't it, Mother?"

"Yes. You may return to the others, Roberta, but for now, please keep this to yourself. I wouldn't want the others thinking the convent wasn't safe or that a maniac was able to break in and run around frightening everyone. Do I have your word?" Mother Job's eyes, unadorned with laugh lines, matched the severity of her facial expression, conveying the fervidness of her message more clearly than her words, and reaffirming in Bobbe's mind that the woman could be and was, indeed, stern when the occasion demanded.

"Of course, Mother," Bobbe said and turned to leave the office.

The balance of the day passed smoothly as the routine of the convent reasserted itself and that evening, following the last period of silence, Bobbe slipped from her cell and hurried to Connie's room, which was down the hall from her own.

After they had been together several minutes, Connie became aware of Bobbe's lethargic attitude and said, "What's the matter tonight?"

"It's nothing, really," she said hesitantly. "I guess this prowler thing this afternoon has gotten to me. I'm still a little scared, aren't you?"

"Well, I am and I'm not," Connie said and stood to cross the room to the small window that overlooked the hills surrounding the convent. "I think if someone did get in, there are more than enough of us to overpower him. Don't you?"

"If you look at it in that way, I guess you're right. I'm glad Reverend Mother decided to tell everyone to be on the alert. If just a few of us knew what really happened this afternoon and the rest of the girls and nuns didn't, I think it would have been unbearable. I would've busted if I couldn't talk about it with someone."

"I didn't know you couldn't keep a secret, Bobbe," Connie said teasingly and returned to sit on the bed. "I don't think I'll ever confide in you again. However, if you know of any juicy bits of gossip you'd like to share, I'll be more than willing to listen."

Motioning for her smiling friend to move closer to her, Bobbe, more relaxed now, whispered, "I know for a fact a girl in the convent—this convent—right here in this building jilted a man to join the order." Leaning forward she leered wickedly and then snickered.

Connie stared wide eyed at her and exclaimed with mock surprise and indignation, "You're kidding?"

"Cross my heart," Bobbe reassured her and drew an "X" on her left breast. "Come on, don't tell me you didn't have a guy you were going with before you joined?"

Knitting her forehead, Connie thought for a moment before answering. "No, not really. Oh, occasional dates and I went steady just to go steady my first year in college but nothing serious." She waited for Bobbe to make her revelation and finally blurted, "Come on, Bobbe, who is it?"

"Me."

"You?" Connie stared incredulously. "You jilted a guy to come to the convent?"

"Yup." Bobbe managed to swallow the lump she suddenly felt forming in her throat.

"Why? For heaven's sake, why?"

"You should know why, Connie. I just felt it was right for me to come here. How long did you think about joining?" Bobbe asked softly but with a defiant edge to her voice.

"I don't really know. I guess from the time I was a freshman in high school," Connie began. "I dated and stuff but the idea was always there. Even through college, when I went steady, the notion was with me. Our pastor and the nuns at the parish school suggested I date so I could actually test the validity of my vocation. Father Schmeichel said, 'If you go to the convent you want to be positive of your vocation and not make a mistake. Find out a little about life and what you'd be giving up before making a decision.'"

Bobbe, who appeared to pale, lifted her eyes from her friend and stared into the night through the window across the room.

"Oh, come on, Bobbe," Connie coaxed when she saw her friend was not about to give up her secrets easily. "Tell me about it. I want to know."

"There's not that much to tell," she said flatly. "I went with Jay—Jay Livingston—for almost three years. Steady, that is. We went to school dances during our senior year but not going together if you know what I mean. The night we graduated from high school we exchanged class rings. That was in forty-nine. I went to work in an insurance office and Jay went off to college. I didn't date anyone while he was gone and then this last July, he asked me to marry him. I wonder—?" Sudden realization crushed into her mind that the night Jay asked her to marry him was the first time any thought of a vocation had ever occurred. Why was she thinking of that now? Staring straight ahead, a quizzical look crossed her face but she said nothing.

"Bobbe?" Connie spoke softly after several seconds had passed, concluding her visitor was not going to continue. "What is it, Bobbe?"

Connie came back into focus when Bobbe blinked her eyes. "I—I'm not sure," she whispered. Should she tell Connie? What if she didn't have a vocation? What had made her believe she had thought about it for a long time? What would the Reverend Mother say? What would her parents think? What would everyone think?

"Connie? Can I trust you?" she asked quietly.

"Of course you can, Bobbe. What's the matter? What's wrong?"

"I mean," Bobbe said again emphatically, "not breathe a word of what I'm about to tell you to anyone—not anyone."

"Scout's honor," she said holding her hand up in a three-fingered salute.

"This is serious, Connie. Please don't joke about it. Okay?"

"I'm sorry, Bobbe." Connie sobered when she saw how intense her friend had become. "Now tell me."

"I—I'm not sure I belong here." Bobbe waited to see what reaction her statement would draw.

After several hushed seconds had laboriously crawled by, Connie asked bewilderedly, "What do you mean, 'not belong here'?"

"I'm not sure I have a genuine vocation. I'm not sure I should even be here." Again she waited for her friend to react.

"What makes you say that, Bobbe?" Connie asked reaching out to take her hand. She found it trembling and damp.

"I never realized it before right now," she said and stood, nervously crossing the room to the window. "So help me, the night Jay asked me to marry him was the first time—the very first time the idea of joining a convent ever crossed my mind. Her voice, flat with disappointment, shook when she spoke

"You mean when he asked you to marry him, you announced out of the clear blue sky that you wanted to join the convent?"

She tried to speak but failing, only nodded her head in agreement.

"I'm no theologian," Connie said standing to join her friend at the window, "but I would say that was about the strongest type of vocation there is. To have it hit you like a ton of bricks during a proposal of marriage from a guy you've liked and loved has got to be the real thing. How come you're so concerned about it now?"

Shaking her head, Bobbe said softly, "I—I don't know. I'm just a little confused, that's all."

"Look, Bobbe, I'm pretty sure everyone who decides to give his life to God has doubts about the decision they've made when they first begin their vocation. I know I had plenty."

"You did?"

"Only mine came before I got here. You decided and then before too much time passed, you were here with a lot of time to think on it. From what you've told me, you've got a vocation and that's all there is to it." Guiding Bobbe toward the door Connie gave her a hug around her shoulders and said, "Get a good night's sleep and everything will look better in the morning."

Pausing at the door, Bobbe turned to face the red-headed girl. "I hope you're right, Connie," she said softly and turned the knob. Her friend smiled reassuringly and without saying anything more, Bobbe left the room. The latch clicked quietly behind her and she walked the few steps to her own cell. Confused thoughts smothered her as she dressed for bed. Kneeling in the center of the room to recite her final prayers of the day, she found the imploring words of supplication difficult to utter and slowly her concentration became lost in the tumultuous thoughts of her sudden discovery.

Automatically turning off the single bare bulb when she finished, Bobbe lay down and dozed fitfully after several minutes of unresolved frustration. The faces of everyone who had attended her reception loomed in her confused dreams, their mocking laughter building in volume until she bolted upright in bed, her face swathed in perspiration. Pulling the thin blankets around her she muttered softly to herself, "Did I ever do anything 'holy' before I decided to join the convent?"

"Mommy! Mommy! Do you know what I'm going to be when I grow up?" Bobbe cried breathlessly as she dashed into the kitchen and threw her arms around her mother's legs.

"What, darling?" Clare asked disengaging her daughter's tight grasp, before crouching down to Bobbe's seven-year-old height. "What are you going to be when you grow up?"

"A Sister just like Sister Albertilla," she exclaimed with a beaming smile. "She's so pretty and nice and good to us kids. I just love her. But—I don't know if I can be." A tiny sob replaced the cheery words.

"Why, Bobbe? Why couldn't you be if you wanted?" Clare asked and wiped a tear from her daughter's eyes.

"I don't have freckles like she does. Do you have to have freckles to be a Sister, Mommy?"

Suppressing a smile, Clare hugged her child. "No, my darling. No, you don't have to have freckles in order to be a nun."

"I don't want to be a nun. I want to be a Sister like Sister Albertilla."

No, Bobbe thought, that was little girl talk. Swinging her legs over to the side of the bed, she rubbed her forehead and smiled wanly at the memory. Every girl in her class had wanted to be like Sister Albertilla. The bud of a vocation was promptly nipped in each girl's mind when they confronted Sister Claver in second grade.

"No," she said softly. "That doesn't count at all."

"I feel sorry for that old Mr. Dudley," Bobbe said between sobs as she gingerly rubbed her recently spanked bottom.

"You feel sorry for him?" Dan asked unable to comprehend his daughter's sudden display of generosity. "You were the one getting the spanking for burying his garbage pail."

"I know, Daddy, but I think it's sad he isn't happy and has to make trouble for us kids who were only having normal fun on Hallowe'en."

"It's only normal and fun when it doesn't hurt people or their feelings, sweetheart," Dan said, nodding his head in sympathetic understanding. "When you do something to a person like Mr. Dudley and he doesn't like it, it's wrong to ever do it again. You kids were warned last year about bothering him and still you went back this year. You're not mean and vindictive. Just be nice to him whenever you see him and ignore whatever he does to you."

Bobbe's face brightened and she said, "You know what I'm going to do, Daddy?"

Dan waited for her statement, hoping it would not be one of retaliation.

"I'm going to pray for him."

"What?"

"I'm going to pray for him and maybe he'll become nice."

Dan put his arm around her shoulder and then began laughing. "Boy, he sure was mad at you kids."

That certainly wasn't anything monumental, Bobbe concluded. However, she decided her attendance at daily Mass and receiving communion every day from the time she had made her announcement was certainly a plus. Or was it? Perhaps it had been just for show. Her thoughts became more mixed than ever.

Lying back on the bed, Bobbe choked a sob she had felt building since awakening so abruptly. At least she could leave anytime during the first year without any trouble from the nuns. Yielding to the possibility she might have made a mistake, she surrendered her eyelids to the tugging of sleep and dozed.

The procession of guests from the reception swirled back through her tired mind in slow motion, mocking her as they laughed and pointed derisively. Unable to awaken, she began running from them but the dream people followed her—never gaining but never falling behind. Dashing up the front steps of St. Paul's church, she opened the door quietly and found her pursuers already seated in the pews, waiting for her. Tiptoeing to the front she found her parents attentively praying and automatically making room for her between them. Turning slightly, she could see the people still laughing and pointing. Suddenly stopping their mockery as though ordered by some unseen power, the congregation sat back and indicated Bobbe should pay attention to the happenings on the altar. When she faced the front again, she saw Father Dolan approaching the pulpit.

"That's it!" she cried aloud as she sat up and instinctively clapped a hand over her mouth. Recalling one of the vignettes the priest had related during the sermon at the Mass he had said in her honor the morning of her reception, she rubbed her eyes to make certain she was awake. A man, whose wife had died when they had been married only six months, began drinking heavily and his personality had changed dramatically for the worse. Then, while downing a glass of whiskey in a drunken stupor, he suddenly sobered and knew what his role in life would be. He became a priest and served God.

Bobbe felt a wave of relief wash over her. Of course it was natural for anyone making a big decision, such as joining the convent, to have doubts. Now, everything would be all right. She was positive. She did belong here. Closing her eyes, she drifted back to that first haze of sleep, which had escaped her, without more dreams of doubt.

The foot of her bed, framed by moonlight spilling in through the narrow window, slowly darkened as a bank of clouds extinguished the luminescence. When the silvered brightness reached in again, it touched the figure of a tall, handsome man dressed in a white suit standing at the bottom of Bobbe's bed. Staring intently at the figure lying before him, his black hair and dark, yet handsome features seemed to be part of the night. Studying the sleeping postulant, his features undulated with smiles and frowns alternately. Animal-like, his amber eyes reflected the light and glowed brightly. Throwing his head back, he laughed soundlessly, his lips parted, revealing white, even teeth.

Gradually, another bank of clouds darkened the room and when they left to pursue their predecessors, the figure was gone.

Early the next morning, Bobbe met Connie in the hall and whispered eagerly, her thoughts of the previous night—her recollection of Father Dolan's sermon and her own re-assurance where her vocation was concerned. "I know now it's right," she finished, "and I'm not going to worry about it anymore."

"I'm happy you were able to resolve the question so easily, Bobbe," Connie said brightly. "You just seem so right here it would have been a shame if you had decided to leave."

The two girls walked toward the chapel for Mass.

The following days fled by in rapid succession and the mysterious incident was forgotten as Thanksgiving ap-proached. Father Grant delivered his annual Thanksgiving Day sermon, which had nothing to do with the holiday, and Mass quickly progressed to its conclusion once he felt he had made his point, for the third time. When Mass was finished, the women ate their silent breakfast. With a special dinner scheduled for twelve o'clock noon, the younger girls retired to their cells to study for examinations which began the following Monday. Grateful for the break in their routine, the students were thankful the convent observed the holiday and the extra time it afforded them to prepare for the tests.

Gentle aromas of roasting turkey, pumpkin and minced-meat pies laced the air along with that of baking yams. Purled around the delightful perfumes was the smell of the special nutbread pudding which Sister Claudia, the head cook, had developed over the years. Indifferently, the hours crept by, held back for each woman by the tantalizing aspects of the approaching noontime feast.

The dinner gong sounded immediately after the Angelus had been completed in the chapel and the nuns, novices, and postulants needed no second call. With appetites honed to a razorlike sharpness by the tempting smells, they hurried to the dining room where twelve large tables filled the hall. One by one the chairs were claimed by women who stood behind them until grace was said.

A gasp of anticipation swept through the dining hall as Sister Claudia and her helpers entered, carrying covered dishes with tiny jets of steam puffing from around the lids. When the last bowl was set in place, a hush fell over the room.

Mother Job called for attention and began the mealtime prayer. "Bless us, Oh Lord, and these thy gifts—"

Another smell slowly made its presence known among the food aromas.

"—which we are about to receive—"

Several of the women's noses twitched in agitation.

"—through the bountiful hands—"

Nervous, isolated giggles erupted when the odor was suddenly recognized.

"—of Christ, our Lord."

"Amen," the women chorused and chairs scraped and clattered against the floor and table legs as they sat. The covers were removed and a horrified silence fell over the room.

"Oh, my God!" one nun finally managed to cry.

"Lord, have mercy on us!" another gasped.

Those nuns and girls who couldn't see, strained to discover the cause of the disturbances and sudden ejaculatory prayers which were being uttered, cried out, and gasped around the room. Then, suddenly galvanized into action, the women stood and rushed for the main door leaving the room empty except for the tables laden with dishes filled with human excrement.

PART TWO

MOTHER JOB

November 22, 1951
to
December 15, 1951

CHAPTER NINE

Normal sounds, which usually went unnoticed, began growing in volume as Mother Job sat motionless behind her desk. Her head moved jerkily, first to the right, and then to the left when she became aware of a monotonous hum—the electric clock marking time slowly from its position on the wall. Looking up, she found the hands almost ready to display three o'clock but she resisted the temptation to pick up the telephone until the next hour was begun. If Bishop King would not return until three in the afternoon, she wouldn't place the call again until shortly after that time. Relieved to the point of being thankful when she discovered the prelate was not home when she called shortly after the awful discovery had been made in the dining room, she had used the intervening hours to prepare herself. How would she broach such a topic to the young bishop?

Countless times since ordering the women to the chapel to pray she had asked herself what was going on, what had happened, but each time there were no answers. Mother Job had played and replayed the macabre scene over and over but could find no sane, reasonable explanation for the incident in the dining hall. What had happened to the food? Where had it gone? A thorough search had uncovered nothing of its whereabouts. There had only been the—

Each of the nuns and postulants who had helped prepare the meal had been ready to swear the dishes were filled with food. But none of them was as distraught as Sister Claudia who had always been a happy, contented person. Distressed and confounded as she was by the disappearance of the food and its horrible replacement, Mother Job was equally con-

110

cerned for the head cook's mental well-being.

There was no one to accuse or blame for such an atrocity. How many times had the Mother General repeated the same arguments and questions in her mind? Now, with only a few minutes left before calling the bishop, she felt completely frustrated, totally helpless. No answers. None. After two hours of debate with herself, she had not thought of the necessary words to present her problem logically. How would she tell him? Her words would have to be chosen carefully to avoid offending him. But hadn't she been offended? Hadn't her Sisters and postulants and novices been offended? Perhaps her best approach was to present her case simply and straightforwardly—use the vernacular for what had happened. She couldn't do that. But what would she do?

Mother Job had always been thankful for the relatively simple life the convent had offered her. Her calling to the religious life had not been a rejection of society as she was certain some had thought. Never, not once, had the idea of comparing her life in the convent with the life she might have had as a married woman, crossed her mind. Not once—until now. Tom's death had eventually been accepted in 1918, shortly after the war's end, and her decision had come more than four years later. What would her life have been like with him? More simple than she found hers to be at this moment, she was positive.

"Forgive me, Lord," she prayed softly, tears forming in her gray eyes. "Help me in this hour of need. Please, help me. Help the others who have been hurt by this awful thing. Don't desert us in this hour of need."

Raising her head she saw the minute hand had slipped to the one and blessed herself before picking up the telephone. After dialing the operator, she waited patiently while the call was placed. With the gratings of the rings echoing in the receiver, she asked herself again, what had happened to the food Sister Claudia had prepared? Where was it? Then the sound of someone picking up the phone on the other end broke into her questions and she snapped to attention, breathlessly awaiting the conversation to begin.

"Bishop King's residence, Father Hasker speaking," the voice said impassively.

"Father Hasker, this is Reverend Mother Job again. Has Bishop King returned yet?" Despite the clipped manner in which she spoke and a slightly higher pitch, her voice did not betray the inner turmoil she was experiencing.

"Yes, he has, Sister, and I've told him of your call. Would you be able to see him tomorrow morning at nine-thirty?"

"Father, I realize the bishop is a very busy man but it is of the utmost importance I see him today. Now. Is that possible?" Her voice suddenly trembled, mocking her efforts to keep it under control.

"I really don't think so. You see—"

"Father," she interrupted, "if you haven't asked the bishop if I could meet with him for a while today, please do so immediately. The matter is extremely grave." Once more she was in control, speaking in a normal manner, yet virtually ordering the priest to do her bidding.

After a short pause, the young priest sighed. "I'll see what I can do. Hold the line, please."

The frustration she had felt at the priest's lethargy instantly became an unbearable suspense, crushing in on her when she heard the phone placed on a table or desk at the bishop's home. Her pulse beat pounding in the earpiece on the telephone, seemed to grow in volume. What had happened to the food? She knew what they had found in the dishes but that didn't explain what had become of the turkey and yams and other things which had been prepared. Fleetingly, she wished her brother, Charley, was with her. She knew he would be better equipped and more able to relate to the bishop what they had found. Charley would use the right word.

Then Father Hasker's voice broke the silence, interrupting her thoughts. "Mother Job?"

"Yes, Father, I'm here." She forced herself to speak calmly.

"Bishop King will see you at seven-thirty this evening, if that's all right with you."

"I had hoped it would be sooner, but it will take almost two hours to drive to Madison anyway. Tell him I'll be there. Thank you very much, Father," she finished, sensing relief pour over her as she replaced the phone in its cradle.

After selecting Sister Raphael to accompany her to visit the bishop, Mother Job appointed Sister Damien to take charge of the convent until she returned. The role of substitute superior was not new to either woman but the Mother General felt instinctively Sister Raphael would be the more steadying influence once she had visited with Bishop King. A reliable confidant whenever the need to talk things out arose, Sister Raphael had entered the convent the same day as Mother Job and the two had been close friends since they met.

When the arrangements had been made to have Sam Tyler, the convent's part-time chauffeur, pick them up at five o'clock, Mother Job elected to use the remaining time to rehearse the awful tale she would have to relate when confronting the bishop.

Precisely at five o'clock, the distraught women entered Tyler's automobile. Noting the air of urgency about the women, he said nothing beyond the few pleasantries they allowed. Once the car had negotiated the horseshoe driveway, Sam made his way toward the road to Madison.

From the third floor window, Bobbe watched the departing nuns. Turning away when the black Buick was out of sight, she smiled evilly and hurried to join the rest of the women in the chapel where they had gathered to pray for Mother Job in her hour of need.

Carefully holding the sedan's speed at sixty miles an hour once they were out of town, Tyler knew it wouldn't do to have the Reverend Mother's ire aroused by going too fast. Normally, a conversation would be taking place between the front and back seat but this evening his passengers were ignoring him. Occasional glances in the rear view mirror revealed the women's drawn faces and barely moving lips offering what he assumed were silent prayers.

"Can't you go any faster, Mr. Tyler?" Mother Job asked impatiently, breaking into Sam's thoughts.

Without answering, he pressed the accelerator down until the speedometer needle bobbed between sixty-eight and seventy. An even greater air of exigency filled the car as the engine and hum of the tires on the pavement rose in pitch. For ten years, since he had retired from the post office, Sam had acted as part-time chauffeur for the convent and in all that time, not once had any one of the nuns he had driven, ever urged him to greater speed.

The passing minutes inexorably swelled into an hour and then almost two before Tyler began slowing the auto to conform with the lower speed limit of Madison. As though on signal, the two women put their heads together to whisper, again shutting their chauffeur out of their problem.

"Sister," Mother Job urged softly, "pray all the time I am speaking with His Excellency. I just don't know what he will make of it." She turned to Sister Raphael and found an understanding yet sympathetic smile greeting her. Although they had prayed almost constantly since leaving the Mother House, the silent recitations had been more rote than dedicated effort. Automatic prayers on which Mother Job had found herself unable to concentrate all of the time. The reason for their mission insisted on intruding, breaking her chain of thought.

"Do you know," she said to Sister Raphael, "that I can only think of one thing now that we're almost there—that I wish I hadn't even called him. We could solve this problem ourselves. Maybe we should go back?"

Siste Raphael's hand automatically went out to comfort her friend. "I understand your hesitancy, Mother, but there is no turning back at this point. Bishop King is expecting us and all of us will rest easier if you share our problem with him."

"I suppose you're right, Sister," Mother Job acknowledged. "What's wrong with me?" She had been deeply disturbed by the incident, which had taken place at noontime. Perhaps more so than the others since her position demanded she be responsible for all happenings at the convent and in the order itself.

"I don't think anything is wrong with you, Mother. We're all upset and nervous over this—this—thing that happened. You're only reacting like the rest of us."

Mother Job smiled and nodded as she turned her head away and stared out the window at the passing lights flashing by. Disliking the fact she had shown so openly her own agitation and confusion she realized indecisiveness was a new experience and could now only pray the bishop would be able to give her comfort and solace at this time.

Through the windshield of the auto, the tall, bare trees guarding Bishop King's brick home loomed into view. The nuns' destination resembled a fortress with its two corner turrets protecting the building proper. The car glided to a stop in front of the huge, dimly lighted porch.

"Please wait here, Mr. Tyler," Sister Raphael said as the Reverend Mother hurried ahead of her companion. "We'll only be a little while."

A chill breeze whipped their veils and cloaks about as they mounted the steps. Stepping back to wait after ringing the doorbell, long minutes passed before they were greeted by a slim, young priest. When he threw the door wide open for them to enter, Mother Job walked past him brusquely and handed him her cloak.

"I'm Father Hasker," he said searching the women's faces for some clue to the identity of the demanding Mother General he had spoken with on the phone.

The nuns introduced themselves and followed him toward the bishop's private office. Selecting a straight-backed chair she found close to the door Mother Job disappeared through, Sister Raphael began praying when she heard the door click shut behind her friend and superior.

Crossing the room, Mother Job approached the slightly built, thin man who stood, waiting with his hand outstretched. After she had kissed his ring, she took the chair the prelate indicated.

"Please, Mother, make yourself comfortable and tell me what is troubling you," he said in a well-modulated voice. A look of concern crossed his youthful features when he noticed her agitated state.

"I don't know quite how to begin," she said with a tiny, wry smile. "This is such an unusual problem—er—incident that took place today."

"It just happened today, Mother? It must be very unusual for you to seek an appointment so quickly," he said studying her intently, waiting for her to divulge the reason for their meeting.

"This noon, when we were about to sit down to Thanksgiving dinner, we noticed a peculiar odor along with the food smells. It—it was—very foreign to Sister Claudia's cooking.

When—when we opened the dishes—there wasn't food in them. It—it—it was human waste." She blurted out the last few words before she lost her nerve or said by accident the word her brother would have used. Sitting straight in her chair, Mother Job set her chin in a defiant position, virtually daring the bishop to question the veracity of her statement.

"You found what in the dishes?" he asked, his eyes widening.

"Please, Your Excellency, I don't think I can or want to say it again. You did hear me correctly."

The bishop stared at the Mother General, disbelief on his face. Terrance King, elevated to the status of bishop at the age of forty-one, had been one of the youngest prelates in the history of the Roman Catholic Church in the United States. His handsome features were enhanced by a boyish charm that few who met him were able to resist and for seven years he had been caretaker of the Cedar Falls diocese, rendering assistance to those in need. Furrows creased his forehead as he studied the woman sitting opposite him. Apparently more upset then she wished to convey, he knew hers was not an ordinary problem based on the few words she had spoken since entering his office. Hoping his shock had not been too evident when the Mother General voiced the reason for her impulsive visit, he waited for her to continue.

"I need your counseling, Your Excellency, as well as advice. I have no idea how I should handle the situation. My Sisters are upset, needless to say. Poor Sister Claudia is extremely worked up." Her heart beat wildly and she could feel a film of perspiration forming inside her coif.

"You have no idea how this happened?" the bishop asked, slowly regaining his composure and accepting the nun's words as unexaggerated truth.

"None. I fear it might be nothing more than a sick, sick joke. On the other hand—"

"On the other hand, what, Mother?" the bishop persisted when he saw her hesitate.

"On the other hand, it might be something more devious."

"What makes you say that, Mother?"

"Sister Claudia and all of her helpers who were in the kitchen were more shaken than anyone."

116

"Why single them out?"

"Because they were the only people who had anything to do with the food after it was brought to the convent."

"Where's the food now?" the bishop asked wrinkling his forehead in thought.

"We have no idea," Mother Job said softly.

"You must have some concept, some clue," King said. "Someone must know where it is."

"All of the women in the kitchen swore they had placed nothing but food in the dishes right before lining up to bring them to the dining room." Breathing easier since they were well into the matter at hand, she felt more comfortable with the bishop.

"I hope you didn't actually make them swear to this, Mother," he said seeking agreement with his conclusion.

"Of course not, Your Excellency. Perhaps it was a poor choice of words but I felt they would have asked God to witness their statements if they had been asked. They were very disturbed. Everyone was. The poor postulants didn't know what to make of it." The sweat inside her coif continued forming and she could feel a drop fight its way through the restraining collar around her neck. Slowly, the starch holding it rigid, softened.

"There was no one there who could have perpetrated this vile thing?" he asked, his steel blue eyes boring into hers, searching her very soul for the understanding he would need to help her.

"No one. Only the sisters, novices, and postulants were present. Father Grant left immediately after Mass. No one."

"Most puzzling," the bishop mused aloud.

"I don't see how a switch could have been made between the kitchen, which is right next to the dining hall itself, and the tables. We prayed grace, sat down and then—" She shuddered at the nauseating scene forming in her mind.

"You have no idea then, how it could have happened?" he asked almost coldly.

"None whatsoever."

Several minutes passed before the bishop spoke again. A look of puzzlement clung to him, alarming the nun more than she already was. Clearing his throat, he said, "No other unexplained happenings or incidents of any type?"

"No, Your Excellency," she said quickly. "I realize this whole thing is most unusual. Considering that, I hope you didn't think Father Grant would have been suspect had he been present in the building."

"Naturally not, Mother."

"You see, I meant there was no one in the convent who didn't belong there. At least to the best of our knowledge there was no one."

"I must admit, Mother," the bishop said, "I have no answers at this point. However, I do not want you to lose faith. You see—"

"Excuse me, Your Excellency," Mother Job cried, interrupting him as the thought of a possible prowler being in the building several weeks before, exploded in her mind. "There was an incident about three or four weeks ago. I had nearly forgotten it."

The bishop leaned forward and said, "What was that, Mother?"

Quickly recounting the story as Sister Madonna and the postulants had reported it, she said, "We finally concluded some deranged person had gained entrance to the convent, had blasphemed the way he did, and escaped without being seen. One young postulant was sitting by the door and the manner in which she described the voice led us to the conclusion it had come from the hall.

"I cautioned the sisters and girls to be ever so watchful for a prowler but nothing unusual or out of the ordinary was reported and it just slipped my mind. However, I don't see any connection unless the same man is a magician."

"What would you have me do at this point, Mother?" the bishop asked after another pause during which he digested the weird classroom happening along with the dinner time incident.

"I need advice on how to proceed," she said simply. "I have no rational explanation to offer my sisters."

"Were the authorities notified after the man's voice was heard in the hall?"

"No. I felt alerting the convent would be sufficient. I did consider it but was concerned word might somehow leak out

118

and others would come around to harass us." Now, she wondered if that particular approach had been wrong. How many madmen were allowed to run loose, terrorizing people?

"Yes, I suppose so," he agreed but was unable to disguise his skepticism regarding her decision. "Regardless, Mother, I think it would be a good idea to notify the authorities when you return. Perhaps the police could patrol the grounds periodically and the women would feel more at ease. As to the switch of the contents for your dinner today, I have no explanation—rational or otherwise."

Her feelings of disappointment bobbed to the surface of her being, showing in her eyes. She hadn't expected an explanation. How could he know what had happened when the convent was over a hundred miles away? Comfort. Solace. Direction. These were the things she needed most from him. Would he deny her these balms?

"My advice, Mother," he continued when he saw her expression of anxiety deepen, "is to inform the authorities and ask for some extra surveillance. I'm sure you will not be bothered anymore. It's highly improbable."

"I suppose I'm overreacting," she admitted sheepishly. "I know now I should have done that very thing when the classroom was disturbed."

"I would like you and your companion to be completely at ease when you leave. Your duties should be of utmost importance in your minds. Not these worries that can just as easily be transferred to the police. However, I will not, I assure you, dismiss them from my attention now that you have told me of them and I will think a great deal on them."

Aware the interview was coming to an end, Mother Job said, "Thank you, Your Excellency. I do apologize for interrupting your holiday."

"Reverend Mother, never apologize for being human. You were upset and rightly so, I might add. I believe you did the right thing in contacting me."

He stood and waited for her to quit the chair. Walking with her to the door he asked, "How many postulants do you have this year?"

"Thirty," she answered brightening at the sudden change in topic. "Nice, bright girls. They all seem to be very dedicated. I'm anxious to get back to them now."

Walking to the door, the bishop smiled warmly and she could feel the veneer of consternation peeling from her. She felt relieved just to have talked with him. Her position as Reverend Mother to the entire order left very few people in whom she could confide. There were older and more experienced nuns with whom she had shared some confidences over the years, and her contemporary, Sister Raphael, had been a comfort to her in several instances. But she knew it would have been very wrong to admit she was as frightened and disturbed by the occurrence at noontime as any of them had been.

"I believe we will stop at the police station before going back to the convent," she said as the door was opened for her by the bishop.

Sister Raphael stood to greet them and after exchanging pleasantries for several moments, the two women left. They found Sam Tyler sitting patiently inside the front door where he had sought refuge from the November night air when it became apparent the nuns would be more than just "a while." After donning their cloaks, they went to the car and once seated in the back, Sam turned the cold engine over and eased out of the driveway. The change in Mother Job was not obvious but Sam knew her well enough to realize whatever had brought them to the bishop was no longer pressing on her thoughts and he had best hold the speed to sixty miles an hour.

"Take us directly home, Mr. Tyler," Mother Job said once the car was speeding along the highway.

Sister Raphael looked at her quizzically.

Catching the questioning movement of her companion's head, Mother Job leaned close to her and said, "It's better if we call the police from the convent and confer with them there."

After digesting the alternate plan, Sister Raphael nodded in agreement.

Again the minutes grew into hours but the pressure of uncertainty and indecision had passed and Sister Raphael mentally planned the next day's work while Mother Job decided what and how the police should be told. Two hours and fifteen minutes after they left Bishop King in Madison, the car pulled into the horseshoe-shaped drive, where it stopped in front of the main entrance.

"Thank you very much, Mr. Tyler," the two women said as they got out of the car.

"Any time, Sisters," he replied. "Good night."

When the car had pulled away, they walked up to the front door of the Mother House, puffs of condensed air jetting from their nostrils.

"I wonder why so many lights are on?" Sister Raphael remarked as she fumbled to pull her watch from its hiding place beneath her cloak and guimpe. "Everyone should be in bed at this hour. Yes, it's almost eleven."

"That is strange," Mother Job agreed, fumbling for her key.

As the door swung open they were met by most of the women who lived at the convent. "Thank the good Lord God you're back, Mother," Sister Teresita said anxiously. "Come with us. We have another problem as bad as the one this noon."

The startled look on the faces of the women about them told the late arrivals something was wrong—drastically wrong.

"What is it?" the Reverend Mother asked hoarsely.

"Come, see for yourself. We can't—" the young nun, acting as spokeswoman, broke off in mid-sentence.

Hurrying down the hall, the group swept Mother Job and Sister Raphael along toward the kitchen. The open doors showed the kitchen workers kneeling in the middle of the room, praying with outstretched arms, their heads tilted toward heaven. The sounds of high-pitched, wailing moans drew their attention to the far end of the room where Sister Claudia knelt, swaying back and forth being embraced by Sister Damien who was attempting to comfort her.

Moving into the kitchen, the sound of splashing water could be heard accompanying Sister Claudia's lamentations begging for Divine help. Carefully stepping around the cook, Mother Job, followed by Sister Raphael and the wide-eyed nuns, moved closer to the sink as one of the nuns pointed a shaking finger toward it. As they approached the gushing faucets, they saw steaming amber liquid flowing into the sink while the heavy, fetid odor of urine assailed their nostrils.

CHAPTER TEN

Cautiously reaching out, Mother Job took the remaining step separating her finger tips from the tap handle. Just as her hand was about to touch the faucet, the flow of urine stopped. The ensuing quiet emphasized Sister Claudia's moaning wail.

"Call a plumber," Mother Job said sternly to Sister Raphael.

"Now? At this hour, Mother?"

"Immediately," she snapped and, turning to face the other women, asked, "What happened?"

Sister Damien, who stood closest to the Mother Superior, stepped forward to offer an answer to the terse question. "Sister Claudia wasn't able to help prepare dinner," she began, "but after we had eaten she came into the kitchen to help wash dishes. When she turned the hot water on—well, what you saw, began coming out. We were unable to turn it off."

"But I just did," Mother Job countered.

"We tried but the handle wouldn't budge a bit," Sister Damien offered and looked questioningly at Mother Job.

Turning to examine the faucet, Mother Job attempted to turn the handle but found it in the off position. How could that be? All she had done was reach out when the flow stopped. She hadn't touched the handle at all. What was happening in her convent? Who was responsible?

"How long did this go on?" she asked lamely, not wanting to betray her own confusion to the already nervous women.

"Since six-thirty this evening," Sister Damien said.

"I see," Mother Job replied. "Everyone go to bed. Sister

Raphael and I will let the plumber fix it and the dishes can be washed in the morning."

"What do you think caused—this—this to happen, Mother?" a novice asked hesitantly.

"It's probably nothing more than our septic tank backing up into the fresh water well," she said, groping for something that would sound logical.

Even Sister Claudia, who was still fidgety and irritable from the disastrous noon meal, seemed quieted by the explanation and meekly followed the women from the room.

Walking to her office, Mother Job wondered about the phenomenom she and the others had just witnessed. She didn't believe her own solution but was thankful the nuns and students had. Or had they? They were intelligent women and would eventually ask more questions when they had time to dwell on the problem. At least they would go to bed and sleep while the plumber worked and hopefully everything would be back to normal by morning. Then the problem would be solved and the nuns would soon forget all about it.

When she reached the door of her office, she grasped the knob but didn't turn it. "How could our hot water tank produce that much heated water for almost four and a half hours?" she softly asked herself before entering.

Sister Raphael, pleading with someone on the telephone, looked up with an expression of thankfulness when she saw her superior standing in the doorway and said quickly, "One moment, please." Clapping a hand over the mouthpiece, she offered, "He wants to come in the morning. I can't convince him to come now."

"Have you told him what the problem is?" Mother Job asked.

"No. I haven't been able to think of a way to tell him without—"

"Let me have the phone," she said brusquely and took the instrument from the other nun who was only too glad to be out of the situation. "Hello? This is the Reverend Mother. Our problem seems to be the septic tank backing up into our fresh water supply. It's really of the utmost importance this be cleared up before morning. There are almost one hundred fifty nuns out here and—"

"Why didn't the other nun tell me that?" the gruff voice burst into her ear.

"The sister you were talking to was unaware of the exact problem. I'm sure that's why she sounded so vague."

"I see. All right. I'll be there within the hour."

"Thank you so very much. Sister Raphael will meet you at the door." Mother Job placed the phone in its cradle.

"Is that really the trouble, Mother?" Sister Raphael asked, her voice harboring a hint of doubt.

"It seems it must be. We'll find out when the plumber arrives. He'll be here within the hour and I want you to let him in."

Excusing herself, Sister Raphael left the office and hurried to the front door. When she was alone, the Mother General picked up the phone and dialed the Cedar Falls police station.

"Police Department," a voice twanged at the other end. "Sergeant Kelso."

"May I speak to the chief of police, please?"

"He ain't in, Ma'am. May I help you?"

"No, I'm afraid not. Who's in charge now?"

"I am, lady. What can I do for you?"

"I'm sorry, I must speak to the chief of police. May I have his home telephone number, please?"

"Are you kidding? If I gave his number out to every nut—er—person that called when he wasn't in, he'd skin me alive. If you can't tell me, you'll just have to wait till morning," he snapped with an air of finality.

"Young man, this is Reverend Mother Job, Mother General of the Bearer of the Divine Word Convent. We have a problem here I feel only the chief can handle. It simply will not wait. Now, may I please have his number?"

A short pause followed her insistent question before Kelso's voice answered, "Okay, Sister, but you come visit me in the hospital and pray for me if he skins me alive. His number's Axman 80183. Got it?"

Smiling as she jotted the number on a piece of scratch paper, she said, "Young man, I will pray for you regardless but I can assure you, you will not be skinned alive. What is the chief's name?"

"Furlong, Sister."

In seconds she had dialed the number and was slowly counting the number of buzzes after the relays had clicked into place. As she waited for the eighth ring, a telephone lifted to complete the circuit and a sleep-laden voice mumbled, "Hullo?"

"Chief Furlong?"

"Yes." The single word struggled through a long yawn.

"Chief Furlong, this is Reverend Mother Job at the Bearer of the Divine Word Convent. We have a problem I must discuss with you."

"Now?" he asked with hope the answer would be something other than yes clearly evident in the one word question.

"Yes. Now," she said emphatically.

"Can't it wait until morning? It's going on eleven-thirty, Sister."

"No, I'm afraid not. It's very urgent."

"Well, give me some idea what it is then. Maybe I can take care of it without coming out to see you at this hour. Then we can talk about it in the morning."

"Did I wake you, Chief?" she asked innocently, aware that compromise at this point would have to be the temporary solution.

"As a matter of fact you did, Sister. Now, how about that problem?" he snorted impatiently.

"Very well. We have been troubled with a prowler, I think, and would like to have a car with some of your policemen in it patrol the convent grounds periodically each night. Would that be possible?"

"What do you mean, 'I think,' Sister?" Furlong said, catching the uncertainty in her voice.

"Well, we haven't actually seen him, but he disturbed a class of postulants the other day and the class heard him. So did Sister Madonna—"

"This just happened now?" The question was laced with an air of suspicion.

"Oh, no. It was about three weeks ago and—"

"And you're just calling me now?" he shouted. "Is this a joke?"

"I assure you it is not a joke, Chief. Today, we had further evidence he must have been in the building around noon-

125

time—"

"Noon? Why did you wait until the middle of the night to call?" Furlong snarled angrily.

"I had an appointment with the bishop in Madison and just returned. It's on the bishop's recommendation I'm calling you. When we returned this evening, we found our water supply contaminated and I suspect this prowler may be responsible for that as well."

"I see." Furlong spoke slowly and paused before making a decision. "All right, Sister, I'll have a car dispatched to your place right now and they'll check it out. Hey, wait a minute. You're not even in the city limits. I can't have a car running up there every couple of hours."

"Oh, dear," Mother Job said when she realized they might be without the comfort of surveillance from the police, "what'll we do now? Can't the rule be broken just this once?"

"It's completely out of the question, Sister. But I'll tell you what I will do. I'll refer this to the sheriff's office and they can send someone up there. That would be in their jurisdiction, not ours. Is that all right with you, Sister?"

"Yes. That's fine. Just so we have someone patroling the grounds as regularly as possible. Thank you, Chief Furlong, and please forgive me for disturbing your sleep."

"That's okay, Sister. That's what I'm paid for. G'night."

Leaving her office, she went to the front door to find Sister Raphael in the large parlor, dozing. Bleary eyed from the late vigil, the nun's head jerked up, wide awake when she realized someone was entering the room.

"The sheriff's department will send a car around several times a night so at least we will have some degree of protection while we're asleep," Mother Job said wearily as she sat down.

"Protection from what? From whom, Mother?"

"Why, the prowler, of course."

"Is there a prowler? No one's seen him."

"Now, now, Sister, you're tired and the whole thing doesn't seem clear to you. Why don't you go to bed and I'll wait for the plumber," Mother Job offered and patted Sister Raphael's hand.

"No, Mother. I'm all right. You're just as exhausted as I am.

126

I'll stay with you. I guess I am a little upset about this whole thing."

Occasionally, heavy eyelids surrendered to fatigue only to snap open when the reason for the nuns' wait surfaced in their tired minds. After forty-five minutes, the sound of a truck pulling into the horseshoe drive brought both women to an alert wakefulness and they hurried to open the door for the plumber before he had a chance to ring the bell and disturb the sleeping women on the upper floors. Explaining to him where the pump house and septic tank were located, the nuns excused themselves and went to the chapel where the plumber was to report when he finished his work.

After a quick inspection of valves and pumps, Art Morgan was convinced there was nothing amiss in the pump house and yawned as he left the small building. He found the septic tank to be in normal working order as well but puzzled at the distance between the location of the pump house and the septic tank. The pump house was directly behind the main building and next to the garage while the water tower was south of the convent. The septic tank, which completed the system, was located down a slight hill, beyond the tower to prevent the type of complaint the nuns had made. As sleepy as he was, Morgan knew water wouldn't run uphill by itself, although it could be pumped. Deciding to make the middle of the night call pay well for his interrupted sleep, he chose to check everything again. Perhaps he had missed something the first time around when he was still yawning every few minutes.

Two hours later he had found nothing.

Quietly entering the convent's back door where the nuns had left him, he turned on the lights in the hall and surrounding rooms without knowing which controlled the kitchen. Hurrying to the spotless room he found the sinks and turned all of the faucet handles. Pure, clear water poured from each tap.

"Art, m'boy, you're a genius," he muttered to himself after turning the spigots off and went to find the women who had employed him.

Wandering into the chapel, Morgan looked about with fascination. A non-Catholic, Morgan had never been inside a church like this, much less a convent. The sound of a muffled whispering attracted his attention and he found the two nuns kneeling before the statue of the Blessed Virgin praying quietly.

"Ah, ma'm?" he whispered hoarsely and jumped at the echo of his own voice. "It's all fixed. I'll send you my bill."

Standing to leave the pew in which they had knelt for over two hours, the women genuflected and turned to face Morgan.

"Thank you, Mr. Morgan. We'll see you out," Mother Job said wearily.

The large front door closed softly with a definitive click behind the plumber and the exhausted women gratefully went to bed. It had been a very long and very eventful day.

The defensive atmosphere, which had held the convent in its grasp, slowly disappeared when the next week passed without incident. Normal routines were handled once more on an almost automatic basis and by the following Friday, the awful Thanksgiving affairs were forgotten by most.

Enjoying the chilled air in the garden before retiring to her room for some extra study time, Bobbe walked alone lost in conflicting thoughts of her future and her desire to be at home with her parents. When the recollection of her father's and mother's faces became too clearly defined, she would find herself suddenly unable to recall their features—as though she were inventing them mentally but could not decide what they should look like. Then, ideas and images of the future would be conjured from nowhere and she would dwell on them, her parents slipping into the dim recesses of her memory. Now she found herself once more losing sight of her parents' faces and a sob escaped her lips. Why couldn't she remember? Is this what happened when someone was separated from loved ones? Inability to remember their faces? Suddenly, she found herself asking if this place, this vocation were worth that particular price.

The next instant brought a vision of the African veldt to her mind's eye and her parents were forgotten. Then a smile crossed her lips when she thought of her performance during the week in class. She had found her tests to be relatively easy

128

and wondered why she had been concerned in the first place. Facts she couldn't recall ever hearing before were written with complete confidence. Sailing through the courses would be child's play if these first tests were any indication of the difficulty remaining to be overcome.

Looking up, Bobbe saw she was alone except for a white-veiled novice who was making her way back to the convent. Although the air had been brisk since the sun had gone down, she shuddered at a sudden chill and thought of returning to the warmth of her cell where she could study and be comfortable.

Now the wind began blowing more, moaning through the leafless trees and evergreens. The gusts began increasing in velocity and Bobbe stopped, listening to the eerie sound. A cold chill penetrated deeper than ever when she heard, intermingled with the wind, a plaintive cry from the back of the garden.

"Bah-h-h-b-e-e-e."

She spun around and faced the end of the garden farthest from the main building where the sound seemed to originate. The chill winter breeze enveloped her and shuddering, she became more aware of the plummeting temperature.

The call came again. *"Bah-h-h-b-e-e-e."*

It was weird. The wind sounded as though it were calling her name.

Curious to find the source of the phenomenon, Bobbe cautiously approached the rear wall of the garden. As she got closer, the wind erupted in stronger, icy cold blasts that whipped her cloak about her body. Standing perfectly still, she could no longer hear the sound of her name.

With a shudder, she turned to retrace her steps toward the convent and screamed.

"Oh, my good God!"

Blocking her path, a tall man confronted her. Appearing to be comfortable in the cold air despite his immaculate white suit, he smiled, displaying large, even teeth.

"Who are you?" Bobbe demanded. "What are you doing in the garden?" Trembling with fright, Bobbe didn't retreat from him and was astounded to find herself responding in a strange, appealing way to his handsome features framed by coal black hair.

"Come, come, Bobbe," he murmured. *"Don't you recognize me?"*

"No. Who—who are you?" she asked hoarsely. What was it about him that seemed so familiar, yet so vague? Her senses reeled as she rose to pinnacles of knowledge and sank in turn to depressions of ignorance.

The garden. Wasn't the garden off limits to men except on those visiting Sundays when fathers and brothers and other male relatives were allowed access? She struggled to speak, to tell this intruder of his trespassing but found herself incapable of forming words into an intelligent sentence. Bathing in the lust of his smile she felt warmth flow through her body and found herself soaring to the heights once more.

"If you don't tell me this instant, I'll call Mother Job. Now, who are you?" she demanded but instantly felt herself slipping once more.

"Don't be upset, Bobbe," he said softly, his voice deep and mellow. *"My name is Dra-woh."*

"What—what are you—doing here?" she whispered, trying to place the strange name. "You're—you're trespassing." Deeper. She was sinking farther than ever.

"Bobbe, sweet Bobbe!" he chortled, her name sounding evil and filthy coming from his lips.

Blanching at the expression, Bobbe's mind reeled as she tried to associate a name and face with the words. Someone used to say that very phrase. But who? Slowly, Jay Livingston's face materialized in her befuddled mind. A smile crossed her full lips when she recognized him. It was Jay who used to call her "Bobbe, sweet Bobbe." But this man, this stranger who did not belong here, was certainly not Jay.

"I've come just to meet you again, sweet one. Don't you remember me?"

Frantically shaking her head, Bobbe's face puckered in desperation when she tried to recall his face—his name. What was his name? The fright she had initially felt, rapidly swelled to panic and she wanted to run but found herself unable to move. Meeting someone from her past, in public or someplace indoors would have been acceptable. But here in the garden? In the waning gray light of a cold day and encroaching black night? The thought was bizarre and weird. Leaving the summit of awareness, she found a new strange calmness forcing itself upon her as she descended once more to the pit of willingness and obedience.

"I have been with you a long time and I know you very well, dear Bobbe," he said in a soft crooning voice.

His glowing, amber eyes bored deeply into her and she knew it was impossible to hide anything from him. "Should I know you from someplace?" she asked in a thick voice.

"You and I have been as one for quite a little while," he said and held a well-manicured hand out toward her. *"From before the time you refused Jay Livingston, I have been with you. I am you and you are me. You have been given to us, and my master has appointed a great mission for you. I possess you and am your master. You no longer have anything to say about what you do. Only I control you. Now, come to me. Come."*

Moving stiffly, Bobbe slowly approached the tall figure.

CHAPTER ELEVEN

Bizarre sensations coursed through the postulant's body as terror, mixed with nausea and fear of the unknown became as one with an overpowering curiosity. As though peering through a tube, she fixed her eyes on the man standing before her. Concentrating on his voice which dropped lower and lower in pitch and grew more coarse with each word uttered, she desperately tried to place it. She had heard his voice before—but where? Mechanically obeying his command, she moved slowly toward the dark, handsome intruder. A struggling impulse to resist fleetingly passed though the rapidly hardening concrete of her compulsion to obey but was quashed by the voice pounding in her ears.

"Come. Come to me now."

Divorced from her will, she moved forward until his face was only inches from hers. His breath, foul with a chemical odor she could not place or identify, filled her nostrils. Gazing into his eyes, she felt the overwhelming power exuding from the glowing orbs.

"I have been with you for a long time. I know everything about you. There is nothing you can hide from me. We are as one, you and I." His gaze grew in ferocity, devouring the young woman standing before him. *"I was with you the time you watched your father fuck your mother. You enjoyed it and played with your own hairless snatch. Didn't you?"*

Nodding numbly, Bobbe asked hollowly, "How do you know that?" She knew she had never told anyone and had felt guilty for days following her eavesdropping. Slowly, the etails reformed in her mind and a feeling of pleasure formed its way into her conscious mind, pushing aside her initial sensations. A smile bent her mouth as she swayed back and forth savoring the memory. "Daddy's big cock slid in and out of Mommy," she whined in a small child's voice and began massaging her genitals through her dress.

Sneering, he pointed accusingly. *"You wanted to play with your little friend's pussy too, didn't you, whore?"*

Mutely, she nodded, recalling how Vickie had wanted to play doctor but was hesitant when Bobbe suggested they undress. There had been many times she had allowed her thoughts to dwell on sex when she was young.

"You thought about sex a lot didn't you, sweet Bobbe?"

Her mind racing, she stared at him dumbfoundedly. How could he know her thoughts? Who was this man who seemed to know her better than anyone in her life?

"I know what is in your mind and heart, my tight-cunted friend. Don't ever try to hide anything from me or you will pay dearly."

Summoning all her strength, she opened her mouth and demanded through clenched teeth, "Who are you?"

"I am Dra-woh, emissary of the Prince of Darkness who is ruler of the earth and flesh. The perpetrator of all crimes. King of wanton desire. I am Satan's protege. Call me what you will, but I am your master."

His voice boomed hollowly through the garden and Bobbe hoped and feared at the same time the other women in the convent building would hear him.

"Only you can hear me, whore."

Fighting to step back and away from the thing in front of her, Bobbe whispered feebly. "I do renounce all of Satan's works and pomps. Get—get thee—behind me, Satan!"

A derisive laugh burst from his mouth as she backed away, attempting to resist. *"You cannot fight me now, little one. No matter how hard you try, you'll learn it is too late to withstand my power. You accepted me long ago when we were asked to take you and now we face each other at last. He has plans for you here and you will cooperate."*

Unable to resist the pull of the words she heard and sensed, Bobbe felt as if her body were being sucked into a pit of muddy quicksand. With spasmodic flashes of thought, she vainly tried to fight back. Close her eyes. Pray. Resist.

But the voice persisted in penetrating her thin defenses. *Open your eyes. Pray—to Satan. Yield. Do not resist. It is fruitless. You are mine.*

"Recall with me now, Bobbe-whore, the night you welcomed the truck driver between your legs. You welcomed the cock of the unholy. Do you remember?" His face seemed to glow as he reminded her of the night before her reception.

All thoughts of withstanding the assault lost in her clouded mind, Bobbe stared straight ahead, nodding in agreement as she recalled the details of that night.

"You picked up someone you thought was a truck driver at a café and asked him if he wanted to screw you.

It was Bill's Truck Stop, she thought.

"That's right, sweet Bobbe-sow, it was Bill's Truck Stop. You took him across the highway to the Wayfarer's Inn and he fucked your virgin hole."

His voice continued recounting the details as Bobbe closed her eyes, reliving the evil thrill she had experienced. Once more she could feel the icy coldness of his touch and the freezing semen gushing into her body.

"Yes! Yes! I remember! I remember!" she cried loudly, a degenerate smile playing on her lips. "I am yours, Dra-woh! Yours! Do with me as you will!"

"Come to me then, sweet Bobbe-fuck and let me sample again the pleasure you gave me then. It has been too long since we have been together."

While his voice droned on, drumming his obscenities deeper into her mind, Bobbe quickly undressed and stood naked in the cold air. A carnality she welcomed and seemed totally at ease with flared within her as violent waves of desire battered her numbed senses. With arms extended, she slowly stepped toward the monster.

"Lie down, sow," he ordered.

Obeying, Bobbe spread her legs and the maleficent being threw himself upon her prostrate body. Locked in sexual embrace, animalistic moans of passion erupted from them to accompany their frenzied thrashings. A scream escaped

Bobbe's lips as the demon drove his gigantic member into her body, making her wish it would tear her body asunder. A random thought compared the bitter cold of his ejaculation the first time to the scalding sensation of a white hot poker being thrust into her body now. Cries of pain and pleasure rose from deep within her as Dra-woh planted his unearthly seed. Exhausted, the girl lay weak and panting at the feet of the man-devil who now stood towering over her.

"Arise, sweet Bobbe-ass, and I will show you some of my mighty powers."

With a painful effort, she stood, shivering from the wetness on her legs and lower body and the cold wind caressing her nakedness.

He gestured with a sweeping motion of his arm and instantly the garden was swathed in warm sunlight, the trees covered with deep green leaves. Birds chirped happily in the evergreen branches and flowers swayed in a warm gentle breeze. She should have felt warm and wonderful all over but the awful cold still held her in its icy grasp. Another wave of his arm and winter held bleak sway over the garden once more.

"You see? I can do everything."

Raising her eyes, she found him smiling evilly and a feeling of loathing and disgust fought its way through the befuddlement rocking her mind. Climb—she must climb from the stinking abyss she found herself in.

"You—you—do not exist here, Satan." The words came in a hoarse whisper.

"I exist. I do exist. I exist because I have been sent to you, my dear. If I had not been sent, then I would not be here. But I am here and you want me with you. I am Dra-woh." A triumphant smile crossed his face and he knew the argument had been won without a fight. "Now go, my sweet fuckwhore. We shall have many more times together while you are prepared. Go."

A sliver of light penetrated her mind for an instant and she pointed a shaking finger at him. "It was you who did those things last week. You."

His coarse laugh rang through the garden as it dropped in pitch becoming a rush of grating noise.

"Your voice. I know your voice, too. It was you we heard in

135

the hall that day."

"Not really, cunt," he said soothingly. "The voice came from within you. But you see? I did show you I could keep my word. I have fucked you. Their God never would, you know. Just remember, I can do whatever I say and I am with you—always."

Her thread of reason was slowly blacking out while deciding his words were sacrilegious and obscene. Enjoyment and acceptance of the statements he made brought her to the brink again, and anticipating future encounters with this being excited her as she teetered before plummeting once more into the black abyss.

"Go now," he ordered. "You will know I am with you." Turning, he walked down the path toward the back of the garden and dissolved into nothingness.

The darkness revealed no sign of him when Bobbe peered around trying to determine where he had gone. A sharp breeze chilled her beyond a state of numbness before realizing where she was and how she was attired. Shuddering at the sensations of clamminess and freezing cold, Bobbe found her clothes near a tree bole and quickly dressed but the cold material against her body made her more chilled than ever.

"What in the world is wrong with me?" she asked aloud, jumping at the sound of her voice. Walking quickly, she hurried to the back of the convent building. Was she getting sick? Why else would she feel so weak and tired? For some reason she could not understand, she felt dirty and decided a hot bath would feel good and stop any encroaching illness.

The halls were deserted when she returned to her room and, undetected, hurried to the bathroom. In minutes she was in the tub, hot water caressing her body. Her breasts ached. Her whole body hurt as though she had been exercising or working strenuously. Puzzled by the tiny scratches marring her otherwise flawless skin, she blamed the lacerations on the barberry bushes in the garden. Lying back in the steaming water, Bobbe watched impassively as the cuts slowly disappeared from her flesh along with the aches and pains and her experience faded into a hazy memory.

But a memory of what? What had she been doing in the

garden that now eluded her powers of concentration? Something must have happened, she told herself. She had the marks to prove it and glanced down at her breasts. Minutes before they had been covered with scratches and bruises grouped in fives. Now nothing appeared on the milky whiteness except her dark nipples.

When the water had cooled, she pulled the plug and stood. Toweling vigorously as the tub drained, she carefully stepped to the tile floor, starting when a knock sounded at the door.

"Bobbe?"

The voice was muffled and she couldn't identify it.

"Bobbe? Is that you in there? It's me, Connie. May I come in?"

"Just a minute, Connie." Bobbe slipped into her robe, crossing the room to unlock the door.

Connie, dressed in her robe and with a towel draped over one arm, smiled broadly. "Hi. You through now?"

"I guess so."

"I thought you were in here. What the heck were you up to?"

"Why? Was I in here that long?"

"Almost an hour."

"I—I wasn't feeling well. You know, like I was coming down with the flu or something. I was chilled and achy, tired all over."

"How do you feel now?"

"Much better. What've you been doing?"

"Studying. What else? I must have—hey, you missed your right leg." Connie pointed to Bobbe's foot and lower leg which were still wet.

"Too much of a hurry to let you in." Bobbe threw the front of her robe back and raised her foot to the tub ledge, exposing her leg to the hip.

"That's sure a weird-looking birthmark you have there." Connie leaned closer to examine the splotch.

"What are you talking about? I don't have a birthmark of any kind."

"You don't, huh? Well, what do you call that? A tattoo?"

Standing on her tiptoes, Bobbe strained to see the backside of her hip in the mirror over the washstand. "Well, for the love of— Where do you suppose that came from?"

Precariously balanced, she examined the oval mark that appeared to have a wedge missing. She knew she didn't have any marks at all on her body. Barely a mole was visible on her creamy skin but here, on her hip, was a dark red mark of some kind.

"I might have bruised it in the garden," Bobbe offered lamely.

"That's no bruise. It's etched into the skin. You know what I think it looks like?"

"What?"

"A pig's hoofprint."

"You're crazy."

"I'm a farm girl. Remember? I know a pig's footprint when I see one."

Bobbe stared at her. "It's nothing, Connie. It'll be all right." She dropped her robe to cover the curious mark and stepped back.

"What kind of animals you keeping in your room, anyhow?" Laughter that should have followed was cut short by a piercing stare from Bobbe.

"It's nothing, Connie," Bobbe snapped hotly. "Don't worry about it. It'll go away." The anger and hostility were instantly replaced by a reassuring smile.

Unperturbed by the unfriendly response, Connie laughed. "Okay. It's your hip. You going to bed now?"

"Yeah. I'm really tired. That old clock gets around to five too quickly and I want a good night's sleep. G'night, Connie." She stretched while walking to the door.

Bobbe flicked the wall switch and her room was filled with pale yellow light that glared in contrast to the blackness it replaced. When her eyes became accustomed to the brightness, she dressed hurriedly and prepared for bed. The thin mattress accepted the girl's tired body but the winter staleness of the room closed in on her and for several minutes she rolled and tossed. Sitting upright and throwing the blanket back, she arose to open the window. The blast of cold air pushing in through the slit she made sent a chill through her but the freshness of it brought a long lingering yawn. Returning to the iron bed, she closed her eyes, drifting off to sleep.

With the exception of several isolated lamps left burning in the hallways, lights in the cells winked out one by one as the women retired for the night. Peace and quietude firmly wrapped itself around the convent, enfolding the sleeping nuns in its embrace. Outside, nothing moved in the fixed stillness gripping the grounds. Painted by a cold, full moon, the landscape hid among abstract shadows and highlights seemingly emphasizing the peculiar calm hanging over the buildings. Snow clouds, which had threatened to cleanse the dreary countryside with a white covering, had passed out of sight still unfulfilled.

Fitfully rolling and tossing, a thin film of perspiration formed on Bobbe's face as she began dreaming of her parents. Feeling the excitement of being with them, she realized they were going on vacation to the Black Hills in South Dakota and leaned forward to talk with them. As though she weren't in the backseat of the automobile, Clare and Dan ignored her. Screaming in her dream, Bobbe called their names when they refused to acknowledge her presence. Totally frustrated, she fell back against the seat and turned to watch the prairie land flash by her window. Gradually, it began to change and she noticed the car was moving slower and slower. Mopping her brow, she noted the drastic rise in temperature and, returning her attention to the scenery, was startled to find it now looked more like the pictures she had seen of Africa than South Dakota. When she turned to ask her parents about the change, she found they were no longer with her and the Chevrolet had become a trucklike vehicle. Sitting behind the steering wheel was a dark-haired man wearing a fez. He turned to look at Bobbe and she recognized him as the truck driver and the man in the garden.

Suddenly slamming the brakes on, he brought the truck to a bouncing halt almost hurtling Bobbe into the front seat. Opening her door, she jumped from the truck and was confronted by a group of small black children who gathered tightly together to stare at her. Their thin arms and legs, nothing but skin and bones, were out of place when compared to their distended bellies. Wide eyes—sad, hungry eyes seemingly incapable of tears peered at her begging for

139

something to eat. Sweat poured down her face and she could feel rivulets of perspiration flowing between her breasts. Reaching to her forehead, she found her hair covered completely and then, looking down, discovered she wore the habit of her order. Stepping forward to comfort the starving waifs, they seemed to float away from her—managing to stay just out of reach of her outstretched fingertips.

A rumbling sound distracted her and she turned to see an ox cart approaching. Forgetting the children, she walked toward the slow moving vehicle and recognized the driver of the crude wagon as the same man who had been with her in the truck. With a wide, malevolent smile, he turned fumbling with something on the seat next to him, before bringing a small black bundle into view. Leaning down, he handed the blanket-wrapped object to her.

"He is in your charge now, Sister. Protect him with your life. Do not let him starve for food or affection."

Bobbe could feel the blanket stir and pulled back the fold to look at her new charge. When she saw the face, she screamed.

The stillness of the convent was shattered by the piercing cries coming from Bobbe's room. Bursting into the hall, those novices, postulants, and nuns who slept closest to her room groggily asked one another who had screamed. Loud moans flowed from the only room whose door was still closed.

Pushing her way through the confused, milling women, Sister Damien fumbled with her glasses before knocking on the thick wooden door. No answer. She knocked again, harder than before.

"Roberta? Roberta, are you all right?"

Still no answer came as the nun placed a hand on the doorknob and gingerly turned it. A rush of cold air engulfed the group as the door opened. Groping for the switch, the window was hastily shut once the pale yellow light flooded the room. Sister Damien froze when she saw Bobbe.

Profusely sweating, the postulant lay uncovered on her bed, writhing and moaning, clutching the bed linen in one hand and masturbating with the other. Another long, piercing scream escaped her lips.

The shriek generated a chill that shuddered through the women. Sister Damien stood between the bed and the doorway of the small room trying to block from view the others pressing in behind her.

"Quickly, go get Reverend Mother and tell her Roberta is sick and that we need a doctor!" the nun ordered over her shoulder without tearing her eyes from Bobbe.

As Sister Damien stepped closer to the bed, Bobbe continued moaning while spittle ran down the side of her face and neck toward her ear. With a crying groan, she rolled to the edge and began vomiting a thick, yellow slime but continued rubbing her clitoris savagely.

"Get a basin or something." Unable to believe her eyes, Sister Damien stepped forward again when she heard someone leave to carry out her bidding and attempted to restrain Bobbe's vigorously moving fingers. Straining every muscle needed, the nun found she was unable to budge the girl's hand from her vagina. Purposely standing closer to Bobbe to act as a shield for the others so they wouldn't see what the postulant was doing, she breathed a silent prayer for Mother Job's haste.

"Please, everyone, leave," the Reverend Mother ordered as she fought her way into the cell.

Bobbe stopped manipulating her organ but continued convulsing as orgasm after orgasm racked her body.

"Sister Damien, select two or three to stay here," Mother Job said curtly, "and have the rest return to their cells." Moving to the bed she took Bobbe's left wrist in one hand and placed her other on the girl's forehead.

"What's wrong, Mother?" Sister Damien asked after dismissing the unneeded women.

Before the Mother Superior could answer, a novice entered the room with a pan from the kitchen and handed it to the Mistress of Novices. Placing the container in position to catch the vomit, Sister Damien looked up and waited for an answer to her question.

Mother Job watched in horror as Bobbe continued to spew the thick liquid from her mouth. "I have no idea. She's very hot. She seems to have a fever. I can't underst— Look out. Your pan is going to overflow."

141

Both women stared at the two-quart saucepan, now almost full, and then looked at the large puddle on the floor next to the bed. With deep, retching gags, Bobbe continued vomiting.

Although knowing it would begin spilling over any second, Sister Damien continued holding the saucepan in position and called to the novices huddled outside the open door. "Get another pan. Bigger this time."

Running footsteps obediently pattered down the hallway.

"The window was open when I came in and it was bitterly cold. Roberta was lying there uncovered and moaning the way you see her now and doing— What do you suppose is wrong with her, Mother?"

"Sister, I *have* no idea. Now, please stop asking me." Mother Job questioned the wisdom in asking Sister Damien to stay when she would have preferred Sister Raphael. "The doctor is on his way and he'll be able to tell us. In the meantime, have some cold towels brought here for her head and let's get that mess on the floor cleaned up before Doctor Geller arrives."

The sound of retreating footsteps disappeared as the two novices who were dispatched to get towels and cleaning utensils, rushed to do their superior's bidding.

"Perhaps we should have the sisters and girls go to the chapel and pray for Roberta."

"Please, Sister Damien, let's not upset the entire convent because one of us happens to have the flu."

Mother Job's admonishment brought a questioning look to Sister Damien's face. "Do you really think it's only flu, Mother?"

Before the Reverend Mother could speak, the novice who was sent to get another container, entered the room. "Here, Sister. Is there anything else I can do?" She placed the three-gallon bucket close to the bed and pushed it toward the place where Bobbe's head hung over the side, disgorging the vile paste into the overflowing saucepan.

"Empty this pan, Mary." Sister Damien set it down so the girl could pick it up by the handle.

Holding it at arm's length, the novice gratefully left the room, which reeked of the putrid, yellow vomit.

"Open the window a little, Sister, and let some fresh air in

142

here." Where were the towels she had asked for? She looked at the bucket as it slowly filled. None of this was possible, she knew. But Sister Damien was already upset enough by Roberta's illness without suggesting there was something out of the ordinary.

Her thoughts were interrupted by the two girls who had been sent to get towels and a mop.

"Here, Mother," one said handing her the towels she carried and quickly left the room before she would be asked to help clean the stenchy mess, now covering half the open floor space of the small room. The older girl dutifully began to mop.

While Sister Damien closely supervised the floor cleaning, the Mother Superior began wiping Bobbe's damp forehead but froze in position as she touched the wet skin. Out of the corner of her eye, she saw a motion farther down the girl's body. Turning slightly so her observation remained covert, she bit the tip of her tongue to prevent a sudden desire to scream. Bobbe's abdomen, undulating at first in a rapid manner, began swelling until her body appeared to be in the last stages of pregnancy. Regaining her composure, Mother Job slowly reached out to touch Bobbe's swollen middle but just as her fingertips were a scant distance from making contact, the girl's stomach flattened to its normal shape. When she saw no further indication of the phenomenon repeating, she glanced up at the nun and novice who were engrossed in mopping the floor. Thankful they had not witnessed the rapid swelling, she returned her attention to Bobbe's face and resumed checking her for indications of cooling but found her still febrile.

"When you finish there, Sister, you'd better get some clean bed clothes and a fresh nightgown before the doctor arrives." Mother Job wondered what they would do about the repugnant stench permeating the room. Would it be wise to move Roberta to another cell while the doctor conducted his examination?

Bobbe stopped vomiting and devoid of the strident moans and retching, the room suddenly fell silent. The novice stopped mopping and looked at Sister Damien without straightening up. Both turned to stare questioningly at their superior.

"Be thankful she stopped. Get those bed clothes. Doctor Geller will be here almost any time." Bending, Mother Job picked up the bucket, now half full and was startled by the weight. She struggled to move it near the doorway and asked the novice to take it away now that the floor was presentable.

When the bed clothes were changed and Bobbe redressed, the Reverend Mother directed the novice to leave and then turned to Sister Damien. "Go to the front door. The others should not be disturbed when the doctor arrives."

As Sister Damien left the room, Mother Job knelt next to Bobbe's head and stroked the girl's brow. Tiny, almost inaudible moans were the only reaction to the older woman's touch. Crossing herself, she began to pray for the novice's recovery.

Just as Sister Damien arrived at the front of the building, she heard a car door slam shut. Opening the entrance, she could see Anthony Geller, slightly stooped and bent from years of service to his fellow man, making his way up the steps. His fresh suit, tie, and shirt matched the neat part in his fog-gray hair but the total appearance was countered with the tired, exhausted expression holding his face. After removing his topcoat and hat, he followed Sister Damien toward the staircase.

"It's simply awful, Doctor. Please hurry." She wanted to grab his hand and pull him faster through the dim hallway.

A benign smile crossed his thin lips. Why did he always have to hurry and why was it always awful? "What seems to be the problem, Sister? You were rather vague on the phone."

"She's screaming and vomiting and moaning and she hasn't opened her eyes once." Sister Damien gasped the more explicit details like an ugly litany while the doctor acknowledged each with a click of his tongue.

The one thing she had seen, that no one else had, was Bobbe masturbating. It certainly was neither fit nor proper to tell this man how one of their novices had been indulging in self-gratification. Perhaps she would tell Mother Job after the doctor left. Perhaps it would be best if something so dirty and awful was not mentioned but simply forgotten.

"Has she been ill before?" The doctor's smooth voice

144

broke into her swirling thoughts.

"Perfect health, as far as we know."

"Lot of flu going around. Probably that."

"I've never seen flu act like this before. Please, hurry."

Exhausted by the eighteen hours he had put in the previous day, the two hours' sleep he had had before receiving the call from the nuns had done nothing to refresh him. Not a young man, Doctor Geller hurried as much as his tired body would allow. For thirty years, since establishing his practice in Cedar Falls, he had cared for the health of the nuns at the convent and they had never been demanding patients. Seldom if ever inconvenienced by them, he struggled now to hurry to the side of their stricken sister.

They found Mother Job standing by the bed with a relieved but puzzled expression as she studied the quiet form of Bobbe, sleeping peacefully on the bed. "She seems perfectly all right now. She's been sleeping like this for some three or four minutes." The Reverend Mother nodded her greeting as she spoke.

"Well, let's take a look at her." Geller moved toward the bed and pulled the straight-back chair over to sit close to Bobbe's head.

Sister Damien searched Mother Job's face for some indication of additional relief now with the doctor here but found the woman's expression more puzzled as Geller conducted his examination. After each test's application, an almost imperceptible shake of his head or click of his tongue would mark the end of that aspect. With each of his gestures, the Reverend Mother's face became more drawn.

At length, Doctor Geller stood and motioned for the women to follow him into the hall. "I can't find anything wrong with her, Mother. She's not subject to seizures of any type, is she?"

"No. That would have been on her medical history. In fact, as I recall her file, Roberta has enjoyed very good health. You can find nothing at all, Doctor?"

"Nothing." The one word seemed almost apologetic in tone.

"What about the vomit?" Mother Job bit the word off as though it were distasteful to say when she recalled the thick

145

slime that had covered the floor only minutes before. That was certainly out of the ordinary. How could he say she was all right—that nothing was wrong with her when only a short time ago—not even an hour—Roberta Moore had been the most sick person the Reverend Mother had ever seen?

"What about it?"

"Yellow. It was yellow and thick—like lumpy paste. It was nothing like ordinary vomit."

"Was anything served that might account for the appearance of the vomitus?"

"No. Nothing even remotely approaching the color or consistency."

"Where is it, Mother? I'd like to see some of it."

Without a word of direction, Sister Damien left the room. As upset as she was, she had noted the sound of fear edging into Mother Job's voice. If Roberta had something contagious, they would all be frightened. The last thing they needed was an epidemic of influenza or something being passed through their ranks. She could recall the number of deaths in her own home town when the epidemic occurred right before she entered the order. Hurrying down the steps, she made her way to the kitchen.

Standing at the foot of the iron bed, Mother Job stared at the quiet form of Bobbe. The sleeping postulant was beautiful—so absolutely beautiful. Why hadn't there been something on her records concerning this type of illness? Perhaps she's never had anything like it before and with God's Blessing and Will, she would never have anything like it again. But there was something else about this episode that nagged at the Mother Superior's mind like the unknown title of a song heard for the first time in years. Unable to put her finger on the elusive memory, she looked up when Sister Damien reentered the cell.

"Did you bring some of it with you, Sister?"

"It's been disposed of by the novices who cleaned it up."

"What about the mop they used?"

"It was rinsed out."

Turning to face the doctor, she managed a weak smile. "I'm sorry, Doctor. There was so much of it."

146

"How much was there, Mother?" He snapped the catch on his bag and stood to face the two women.

"Quarts and—and—there must have been several gallons of it." She knew the words made no sense but resolutely nodded her head when she recalled the amount on the floor, the overflowing two-quart saucepan and the half-filled three-gallon bucket. It sounded preposterous, but she knew the amount had been there—had come from Roberta's mouth. Sister Damien had seen it and when she looked at the Mistress of Novices, she found the woman's head bobbing in agreement.

Geller cocked an eyebrow but said nothing. It was too late and he was too tired to challenge the head of the convent's word and get into a discussion about the capacity of the human stomach. "I see," he said simply, hoping his voice did not sound too patronizing.

"Isn't that unusual, Doctor?" Mother Job persisted.

"Well, yes—I suppose you might say that. However, the only thing we have to go by is what her body tells us now. And it's saying there is basically nothing wrong with this young lady. I would suggest a good night's sleep for everyone and I'll give her a sedative so she'll sleep comfortably." Reopening his case, he prepared a syringe and administered the injection.

Bobbe remained motionless as the needle punctured her skin and the fluid was pushed into her bloodstream.

"What about the smell?"

"What did you say, Sister?" Turning to her companion, Mother Job waited for her to repeat herself.

"I said, what about the smell? It was so powerful—so bad. I'm surprised it's dissipated so much considering how strong it was earlier."

"You're right. I hadn't noticed." Mother Job moved about the room, sniffing deeply. "It's barely perceptible but it's still here. Can you smell it, Doctor?"

Inhaling deeply, the old man slowly shook his head. "I don't smell anything, Mother."

"It's a chemical smell. It was so powerful before I couldn't quite put my finger on what it reminded me of but now—now that it's diminished I would say it's definitely a chemical smell."

"Like matches when they're first ignited," Sister Damien offered, while sniffing the air. "Sulphurous. Yes, sulphur is definitely in the air."

Again, the doctor inhaled deeply. "If anything, it smells like cleaning compounds and furniture polish in here. I'm not trying to be difficult, Mother, but really, that's all I smell."

Ignoring the man, Mother Job continued her olfactory perusal of the air. "I believe you're right, Sister. There definitely is sulphur but I think there's something else mixed in with it. I can't quite identify it."

"If there's any recurrence or if she feels ill in the morning, call me and I'll look in on her again, Mother."

"What? Oh, yes, Doctor. Come, we'll see you to the door." Indicating with an outstretched arm that he should precede them, she waited until Sister Damien and he had quitted the room before she extinguished the light and closed the door softly behind her.

When they reached the front door, they waited while Geller put his coat and hat on. "Thank you very much, Doctor, for coming here in the middle of the night," Mother Job said reaching for the doorknob.

"Anytime, Sister." Then he was gone into the blackness, and once they heard the roar of his car engine they turned out the lights as they retraced their steps to the upper floor.

"You go to your room. I'll look in on Roberta and make sure she's all right before I retire." The two nuns separated at the top of the winding staircase and Mother Job approached Bobbe's room silently. Opening the door without making a noise, she found the room icy cold again but the faint trace of odor was completely gone.

A soft moan from Bobbe as she rolled restlessly on the bed drew the Reverend Mother to her side like a magnet. Without warning the groan became a short, high-pitched scream and she clutched her lower abdomen tightly. As muscular contractions twisted the girl's body, the nun found she could barely hold the stricken girl on the bed. Marveling at the postulant's enormous strength, she gasped when the cramps stopped suddenly and Bobbe relaxed, returning to deep sleep. Bending forward, she placed her ear to the girl's breast and when she detected a steady heart rhythm, the tension fell from her face and body. Pulling the straight-backed chair to the side of the bed, Mother Job sat down to keep an all-night vigil.

Her head lolling forward on her chest, the Mother General snapped awake and fumbled for her watch. Five-thirty. She would have to leave soon to dress for Mass. Apprehensively, she watched Bobbe's eyelids flutter as the girl awoke.

"Why, Reverend Mother? What are you doing here?" Sitting up, she incredulously returned the woman's stare.

"You were sick during the night, Roberta. Don't you remember?" The older woman stood and approached the bed.

"Me? Sick? Why I feel great. I had a good night's sleep and feel wonderful. What—what was wrong with me? I don't remember being sick."

"I guess you must have had a bad attack of the flu—or something."

"Wait a minute. Last night, I walked for a while in the garden right after the sun went down and when I came in a few minutes later, I felt strange."

"Strange?"

"Yes, as though I were getting sick. Chilled and achy all over. I took a hot bath and went right to bed."

"The doctor couldn't find—"

"The doctor? Did you call the doctor for me, Mother?"

"Yes. You were quite ill. However, he couldn't find anything wrong and didn't seem to be very concerned when he was here."

"How—how was I sick?"

"Before the doctor arrived, you had a high temperature and threw up quite a bit and screamed and moaned as though you were in great pain."

"I did all that? What, I do have a different gown on." She fingered the material when she noticed the change in night clothes. "What did I do? Mess things up?" Blushing, she felt embarrassed for not remembering such a thing.

"You might say that, Roberta." The older woman didn't think it wise to go into details and mention the vast quantities of vomit or the fact her abdomen had swelled. Instead she found herself questioning if she had actually seen the girl's middle puff up as though she were pregnant. If the doctor had no explanation for the symptoms as they had described them, and was not disturbed or alarmed, there was no reason to upset Roberta. On the other hand, she felt the same odd something nagging at her mind as she tried to rationalize the night's events for Roberta. "How do you feel now, Roberta?"

"I feel fine, Mother." She got out of bed and stretched. "I really do."

"You don't feel as though you should stay in bed today?"

"Mother, really. I'm perfectly all right. I don't even remember being ill. I feel great."

"Very well, then. Get dressed." She checked her watch again. "It's twenty of six. Don't be late for Mass."

As Bobbe began to dress, Mother Job left the room, walking down the hall shaking her head. She was tired—tired to the marrow of her bones. Catching only fitful snatches of sleep while she had sat next to Bobbe's bed, she groggily made her way to her room.

How could it be possible for Roberta to feel all right this morning? She should be unable to get out of bed. She should be weak because of everything she had thrown up. A knot formed in the Reverend Mother's stomach when she recalled the bizarre scene of the yellow-white pasty substance gushing from the postulant's mouth. It was impossible—totally impossible for a human being to vomit that much. Had she actually been that much? Had she really seen the girl's abdomen swell and inflate the way it had? Something was wrong. But what? The only thing she could be positive of now was the fact her own mind was muddled from lack of sleep and she would have to remedy that before giving further attention to the problem.

She hurried to Mass and then fell into bed without going to breakfast.

CHAPTER TWELVE

After Father Grant left the altar, Bobbe remained in her pew while the other women filed out. Her eyes scanned the open missal she held, but her mind, lost in gyrating thoughts, didn't comprehend the words. Sick? Ill? Her health had never been a problem and now the Reverend Mother was trying to tell her she had been sick—very sick the previous night. A doctor had been called but she remembered nothing of the incident. What was wrong with her? Because of the change in night clothes and bed linen and the fact Mother Job was in her room when she awoke, Bobbe had accepted the fact as truth. But why didn't she remember anything?

Turning, she found herself alone in the chapel and when a sudden, ravenous appetite swept through her, she stood and quickly genuflected. Outside the polished doors, she found Connie waiting with another postulant both of whose rooms were close to her cell.

"How do you feel, Roberta?" Mary Ellen Tolworth asked.

"Fine." For some reason Bobbe found the overweight girl unappealing and most of the time not the least bit friendly. The shell Mary Ellen had pulled around herself served to keep people at bay—people who might get too close and tell her the truth about her appearance.

Bobbe decided she was being uncharitable.

Still, she seemed to fit Jay's description of the type of women who sought refuge in the convent. Not true. Mary Ellen was dedicated and had a calling, a vocation. A need to serve God.

But did she? Bobbe stared at the heavy girl and then

turned away when Connie spoke.

"What was wrong with you last night?"

"I really don't know. I told you I had felt chilled and strange when I saw you after I bathed. But I thought it was going away."

Connie smiled and put a comforting hand on her friend's arm. "I just hope it's not contagious. My gosh, I wouldn't want to get sick like that for anything."

"You would for God. Wouldn't you?" Mary Ellen managed a smile that resembled a smirk, when she reminded the two girls of their reason for being in the convent.

"Oh, of course we would," Connie turned and began walking toward the refectory.

Bobbe caught up to her while Mary Ellen trailed after them. "I'd do anything for *him*." Her voice, although empty of emotion, managed to say the words without Connie noticing the slight change.

After a big breakfast, during which Bobbe managed almost three helpings of everything, the postulants along with the novices and nuns went to their duties.

Mother Job opened her eyes and stared at the ceiling of her cell. What time was it? The room was so bright. Had she overslept? Why hadn't anyone called her?

Then the interruption of the previous night forced its way into the fore of her memory.

Stretching, she got out of bed and quickly dressed. How many more unusual incidents could she manage? The intruder who shouted obscenities in the hall. The awful experience of Thanksgiving day. The septic tank backing up or whatever it was that had happened. Now, Roberta's strange illness and almost miraculous recovery. What did it all mean? Were these experiences designed by God to test her? She had patience. Wasn't her namesake the patron of those being subjected to trials and tribulations? She would manage to survive somehow because she had faith and trust in the Almighty. But what was the purpose of these weird occurrences? Unable to comprehend, she suddenly blessed herself and whispered a prayer. "Forgive me, Oh, Lord, for trying to understand the ways in which You work. My curiosity is the one fault I have had trouble in overcoming. The devil plays on this weakness in my moments of forgetfulness. Give me the strength to resist him, Oh, Lord."

As she left her room, she muttered, "Begone, Satan. Begone."

She hurried to the kitchen but found there was no coffee left from breakfast. Accepting the offer of Sister Lawrence to make some instant coffee, which would be brought to her office, Mother Job left to tend her duties.

While sorting the mail the Mother General found herself wishing for someone other than Bishop King in whom she could confide. For some inexplicable reason, she had felt peculiar in his presence when they had discussed the changing food on Thanksgiving Day. Although he was a sincere friend and had not appeared to be uncomfortable when she had explained her reason for being there, Mother Job found the memory disturbing and wished for a different confidant. Now, she would have to visit with him again.

Her impromptu prayer when leaving her room had triggered a thought, jelling her nagging question of the night before, and she wanted to explore it more fully after caring for some of the more vital aspects of her problems. The first thing she had to do was call the bishop.

Drumming her fingers as the operator placed the call, she breathed a prayer he would understand her feelings of perplexity. She listened intently when she realized the bishop's residence was answering.

"Bishop King's residence. Mrs. Kelly speaking."

"Long distance calling for Bishop King. Is he there?"

"No, ma'am. Bishop King is out of town and will not return until Monday evening. May I take a message?"

Mother Job's heart sank.

"Can he be reached at another number?" the operator persisted.

"Yes. He can be reached at Saint Philomena's parish in Cedar Falls. The number is—"

Mother Job felt weak with relief.

"This is Cedar Falls calling. My party will contact him there. Thank you very much." The connection to Madison was broken and the operator continued speaking to Mother Job.

153

"Did you hear, ma'am?"

"Yes, I did. Thank you. I'll place the call."

Her finger found the dial almost difficult to move after finding the telephone number for Saint Philomena's rectory. After four rings she heard the receiver lift and a voice speak almost simultaneously. "Saint Philomena's rectory. Mrs. Verona speaking."

"This is Mother Job at the Order of the Bearer of the Divine Word Convent. I understand Bishop King is there. May I speak with him?"

"Bishop King hasn't arrived yet. Could I take a message?"

"Yes. Please have the bishop call me as soon as he arrives. It's of the utmost importance. I must speak with him. The convent's number is JUlien 2-3038. Do you have it?"

"Yes, Mother." Proving her efficiency, the housekeeper repeated the message and was gone.

Perhaps his schedule would permit Mother Job to see him face to face. She would certainly feel more secure in that position than on the telephone.

A knock on the door interrupted her thoughts as Sister Lawrence walked in without waiting to be asked. "I thought you might be hungry, too, Mother, and took the liberty of bringing you some toast." The small tray was placed on the tidy desk and the nun left after excusing herself.

The toast disappeared and the coffee helped bring the Mother Superior to a more alert state of mind. She worked her way through the stack of mail rapidly and after filing the last bit of paper in the bank of green cabinets, the phone rang.

"You have a call on extension one, Mother. It's Bishop King," Sister Edward said when she picked up the receiver.

"Thank you, Sister," she said with a sigh of relief and pushed the flashing button. "Your Excellency?"

"Yes, Mother. How are you?"

"Very disturbed and in great need of consulting with you again. I fear we may have a very serious problem here."

"What does the nature of the problem appear to be, Mother?"

"It involves the incidents I discussed with you last week and several other strange and really frightening occurrences since then."

"I understand. I'm here for an anniversary Mass tomorrow—a distant cousin is celebrating his twenty-fifth year in the priesthood. There's a family dinner this evening, but I believe I'll be free this afternoon for a while, right after lunch. Do you want to come here or would it be better if I came there?"

"Oh, Your Excellency, I don't want to inconvenience you but if it wouldn't be too much of an imposition for you to come here, I believe it would be best."

"Fine, Mother. What time would be good for you?"

"Would one-thirty be all right?"

"One-thirty it is. I'll look forward to seeing you then."

Smiling with relief, she replaced the phone in its cradle. She left her office, making her way toward the library feeling more at ease about visiting with the bishop on her own home ground. There was enough time to check a book in the library she had read many years ago, the title of which had come to mind when she had breathed the prayer in her room earlier.

Going to the card file behind the desk, she looked about before starting her search. The library was deserted. Opening the file marked "B," she fingered her way through the list of books registered in the title file. A look of recognition crossed her face as she withdrew a card with *Begone Satan* typed across the top.

Jotting down the location, she found the book in the last row of shelves and paged through it as she walked to a table. The thin booklet, which she had read sometime in the past, concerned a mysterious event occurring many years before in Iowa. For some reason she felt she would be on firmer ground when the bishop arrived if she reread the account again.

The only sound in the large room was the rustling of paper as she turned the pages. Reading hurriedly, Mother Job absorbed the details of a woman possessed by the devil who, after many years of controlling her, was ultimately driven out through the rite of exorcism.

Gasping suddenly, she winced and slowed her pace of reading. "'At times,'" she formed the words aloud in a soft, quavering voice, "'torrents of spittle and filth spouted forth in quantities that were humanly impossible to lodge in a normal human being.'"

The pamphlet slipped in her hand as she recalled the yellowish slime Bobbe had vomited. With a sad shake of her head, she continued the account. Body distended. Deep, loud voices coming from the possessed woman. Abominations imposed on those about the inflicted person.

"Oh, God. What have we done to deserve something like this? Good Lord in heaven. Don't let it be. Not here. Not one of our own." Her voice cracked with emotion as she whispered the prayer.

Badly shaken, she fought a sob building in her throat. Surely the situation outlined in what she had just read did not match exactly with the incidents that had taken place over the last few weeks. Many indications of possession were given in the thin book but very few were of a similar nature to the abnormal occurrences at the convent.

Standing, she closed the book and looked at her watch. Bishop King would arrive any minute and she wanted to greet him personally. She would take the booklet with her in case she wanted to refer to it and prove her point. Such a point to prove! The devil. Here? In the convent? Her convent? Impossible!

Please, dear God, she mentally prayed hurrying down the hall, don't let this thing happen. Not here!

When she reached the foyer, the bishop was at the front door. She hurried to greet him before he rang the bell. Once seated in her office, she wondered how she should begin. How would she tell this young prelate of her suspicions? Of the possibility a postulant might be possessed by a filthy demon? The devil!

"Well, Mother, what is this problem?" King asked after he noticed her discomfort.

"Your Excellency, I don't want you to think I am subject to wild or overly imaginative ideas. But—"

The bishop held up his hand to interrupt her. "Mother, I have always had the highest regard for you and could not think any such thing. Have you solved the problem you recently discussed with me?"

"No, Your Excellency." Mother Job quickly recounted their experience with the plumbing when she and Sister Raphael returned. "I'm afraid I lied to the sisters when I told them it was probably our septic tank backing up into the fresh water well. I'm not certain if they believed me or not. They went to bed and we called a plumber who fixed whatever it was that needed fixing and we haven't had any trouble of the kind since."

"I believe you did the right thing telling them about the septic tank. But it sounds as though that particular problem is solved." A quizzical expression crossed his handsome face.

"Last night, one of our postulants, Roberta Moore, had an almost unbelievable sick spell."

"Unbelievable?" His eyebrows arched.

"Yes, Your Excellency. She vomited literally gallons of a thick, foul smelling substance. Her screams were horrifying. Her stomach inflated like she was—well—like she was pregnant." She paused to see what impact her words were making on the young bishop.

A twitch played at the corners of his eyes but the steady gaze held firm and he remained silent so she could continue.

"We called Dr. Geller but he found everything to be normal when he examined her. She's a beautiful child and I only tell you this because I feel it may be something more diabolical than just an unusual illness."

King blanched as she finished. "You don't really mean something of the devil, do you, Mother?" His voice was even but the words were clipped and frozen.

Unblinkingly, she returned his stare. Now, it was in the open. The bishop had uttered the one word she had not been able to bring herself to voice aloud. The bishop had given substance to the suspicions that had been gnawing at her since her all-night vigil at Roberta's bedside. With the idea exposed, she could present her case, thin as it might sound in spoken words.

"Yes, Your Excellency, I do. The voice in the hall or whatever it was, the horrible incidents on Thanksgiving Day, and now Roberta's problem are to me all totally unnatural occurrences and not the workings of God. This morning, she felt completely rested as though nothing had happened last night. Why, she didn't even recall being sick." Again, she waited for him to argue against her ideas but he remained reticent. What was wrong? Couldn't he see the details in the

157

same light as she? Perhaps she wasn't explaining herself properly. Was there anything she hadn't touched on?

"It is highly unusual, Mother," he finally offered. "Is there more?" If he was interested, his noncommittal expression refused to deny the fact as he waited for his hostess to speak.

"I went to the library this morning and found this booklet written in the early thirties about a woman who was possessed, someplace in Iowa. I found some striking similarities between that case and our troubles here." Holding up the pamphlet so the bishop would know the reference she was describing, the Mother General suddenly felt disappointed in his reaction.

A look of clouded, controlled anger swept across his face as he spoke intently, almost accusingly. "Do you suspect someone of being possessed by a demon, Mother? *Someone here in your convent?*"

"I don't know what to think. I believe it may be possible only because of the impossibility concerning the odd happenings. The things that have happened here are outside of nature's realm. The food turned into something other than food, as if by magic. Hot urine running for hours when hot water couldn't possibly run that long. Roberta being as ill as she was last night. Roberta's class hearing the voice in the hall. It seems as though some unholy force is at work here." She knew her words and voice sounded defensive and the harder she tried to make them forceful, the weaker her argument sounded. Even to her.

The bishop coughed and cleared his throat before speaking in a more even and kind voice. "You keep mentioning this Roberta. Is it she whom you suspect of being possessed?"

With a shrug, Mother Job stood and crossed the room to the file cabinets. "I don't know, Your Excellency. Would you like to see her file?"

"By all means."

Handing the thin Manila file folder to him, she returned to her seat and waited for him to peruse the contents.

The clock on the wall hummed its way through several minutes before he raised his head. "There certainly isn't anything here out of the ordinary. It appears normal to me."

"That's the maddening thing about it."

"I'm familiar with the case history portrayed in that particular booklet. The sciences of psychiatry and psychology were still in their adolescence when the woman was finally determined to be possessed. Today the Church looks differently on possession than it did in the past when that pamphlet was written. Granted the devil did indeed possess that woman's soul, the important aspect is the Church did not decide this until after many years of trial and observation. Further back in history, during the Middle Ages, for example, there were six signs of willful susceptibility to the devil. Abortion. Murder. Evil love. Jealousy and hatred. Inability to perform the sex act. Deprivation of reason."

Amazed, Mother Job stared at the bishop. "Your Excellency, you're so well briefed on the subject."

"It's part of my duties as a bishop. You see, only a bishop can give permission for an exorcism to be performed. I don't consider myself an expert but I do know considerably more than most people or priests."

Catching the subtle reprimand, Mother Job nodded in understanding and waited for him to continue.

"Those six signs I just mentioned were the key to determining if a person were truly possessed. If one or more signs were present, the afflicted would be exorcised in due time. Then, in the eighteenth century, when work with the mentally ill began, the attitude of the church slowly changed. For instance, sexual difficulties were eventually attributed to a neurosis. Not the devil. Eventually, science had rational explanations for all six indicators. Today a person suspected of being possessed must first be examined by a psychologist or psychiatrist before the Church will study any details. I might add most cases are resolved in this manner—through the sciences. However, and I'm not denying the possibility of a true case of possession occurring today, when the sciences are unable to correct the situation and the Church feels the presence of a demon is truly, undeniably in existence, the permission to perform the holy rite of exorcism is granted."

Absorbing the disturbing facts, Mother Job wondered how they would determine if one of the convent members were truly possessed. "Isn't there an easier, quicker way to determine this, Your Excellency? You said this particular case in Iowa had been observed for years before it was decided the devil indeed possessed the woman. How are we to solve this problem here, Your Excellency?"

"We're not absolutely certain a problem does exist. There should be reasonable explanations for all the unusual occurrences that have taken place here. Logic virtually demands it. You see, Holy Mother Church is quite conservative in declaring visions and miracles the authentic work of God and is just as reserved in her thinking when it comes to the other end of the spectrum. The needless bloodshed of witch hunts and possessed souls that took place in the past prompted the Church to take a wait-and-see attitude. At one time, anyone suspected of witchcraft or being in league with the devil was put to death. More than likely most of them were completely innocent of any wrongdoing."

He watched her closely as the slow moving procedure of the Church was outlined and found restrained curiosity showing on her face while her hands nervously twisted the blue pamphlet *Begone Satan*, into a tube. "Before a person can be considered possessed today, one of three signs that are accepted as proof must be acknowledged to be present in a bona fide manner. A foreign language must be spoken by the suspect—language he—or she—could have no knowledge of whatsoever. The subject must have knowledge of the future and the hidden past. Lastly, physical phenomena beyond the natural flow of life must be present where the subject is concerned."

"Physical phenomena, Your Excellency? I don't understand."

"Phenomena such as heavy objects moving unaided—"

Mother Job gasped. "Or food turning into something other than food."

"Even if all three signs were manifest, we would still have to give consideration to the sciences, Mother." His voice emphasized the importance of the words he uttered. She would have to accept the procedures if the suspicions proved to be remotely correct.

"Won't that be difficult, Your Excellency?"

"Difficult? How do you mean, Mother?"

"Who will do the investigating or examining? We can't as a

community just have anyone come in here seeking out the devil. How would we know the information would be kept completely confidential? Taking Roberta out of the convent to a consultant would be equally dangerous, if not more so." The curious aspect of her nature was now smothered by the anxiety and apprehension she felt growing because of the situation at hand.

"There is one more aspect we haven't considered, Mother. We are not absolutely certain there is a case requiring the services of a psychologist or psychiatrist. What has happened here could be a case of extraordinary phenomena only. Possibly a poltergeist. A poltergeist is—"

"I'm familiar with the term, Your Excellency. If I may be permitted to clarify what you've been saying, there are several possible explanations for our problem. Mental illness. Extraordinary phenomena or—possession. How are we going to determine which it is?"

Knowing he had to satisfy the nun sitting opposite him as well as the position of the Church, Bishop King stood without answering the question immediately. He leaned on the file cabinet after turning to face her.

"With your permission, Mother, I'll assign a priest to the convent as permanent chaplain for a while and relieve Father Grant of his duties here. I'm sure he'll be content to stay at his other post as chaplain at the hospital. The man I have in mind for his replacement here is a Capuchin Father who is most experienced in this particular field. I know he has conducted no less than fifteen exorcisms in the last twenty years or so."

"Fifteen?" The word was a breath of surprise Mother Job was unable to conceal when the almost commonplace aura the number seemed to suggest registered in her mind. "I had no idea such a thing occurred with any degree of frequency."

"Well, most cases remain extremely confidential and seldom receive the publicity the Iowa case did. Actually, it is much better for all concerned if an exorcism is kept secret. Surely the poor soul who is infested should not have to endure the stigma of being known as the 'one possessed by the devil.'"

"What will—ah, what is his name? The Capuchin?"

"Father Balthasar Becker. A most pleasing individual and a

more than worthy adversary of the devil. A very intelligent man."

"What will he do, this Father Becker, once he's here?" Her voice betrayed her feeling of doubt. What could he witness she hadn't already seen? But then, he was experienced in these things and she knew so little.

"I'll instruct him to observe the day-to-day activities of the convent and, if you desire, the activities of this—ah—" He stopped and looked at the folder on the desk. "—Roberta Moore. He'll know what to look for under the circumstances as you outline them."

Her voice, filled with relief, took on a more relaxed attitude. "How quickly can he come?"

"I'll call my office and have Mrs. Kelly, my secretary, get on it immediately. I only hope he's available. If he's not, there are others."

A feeling of peace pushed its way into her being, replacing the fear and unmitigated alarm she had felt since being awakened in the middle of the night by Bobbe's illness. "You have no idea what I've been going through the last few hours, thinking perhaps one of our convent was possessed and a possible danger not only to herself, but to the rest of us. Now, hearing how remote the chance of someone being possessed actually is and knowing there will be someone here who is knowledgeable on the subject gives me a feeling of great relief."

"The chance of possession is remote, and I'm sure the odd happenings will be explained satisfactorily sooner or later. I will caution you of one thing. Do not inform anyone of the real reason for Father Becker's presence."

"Of course. I've already made up my mind not even Sister Raphael or Sister Damien will know." She hesitated before asking the one question that would make the priest's presence totally acceptable. "Father Becker will report to me?"

"Until something is actually observed by him, I don't feel there will be anything to report. However, if you want to know his findings, I'm certain he'll be happy to share them with you." He paused before adding, "Yes, in fact it'll be necessary you do know. In the event he determines there's no real possession and a psychologist or psychiatrist should be consulted, you certainly will have to be in on everything from that point."

Mother Job breathed an inaudible sigh of relief. The suspicion and investigation would be kept within the confines of the convent, at least for the time being.

"I'll call Mrs. Kelly as soon as I return to Saint Philomena's and have her locate Father Becker for me. When I return home Monday, I'll call him and report back to you immediately afterward. Is that satisfactory to you, Mother?"

"Very much so, Your Excellency," the Reverend Mother said and stood. She accompanied him to the front door and held out her hand to take his before he left. Kneeling she kissed his ring and stood.

When she was standing again, he said, "I think it might be a good idea if you didn't read any more of *Begone Satan* right now. You might misinterpret something around here and that wouldn't be good, would it?" Although his voice and choice of words were gentle, there was no attempt on his part to camouflage any further that the word of warning was a direct order.

She nodded silently.

"One other thing, Mother. You will find solace in the prayer to Saint Michael that's recited after Mass."

"Thank you, Your Excellency. I'll wait for your call on Monday." She closed the door after the prelate and retraced her steps to her office.

Bishop King hurried to the black Cadillac sitting at the curb. As he opened the driver's seat, his attention was directed to the top floor of the convent where he saw the figure of a young postulant standing, peering out a window directly at him. Thinking better of raising his hand in a salutation, he got in the car. The motor turned over easily and he manuevered the large auto around the horseshoe drive expertly. Driving was the one pleasure he would never deny himself.

Bobbe watched Bishop King hesitate before getting into the black automobile and then drive off. She smiled crookedly and then turned when she felt two hands on her hips. Spinning about, she faced Dra-woh.

"He is gone."

The voice of the man in white caressed her and she thrilled at the sound of it. "Will he interfere with my training?"

"No one will bother us. You are too important to the master."

The little laugh in her throat grew until it became a bubbling gurgle of unholy mirth. Throwing her head back, her teeth glistened in the afternoon sun, her eyes reflecting the light, as she wallowed in the attention of the demon standing next to her.

CHAPTER THIRTEEN

Her spirits lifted by the words of Bishop King, Mother Job hurried back to her office. A feeling of confidence, one that had escaped her for the last hours since Bobbe's illness, worked its way back into place. It was incredible, simply incredible, how the mind could create fears and anxieties when it was allowed to run rampant. She knew the bishop was right in his decision and the convent's new chaplain, Father Becker, would not find any indication of the devil in her convent.

A shudder was born at the thought of the devil and the prayer to Saint Michael the Archangel coursed through her mind. . . . *by the power of God, cast him into hell with the other evil spirits, who prowl about the world seeking the ruin of souls. Amen.*

Finishing as she reentered her office, her eyes were drawn instantly to her desk where she saw the rolled and dog-eared pamphlet she had twisted in her hands while visiting with the bishop. Sister Maxine, the librarian, would be furious about the condition of the book. Rolling it in the opposite direction, Mother Job flattened it out, straightening the bent pages. Satisfied the thin booklet was not injured as badly as she first thought, she began thumbing through the pages of violence, desecration, and ultimate victory over the legions of hell. The words of the prelate forgotten, she sat behind her desk, eyes riveted to the pages while she reread the terrifying story.

The balance of the weekend passed quickly but Mother Job, once more alerted to the possibility of possession by the booklet and her recollection of the bizarre events of the last few weeks, referred to the Iowa case history, comparing it to isolated incidents of no consequence. Her anxiety built steadily and when Bishop King called Monday before lunch, she hurried to her office to take the message. Why was he calling so early?

"Father Becker is not available at this time, Mother." Although his words were disappointing, his voice seemed relatively unconcerned.

Mother Job's heart sank. What would happen now? "What do we do, Your Excellency? Do you have an alternate suggestion?"

"Just one requiring a small amount of patience on your part, Mother. His schedule is filled until the fourteenth of December. Then, he's free and could arrive at the convent on the fifteenth. Would that be satisfactory?"

What choice did she have? Becker sounded as though he were the best and only solution to their problem. "That'll be fine, Bishop King. We have managed so far and another week or so will not be an impossible imposition."

After they had said their good-byes, Mother Job wondered if the Capuchin might be conducting an exorcism right now? Highly improbable. From what the bishop had said, there was no time formula where the rite was concerned and he had been most definite about the arrival date of the new chaplain. In addition, she was positive Bishop King would not have revealed the information, had she been foolish enough to ask. That sort of thing was kept strictly confidential. Comforted by the thought the matter would be held a closely bound secret, should the chaplain determine the devil was among them, she made her way to the refectory. *The devil among them, indeed!* They'd show *him!*

The thought of how to inform the other nuns about the new chaplain crossed her mind. It would seem more natural if Father Grant told them, since the bishop had said he would be contacting the older priest that afternoon. Yes, that way would least likely arouse anyone's suspicions. Suspicions? In the convent? The idea made her shake her head sadly. This whole thing had to pass. They had to be delivered from this trouble. She would have to be extra alert during the interval until Father Becker arrived.

Oh, Lord, protect us, she mentally prayed as she entered the dining hall.

Standing in the shadows of the hall outside the chaplain's quarters, Bobbe watched as Connie and another postulant left carrying a bucket, mops, and dust cloths. They had been assigned to clean the apartment for the impending arrival of Father Becker. Watching unemotionally as the girls passed within a few feet of her, she stepped from her hiding place once they were out of sight. Stealthily crossing to the entrance, Bobbe turned the knob and slipped inside, closing the door behind her.

Although the days had passed without incident, no one noticed the melancholy gripping Bobbe as she sat in the community room the day before Father Becker was to arrive. She had been late for lunch by a few minutes and, after receiving her mail, accompanied Connie to spend her leisure hour reading her letter from home.

"You read your letter, Bobbe," Connie said settling herself at a sewing machine. "I received permission to do a little repair work on one of my dresses."

"You certainly must be ambitious." Bobbe slit the envelope open and withdrew the letter.

"Working in the chaplain's apartment all morning gave me an appetite for work as well as food." Connie smiled and concentrated on inserting a new bobbin.

Settling into an overstuffed easy chair, Bobbe began reading her mother's letter.

Wednesday
December 12, 1951

Dear Bobbe,
  Things are still quiet around the house. Your father and I have really had a time adjusting to your absence. But please, and this may sound like an afterthought, don't think we're not happy for you or that we feel a loss because of your decision to enter the convent. We love you very much and only want for you what you want for yourself. Enough on that.
  I've almost finished my Christmas shopping and have

gotten the things you suggested as gifts for yourself. I guess we'll have Aunt Kate here for Christmas dinner. I think we'll miss you the most that day. I do like your idea about thinking of you as living in another town and working at a job. You're right about us accepting it easier that way and not thinking as though you have gone out of our lives completely. Naturally, you're not, are you? You're with us every minute in our hearts and minds. Your father and I are really looking forward to visiting Sunday in February. That day just seems as though it will never get here.

I know it doesn't make any difference to you but I'm sure you'd want to know about Jay. He's getting married the day after Christmas to Crystal Brauerman. I understand they began going together shortly after you left. Now they're going to be married. How about that?

There was more to the letter, but Bobbe's eyes remained riveted to the paragraph concerning Jay. He was getting married—and to Crystal Brauerman, of all people. Crystal had never been one of her favorite people and she found it difficult to believe Jay had fallen in love with her. With a shake of her head, Bobbe tore her eyes from the page and stared out the window toward the garden.

She was out of Jay's life and he could do as he pleased. Why should she be concerned? Didn't she have her own life to lead? Then the question of Jay's love for her and how sincere it had been suddenly filled her mind. Obviously his love had been no deeper for her than hers for him.

Her eyes began feeling hot and she knew a cascade of tears was about to erupt. Walking quickly from the community room she hurried to the staircase. Seconds later, she threw herself on the bed, sobbing.

"I don't care," she gasped aloud. "I don't care!" But she couldn't repel the feeling she had lost something—something that had been hers and was now being taken away—something she had not wanted to give up. Her weeping eventually stopped but an occasional sob shook her body after she drifted off to sleep.

The next morning, Father Grant turned to deliver what the women in his congregation assumed would be a usual sermon. But when he began talking and it was evidently a farewell address, all eyes and ears were attentively alert.

"I have enjoyed my years here at the convent, and I know I will most certainly miss you good nuns. However, when God's Will is directed toward you for a specific mission, you humbly obey His Will. If I can impart no other message during my stay here, be subservient to Him and do His bidding.

"I will be leaving after Mass and as I understand it, my replacement is to be Father Balthasar Becker. Father Becker is a Capuchin priest. He will arrive sometime today. He will care for your spiritual needs as I have tried to do.

"Now, it is time to say good-bye. I'm sure you all are aware of the origin of the farewell phrase good-bye. It originally was God be with ye. So I say now, God be with you."

Turning back to the altar, Father Grant continued with the Mass. When the nuns, novices, and postulants filed up to the railing to receive the host, the old priest approached them carrying a ciborium filled with the blessed wafers. He seemed older and slower as he administered holy communion to each woman for the last time.

Bobbe thrust her head back and with mouth open, she waited to have the Host placed on her tongue. Undulating colors of blue, purple, and black mixed with flashes of yellow, vermillion, and blazing white began blocking her vision. Dizziness swept over her and she clung to the rail in front of her to keep her balance. Losing consciousness, she released her grip and felt herself falling backward. Far off in the distance she heard a cry beginning to build.

"Be-e-e-h-h-h-ck-e-e-e-r."

Her stomach churned as the sound built within her. Gagging, she could feel thick mucus building in her mouth. With a loud groan, she hit the floor.

Writhing and convulsing, Bobbe kicked and struck anyone trying to help her but the seizure lasted only a few seconds. Several nuns, Mother Job among them, picked her up and carried Bobbe's limp body from the chapel to her room.

Assuming the attack was finished, Mother Job turned to the nuns who had helped. "I'll stay with her for a while. I think she'll be all right. The rest of you return to the chapel for the finish of Mass."

"Yes, Mother," the voices chorused in a half whisper.

"Say a prayer for Roberta," she added as the last one left the cell. Turning to face the quiet figure on the bed, she blinked a tear away. "Why couldn't you wait?"

Once more the fears she had put to rest over the last few quiet days came crashing back into her mind, bombarding her with the same questions she had wrestled with in the past. A moan drew Mother Job's attention to the bed and its occupant.

Bobbe opened her eyes, a startled expression crossing her face. "What—what happened?"

"You fainted at the communion rail, Roberta." Torn with doubts as to how she should handle the postulant, Mother Job decided it would be best to act as though nothing out of the ordinary had happened. Pursue it as though nothing was thought to be amiss.

"I don't remember anything, Mother. What did I do? Just pass out?" She sat up and held her head in both hands before raising her face to the Mother Superior.

"You—uh—you had a convulsion, Roberta. Have you ever had any before? I mean, you—well, there wasn't anything on your medical records indicating a history of convulsions or seizures." Was she doing the right thing? She wasn't even certain if it would be wise to mention the subject of convulsions to a person who had just suffered the first one.

Bobbe's expression changed from puzzlement to one of incredulity. "A convulsion? Me? No! No, never. Not me."

"Don't excite yourself, Roberta. If you like, we could call a doctor and have him examine you." She tried to keep her voice calm but found herself wanting to leave the room immediately.

"No. No doctor. I feel fine. Are you sure it was a convulsion?"

"I'm almost positive it was. I'm no expert but I would say it was a seizure of some sort. Were you hungry?" Perhaps this was a genuine fainting spell. She hoped it was. Perhaps *she* was overreacting. Perhaps the devil *was* among them. "Quite often, fasting for communion will make you feel dizzy and ill, Roberta. Did you feel sick prior to communion time?"

Bobbe's forehead puckered in thought when she recalled

the events of Mass right before she left her seat to approach the communion rail. "No. I felt good, as I recall, Mother. I feel fine now, as a matter of fact. I'm hungry but no more so than normal. I'm sure I'll be all right." A timid smile crossed her face. "I certainly can cause problems, can't I, Mother?"

The Reverend Mother placed a reassuring hand on her shoulder. "Now, don't feel badly about this. Good heavens. A person can faint without causing a disturbance. You have felt all right, haven't you, since the night you were so sick?"

"Perfectly fine, Mother."

"Do you feel like eating now?"

"Yes. I'm hungry."

Mother Job indicated the postulant should precede her from the cell and followed Bobbe into the hall. Walking down the stairs, the postulant followed her superior by a step.

"If anything bothers you or you feel distressed about anything, Roberta, please feel free to come to my office. I'll visit with you any time."

Bobbe stared at the back of the nun's head. What a strange thing to say. Weren't the postulants and novices supposed to consult with Sister Damien about questions or problems? "What time does the new chaplain arrive, Mother?" A change in topic of conversation might be in order, she thought.

"Not until this evening, after dinner. You postulants and novices will have an opportunity to meet Father Becker tomorrow morning after Mass."

Bobbe's face contorted into a snarl at the mention of the Capuchin's name but resumed its normal appearance when the Reverend Mother turned at the bottom of the steps and smiled. When they reached the dining room, breakfast was already being served.

Because the new chaplain's arrival that night had everyone in a state of excitement, the subject of Bobbe's fainting spell was soon dismissed from the minds of the women. Mother Job made a mental note to include the incident in her first talk with the Capuchin.

The day passed uneventfully as the women anticipated the priest's appearance. Following the evening meal and the conclusion of the day's organized prayers, Mother Job hurried to her office to wait the final minutes before she would meet Father Balthasar Becker. Just as she was about to sit behind her desk, a quick nervous knock sounded and before she could answer, the door opened and a white-veiled novice stepped inside.

"Father Becker is here, Mother."

The young nun stepped aside and Mother Job gasped when she saw the giant filling the doorway. The huge, barrel-chested man, clad in a rough cassock, was striding into the room, exposing his sandeled feet. Craning her neck, Mother Job peered upward past his bright red beard to his bald head before returning to the eyes of the six-foot-six-inch priest.

"Mother Job?" His voice matched his three-hundred-pound body.

"I'm Reverend Mother Job," she said weakly, taken aback by the goliath in her office.

"I'm Father Balthasar Becker." A large, hamlike hand, fastened by a thick wrist to an arm that resembled a sturdy oak branch, was thrust out to be shaken.

"How do you do, Father." Her hand was swallowed and lost in his. "It's good to see you." She indicated a chair for him to sit but he waited until she was seated herself before easing his large frame onto it.

With a delighted smile, the novice left, closing the door quietly behind her.

"His Excellency, Bishop King, advised me you may have a problem here and gave me some details as to what has happened. Has anything occurred of which the bishop is not aware?" The direct method of approaching any problem had stood him in good stead throughout his adult life and, seldom a man to engage in light talk, he preferred doing away with needless conversation. Especially at a time like this.

Mother Job studied him, deciding his age could be anywhere between fifty and seventy although the bright hue of his full beard seemed to indicate he was on the younger end of the scale. His eyes, she found, were his most arresting feature. At first she had thought them to be black but now, with the ceiling fixture spilling its light over him, she could tell they were a deep brown.

The words of Bishop King suddenly focused in her memory. "*A most worth adversary to the devil.*" Now, she

172

had no fears. She felt relieved, almost comfortable in his presence.

Sitting forward, Mother Job looked straight into the brown eyes. "Yes, Father, this morning at communion. The postulant in question, Roberta Moore, suffered a convulsive seizure right before she was to receive the Host. She foamed at the mouth and fell to the floor kicking and striking out at those who tried to help her. She recovered almost immediately once we got her to her cell. Within a few minutes, she was ready to go to breakfast as though nothing had happened."

Thick, fat fingers ran through his beard in a combing gesture. "Hmmmm. Well. Has she ever suffered a fit before?"

Rankled at his poor choice of words describing the event, she formed her answer carefully in her head before speaking. "No. There was nothing on her medical history form and I asked her if she had ever suffered any *seizures* before. She said nothing like that had ever happened to her—not before this morning, that is."

His eyes sparkled with an inquisitive gleam. Oblivious to the nun's attempt to correct his choice of words, he shifted his weight in the straight chair. "Well, that in itself is not conclusive evidence. We'll make a note of it and put all the pieces together as they present themselves. We'll talk from time to time about this in addition to my duties as chaplain and the convent's confessor. Should you observe something you feel is out of the ordinary, please report it to me at once. If I feel there is a case of possession here—a genuine case—calling for the holy rite of exorcism, I shall confer with Bishop King and we will abide by his decision."

The deliberate manner in which he spoke told the Mother Superior she was dealing with a man who knew his business and feared few people on the face of the earth. Still, she found the aura of humbleness holding him in a gentle grip, a comforting quality.

"Very well, Father. It is getting late and I'm sure you'd like to relax this evening after your journey. If I may, I'll show you to your quarters."

Jumping lightly to his feet, the Capuchin held the door for the nun and followed her into the hall where he picked up his small valise.

"The rooms haven't been used for a few years ever since Father Grant started serving here. He lives at the hospital. However, two of our postulants cleaned the apartment thoroughly just yesterday. I hope you find it comfortable."

"A simple cot to rest on a few hours each day is all I really need, Mother Job. My needs and wants are as simple as a new born babe's. A place to sleep and something to eat. Beyond that I find my comfort and solace in God and helping those of His children who need assistance."

"Did you have a good trip, Father?"

"Very nice. It was a pleasant train ride."

Mother Job tried to make polite conversation as they walked but the fist of cold fear gripping her heart again, suddenly filled her with dread. The man she was showing to the chaplain's quarters was an exorcist—one who fought the devil and his demons first hand. As if complementing the giant priest, the reason bringing the Capuchin to the convent loomed bigger than ever in her mind.

She left him at the entrance of the apartment when he assured her he would have no trouble settling himself. Closing the door gently, he glanced about the bare appearing, unlived-in rooms. A small parlor with an empty desk against one wall was stark in its decor of mohair-covered davenport and chair. Above the desk the outline of a crucifix which had been present once but no longer there was clearly evident in the lighter shade of wall paper. Next to the desk there stood a dull brass floor lamp with a semitransparent shade. Opening the only door other than the one through which he had entered, he found the bedroom. It was as Spartan as the living room, and he smiled gratefully.

Becker crossed the room and dropped the black suitcase on the bed. Withdrawing from the yawning mouth of the satchel a cassock and necessary pieces of underwear and handkerchiefs, he opened the closet door and stood immobile. Hanging in an inverted position was the missing cross from the living room, the heavy brass figure of Christ, bent grotesquely out of shape.

PART
THREE

BALTHASAR
BECKER

December 16, 1951
to
December 26, 1951

CHAPTER FOURTEEN

Following Sunday Mass and breakfast the next morning, Mother Job rushed to her office where the Capuchin and she would have their first in-depth meeting. Seconds after she entered the priest joined her.

"I trust you had a good night's sleep, Father?" Mother Job felt diminutive, almost insignificant in the presence of the huge priest. But now that both were seated, she felt more on an equal basis with him. For some reason he did not seem so huge.

"Very good, Mother. There is something about a convent's atmosphere that is exceedingly restful. None of the tensions of the world ever seem to penetrate the shield of peace and calm God allows you women."

A benign smile, hidden within the hair of his beard, betrayed itself in his eyes. He knew only too well how the incidents of the past two months had disrupted the tranquillity of the convent and he wanted to put the Mother General at ease as much as possible. In time perhaps, he would tell her of the crucifix's defilement. But not now. Aware that fear of the unknown could be alleviated with knowledge, he wanted to give her as much information as he could. Armed with proper concepts, she would better appreciate the nature of the problem they would have in determining the status of the case at hand.

"What do you know about 'possession,' Mother Job?"

"Very little, Father. In fact the booklet *Begone Satan* is the only thing I have ever read concerning the subject. Bishop King did fill me in on the Church's position in cases like this.

How it moves cautiously and slowly before determining if a person is truly possessed. Outside of that little bit, I know virtually nothing." She hoped the Capuchin would talk freely, giving her as much information as possible so she would be able to help him in his day-to-day observations.

"I see. Well, knowing the Church does move slowly in matters such as this will make you understand the gravity of the situation. You see, the first thing we must determine is the problem itself. The choices we have to work with are possession, natural manifestation of phenomena, and mental disorder." His voice, smooth and deep, rang with an air of professional expertise, knowledge, and experience all of which belied his simple appearance.

Nodding, she said nothing, watching instead his red beard, which appeared to take on a life of its own whenever he spoke.

"Natural phenomena are tough to contend with since we must ask ourselves if there are really such things as ghosts and goblins who wander the earth, going bump in the night."

Quickly raising her eyes from his beard to stare deeply into his when he paused, she glanced uneasily toward the clock on the wall before speaking. "How can ghosts and the like be considered 'natural,' Father?"

"If ghosts are to be denied, then the concept of the immortal human soul must be denied as well since ghosts are supposed to represent the earthbound spirits of the dead. The Church accepts the natural concept of the immortal soul as the basis for its existence. Without the soul, the Church has no reason to persist."

She nodded and waited for him to continue.

"I believe most so-called mysterious happenings and events could be explained in a very reasonable manner if the proper investigation is conducted. We do have science on our side and Holy Mother Church demands we consult those sciences that are capable of explaining some of the phenomena often mistaken for signs of possession."

"Could you explain that a little more, Father? The bishop touched on it but didn't go into any detail."

Her anticipation of his explanation was quickly interpreted as eagerness by the priest and he made a mental note of her attitude. "Well, as men involved in the beginnings of psychiatry and psychology gathered evidence, some of the phenomena of possession suddenly had rational explanations. However, both could only go so far. The study of psychology is at best an empirical science and cannot address the possibility of a malevolent spirit being present or even acknowledge the possibility one might exist. They confine the interpretation of such a case within the boundaries of their own realm and look upon the manifestations of the 'unholy' as a maladjustment of the poor individual who is infested." A smile, caused by his statement's wryness, twitched unseen at the corners of his mouth.

"Are you saying then you don't have much faith in the findings of these sciences?"

"On the contrary, Mother. I have every faith in them as far as they go. By allowing them to eliminate, if you will, the aspects of an individual's case they can handle within the scope of their science, what is left unexplained, is examined by the Church as the possibility for the case of possession. This method allowed the Church to understand better the circumstances surrounding the phenomena themselves. Prior to the advent of psychology, the Church had the six signs of the Middle Ages to work with. They were—"

"That much I do know, Father. Bishop King told me about them."

He rubbed his hands together, thankful she was apprised of at least some basic knowledge. "Good. As I was saying, when the Church had only those six signs to go by, She was operating in the darkness of ignorance. A person suffering from a simple neurosis, which would be passed off today as a mere problem to be solved quickly, would be put through the rigors of exorcism and in most cases was probably not helped at all."

His gentility and understanding moved Mother Job to wonder how such an irenic man could be appointed exorcist. Ignoring the question, she refocused her attention on the priest's words.

"In one of the situations I was involved with, the husband of the woman who was infested with an unholy spirit, absolutely refused to allow anyone but myself into the house or near his wife. When the rite of exorcism was completed successfully, the poor man suffered a nervous breakdown. In the past, the man would have been exorcised, more than likely, and I might add, it would have been unsuccessful. However, because we better understand psychology's position in the scheme of things, he recovered within a matter of a few months and both are well and happy today. Quite often it is virtually impossible to determine which of the two problems you are dealing with until some time has passed and certain observations have been made. It's not like diagnosing a head cold or sore throat. Another time—" Stopping short, he questioned the advisability of sharing his experiences with this troubled woman. Wouldn't the accounts cause her more anguish? "—I will tell you of some of the other cases I have been involved with over the years."

Confident she had not noticed his brief pause while deciding not to relate more of his background, he managed a smile. "I do know the pomps of Satan well, Mother, although I must admit I have never locked horns, so to speak, with the Abomination, himself. He has underlings and condemned souls whom he dispatches to wreak havoc on the faithful of the world."

"Then Catholics are the only ones ever possessed, Father?" She felt her voice, high pitched after being silent for several minutes, sounded too loud—too excited. But if only the faithful of the world were afflicted, then surely only Catholics were afflicted.

"Heavens no, Mother. Aren't Protestants God's children as well as Moslems and Catholics? Heathens and pagans as well as members of other religious sects and denominations have been infested as much as Catholics. I'm afraid the devil shows no preferences for one sect over another."

"I'm afraid that was awfully narrow thinking on my part, Father."

"Anyone is susceptible to his whims and fancies. If, and I say *if*, someone is possessed here, it would not be the first time Lucifer and his minions have invaded the confines of a holy place. There are many instances in the past. All well documented. Some questionable at best when today's methods are taken into consideration."

179

"Do you mean by a holy place—in a convent?"

Becker studied the woman for several moments before answering. Would this woman, whom he had just met, be able to understand the complexities facing them and still be objective enough to learn of past cases without comparing them to her own situation? Did he have a choice not to tell her now that he had mentioned the past?

"Yes, Mother Job. In convents. But you must bear in mind the times and limited expertise available to the Church and Her exorcists and people in power."

"Please, Father. You must tell me more. You can't just mention it in passing and expect me to let it pass."

He placed a huge hand on his bare head, massaging it in a quick, frustrated motion. "Mother, most of those cases would be referred to the sciences today. However, I understand your own anxiety and hunger for knowledge. The most famous case is probably that of the nuns of Aix-en-Provence in France where an apparent epidemic of possession occurred in the seventeeth century."

"What order of nuns were they?"

"Ursuline." He tried not to notice the tiny smile of relief that crossed her face. "Another well-documented case involved the Premonstratensian Convent in Unterzell, Germany. A third that comes to mind was that of a priest who was involved as chaplain at a convent."

"A priest? A chaplain?"

"Don't be shocked, Mother. After all, women and nuns certainly had no corner on mental illness or false accusations or being framed, if you will, by uneducated people."

"Basically, what happened at these convents?"

"The afflicted would display symptoms such as cramps, bodily contortions, and hallucinations."

Her blank look prompted him to continue. "Cramps wherein the person in question would suffer a physical disorder for a short period of time and recover. Bodily contortions were nothing more than falling down and writhing on the floor. Hallucinations wherein screams in the convent's chapel would disrupt services. Those are broad generalizations and not necessarily the works of a demon. More than likely the machinations of a disturbed mind." He stopped when he saw the woman across the desk turning ashen gray.

"What is it, Mother?"

"Roberta certainly suffered 'cramps,' if that's the proper terminology, the night she threw up that awful yellow stuff. Yesterday morning, she was subject to a seizure at the communion railing. That could be classified as bodily contortions. And, although she hasn't disrupted chapel services other than the one time in any way, she certainly screamed loud enough the night she was ill."

"Please, Mother. I beg of you. Don't try to make this girl's symptoms fit the signs of possession used two hundred years ago. They're no longer applicable. Remember, there are only three acceptable indications. They're—"

"I know. I know. But you have to admit we have had certain physical manifestations around here. The two incidents on Thanksgiving and—"

Holding his hand up for silence, the priest stood. "This whole thing is not to be rushed—under any circumstances, Mother. It simply will not be allowed or tolerated. Patience is the one virtue that should be the order of the day."

"Of course, Father. I'm truly sorry. How long should an exorcism take, if a person is actually possessed?"

The contriteness of her statement was obvious in her pained expression. Turning, Father Becker crossed the room to the window and peered into the countryside which lay before the convent like an unhappy gray painting of winter without snow.

"There is no set formula for the time it takes to complete a successful rite. It could go on for years. I know of one case in which it took the exorcist some eighteen months to drive the demon from the infested person. On the other hand, I believe you mentioned *Begone Satan.* That particular situation took twenty-three days if I remember right."

Nodding her head in understanding, she camouflaged her thoughts of despair. Overwhelmed by the thought of eighteen months or even years as the priest had said, she wondered if the convent's members were up to the rigors apparently needed to withstand such an ordeal.

With an effort the large man resumed his seat after leaving

181

the window and, his fingertips touching, stared at Mother Job. "Let's get down to cases. These happenings that have taken place in the convent, when did they start?"

"Around the first of November. Yes, just about six weeks ago." She picked up the calendar and consulted it for accuracy to reinforce her own memory. "Yes, around the first of November."

"The first instance was the voice in the hall. Is that right?" She nodded.

"Then the food incident on Thanksgiving followed by the trouble with the plumbing. Is that correct?"

Another nod and shudder as the events were mentally relived for a brief second.

"To keep the order of happenings straight in my own mind, when did the novice get so ill? The bishop felt it belonged on the list of extraordinary events." Reaching into the folds of his cassock he pulled out a blue-covered notebook and pencil stub. Flipping it open to the first page, he waited to record the fact.

"It would have been the week—after Thanksgiving. Yes, that's right. The second Friday after Thanksgiving." She returned his even gaze, denying the turmoil of her own thoughts. If the priest or the bishop had been with Roberta, there would be absolutely no doubt about the uncommon incident.

"What exactly was the nature of her illness, Mother?" The warm compassionate expression had changed until now it was almost cold in skepticism. Seemingly, his words demanded everything the nun was about to say, be proven.

Recounting the incident, Mother Job held back none of the sordid details. Every bit of information, no matter how small or insignificant, was essential.

The Capuchin sat still, absorbing the disgusting account. When she finished, he moved slightly, breaking the tension. "Anything else, Mother?"

"Just the seizure Roberta suffered before you arrived." The evidence suddenly sounded thin—ridiculous. The nun wondered if she had panicked over nothing. It didn't even sound convincing to her as she outlined her suspicions to the priest. Still she found him earnest and his attention had not wavered

182

for a second while she had been speaking. Nor had there been the slightest sign of emotion.

"There was absolutely nothing else, Mother? No other voices, or incidents that seemed out of the ordinary?"

There must have been something else. Something she had not thought anything of at the time. But what? What would it take to convince this exorcist? How could she tell him something if there wasn't anything? Replaying over and over each episode in her memory, Mother Job mentally followed the activity of the convent after each occurrence. Then, thinking the aftermath, when she as well as most of the women were more prone to be alert because of the unusual aspects of each circumstance, might not be as important as the time prior to the events, Mother Job began examining the antecedent of each. What had she done the morning the voice was heard? A look of surprise mixed with discovery crossed her face.

"At the time I didn't give much thought to it. In light of the remarkable events following, I'm not surprised I forgot."

"Forgot? Forgot what, Mother?"

"Sometime before—no, it was the same day the voice was heard in the hall, I had occasion to visit with Roberta. Several days before, on the Feast of All Saints, she had left Mass right after receiving communion. She told me she had vomited the Host up and it had turned black. My Lord. I never gave it a thought before just now. The voice in the hall completely overshadowed it. Does it have any significance, Father?" Her voice, heavy with the excitement of discovery, quavered as she leaned forward expectantly, staring at the Capuchin.

Becker returned her gaze steadily. "I can't say, Mother." His words came softly, belying the huge chest where they originated. "You aren't hoping this *is* the work of the devil, are you, Mother?"

Her gasp sounded like the dying whimper of an animal. Jumping to her feet, her lips trembled as she spoke in a hoarse whisper. "Father Becker! How dare you? That is the cruelest thing anyone could suggest under the circumstances. I demand an apology. Here and now." Her face, now flushed a bright vermillion, twitched as she waited for him to speak. How could he justify such a question?

Calmly motioning for her to be seated again, the large priest spoke in a kind, gentle voice. "Mother Job, I must make certain you are in the right frame of mind at this point. What we may face could prove to be a severe test of our own personal faiths. It is completely wrong for a person to think he is so strong in his religious convictions and faith that the taunts and tricks of the devil are welcomed as a test. It's not uncommon for a person who is close to the one suspected of infestation to wish for an encounter with the devil to chastise the unholy spirit for harming the loved one. If you feel I should apologize then, I do so. But please remember, if this is a genuine case, you and your sisters and I will be in for a torturous experience—to say nothing of the one possessed."

Dropping her eyes to the desk top, Mother Job's breath slowed to more relaxed intervals. "Of course, I don't want to meet with Satan or his demons. This whole thing is horrible and I wish for nothing but the normalcy of the convent again. Forgive me if I misunderstood you."

With a wave of his hand, the incident was dismissed from both minds. "This thing about the Host turning black on All Saints Day concerns me. This was the same day as the voice in the hall?"

"No, Father. She told me about it two days later."

"Perhaps— Did anything happen December eighth?"

"The Feast of the Immaculate Conception?" Her thoughts quickly dissected the day and its events. Nothing. "Nothing happened then. Why, Father?"

"I thought perhaps, we might find a pattern concerning the holy days of the Church. But, if nothing happened—" His voice trailed off. How many dead ends would they encounter before they had sufficient evidence one way or the other? "I want you to observe with me, Mother. Anything out of the ordinary, especially where this postulant is concerned, I want reported to me immediately. However, I cannot overly stress the importance of secrecy at this time. Tell no one else. It could be, if Satan is afoot, that one of the others is possessed and he is allowing us to think it is—uh—"

"Roberta?"

"Yes—Roberta." Becker stood and faced the Mother General. With a dour look etched into his bearded countenance, he wheeled and strode to the door. Pausing at the entrance, he turned to face her once more. "I know you have been praying, Mother, but the situation at hand demands even more intense prayer. It is that serious." Without waiting for a response, he opened the door and left.

"Are you going to miss your folks on Christmas, Bobbe?" Connie asked as they walked toward the chapel. Although it was Sunday, the new chaplain had set time aside for confessions in the afternoon instead of the next day, which was Christmas Eve.

"Naturally. Christmas was always a big time at our house. From the way my mother wrote, it will be pretty quiet around there."

"Feel guilty?"

"No. Why should I?"

"I do in a little way."

"That's silly. You're here close to God aren't you?"

Connie nodded with a smile and opened the door to the Chapel of Saint John the Baptist. Kneeling in separate pews the girls began reviewing their lives since their last confession to Father Grant.

Bobbe wondered what the Capuchin would be like as a confessor. Father Grant had been as mechanical and repetitious in the confessional as he had been in delivering homilies. She'd soon find out. There were only a few others in the chapel and most of them had apparently received the sacrament since one by one they soon left.

Reflecting on her routine life in the convent Bobbe noted the lack of opportunity to sin. How precious to live in such a benign, safe place away from the trials of the outside world. Her only offenses here with the nuns were sins of omission and erratic, sometimes sinful thoughts. With an effort, she recalled the feelings of jealousy and envy that had overwhelmed her when she read her mother's letter wherein she learned of Jay's impending marriage. Hatred for Crystal had inundated Bobbe when she thought of her being held by Jay. Visions of their wedding night had etched themselves deeply in her mind with enjoyable variations occurring when she replaced Crystal in Jay's arms. Desirous thoughts. Lustful thoughts. What would Father Becker think of her? How would he know who she was? Her mind slowly settling on the words to use, she stood and approached the confessional.

The muffled voices coming from behind the closed doors, alerted Bobbe as to who was preceding her. Stopping while she was still fifteen feet away, she knew she would be unable to understand the words being spoken by Sister Mathias, the oldest member of the order. Hard of hearing, the elderly nun seemed to be the only one in the convent who didn't mind if everyone else heard her confession of sins along with the priest and God. Then the door opened and the tiny, bent figure shuffled out.

Entering the small cubicle, Bobbe knelt before the curtained window. She began speaking in a whisper. "Bless me, Father, for I have sinned. My last confession was three or four weeks ago." The last time should have been calculated precisely before entering, she decided. What would he think of a nun-to-be who couldn't be more exact than that?

"From what the other nuns tell me, it was three weeks ago." His voice, soft and even, seemed to exude a certain good-natured humor.

Relaxing some, Bobbe began recounting her sins as she had prepared them. After everything had been said to the point of her thoughts of Jay, she began after a short pause. "When I heard—" Why should she tell him? It was none of his business what she thought. For no reason she felt a flaming hostility to the priest leaping to life within her. A sensation of nausea swept through her. "—you were coming, Father, I was anxious to meet you."

"That's fine," Becker said from behind the protection of the curtain recognizing the confession's ambiguity as that of a young postulant or novice. "All of you novices and postulants are to be envied for your role in life. Each has been selected by God to do that work which is necessary to bring as many souls to Him as possible. You will teach people about Him and the salvation each can have with Him. Remember this when we celebrate Midnight Mass tomorrow night. It is His birthday we celebrate and He was born unto woman so He could die for each one of us. For your penance, say four Our Fathers and four Hail Marys for a special intention of mine, if you would." The prayer of absolution followed. Said rapidly in Latin, the words all seemed to run together until he intoned the blessing. Slowly and distinctly Balthasar Becker spoke the words of absolution. *"Ego te absolvo, in nomine Patris, et Filius et Spiritus Sanctus.* Amen. Go in peace and pray for me."

As the words of the blessing were spoken Bobbe's face contorted in rage and discomfort racked her body causing her to slip from the kneeler.

"Are you all right?" Becker's voice was soft and concerned.

"Yes, Father. I—I slipped."

Standing, she left the cubicle. After saying the prayers of penance directed by the Capuchin, she left the chapel, filled with the feeling of peace going to confession always brought her.

The next evening the strains of Christmas carols wafted through the halls of the convent from the community room. Members of the order were gathered about the upright piano where Sister Pauline played the familiar melodies. When Father Becker entered, he stopped, reflecting on the tranquil scene's warmth.

"Good evening, Father," Mother Job said as she broke away from the gathering of nuns. "Merry Christmas." Her voice was cheery with relief.

"Good evening, Mother, and may yours be a blessed one."

Motioning for him to follow her to a far corner of the large room, she made certain no one was within hearing distance of them when she stopped. How could anything be wrong here? The spirit of Christmas was everywhere in the building. But the sight of the giant Capuchin was constantly a reminder of the reason for his presence whenever the Mother Superior saw him in the halls. And that reason would rear like the ugly head of a poisonous snake ready to strike. Since his arrival, she had had nothing to report and he too had not witnessed anything out of the ordinary.

After listening to the closing stanza of "It Came upon a Midnight Clear," Becker turned to the nun and spoke in a soft voice. "I dislike the absence of activity, Mother."

"Do you mean you have reason to believe something is wrong?" She stared at him intently waiting for his reply.

"I suspect anything and everything as well as nothing. There were certain happenings that occurred before my arrival, and since I have come, absolutely nothing has happened. This, I don't like."

"Why, Father? I should think the lack would be encouraging."

"We cannot deny the disruptions that took place here in the convent. If they were caused by a mentally disturbed mind, something should have happened again by now. But, as you know, nothing in nine days."

"Perhaps then, there's nothing to be concerned about."

"Maybe, Mother, maybe. But—" His voice trailed off and with a shrug of his shoulders the priest left the community room. It was almost midnight.

Shortly after the priest's departure, the nuns began leaving the gathering in the community room to make their way to the chapel. As each one entered the small church, bewilderment crossed the face of every woman. For some reason the statues of the Blessed Virgin and Saint John were covered.

Already dressed in the vestments for Mass, Father Becker stood at the communion rail. When Mother Job entered, she hurried to him when she saw the covered statues.

"Is something wrong, Father?" Her whispered words were fraught with emotion.

"Make certain the covers are kept on the statues, Mother. I'll explain to you alone after Mass is finished." He turned to approach the altar to offer the sacrifice of the Mass without the aid of the altar boy who had been dismissed shortly after Thanksgiving.

Mother Job left the railing separating the sanctuary from the pews and took her seat.

The Mass was offered quickly and Father Becker delivered a brief sermon. When the time for communion arrived, the women left their pews to approach the railing to receive the Body of Christ under the appearance of simple unleavened bread. One by one their heads were tipped back to receive the wafer.

As the huge priest approached Bobbe from her right she began to mutter in an eerie, hollow voice. "Lairlirn Morwarng, youhjian woo! Youhjian woo! Yuu woo meir-jyuu—juaanyir buh-sheng woo. Jauhu woo, Morwarng! Lairlirn, youhjian woo!"

CHAPTER FIFTEEN

Although the Capuchin had heard Bobbe utter the strange words, he continued administering the Host after it became apparent the postulant was not going to receive communion. The nun next to Bobbé turned after the priest had passed to the woman on her left and stared with a look of wonderment. When the troubled girl stood to return to her pew, the nun followed closely, her eyes riveted to the back of Bobbe's head.

The unused Hosts were replaced in the tabernacle and Father Becker rushed through the remainder of the services. After varied lengths of individual prayers the women began filing out of the chapel singly and in pairs. Mother Job walked hurriedly to the sacristy to find Father Becker and hear his explanation for the covered statues.

Under the impression she had received communion, Bobbe was among the last to leave the quiet chapel. When she reached the hall outside, a group of nuns, headed by the older woman who had been kneeling next to her at the communion rail, approached her.

"What were you praying, Roberta?" Sister Theophilia asked intently.

"What?" Bobbe stared at her, dumbfounded by the strange question.

"At the communion railing, you were praying. What were you saying?" the older nun persisted.

Bobbe's eyes flitted from one woman to the next until she had searched each face for some sort of explanation before returning her puzzled stare to Sister Theophilia. "I have no idea what you're talking about, Sister."

"You said something when Father Becker approached you to give you communion," Connie offered, stepping forward to be near her friend who was obviously bewildered and upset.

Frightened, Bobbe looked at Connie as though her friend were about to lie—about to betray her. What was happening here? She had said nothing. Nothing at all. She had received communion like everyone else and simply returned to her seat. She had said nothing. *Nothing.*

"I heard you too, Roberta," Sister Theophania offered timidly, smiling sweetly.

"I—I—" Bobbe fumbled for words. Did she need a defense against these women—these women whom she was to think of as sisters? What was she to say? Were they all crazy? Maybe the hour was too late for them and they were sleepy and tired and hearing things.

"Glossalalia," the one nun offered from the back of the group.

"What?" Several of the women chorused the one-word question and stepped back, turning to see who had spoken.

Sister Cosmas stepped forward to the circle of black-clothed women. "I said, glossalalia. 'The language of the angels.'"

A murmur ran through the group as some of them looked wonderingly at each other. When Sister Cosmas saw no one understood the term, she held her hands up for silence. "Roberta was praying when she received communion."

"I said nothing, Sister," Bobbe insisted, feeling as though she had been accused of a crime. Disliking the manner in which Sister Cosmas had assumed the role of prosecutor, she stepped back toward the chapel doors but stopped when she saw the nun smile dulcetly.

"Roberta is blessed. You see, those who speak in the language of the angels seldom are aware of the fact."

Another murmur ran through the group.

"What are you talking about, Sister?" Bobbe stepped forward aggressively despite her puzzlement.

"My child, you have been truly blessed. To have you among us is surely a good sign. How long have you spoken? Certainly, someone has told you of this gift before now, haven't they?"

191

Sister Cosmas asked eagerly.

"Sister, I have absolutely no idea what you're talking about. I didn't say anything at the communion railing. Why won't you believe me? Why won't any of you believe me?" She fixed her eyes on Connie when voicing the last plaintive question.

"But you did, Roberta. I heard you. Most of us heard you. Sister Cosmas, tell her what it is." Sister Theophania indicated the others should be quiet so the troubled postulant could hear the explanation.

"People blessed with the ability to speak the language of the angels, like Roberta did at Mass, speak singularly to God. Sometimes they speak in groups. We ordinary people cannot understand what it is they say, but naturally, God does. The last parish school I was assigned to before my retirement was at Saint Stephen's in Illinois where there were three people so blessed and every Sunday before nine o'clock Mass they would gather at the communion rail to speak directly to God in the language of the angels. Just think how wonderful it is to have one of us so gifted and blessed. Surely this is a sign from God." Sister Cosmas clapped her hands together happily as the other women beamed and smiled.

"Wait a moment." Another voice came from the back of the group and Sister Marie Therese pushed her way to the front. "Don't be so sure of that."

"Why?" Sister Cosmas turned, thrusting her pointed chin toward the dissenter in a defiant gesture.

"I think she was speaking Chinese."

"What?" the group chorused in a shocked voice.

"That's impossible!" Bobbe blurted the terse objection shaking her head dazedly. Were they all crazy? First they had her speaking to God on a direct line and now one of them insisted she had been speaking Chinese. She'd never even met a Chinese person. What in Go—? What in Go—? Now she couldn't even utter His name. Was something the matter with her? She knew she hadn't said anything. Certainly she should know if she had. Why were they all claiming she had? Fighting the urge to cry, she was unable to hold back a sob that erupted unnoticed by the other women.

"When I was in China I heard enough Chinese dialects to recognize the language," Sister Marie Therese said sternly.

"You were there only a little over a year before everyone was driven out," Sister Cosmas countered angrily in an attempt to discredit the opposing viewpoint.

"I don't understand the language but I certainly recognize it," the younger nun protested lamely.

Milling in front of the chapel's carved doors, the women continued chattering about the phenomenon they had just witnessed and plied a bewildered Bobbe with more questions for which she had no answers. Held in a semicircle of black, she pressed against the wall next to the ornately carved doors. Through the bobbing and milling heads, she saw Mother Job coming out of the chapel and began fighting her way toward her. "Mother Job! Mother Job! Help me!"

At the sound of their Mother Superior's name, the women fell silent and stepped back. Taking full advantage of the opening the nuns created, Bobbe rushed forward to the approaching woman.

"Roberta. Come here, Roberta." Her voice was sharp and agitated when she saw the anxious postulant hurrying toward her from the gathering of nuns.

The women fell silent, staring at their superior whose face was as white as her collar.

Genuflecting at the corner of the altar, Mother Job turned to enter the sacristy while the others left the chapel. Becker was putting away the vestments he had worn at Mass when she found him.

"Father, what happened?" Her voice betrayed the anxiety she was desperately trying to control.

"Abominations of the devil? The work of a sick mind? An intruder from the outside? I'll show you and see what you decide." Leading her to the sanctuary, he began his explanation. "I had to change the linens on the altar before any of you got here for Mass. They had been dirtied with a peculiar white and yellow substance that looked like chewed up macaroni and it smelled terrible, simply awful. Quite a lot like mold and sulphur combined with a strong acidic odor." Gesturing toward the statue of the Blessed Virgin, he passed in front of the main altar, and approached it. "But the worst was this."

With a tug he pulled the hastily placed cover from it,

exposing Mary's sorrowful face. As the cloth fell, her arms, no longer empty, were bared. Now the severed plaster head of Saint John the Baptist rested in the statue's suppliant hands, the beatific smile, a grotesque smirk.

"Oh, my good God!" Mother Job gasped as she fought the urge to scream. Sucking in a deep breath, she regained control and turned to the giant priest. "Who could have done such a terrible thing? Roberta?"

"Remain calm, Mother. I want you to confine, if it's possible, this postulant to her quarters. I suspect, very strongly, the works of a demon. However, I must make absolutely certain before I consult with the bishop. Contact Father Grant and have him stand by in case the services of a chaplain are needed. I must talk with the parents of this girl. How far is her home from here, Mother?"

"About two hundred fifty miles, Father."

"What about transportation?"

"I believe a train leaves around six in the morning and comes back sometime in the evening. This is the train some of the nuns use when they go to that area." What would happen if this man left the confines of the building? Would they be safe from this—this—? She was unable to think the word much less speak it aloud. How long would he be gone? Could they survive if the "thing" were openly to make its presence known? And what had Roberta said at the communion railing? They hadn't even talked about that.

"Leave the statues covered, Mother, until I return," Becker said throwing the makeshift cover over the gruesome sight. "The devil. And on Christmas, too. Ah, me." He turned and went back to the sacristy to finish putting the implements of the Mass away without giving her an opportunity to ask what Roberta had said.

Genuflecting at the corner of the main altar, Mother Job hurried to carry out the Capuchin's request concerning Bobbe. She would have to remember the communion incident when they talked next. As she left the chapel, she found the milling nuns, novices, and postulants chattering and asking questions of someone who was hidden from view. Then, catching sight of the object of attention, she cried out.

"Roberta. Come here, Roberta."

Pushing her way through the crowd which fell back to make Bobbe's passage easier, she cried out for help. Rushing to the woman's side, the frightened girl hoped she would find succor there. Instead, she saw the icy cold, frightened look in Mother Job's eyes and stopped several feet away from her. Even Mother Job was acting in a peculiar fashion now. Where would this insanity end? She wanted to turn and run. Run away, screaming how everyone had lost their minds.

"Roberta. Please go to your room right now and go to bed. Under no circumstances are you to leave your room. Do you understand?"

Bobbe nodded in an uncomprehending gesture. Maybe she could barricade the door and be safe from these crazy people. Why should she be confined to her room? What had she done that was so awful? What if she did speak at the communion railing? Certainly, being confined to her room for that was a little stiff for a penalty. What if she had been speaking to God directly? She shouldn't be punished for having a direct contact with Him. Protest. Rebel. Yes. That's what we should do. Protest the unfairness of all this. Rebel against the injustice. She opened her mouth to speak but froze when she heard the voice within her.

"Not now. We have other plans for you. Obey."

"Yes, Mother." Her voice carried the injury and hurt of the situation but was filled with remorse and contriteness at the same time.

"I will talk with you in the morning. Do you understand?"

"Mother?"

"Yes?"

Her voice was barely audible as she struggled to make a final protest. "I didn't say anything at the communion rail. I really didn't. The rest of them say I did. And that I was speaking in the language of the angels or something. Sister Therese claims I spoke Chinese. Did you hear me say anything, Mother?"

Mother Job's face whitened even more when Bobbe mentioned Sister Marie Therese's explanation. Chinese? A foreign language? One she was positive someone like Roberta would not have any knowledge of? How could she do this unless she were truly—?

195

"I will talk to you about this later. Right now, I want you to go to your room and go to bed as I directed. I'll discuss this with you in the morning. Do you understand?" She stared at the frightened girl and caught herself shuddering involuntarily. *My good Lord God. Am I looking at the devil?*

"Yes, Mother." Bobbe spoke meekly and turned to obey. Shoulders slumped, she made her way to the stairwell and slowly walked up the two flights to her room.

After undressing and donning her simple nightgown, Bobbe turned out the light and lay down on the thin mattress. The late hour brought sleep to her immediately and she remained lying on her back while the convent quickly quieted down for the night as the nuns retired.

Fitful jerks of her head and body plagued Bobbe, and after several minutes, she opened her eyes and got out of bed. With her robe thrown carelessly about her shoulders, she opened the door and padded barefoot down the hall toward the back staircase. Noiselessly, she made her way undetected by anyone to the back of the building and past the kitchen. Opening the back door, she slipped into the cold early morning air and ran directly to the back of the garden.

"Dra-woh?" The name was whispered every few feet. "Are you here? I want you so badly."

The tall figure of the demon materialized before her.

"Dra-woh. Oh, Dra-woh." Throwing her arms around his neck, she whimpered in the hushed silence of the garden.

"Ah, sweet Bobbe-fuck. You have come to see me. Do not be troubled by what those sows have said. They will soon forget what has happened tonight and you will be able to continue. The master has plans for you. You are going to be important in time to come."

The demon slipped the robe from her shoulders and stripped off the simple nightdress. The mark on her hip glowed brightly, burning itself deeper into her flesh as they embraced. Throwing her to the ground, he covered her nude figure with his own body. An abandoned scream of pleasure escaped her lips when she savagely bit him on the shoulder. The locked couple thrashed about, grunting lustily as their passion was fed and prolonged and ultimately satiated. After the demon had deposited his filthy seed in her, Bobbe lay

196

weak and spent.

Rising to his feet, he glared at her. *"Now, go savor the pleasures of the red-headed sow's virgin body, Sweet-cunt."* His voice a rasping growl, he ordered the helpless girl to do his bidding.

The nude figure glided toward the back of the dark convent building, reentering as silently as she had left it minutes before. Without a sound, she made her way up the back stairs again, hurrying toward Connie's room.

Opening the door, Bobbe could hear the postulant's slow, even breathing. The intruder approached the bed sound-lessly to kneel alongside it. Snakelike, one arm slid under the covers groping for Connie's legs. When her fingertips found a warm, smooth thigh, they traversed upward, toward her body. Gently caressing the small hairy triangle, Bobbe's fingers fondled the inert clitoris and Connie writhed and moaned before she sat up in bed.

"Who's there?" The words knifed through the dark silence.

At the sound of the startled voice, the girl fell back to the floor as Connie jumped from the bed only to stumble over Bobbe's prostrate figure. Sprawling face down next to the nude body, the frightened postulant scrambled to her feet, and, searching along the wall for the light switch, flooded the small room with the familiar yellow glare.

"Bobbe?" Her voice gasped when she recognized the naked girl lying on the floor of her cell. Kneeling next to the motionless form, Connie gently took her friend's wrist in an attempt to check her pulse. Unable to find one, Connie leaped to her feet and ran from the room. "Mother Job! Mother Job!" Her screaming words echoed hollowly through the dark, deserted halls. "Somebody! Come quickly! Bobbe's dead!"

Doctor Geller bent over the motionless form of Bobbe Moore, which was now covered by a sheet, listening intently through his stethoscope for some sign of life. Only a deathly stillness met his ears. Nothing. No indication of life whatso-ever. With a deep sigh, he stood up and studied the postulant lying on the bed before him. She had been a beautiful girl. So young and, although he had only seen her once when she had been ill or so the nuns had thought at the time, he assumed she had also been a vibrant girl. Now—now she was dead. A cadaver. He pulled the instrument from his ears and threw it into his bag. Closing the case, he turned to face the Mother General.

"I'm sorry, Mother Job. There was nothing I could do. She was dead before I got here. I—" There had been similar situations in the past but there had always been reasons for death to claim someone. Here he could find no reason. What should he say? What could he say? The older nun he faced, in fact all of the women here were family to the dead girl in a certain respect. But, since this was her first year, she was still somewhat of a stranger. What could he say when one so young died for no apparent reason—especially on Christmas morning? Shaking his head, he left the room without saying anything more. He nodded to Father Becker, who had interrupted the last rites when the doctor had arrived, indicating the priest should continue. His work was finished. Let the Capuchin finish his and send the girl's spotless soul to its Maker. The women gathered in the hall rendered prayers for her. Others prayed in the chapel. Perhaps she was better off than any one else in the building or world.

Becker entered the little room as the doctor was shown to the door by Sister Raphael. Nodding to Mother Job who clutched a handkerchief, he crossed the room in two strides and approached the body. He laid the small purple stole on Bobbe's remains to help cleanse it of any unmentioned sins and reached for the vials of oils and ointments. It was finished here. Done. But the devil had not won. She was going to be with her heavenly Father and was safe from the works of the devil for all time. A tear formed in one eye and plunged into his beard as he mumbled the Latin prayers quietly.

Then, Bobbie opened her eyes and snickered.

Stunned, Becker stopped praying. The snicker grew into an hysterical laugh sending chills flowing down the spines of the attending priest and the nuns who stood in the hall. Frozen in fear, the chaplain and Reverend Mother watched with staring eyes the convulsing postulant who was doubled up in merriment.

His features, now taut and alert, reflected the exorcist's

understanding of what they were witnessing. Becker blessed himself and stepped back, ready to sprinkle the girl with holy water from the small bottle he held in his huge hand.

Before he could act, Bobbe sprang from the bed with the agility of a jungle beast and raced from the room, exploding through the cluster of women who had jammed their way into the doorway when they heard the laughter. What had been tears of sorrow now became a saline flood of horror.

CHAPTER SIXTEEN

The high-pitched laughter ricocheted through the halls mingling with the women's shocked cries of surprise and terror as Bobbe raced down the hall. The huge priest quickly approached the weeping nuns with Mother Job directly behind him.

"Sisters, please, go to the chapel and pray as you have never prayed before in your lives. Pray the Litany of the Saints. Hurry!"

Turning, the women responded like sobbing robots to carry out the chaplain's bidding.

Directing his attention to the Mother Superior, the Capuchin spoke in a steady even voice. "We must find her, Mother. Has Doctor Geller left?"

"I believe so, Father. Shall I check?" She half ran, half walked to keep up with his longlegged stride when the priest began hurrying in the direction the postulant had taken.

"No. I'm sure when he pronounced her dead, she was dead as far as his findings were concerned."

"Where do you suppose Roberta went?" Her voice shook, betraying the lingering memory of the girl's hideous laughter piercing the quiet night when she leaped from the bed.

With a shrug of his broad shoulders, he quickened his step. "I have no idea. We'll have to search the building until we find her. Right now she constitutes a threat not only to herself but to the others as well. All of us, Mother."

"Are you completely convinced a demon possesses her soul?"

Again, he shrugged his shoulders and stopped at the first

closed doorway they found. Easing it ajar, he swung the door back on its hinges and turned on the light. The storeroom was empty. They continued down the hall, opening each entry, searching each room. Every cell along with each closet and storage area was examined closely. Finding nothing on the third floor, the priest and nun extended their search to the second floor where classrooms and cells were looked into and searched without finding a trace of the missing postulant. Satisfied they had exhausted all possible hiding places, the searchers went down the last flight of stairs to the first floor and quickly began opening doors to more classrooms, offices, and visiting rooms, flooding each with light and entering only when a possible hiding place presented itself. The chapel was looked into briefly when the buzz of voices, beseeching God the Almighty and the Saints in heaven for help, filled the air. But no Bobbe.

The bell tower door opened grudgingly, revealing undisturbed dust on the floor and steps leading to the belfry. Becker pulled the door shut, directing his steps down the hall toward the back of the convent.

The kitchen and dining hall were searched without finding a trace of the postulant. The door to the basement was found locked and a quick perusal of the large, open cellar turned up the same results as the other floors.

"Did we miss anything, Mother?" His breath came in short gasps when he stopped moving for the first time since their quest had been initiated.

"We didn't check the opposite end of the wing on the third floor—"

Becker held a hamlike hand up for silence and whispered hoarsely when he spoke. "Listen, Mother. What's that?"

The quiet padding of bare feet running filtered down to them through the open stairwell.

"Quickly!" He signaled for her to follow him and he was off, running up the stairs two at a time, his fatigue forgotten. Reaching the top step, he waited until Mother Job caught up and they repeated their search of the second floor. Thoroughly. To no avail.

"Come, Mother. We'll check the wing that was overlooked on the next floor."

Exhausted, they slowly made their way up the steps. Checking that portion of the third floor, which had escaped their scrutiny before, yielded nothing. Inspecting each room and cranny, they worked their way back toward Bobbe's cell.

"Wasn't her door left open?" The priest moved toward the innocent appearing but ominously closed doorway.

Nodding her head, Mother Job tugged on the sleeve of his cassock. "Be careful, Father." Her voice, husky with terror, rasped dryly as they edged closer.

Slowly turning the knob and lifting on it to prevent an ill-timed squeak sounding from a dry hinge and announcing their presence, Becker quietly opened the door. Flooding the tiny cell with yellowish light, they found the postulant sleeping peacefully in bed, dressed in her woolen nightgown.

Unable to contain her tears any longer, Mother Job began sobbing. "Father—what are—we to—do?"

Placing a comforting arm about her shoulders and leading her from the room, he remained silent until they reached the first floor. "Go to your office, Mother. I'll send the others back to bed and then you and I will talk." His words were kind but firm when he realized the nun was regaining her composure and would welcome the chance to air her feelings with him.

Without a word of question or dissent, she turned and made her way, shoulders slumped forward like a woman many years her senior, to her office.

Father Becker strode determinedly in the opposite direction toward the chapel. Walking to the front of the small church, he genuflected and turned, waiting until the women's eyes were on him before he spoke. "Sisters, you may retire now. Roberta is sleeping quietly in her bed. She seems to be fine. We must thank God for sparing her tonight. Everything is under control now. Good night."

He refaced the altar and knelt for a moment, breathed a silent prayer for strength in the impending meeting with the demons of hell. Sensing the absence of the nuns after the last one had left, he began praying softly. "Stay with me, God and send your strongest enemy of Satan, Saint Michael, the archangel, to do battle with him."

When he mentioned the angel's name, the heavy door to the chapel slammed shut, dispatching a reverberating echo through the now deserted halls like an explosion.

Unruffled by the noise, he rose and turned to face an empty chapel. An almost delighted smile played on his lips as he strode confidently down the aisle and into the deserted halls. Making his way toward Mother Job's office, he prayed again to Saint Michael. The archangel was still a powerful ally to have in a situation like this. Considering the reaction in the chapel when he mentioned the angel's name, he was more certain now his mission here was a genuine one. The girl, Roberta, had been dead and pronounced so by the doctor. Now she was very much alive. Geller had been unable to find a single life sign and Becker had had enough experience himself administering to the dying to recognize death.

Hadn't he witnessed almost too much for one man? Hadn't he paid enough of a price to win his own salvation? How many others had to do battle over and over again with Lucifer and his minions? Still, here he was, ready once more to enter into deadly combat with the devil.

Why had he become a priest? Would he, knowing what it had held in store for him, still consider the priesthood if he had the opportunity to relive his life? Why? Why *had* he become a priest of God?

He could still hear his mother's voice saying: *"You must be a good boy all your life, my son."* She had said it so many times but he remembered it most graphically and always associated the statement with the death of his father. His mother had become overly protective of him. Because of her exaggerated love and concern for him, he had had no friends through his grade school years. And, in her attempt to protect him from the world and insure his safety, she had arranged to have him attend a boy's school run by Capuchin priests and brothers. It had been there he discovered his vocation. Or had it been discovered for him?

"You must be a good boy all your life—" The words rang in his ears now. He *had* been good. He *had* fought the arch-enemy of God time after time and he was wearing out. He knew he was wearing out. Each encounter exacted its toll—a little more of his life's essentiality drained away by the effort and strain. One day, he hoped he would not have to battle

with Satan anymore.

"You must be a good boy—" He struck his breast humbly and whispered, while an audible sob retched in his throat. "I have been good, Mama. I have been good. Leave me alone! Please? You did your work well. I have been good."

"You must be—"

Raising his voice, the giant Capuchin prayed more loudly. "Saint Michael, be with me in this hour of need. Do not let the evil present here affect me. Do not let it eat at my soul—my conviction—my faith. It is he who creates these doubts in my poor humble mind. Cast him into hell with his other evil spirits and protect me at all times."

The skin on his neck crawled when he heard a low moaning sound, which seemed to rise from the bowels of the earth below the convent building, call his name. *"Be-e-e-h-h-ck-e-e-r."*

Quickening his pace, he found himself outside the Mother General's office. Before opening the door, he blessed himself with the sign of the cross and then entered to find her sitting behind the desk. Only reddened eyes betrayed the emotional outburst she had fallen subject to minutes before and she appeared ready for the priest and anything he might say.

"Did you heard anything just now—before I entered, Mother?"

"Just the wind, blowing around the building. It seems to be picking up. Why?"

"Huh? Oh, I heard the wind too and thought it sounded cold. However, I don't think we want to discuss the weather. What's your opinion of this—this apparent miracle, Mother?"

Did he have to ask? She knew he was serious and wanted more than just a casual answer. "If I live to be a hundred, I shall never forget the feeling I experienced when Roberta started laughing." She shuddered when the frightening scene was triggered in her mind by the question.

"Do you think it was the work of a demon, Mother?"

"If none of the other things had taken place I would say we had witnessed a miracle of God. But in light of what has taken place, I would—" Her voice trailed off. She could not bring herself to say it was the work of the Devil even though she had been the first to suspect. Looking at the Capuchin, she found a look of understanding and compassion.

"—say it was the work of Satan?" he offered, finishing the sentence for her.

"Yes." Her voice sounded tiny as she noticeably shuddered.

"Something happened the first day I arrived, Mother. I elected not to tell you only because I was concerned it might possibly upset you more than you were at the time." He quickly explained about the crucifix he had found in the closet of his apartment and watched her face sadden as he unfolded the details.

When he was finished, she leaned her elbows on the desk but fought the temptation to rest her chin in cupped hands. "I should have told you this earlier, right after Midnight Mass, but I thought considering the hour and all it could wait until morning."

Instantly alert by the apologetic preamble, Becker sat forward waiting for her to explain. "Yes, Mother. What is it?"

"Sister Marie Therese claims Roberta spoke Chinese at the communion railing. You do remember her saying something?"

"Yes. Yes, of course." His forehead knitted together as he pondered the statement. "How certain is she? How well does she know the language? Does she know what the postulant said?"

"She seemed quite positive when I talked with her after I sent Roberta to her cell. But she doesn't understand Chinese that well. She was there less than two years before being driven from the province she lived in. She learned the language here at the convent but I fear most of what she knew has been forgotten. It's a difficult? language and unless used every day a person—"

"Yes, of course, Mother. I understand." Narrowing his eyes, he wondered if the third sign would manifest. There had been physical phenomena beyond the natural flow of life prior to his arrival and certainly the doctor involved tonight would be positive he had been right until confronted with a living postulant named Roberta Moore—the same girl he had pronounced dead. If what the girl spoke at the communion railing was indeed a Chinese dialect, how would she have learned something so unique, so difficult? Would she begin telling things from some of the members' past lives? Would they be embarrassed? Would she talk of the future?

Instantly, another thought struck him. What would the bishop say? Would he insist on the sciences being consulted before giving permission? Or would he agree to take the word of Balthasar Becker, the exorcist?

Looking up, he gazed deeply into the Mother General's tired, red eyes and found the strength he expected. It was strength he would rely on should he feel himself reaching the breaking point once the rite was underway.

When she realized he was staring at her, she coughed embarrassedly and glanced at the clock on the wall. "What do we do now, Father?"

Without answering, he looked at the watch on his wrist. "It's four-thirty now. I'll have to wait until eight or nine o'clock before I call the bishop and request permission to begin."

Too long. It was too long to have to wait before they began driving this unholy thing from their presence. She shook her head in a reprimanding gesture. Now was the time for strength and calmness. She had survived this ordeal thus far by being patient. Now was not the time to lose her nerve. But the devil must go from their convent. He did not belong. This was no place for him.

"Do we tell the others, Father?" Surprisingly, she found her voice under control and felt pleased by her ability to cope with the problems they faced.

"By all means. I assume they are all strong in their faith and will be equal to any tactic the demon may try. Besides, eventually they'll know, without our telling them, that something evil is among us. I wonder if any suspect now? We'll tell them, however, only after I've talked with the bishop and received permission to conduct the rite. Not before. Can you control the questions they might ask until then, Mother?"

The questions she felt might be asked crossed her mind. There would be many, and the only way she could avoid revealing the true circumstances they faced would be to parry each with a well-worded thrust of her own. Like a skilled swordsman, she would have to avert the point of the queries with counter-queries.

"Yes, Father, I can. What about her parents? I understand they should know. But what about your trip to see them today? You won't go now, will you?" Her eyes begged him to stay while she mentally pleaded, we need you here, you pillar of strength, you knowledgeable devil-fighter. Without you here, we'll surely lose this battle. All of us will be consumed.

"No. I won't be able to go. Every sign that's manifested here indicates true possession and not a physical or mental disorder. Even if we had the luxury of time and convenience to consult the sciences, the results would be the same. My place is here, to drive him out of the girl and send him back to the hell where he belongs."

When the doubts he had been subjected to in the hall momentarily forced their way back into his memory, he involuntarily sighed. "You know, Mother, when I took my holy orders, I never dreamt I would have to use the order of exorcism so much. It may be one of the minor aspects of the priesthood but it has played a major role in my life."

"Is there anything special you'll require as far as equipment is concerned, Father?"

"There's nothing out of the ordinary, Mother. Holy water, a crucifix on a pedestal, at least four of your strongest nuns, and prayers—prayers like your sisters have never prayed. A constant flow of prayers to God, begging Him to let this hour pass without consequence."

An inquiring expression crossed her face. "Four of my strongest nuns? Why?"

"To help restrain the poor girl. She'll be given strength that will defy explanation. The demon will enter her body and make her perform acts that'll nauseate those who witness the struggle. They'll have to be physically powerful as well as strong in their faith in Almighty God."

"You make it sound as though the demon can come and go as he pleases where Roberta is concerned."

"Precisely."

"I thought the demon would be present all the time."

"Normally, that is the case. However, there are instances on record where the infested person has functioned normally between 'attacks' and anyone would have been hard pressed to detect anything out of the ordinary. A good example is the

207

woman who was the subject of *Begone Satan*. The early indications that something was wrong were her inability to utter the name of God, Jesus, and certain prayers, and the incapability of ingesting a Blessed Host. Outside of that there appeared to be nothing wrong. A soul can be possessed by an unclean spirit for years before the demon makes a move to claim dominance of that person outwardly."

Shaking her head dumbly at the implication of the priest's words, Mother Job began silently listing the women she would press into service. Sister Michael would be a good selection if for no other reason than her name. Sisters Gregory, Boniface, Timothy, John, and James were all large, husky women who should be able to control Roberta. It was ludicrous to think the postulant, who could not have weighed more than one hundred ten pounds, could best the likes of the nuns she had chosen. Then she recalled Roberta's display of tremendous strength the night she had been ill and changed her mind, hoping the nuns she would use could restrain the girl.

Naturally, Mother Job would want Sister Raphael to be on hand to assist her and act as liaison to the rest of the convent. In the event information or requests were necessary and the Reverend Mother could not carry out the task because of more urgent demands, Sister Raphael would be more desirable than Sister Damien.

Father Becker spoke, breaking into her mental plans. "Mother, we had best get some rest before I contact the bishop. However, you should first inform those nuns you wish to have assist during the rite. The others can be told later."

Standing, he stretched his oversize frame. He had never welcomed the prospect of encountering demons, and since his first exorcism, dreaded the vile tricks they could perform. There was no reason to believe this rite, to be executed in a convent, would be any easier than the others.

"Good night, Mother." His voice was quiet as he turned and left the room. A few hours' sleep would be all he could afford at this point. When he reached his apartment, he lay down on the bed without bothering to undress and was asleep in seconds.

Shortly after the Capuchin had left her office, Mother Job

turned out the lights and hurried up the stairs toward her cell. Father Becker's explanation of other convents being infested with demons hammered at her consciousness. Why did the awful thing that was happening here have to be? Why their convent? It had happened in other convents but why did it have to be their convent? Why?

The persistent questions continued unabated until she stopped in the hallway leading to her third-floor room. What if she hadn't become a nun? She wouldn't be here now. She wouldn't have to face the upcoming struggle she knew would only be more awful than the giant priest had said. It simply had to be the most horrendous experience a mere mortal could possibly face on earth.

Why *had* she become a nun? What if—? What if Tom hadn't been killed in the war? They would have been married when he arrived home from Europe. She wouldn't be here. When the news of his death, the day before the Armistice was declared, came from his parents, her life seemed as empty and dead as her fiance. For a while, she had even hated her parents who seemed thankful Tom had died. How many times had her parents told her she was too young for marriage? Each time they had presented their argument, she would counter with the fact seventeen was not too young. And then, at seventeen, her life was over. Or so she had thought.

College and its empty pretenses of happiness and fulfillment was tolerated and she graduated to become a teacher. Her profession opened an entirely new outlook for her and added an exciting, gratifying dimension to her life. The students in her classes became her reason to exist, and she found helping them filled, in another way, the void Tom's death had created. Then, when she had decided to enter the convent, her own life regained its meaning and attained fulfillment once more.

While preparing for bed, she wished fervently none of it had happened. So what if she were the youngest Mother General in the history of their order? She could have been the mother of grown children at the same age. Maybe even a grandmother. A smile, which felt peculiar on her drawn face, crossed her lips at the thought of being a grandmother.

"Forgive me, dear God. I do not regret my vocation. I love You and rededicate my life to You," she cried aloud and crossed herself. Never, not once since becoming a postulant had she ever questioned or had concerns of any kind about her vocation. Could these seeds of doubt have been planted by the demon? She quickly said the prayer to Saint Michael the archangel and felt more at ease.

The reason for her uncertainty suddenly filled her mind. Roberta Moore. How was she right now? Was she sleeping well? Concern for the postulant prompted her to slip into her robe and hurry down the hall toward Bobbe's cell.

Slowly approaching the door, she could feel her hair crawl, and a film of perspiration slicking her forehead. Mother Job quietly turned the knob and peered in to see the girl sleeping peacefully in the shadowed room. She was so young. So beautiful. Why? Why did it have to happen here?

The Mother General closed the door without a sound and, praying to prevent a recurrence of her own mistrust, tiptoed down the hall.

The door to Bobbe's room had barely closed when the tall figure of Dra-woh materialized in the shadows next to the bed. Positioning himself at her feet, he continued his unholy vigil. *"You shall be* his *forever."* His voice rang hollowly through the tiny cell as he smiled. *"Forever."*

When dawn broke on Christmas morning, the convent lacked the joyousness of past years and the attitude of the women was as dull and gray as the overcast sky. Their morose solemnity filled the halls while the silence, voluntarily imposed by themselves, struggled to shriek. The cheery voices and carols of the night before had been prematurely packed away for another, happier time. Under the direction of Father Becker, the nuns would pray in shifts. Without telling them the reason, he managed to convey an ominous meaning to his words when he instructed them to begin their vigils.

After a schedule had been drawn up, Becker hurried to meet with the nuns Mother Job had selected to assist him in the exorcism. Making his way to her office, he smiled broadly and rubbed a hand over his bald head. He felt like a general going to brief his troops and officers before sending them into battle. And just what was he if he wasn't a general preparing for war?

The door to Mother Job's office was open and he strode in, easing it shut behind him. The women present jumped to their feet.

"Please be seated, Sisters." He found a place to stand next to the bookcase beneath the electric clock and faced the women. Officially, these would be the first to know the problem facing them involved a demon. The rest of the women had only been told Roberta needed prayers as no other person in the order had ever needed them. Concluding she was ill and had been granted one more chance at life through Divine intervention, they had obediently complied with the request. Becker knew he couldn't panic them with the information that one among them was infested with a demon and not be able to reassure them at the same time he had the bishop's permission to perform the holy rite of exorcism.

The women he faced now were a different matter. These he wanted appraised of the situation so they could prepare themselves as much as possible for the difficult task ahead. The apprehension and curiosity etched in varying degrees on their faces were evidence none of them suspected why they had been called to the Mother Superior's office or why their chaplain was present.

"Sisters, we have a problem that is difficult to explain. Not really difficult—perhaps horrifying would be a better word. I feel strongly, and I do base these fellings and conclusions on much experience, that one of the postulants, Roberta Moore, is possessed by a demon."

His strong voice reverberated for several seconds while he observed their reactions to the shocking news. The six women remained still and composed. None showed any indication of panic. Pleased thus far with Mother Job's choices, he glanced over to find her face pale and immobile.

"I asked Mother Job to select four nuns, and I see we have seven here, to assist me in exorcising this devil who has invaded your convent."

He paused again but found no sign of fear at the thought of actually being present during the rite. His bearded mouth turned upward in a reassuring smile. "Over the years, the Good Lord has seen fit to involve me in fifteen episodes of this type and with the help of the Almighty, I have managed to survive them."

Their undivided attention convinced him they would be a good army to command.

"At this point, I do not have the bishop's permission to perform the rite of exorcism yet, but I will call him within the hour and seek it. I'm sure he will grant it and then our work—yours and mine—will begin.

"I wanted to have this opportunity to tell you some of your duties and to allow time to prepare yourselves. I will need at least four of you in the room with me at all times. You will have to restrain physically the girl and pray with me those prayers that have been designated to drive this thing from her immortal soul. At best, it will be the most difficult task you will ever be required to perform in this lifetime. The only requirement I'll make of you is immediate compliance to any order I give and that you pray with all the devotion with which you are capable. I will hear your confessions now so you may be pure of soul when we start. I would suggest a general confession since the demons will have no way of knowing your past sins once they have been confessed."

"What do you mean, Father?" Sister James leaned forward waiting for the answer to her question.

"The devil, once speaking through one he possessed, said he knew only those sins not confessed or forgiven. But when the sacrament of penance was administered, he had no way of knowing what sins had been committed. I do caution you to keep in mind he *is* the prince of lies, and I don't know if it's a reliable statement."

"He told you this?" Sister Boniface's face reflected her awestruck whisper. The women fidgeted in their seats as they began a delayed reaction to the information the Capuchin was passing on to them.

"No. Not to me personally. It was made to another Capuchin who struggled more than three weeks cleansing the spirit of a possessed woman. It is strange, but in fifteen exorcisms I have never once encountered Lucifer himself. Always his underlings. Beelzebub, Ximinia, Bel, Zachar, and even Judas Iscariot appeared once along with the demon holding the soul of a possessed boy I was exorcising."

Impressed by the professional, almost offhand manner in which Becker had informed them, the nuns quickly pledged their support to the bearded priest.

"Now, Sisters, in light of the fact the balance of the community does not know of your problem yet, I would suggest we use Mother Job's office as our confessional. I'm sure the nuns and girls who are in the chapel would wonder about your going to confession again after having received the sacrament only two days ago."

His eyes twinkled and the nuns smiled bravely in return as they filed out of the office to await their turn.

While Father Becker made the telephone call to the bishop from his apartment, Mother Job remained in her office, trying to concentrate on the stack of papers before her. Staring at the unfinished work for an hour, she jumped when a sharp knock broke the silence. Thankful for the interruption, she found her mouth dry when she spoke.

"Come in."

The giant priest burst into the room, sitting down heavily. "The bishop feels we should wait awhile and observe just a bit more. There are certain areas he feels we haven't investigated." Sitting forward, he held his head in both hands while staring at the floor.

"I know she's possessed, Mother. He refuses to accept the evidence at this point. I only hope and pray to God we won't be too late."

CHAPTER SEVENTEEN

"What will you do now, Father?" Mother Job asked unable to control the anxiety in her voice when she saw the distraught look on the priest's face. His words, echoing in her head, crushed the hope of quickly ridding them of the demon who had invaded their convent. How long would they have to wait? Why was Bishop King being so stubborn and immovable?

Shrugging his shoulders, the man's face reflected dejection mixed with his resignation to the bishop's order. "I guess I'll have to go to Springfield after all and visit the girl's parents and the pastor of her parish. The Lord knows I don't want to leave here considering the events of the last few hours but Bishop King reminded me that in full consideration of the severe situation we face, the Moores should be informed and consulted if at all possible. Perhaps they can give us some insight to the girl's problem." With a great effort, he turned his beefy body in the chair to look at the clock. "How am I to get there now? The train is long gone."

The Mother General's mind raced wildly. Leave? Would he abandon them? They'd be defenseless against this—this—thing. She recalled how the Capuchin had asked her to have Father Grant stand by during his absence when the Capuchin had initially planned his Springfield visit. But now—now the exorcist was positive there was a demon to contend with and he was about to leave. Who would protect them? Prayer. They would have to rely on the Almighty until Father Becker returned.

Pursing her lips, she concentrated on the immediate problem of getting the priest to Springfield and back in the fastest manner possible. "I believe there may be a bus for Springfield around noon. Shall I check, Father?"

"Yes, Mother. Try. Try." He ran both his hands over his head and face in frustration, closing his eyes when the nun picked up the telephone book to thumb through the pages.

What should be said to these people, strangers whom he didn't know—the parents of a girl, a lovely girl, who had elected to dedicate her life to God and whom he knew to be possessed by an evil spirit?

What should be said? *"Don't be upset, dear people, but I suspect your daughter is possessed by the devil."*

Only crass, uncaring parents would stand a remote chance of surviving such a statement.

"Tell me, just what happened in her youth that would allow Satan and his evil forces to gain control of her soul and body? Was she a rotten little kid or is this something new for her?"

Standing, he crossed the room to the window and watched gently falling snow drifting to the ground. What could he say? Never—not once had he been called on to do something like this in his past experiences. In every other case he had been called in after the fact of possession had been well established. Would it be wise to reveal the true nature of the case immediately at the outset of their conversation and run the risk of dire consequences? Such news could only be devastating to the mind and spirit of her parents. He would have to refer initially to the problem as an illness.

The sound of the phone being laid in its cradle brought the large man about to face the nun.

"You're in luck, Father. The bus leaves Cedar Falls at eleven-thirty this morning and arrives in Springfield at six this evening. Since there aren't any buses leaving there until tomorrow, I'll check with the railroad station and see if there are any connections during the night." Without waiting for confirmation from the priest, she picked up the phone and dialed the number.

Turning back to the window, Becker continued focusing his attention on the quandary facing him. *"The nuns at the convent believe your daughter, Roberta, has suffered a complete breakdown and your anxiety is completely*

215

understandable. She's so young. However painful it might be, certain questions must be asked and answered, concerning her background. Did anything ever happen when she was a little girl to make her fantasize or pretend she was someone else?" There would be nothing out of the ordinary found with a question like that. All little girls pretend to be somebody else at one time or another. Mental illness is not the result of playing house or dressing up in grownup clothing, pretending adulthood has mysteriously been bestowed.

"There's a train that leaves at ten P.M. and arrives here at three-ten in the morning, Father." Mother Job waited without saying more, hoping he would rebel and refuse to go. Still, she knew he must obey. He had to go—and leave the convent and nuns fending for themselves.

Completely unhappy with the unexpected turn of events brought on by the bishop's directive, Becker knew he was not concealing his reactions too well. Reluctantly, he nodded his approval.

"I'll call Mr. Tyler and have him take you to the bus depot, Father."

"I'll get ready, Mother." Accepting the inevitable, he left the room.

Bobbe tentatively opened her eyes, blinking at the brightness of her room. How could it be so light at five in the morning? Stretching, she sat up in bed and smiled broadly. It was Christmas Day. Feelings of excitement awakened within her as she propped her knees up and hugged them.

Warm thoughts of Christmases past brought an aroused longing for her parents to mind, which began gnawing at Bobbe's heart. Were they missing her? Foolish question. Their letters told how her absence grew more difficult for them to bear.

Raising her head, Bobbe caught sight of her wristwatch and remembered the unusual brightness of the cell. Her eyes widened when she saw the time. One-thirty? Impossible. She held it to her ear, and detected the gentle tick. It *was* one-thirty. How could she possibly have slept through morning Mass and breakfast *and* dinner? Could her watch have stopped during the night and started again? If that had happened, what time was it now? If she was late for Mass there'd be a lecture by Sister Damien, which was the last thing she wanted on Christmas Day—an encounter of the wrong kind with the Mistress of Novices. Throwing the covers back, she went to the window. Large, fluffy snowflakes were drifting about, gently settling to the earth. Already several inches of thick, wet snow blanketed the countryside, gift wrapping each tree and bush in shimmering white. The overcast sky was too light in color to be early morning.

After dressing, Bobbe rushed into the hall but found it deserted. No activity. No sound. Dashing down the stairs to the first floor, she warily approached the chapel doors. After easing them open, she stepped inside and found twenty black shrouded women kneeling in the front pews, singing a Christmas carol. Where was everyone else?

Tiptoeing from the church, she went to the main hallway off which most of the offices were located and stared unbelievingly at the clock. One thirty-five. She *had* slept through everything. For some reason she was unable to understand, they had allowed her to do so. But why? Why would they do something like that? Had she won a drawing, which bestowed the privilege of sleeping late on Christmas morning? No. That was preposterous. But how absurd was it to think she had been allowed to sleep? Why? Had she been up and gone to church, eaten, and gone back to bed without remembering? That was a stupid thought. But then, there had been things she had gone through, like being ill enough to have a doctor called, that she couldn't remember. Even though Mother Job and the others insisted it had actually happened. Was something the matter with her?

Her stomach's growling brought an expression of relief to Bobbe's face. At least she was hungry. That much about her was normal. Turning, she walked toward the kitchen. Maybe she could find a snack to ease her hunger pangs until dinner this evening. Both the refectory and the kitchen were deserted. The noon dishes had been washed and put away. Usually someone would be here, puttering with early preparations for the evening meal. Something was wrong, but what? Swinging the refrigerator door open, she found several plates of leftovers from the noon meal. A platter of roasted chicken drew her attention anad after selecting a thigh, she closed the door.

When she passed a window, Bobbe caught sight again of the falling snow. Hurrying to the back door, she tentatively stepped outside to find the temperature almost warm, the air clean and fresh but not cold. She stepped all the way out, closing the door behind her. One quick turn around the garden to clear her head and she would find out what was going on.

The Christmas-card garden seemed to beckon the girl strolling about. Deeply breathing the fresh clean air, unmindful of the dampness her short hair was accumulating from the snow melting on her head, Bobbe slogged through the ever-deepening snow. What was it about the garden she found so fascinating? There wasn't anything special about it, ordinary trees planted at irregular intervals with low bushes lining the walks. Perhaps it was the spring flowers she loved the best. But that was impossible. She had never seen the garden in springtime. Still she knew exactly what the flowers would look like in the early part of the year. But hou could she possibly know that?

A slight noise behind the postulant drew her attention and she turned to find Dra-woh approaching her.

"Hello. Merry Christmas." Bobbe's voice was lilting, an innocent smile curving her full lips.

Throwing his head back, Dra-woh laughed mirthlessly. *"Now that is funny, sweet Bobbe-cunt."*

Recollections of previous meetings in the garden bobbed to the surface of her mind, her inculpable expression mutating into an evil smile. Then, she suddenly recoiled from him.

"You. I—I saw something last night that frightened me terribly. I was sinking into a black swamp and you were there looking at me but you didn't help me. I heard Father Becker saying some prayers and the other nuns—were—were crying—and—and—there were hands on me. Hands all over me."

Her eyes, wide with agitation and anger, stared past the figure standing before her when she shuddered violently at the memory.

"Hands felt me all over, poking and prodding. It felt like a—a doctor was examining me. What was wrong with me? Was it a dream? It seemed like a movie and I was watching it but I was the main character as well." She brought her eyes to focus on his and they stared deeply into each other's.

"You died," he chortled gleefully. *"When that dirty bastard, Becker, began praying over you, I played a good trick on him. I brought you back to life. I scared the living shit out of that prick."*

Smiling evilly, Bobbe put her arms around Dra-woh's neck and kissed him, her tongue darting into his foul-tasting mouth, no longer mindful of the chemical taste.

Pushing her away, he snarled savagely. *"Not now, slut-bitch. You'll have me near you for a long time while I train you for your mission. Right now, I think it is time for you to pray."* His voice modified to a purr as he instructed the postulant. Her look of bewilderment brought a chuckle to his throat that grew until he threw his head back, laughing insanely.

"Yes. Pray. Do you hear me? Pray. Go kneel in front of the statue of John at the front of the garden and pray your fucking head off. Go. Now."

Turning, Bobbe obediently walked to the front of the garden and knelt at the snow-covered shrine. Folding her hands, her lips began forming a silent pantomime of prayers.

Sister Damien was not happy when she entered the community room. Her knees hurt from too much praying. Quickly blessing herself with the sign of the cross, she mentally chastised herself. One could never pray too much. But, darn that Roberta Moore for getting sick and acting up again. Because of her, the entire community of women was assigned to two hour shifts of prayer in addition to the other services. She had already calculated her tours of devotion and knew she would be going during the wee morning hours. Around the clock, the chaplain had said. *That Father Becker.*

Selecting a magazine from the table, the Mistress of Novices dropped into the softest chair in the room, next to the window overlooking the garden. Page after page was turned without finding something to hold her attention. Closing the pamphlet, she thanked God for the beautiful snowfall making His Son's birthday a memorable one. Looking out the window toward the shrine of Saint John, she screamed shrillingly.

Bobbe's kneeling figure hovered in midair, her face scant inches from the statue's countenance.

Others, who were sitting in the community room, looked up startled by the cry. Rushing to Sister Damien, they followed her trembling finger to Bobbe floating ten feet off the snow-covered ground.

Connie Devler gasped and cried out. "Come on. Let's get her down before she falls." Running for the door, the postulant was followed by several of her classmates.

The sound of their running feet echoed through the halls and without slowing to a walk as they passed the chapel rushed to the back door in the kitchen. Bursting through the back entry into the garden, they slammed to a halt. Awestruck and speechless, they stared at Bobbe kneeling devoutly in the snow.

"Roberta? Are you all right?" Mary Ellen called.

"Bobbe?" Connie approached slowly, warily.

Turning, Bobbe saw the fear and surpise etched on the faces of her friends. Now what was wrong?

"Of course, I'm all right. Why?"

Fear and surprise gave way to bewilderment and puzzled stares. Connie stepped forward and took Bobbe by the arm, helping her to stand. "Don't you know what just happened? Don't you remember?"

"I—I was praying here. What's so unusual about that?" Her voice had a distinct edge of irritability. What was wrong with them?

"Let's you and me go for a walk, Bobbe." With a look of authority, Connie dismissed the rest of the postulants. Because of her closeness to Bobbe, she felt she would be best able to talk with her. When the other girls had entered the building, Connie steered her friend toward the back of the outdoor sanctuary.

"Don't you really remember what just happened?"

"Well, I remember I was walking in the garden, trying to

figure out how I had been allowed to sleep so late on Christmas. See, there are my footprints in the snow." She pointed to the single set of tracks, which led to the back of the garden and then another set returning toward the shrine. "Then, I think I remember a voice telling me to go to the statue and pray. That's all. Oh, then naturally I remember you and the others coming out yelling at me. What did happen, Connie?"

Would Bobbe believe her? Connie asked herself if the entire group of nuns and girls in the community room had possibly suffered a mass hallucination. Choosing her words carefully she began.

"You—were—floating in the air. In midair."

"I was what?" Bobbe's voice squeaked in disbelief. "Are *you* all right, Connie? What you're saying's impossible, you know. Besides, I'd remember something like that. Uh, they don't have a little Christmas wine in the community room, do they?" She giggled lightly but stopped when she saw Connie was not joining her in the dissuading laughter.

"I'm not kidding, Bobbe. We all saw you. And after what happened last night, I'm starting to wonder about you."

Bobbe stopped walking at the thinly veiled reference to the previous night. Something nagged at her memory—something she had just recalled—but, it remained nebulous and elusive just out of mind's reach. Clearing her throat, she stared at Connie, a look of desperation inching across her face. "What about last night? What happened?"

"Now, I suppose you're going to tell me you don't remember anything about that, either?" Connie impatiently snorted the question.

"Really, what happened? I don't remember anything from the time I went to bed after midnight Mass till waking up a little while ago."

Detecting the sincerity on Bobbe's face and sensing an honest ignorance of the previous night's disruption, Connie smiled comfortingly and began. "Last night, no, early this morning really, I woke up with the strange sensation of someone being in my room—fooling around—with—with my body. Now, I ask you, can you imagine a nice postulant like me having a nasty dream like that?"

221

Bobbe frowned, letting the attempt at humor pass. "Go ahead."

"Well, I got up and found you lying on the floor of my cell, naked as the day you were born. I thought—"

"Naked? You found me naked? In your room?"

Connie held up her hand. "Wait, there's more. I thought you were dead and ran out in the hall screaming you were."

"That I was what? Dead?" Bobbe's look of incredulity emphasized her words.

"You have no idea how frightened I was. I guess I panicked. At any rate, the doctor actually did pronounce you dead and—"

"He what?" Now it wasn't funny any longer. Feelings of indignation swiftly rose to the surface of Bobbe's mind. Having someone like Connie mistake a person for being dead was one thing. But a doctor? And what would she have been doing in her friend's room, late at night, lying on the floor completely nude?

Nothing in this place seemed to make sense anymore. Maybe she should talk with Mother Job, call her parents, and have them come to get her. She recalled her father's words about being there before she hung up the phone. That kind of love and concern she could understand. None of this attention she was drawing to herself made sense.

"This is the silliest thing I've ever heard, Connie. Are you sure you're not making the whole story up?"

"A lot of us were in the hall when the doctor came out and told Father Becker. Father Becker went back into your cell where we had carried you, to finish giving you the last rites. A few minutes later, after the doctor had left, all of us heard you giggling and laughing. Then, all of a sudden, you came charging out and tore down the hall. The rest of us were sent to the chapel to pray and, for what it's worth, we've been praying in shifts ever since. Later, Father Becker told us you were back in bed sleeping peacefully. I guess they elected to let you sleep this morning instead of waking you—in case you actually were sick—or whatever. Bobbe, what gives?" Patiently, Connie waited for her friend's explanation.

Bobbe's face, matching the snow, went slack as Connie finished. What *was* happening? "*I—I don't know what's happening.* I feel as though I'm being made into a fool. Ever since I got here, I've felt like I'm a puppet some of the time and a senseless dolt other times. Remember when I questioned my vocation? I think I'd just better reevaluate the whole situation again and call my parents. I think I should get out of here."

"Can't you tell me anything?"

Bobbe's forehead screwed up in frustrated thought while she attempted to recall the incidents in the garden before Connie came out. Isolated snatches flashed by unidentified, until she managed to concentrate on one that seemed more clear than the others. What had prompted her to go to the shrine and kneel in the snow? *The voice.* The voice had ordered her to pray. Should she tell Connie about the voice? Connie would think she was crazy. Maybe she was crazy—insane, considering everything they claimed she had done.

"I've heard strange voices at times, telling me to do things." The sound of the words coming from her mouth seemed unreal as she spoke about the thing lurking just under her conscious level. She began trembling as Connie stared at her.

"Voices? Telling you to do things? What kind of things?" Connie slipped an arm around her friend's shoulder, hugging her protectively.

"That's just it. I don't remember. I don't have any idea what's going on around here. Maybe I should talk to Father Becker."

Recognizing Bobbe's consternation and frustrations, Connie began guiding her toward the back of the convent building. "Yeah. That sounds like it might be the best thing to do. He seems like a nice person and I'll bet he can tell you what's going on."

They stopped at the foot of the steps leading to the back porch when the door suddenly opened and Mother Job appeared in the entrance.

"Constance. Come here, please." Her voice was composed and her expression was one of control. The only air of urgency was Sister Damien's face peering over the Mother General's shoulder.

Connie patted Bobbe's hand. "Don't worry, Bobbe, everything will be just fine."

She ran up the steps to meet the Reverend Mother.

"Come into my office, Constance. I want to speak with you. Roberta. Stay with Sister Damien."

Bobbe stood at the foot of the steps looking upward into the face of the frightened Mistress of Novices.

CHAPTER EIGHTEEN

The incongruous reason for his trip weighed heavily on Balthasar Becker as the bus approached Springfield. The trip had been a lonely one and the scarcity of passengers emphasized the importance of the day. Only those who had drastic reason traveled on Christmas. And his reason was more than drastic. His willingness to comply with the bishop's directive coupled with his own knowledge that the trip was of vital importance gave him a sensation of desperation when he thought of the despicable reason motivating him. To travel on the birthday of Christ, carrying the information a postulant was possessed and in grave danger was bad enough. To have to tell the girl's parents was a cup he would gladly have passed to someone else. But to whom?

The bus turned a sharp corner, pulling to the curb in front of the Springfield terminal. With a wheeze of air brakes, the bus lurched to a halt and the driver swung the door open.

"Springfield," he announced in a dull, tired voice.

Becker quickly stood and climbed off the bus. At least he would not arrive unannounced. Mother Job had suggested she call the Moores and tell them of his impending visit without alarming them as to the reason, and at the same time make certain they would be available to the Capuchin. Then to save further time, she offered to call Father Dolan at Saint Paul's rectory and have him meet Father Becker at the Moore residence.

Hailing a cab, Becker gave the address Mother Job had written down for him. In less than five minutes he was going up the front walk of the Moore residence. The warm glow of

225

lighted Christmas wreaths in the windows of the house brought a tear of sadness to his deep brown eyes. Wasn't there a story or legend concerning lights in windows during Yuletide? Weren't they supposed to guide the Baby Jesus to a place of warmth and love? And what was he bringing to this house? Shaking his head and breathing a silent prayer for strength, he rang the bell.

Almost at once the door swung open and Dan Moore greeted the priest. "Come in, Father. Come in. Merry Christmas. I'm Dan Moore, Bobbe's—I mean, Roberta's father."

"I'm Father Balthasar Becker." The Capuchin filled the doorway as he entered, forcing himself to return the festive greeting. "A Merry and Blessed Christmas to you, too, Mr. Moore."

"Let me take your coat, Father. We've been expecting you ever since Mother Job called." After the priest's coat was placed in the hall closet, Dan indicated the priest should precede him into the living room.

Becker blanched when he saw the older, white-haired lady sitting on the couch.

"This is my wife, Clare, and my aunt, Mrs. Kate Moore," Dan said, nodding toward the women.

The priest greeted them cordially but was laying plans to rid the room of the older woman. She would only prove to be an additional obstacle to overcome once he launched into his terrifying account.

"Sit down, Father," Clare said nervously, suggesting the large easy chair in the corner with an anxious nod of her head. "Whatever brings you to Springfield on Christmas Day?"

"It's about Roberta. She—"He stopped and bit his tongue. He had not expected them to be so forthright and was not prepared for such a quick entry into the reason for his trip. He had anticipated some small talk first. There should have been questions or statements about the first serious snowfall of the year and its opportune appearance on Christmas Day. Couldn't they have asked something about him? He turned to Clare who was sitting forward with a troubled look.

"Bobbe?" The single word was spoken anxiously. When the priest hesitated, she said, "She's all right, isn't she? She's

226

not sick, is she?"

What difference? The priest shifted in his seat. What difference if he dropped the bomb fifteen subtle minutes from now or blurted it out in his first sentence? The results would be as devastating to the parents no matter which route he chose.

"I'm afraid she is. But not in the usual sense." He was positive that statement would be worth some good questions. The one aspect he had hoped for was time in which he could find something out about the Moores. What kind of people were they? Could they grasp what he was about to tell them? With a little time and some knowledge of their temperament, he could choose the right words that would ease into their hearts and minds the loathsome burden of his findings. But now, that chance was gone.

"What do you mean by that, Father?" Dan asked as he leaned forward, a concerned expression worming its way among the wrinkles of his face.

"I—"

The doorbell rang and Becker found himself breathing a prayer of thanksgiving for the momentary reprieve. The time would give him a chance to plan his altered course. Leaning back in the easy chair, he studied the multicolored tree, which now seemed ironically out of place.

"Father Dolan?"

Dan's words brought a look of added concern to Clare's face when the appearance of another priest at their door on Christmas night suddenly brought exaggerated suspicions to her mind. Something was wrong with Bobbe. But what? What had happened to her little girl?

Dan escorted Father Dolan into the living room and after the introductions were made, all eyes in the room fixed on the huge Capuchin.

The silence was broken when Kate Moore stood and wisely said, "I suppose I should go lie down for a while. It's been a tiring day." The priests and Dan jumped to their feet as she left the room.

Becker blessed her wisdom and departure equally. When they were reseated, he began. "There have been one or two isolated incidents at the convent, which we feel Roberta may

227

have been responsible for and—"

"Incidents?" Dan asked excitedly.

"Bobbe? Responsible?" Clare's voice trembled as she spoke.

Holding his hand up for silence, Father Dolan calmed them with a comforting look. "What do you mean, Father?"

"Roberta apparently shouted some obscenities in a classroom and—" his voice trailed off into nothingness. He couldn't tell them everything but considering their looks of shock and disbelief, he decided he would, if necessary. The three people only stared at him in dumb amazement.

"Surely, you're joking, Father." Dan, a look of expectation trying to crowd the feeling of horror from his face, spoke first, hoping the strange priest would clarify his statements before they misinterpreted them.

"No. I'm not, I'm afraid." He knew he'd have to tell them everything. They were entitled to know. Tell them everything the demon had forced their daughter to do. God damn Satan and his works and evil spirits. It wasn't right these people should have to endure this torture. *God damn him! God damn the devil!*

"That's just one incident." Fighting to keep his voice calm and soft, he took a deep breath. He begged God's forgiveness if he were wrong in simply telling them the facts outright and asked for the strength the parents would need to receive the despicable news. "I—that is, we, the Reverend Mother and myself, have reason to believe your daughter may be possessed by an unholy spirit."

The last words seemed to hang in the air, beating into the minds of the three people who sat aghast at the statement the Capuchin had just made. The dreaded silence seemed to reach out in an attempt to choke the four people in its suffocating grasp. When Clare and Dan and their parish priest looked into the eyes of the giant sitting opposite them, they found sincerity and compassion, sympathy and utter sadness.

Several long seconds ticked away before Father Dolan spoke. "Are you certain, Father?"

"Quite sure, Father Dolan. I have already asked permission of the bishop to exorcise the spirit but he has withheld his consent until I have visited with you people. I was upset about the delay and hope to be able to begin when I return." Becker shifted uneasily in his chair. Where could he go from here? Everything was out in the open. Would they be able to answer questions now?

Quietly sobbing, Clare stared at the floor. What was happening to her baby? Why did it have to be her Bobbe? She tried to raise her eyes to meet the looks of the three men in the room but felt intimidated. What else might she learn?

Becker quickly explained in detail all the unnatural incidents that had occurred since Thanksgiving. Slowly, he could see understanding of the situation working its way into the bearing of the parents and the priest.

"There seems to be no rhyme or reason to any of it, Father." Dan seemed to accept the fact and now wanted to know the rationale behind his daughter's infestation.

"At this point we know of no explanation for the situation. However, it may become evident when the rite is performed." Becker had accepted the stunned silence at the beginning of his revelations as a normal reaction. How could it be anything but difficult to accept?

Covertly glancing at the clock on the mantel, the Capuchin began pressing for answers to the questions he had formulated on the bus. "Was Roberta ever in any difficulty with a boy when she was growing up?"

"She broke off with Jay Livingston when she decided to enter the convent," Clare offered.

"Jay's about the nicest young man in town. He would have made a great husband for Bob—Roberta," Dan added. "He's the only one she ever dated to any extent."

"To the best of my knowledge they had a good relationship," Dolan said after several minutes of considered silence.

"What about her religious habits? Had she been particularly religious?" Becker's attitude seemed to convey his inner feelings of desperation. There must be some concrete evidence he could take back to the bishop.

The three volunteered the information that Bobbe was no more or less religious than any young lady her age.

"How long had she thought of becoming a nun?"

Becker's manner put Dan in mind of an attorney cross-examining a witness suspected of perjury.

Clare glanced at Dan before they both turned to face Father Dolan. "She just announced it one day. A Saturday morning," Clare offered in a small voice.

"Yes," Dolan spoke up, "I believe I was the first one she told."

Was this the tiny, seemingly unimportant piece of evidence he was seeking? Becker pressed for information, finding that after the priest, the Sisters at the school convent had been conferred with and finally her mother and father had been told. The boy in question, her steady date, had been told when he proposed marriage the night before. Strange. But was it worthy of consideration? Many valid vocations were the apparent whims of individuals who ultimately led successful, fulfilling lives as members of a religious order or the priesthood.

"No indications of a vocation prior to that?" Why did Becker feel as if he were drowning and trying to grasp at insignificant waves for salvation? Did nothing have substance anymore?

Her vocation had been totally unexpected. After making the announcement in July she had entered the order the following September. Less than four months had elapsed since then.

Becker stroked his beard. That was not much time at all. Taking into account the undeniable suspicion she might be possessed, the information could only mean the unholy spirit infesting her had prompted the girl to enter the convent. But for what reason? Easy access to a group of holy women for the devil to torment? Perhaps the answers would come out during the exorcism.

Several minutes later, Becker glanced at the clock again and stood, bringing the other three to their feet. There were no further clues to be had he was positive, and persisting in questions would only lead the parents to a more confused state than they were in already.

"I must go. I have a train to catch at ten o'clock and I'm afraid I'll just have enough time to catch it now. Could you take me to the station, Father Dolan?"

Dolan nodded and moved toward the hall.

"Little mother," the Capuchin said to Clare, "I know you'll worry, even if I tell you not to. So I'll tell you instead your daughter needs your prayers more than she needs useless worry. Your heart is shattered but you will find solace in God. Pray to Him to give me the strength to cope with this unclean spirit. I shall, with the power Jesus Christ has given me, cleanse her spirit so she is once again your daughter and a child of God."

When he rested his large hands on her shoulders, Clare felt tiny, almost insignificant, before the tall priest and yet, a strange feeling of ease and calm washed over her when he touched her.

"Kneel and I will bless you," Becker said softly. "May the grace of the Almighty, God the Father, God the Son, and God the Holy Ghost descend upon you and help you and your daughter, Roberta, in this, your hour of need."

Father Dolan, who had knelt to receive the blessing, stood with Dan and Clare. Slipping into their overcoats, the two priests were on their way to the railroad station, having left the Moores only after a promise to return had been extracted from Father Dolan.

They drove to the station in silence and stood on the platform waiting for the approaching train to stop. The Capuchin looked down at the small man standing in front of him. "I assume, Father, you'll use the utmost discretion in speaking of this affair here in Springfield?"

The banging side rods of the steam engine drowned out the older priest's voice but the nod of his head and the serious expression on his face left no doubt about his answer. The train eased to a stop, steam wheezing from hidden pipes and traps under the dimly lighted passenger cars to billow about the cold air in exaggerated clouds.

Dolan watched the tall priest board the train. "Keep in close touch if you can, Father Becker, so I can comfort the girl's parents. It's simply terrible."

Becker turned on the steps and held out his hand to shake. Dolan's was lost in the expanse of muscles, bones, and skin but returned the comradely gesture with vigor.

"I will definitely keep in touch, Father. I have your number and will call if I need you for anything. I'll have Mother Job

231

contact you if time doesn't permit me to do so." He forced a smile and waved before mounting the remaining steps to the vestibule. With an effortless push, he shoved the heavy door aside as though it were made of cardboard and disappeared into the bowels of the coach.

Bobbe stared out the window of her cell at the blue-white countryside below while overhead, stars shone brightly against a black backdrop. Tears welling in her eyes caused the scene to wiggle and flutter surrealistically. She was being treated like a prisoner. What right did Mother Job have in ordering her confined to her cell? With a nun sitting outside? Was this a convent or a prison? Perhaps Jay had been right. She was throwing her life away.

Jay. Where was he? She needed him desperately. But for some reason he couldn't come to her now. What was it? Something about the day after Christmas. He was getting married. To—to—Crystal Brauerman. Not to Bobbe Moore. She was losing him forever to that—that Crystal Brauerman.

As soon as she could get close to a phone, she'd call her father. He'd come get her. Right now. Before she even hung the phone up.

"You must obey!" The voice was like a murmur of the wind but she understood it clearly. Who must she obey? Why? The nuns? No more. They were treating her in an awful manner. She wouldn't stay here right now except Sister John was sitting outside her door. Sister Timothy had been there all afternoon, ever since Connie had told her some wild talk about her dying the night before and floating in the air. Everyone was crazy in this place.

"You will obey!" Now the voice was joined by others in a soft, muted chorus.

Slowly, her eyes glazed and she quietly went to the iron bed to lie down. Staring at the ceiling, her mouth formed the words, "I will obey."

The voices chuckled and laughed softly while Sister John sat in the hallway praying her rosary.

CHAPTER NINETEEN

His exhaustion and weariness prevailed when the Capuchin dropped into a seat of the coach, leaving Father Dolan standing on the station platform. Sleep had mercifully dulled his sense of fatigue and the pythonic man's startling recuperative powers were allowed to restore his vitality while the train sped wailing through the night, belching smoke and steam. When fifty miles separated him from Cedar Falls, Father Becker opened his eyes, his body jerking awake. His sleep had been deep and dreamless and it took several seconds for him to recognize his surroundings. The mournful cry of the steam engine's whistle shrieking a warning brought his confused thoughts into sharp focus. Standing, he made his way to the men's room. A splash of cold water on his bearded face finished his awakening, and, completely orientated, he returned to his seat.

Forty-five minutes later, the train reduced its speed as it approached Cedar Falls and ultimately stopped in front of the railroad station with a jolt and loud hissing amid clouds of steam. Becker pushed his way through the door and into the vestibule where he hurried down the steps, ignoring the conductor's perfunctory word of caution.

The priest hailed the only cab waiting at the station and, after a brief ride through the deserted streets, arrived at the front door of the convent. When he had paid the driver and the car roared out of the horseshoe-shaped drive, the thought of the unusual Christmas he had spent tantalized him while he approached the large front doors of the building. What awaited him inside?

Fumbling with the key Mother Job had given him, he turned the lock easily and once in the dim light of the entryway checked his watch. He felt remarkably alert after sleeping almost six hours and decided a quick visit to the chapel would help immeasurably in refocusing his energies on the problem at hand. Another hour's sleep would complete the job of refreshing him before saying Mass for the good nuns. Good nuns! A smile crossed his face while he walked along the deserted hall wondering where that particular expression had come from. Of course, they were good. Most of the time they were good. Now, however, one was apparently possessed and causing more than a stir as well as grief for those about her. Perhaps the nuns praying to the Almighty would make this particular exorcism easier than the others in which he had been involved. The memories of his previous experiences with demons rankled his mind, and, pushing the carven doors of the chapel open, he decided he should not count on anything other than the unexpected. Especially where Lucifer and his kind were concerned.

The gentle hum of voices softly reciting the rosary burbled through the chapel's peaceful atmosphere. Easing his bulk into the last pew, he bowed his head devoutly, humbly.

Mother Job, kneeling in back of the group of nuns assigned to this span of time to pray for Roberta, had heard nothing when the priest entered but sensed his presence behind her. Sister Damien, who was next to the Mother Superior, continued leading the rosary as the Mother Superior stood and left the pew.

Hurrying toward the rear of the small church, she stopped near the Capuchin and whispered hoarsely, "Father, I think we should talk in my office before you retire."

Without waiting for an answer, she left the chapel.

A few minutes later Becker settled his frame into the chair opposite Mother Job's desk, noting the nun looked every bit as tired as he had felt when boarding the train in Springfield. A wan and rueful expression held the woman's face while he gazed at her, waiting for her to speak.

"This is a terrible time of the day to be conferring with you, Father, but I have something to tell you and I would also like to know what happened today—yesterday—when you visited with the Moores." Her voice was tired, matching her appearance.

Galvanized into action by her words, the priest sat up. "Another incident, Mother?"

Startled by his sudden movement, she waited several seconds before offering her information. "Roberta apparently awoke shortly after one yesterday afternoon. No one knew she was up until Sister Damien happened to look out the window of the community room and saw her floating in midair before the statue of Saint John. Sister Damien screamed and when some of the younger girls ran out to help Roberta, they found her kneeling in a normal way, praying. The nuns in the building who watched said she just floated to earth like a feather."

Stroking his beard with a huge paw, Becker snorted. "Levitation. Ah, this demon is tricky. You see, Mother, he must be trying now to mislead us into believing this girl is possibly in league with God or some holy spirit."

"Couldn't that be, Father?"

"Couldn't what be?" His voice was suddenly gruff.

"Couldn't Roberta be blessed instead of possessed?"

"Only if what we believe to be holy and good is all wrong. Don't forget the evil work already done through her. The changed food, the fouling of the water in the pipes, the beheaded statue of Saint John the Baptist—"

The recitation of the events brought a shudder to her exhausted body. Of course Roberta could not be blessed. Not with those manifestations occurring since her arrival.

"Did anything else happen, Mother?" Now his voice was soft, his manner consoling, when he realized his words and attitude had upset her.

"Constance Devler, another postulant and a good friend of Roberta's, walked with her right after she was found kneeling in front of the statue. Constance told me how they talked about the incident and that Roberta seemed unable to recall anything of it. Constance then went on to tell her what happened Christmas Eve and she claimed to remember nothing of that either."

Becker nodded his head in understanding as Mother Job gave her report. "It's very seldom the afflicted person remembers certain aspects of the possession. Especially those acts that are totally against nature. Was there anything else she said?"

"Yes. Constance said Roberta told her she had been hearing strange voices lately."

A glint of recognition crept into his eyes. "Does she remember what the voices have said to her?"

In her exhaustion, Mother Job missed the subtle change in the priest and continued her dissertation without asking what he was thinking. "Apparently not. However, she did recall being told to go and pray in front of the statue. She did remember that."

"How has she been since then?"

"I told her to stay in her cell and have posted a guard outside her room—just in case something should happen." Her eyes sought his approval when she realized how harsh her directive had been when she told him of it.

"I believe, under the circumstances, it was a wise decision, Mother."

She managed a sigh of relief.

"Well, when everything you've just told me is added to what has happened in the past and it is considered in the proper light, the only answer seems to be possession, doesn't it, Mother?"

Nodding dumbly, she coughed to clear her throat. "Did you find anything out in Springfield, Father?"

"Yes and no. I found she led a perfectly normal childhood, without a hint of nervous disorder or mental problems. I suppose that in itself can be interpreted as significant."

A look of puzzlement crossed her face. "I—I don't understand, Father."

"When an absolutely normal person behaves in a totally abnormal way, it is always significant. I grant stress can make an evenly dispositioned person cross or ill-tempered on occasion and that's common enough. But when a healthy girl becomes deathly ill, and a doctor can't find anything wrong, and the girl wakes up in the morning completely rested it's very much out of the ordinary, to say the least. Significant. Being pronounced dead by a medical man and running around a minute later is totally unbelievable. But it happened.

And it's significant. Floating in the air certainly is not an everyday occurrence, either. Again, significant."

Mother Job slowly nodded in understanding but remained silent waiting to hear the priest's account of his trip.

"The only remarkable thing I found was the fact her vocation was a complete surprise to everyone. Her parents. Her pastor. And again, most significantly, to the young man she had dated for almost three years. I find her announcing her vocation the night she's proposed to, most abnormal. Still it could have been expected when everything is taken into account."

After digesting the facts for several minutes she spoke solemnly as though her acceptance was complete. "What is our next step, Father?"

"Tomorrow morning—this morning, I will go to see the bishop immediately after Mass. By heavens, he *has* to give me permission now. We can't wait any longer, knowing what we do."

"You had best get some sleep then, Father. I'll call Mr. Tyler as soon as possible and arrange to have him take you to Madison."

"You're most kind, Mother." Standing he turned to leave but stopped when another thought occurred to him. "You had best think of how to break the news to the rest of the community. This other postulant—did you tell her anything?"

Mother Job's face reflected her sense of disappointment. How could he suspect she would leak something of this nature to a mere postulant? When she spoke, her voice bristled with a deviant hostility. "No, Father. I simply told her you would talk to Roberta when you returned."

"Good. That's good, Mother. Good night—er—morning." He quietly closed the door behind him and hurried along the gloomy halls wondering what had come over Mother Job. Such a strange woman. She could be warm and thoughtful one moment and cold and short the next.

Unmindful of his tactless manner in phrasing his question, Becker hoped the whole ordeal of the past few weeks wasn't unduly affecting her. When the rite began he prayed she would be able to withstand the treachery of Lucifer and his

237

horde. He yawned, welcoming the prospect of an additional hour's sleep.

When he turned the corner and entered the corridor leading to his rooms, Bobbe, standing in the shadows of one of the classrooms, stepped into the hall holding Dra-woh's hand. They smiled, watching the retreating priest, his shoulders slumped tiredly forward.

Turning, she gazed up at the tall, handsome demon standing next to her with expressionless eyes. "What would you have me do, Master?"

"Don't worry about the priest. He's a fake and won't be any trouble. Come with me now. I feel like fucking your holy cunt." His sinister chuckle slivered through the halls.

"Where shall we go, Dra-woh?" Her face, an unemotional mask, remained tilted upward, her blank eyes fixed on him. Once before, it seemed a thousand years to the girl, she had looked at someone—it—it had been Jay—in the same way. She had told him something. Something that had upset him and she had gone home and cried. Focusing her mind, she tried to recapture the moment but was interrupted when the thing standing next to her spoke again.

"We'll find someplace, Bobbe-sow."

Hurrying along the halls, Dra-woh roughly dragged Bobbe past the chapel doors bringing a squeal of pain to her lips that was smothered when he stared at her. Pulling as roughly on his arm as he had on hers, she stopped and grinned wickedly.

"Dra-woh, let's go fuck in the church."

When he spoke, his voice was a savage snarl. *"Are you crazy? Anyplace but there. I can't go in there. It's bad enough when you have to go inside so they don't suspect I'm around. Besides, can't you hear those holy whores in there praying their sacred bullshit?"*

She nodded apologetically. "Where, then?"

"Dumb fucking slut-bitch-Bobbe. Why do you suppose I have you do everything? Stupid sow!" The words dribbled from his lips in a guttural mutter, as he ignored her question.

When they reached the kitchen, he pushed the heavy doors open without effort, pulling Bobbe inside. Quickly stripping off the girl's nightgown, Dra-woh ordered her to lie on the huge stainless steel work table which Sister Claudia worked hours on to keep meticulously clean. A quicksilver stab of pain racked her body as the demon's gigantic penis pierced her body again.

When he finished, he ordered the exhausted postulant to scour and polish the table. Satisfied the evidence of their copulation was erased, Dra-woh released the girl to return to her cell so she could attend Mass at six o'clock in a normal fashion. Before leaving, the evil monster roughly grabbed Bobbe's shoulders, growling his instructions in a raspy voice.

"Soon, I will have company with me. Your training will begin then. While you are trained for our master's mission, all of us will have a good time torturing everyone here."

With a blank look of benightedness, Bobbe stared submissively at the thing holding her but said nothing.

"That nun-fucker Balthasar Becker is getting close, too. I'll have to show him up somehow. Go join the other sows, slut."

The figure of the man-demon shimmered and writhed while Bobbe stood uncertain, watching the final shadow evaporate. Then turning, she started out of the kitchen and headed for the chapel but stopped after taking several steps. A look of puzzlement held her face in a stilted mask for several minutes. What was she supposed to do? Hesitantly, retracing her steps to the kitchen, she reluctantly walked toward the rear staircase. Mounting the steps deliberately, one at a time, she reached the third floor. Her bare feet made no sound on the tile floor as she hurried toward her cell. When she turned the corner, Bobbe saw Sister James, who had relieved Sister John from watch duty at her cell door shortly before Dra-woh summoned her from the room. She could hear the nun praying the rosary in a muted whisper.

"Holy Mary, Mother of God, pray— "

The nun froze in a statuelike pose as Bobbe approached, just as she had done before, when the girl had left the cell. Easing the door open, the postulant slipped silently into the small room.

"—for us sinners, now and at the hour of our death. Amen." Sister James continued with the prayer unaware she had paused in her recitation.

Bobbe sat on the edge of her bed and, yawning, slowly

stretched. Standing, she undressed and slipped into her simple uniform. After brushing her hair into place she went to the door.

"Is it all right if I go to Mass, Sister?"

Sister James jumped at the sound of the girl's voice. "I guess it is, Roberta. I'll go down with you."

The two women made their way silently toward the front stairs, too embarrassed to talk because of their unusual role of jailer and prisoner.

With thoughts of his impending conversation with the bishop boring deeply into his mind, Becker rushed through the services of Mass and communion for the nuns. Permission *had* to be granted to begin the rite. Baffled at what he would do should the prelate still withhold his authorization, the Capuchin had recalled while preparing for Mass, how the bishop had not even allowed him to tell of the latest developments until the girl's parents were consulted. When that had been accomplished, any new evidence could be submitted along with the results of the interview and the decision would be properly made. Becker knew he'd have to emphasize the points that would convince the young bishop.

Now, as the priest walked to the communion rail with the ciborium, he spotted Bobbe kneeling with the other communicants. Gradually, while Father Becker approached her to administer the Host, her face wrinkled and contracted into a grotesque mask, her mouth clamped tightly shut. The girl's eyes rolled up and out of sight until the whites stared blindly at the patiently waiting Capuchin now standing in front of her. When it was apparent she was not going to take the proffered wafer, Becker moved on to the next woman.

Reciting the prayer automatically and continuing to administer the Host, the priest's mind raced. The demon was forcing the girl to conduct a frontal attack on the Body of Christ. He would have to talk with her after Mass—and before he spoke to the bishop. Perhaps he would discover additional information that would help sway the prelate's decision. When the last woman had received communion, he returned to the altar and hurried through the remainder of the Mass, constantly praying all would go well.

By the time he had disposed of the Mass vestments, he found the women well into their breakfast. Motioning for the Reverend Mother to come to the corridor, he waited while she made her way through the dining hall to join him. He told her of his intentions to talk with Roberta before contacting Bishop King and asked for the use of her office.

He sat in the unfamiliar chair behind the desk, facing the door, waiting only for a brief time before a soft knock broke the silence.

"Come in." Becker's quiet tone denied the surge of emotion coursing through him.

Bobbe timidly entered the room. "You wanted to see me, Father?"

"Yes, child, come in and sit down." He stood, pointing to the chair he had placed opposite the desk.

After she was seated, the priest studied the beautiful girl whose innocent appearance could have deterred the Capuchin's suspicions if the manifestations had not occurred and he wasn't convinced she was infested by an unholy being.

"Tell me, Roberta, why did you make such a horrible face at me this morning when I wanted to give you communion?" Since the demon had made a frontal attack on the Host, he felt a frontal attack on the demon was in order. At least, the thing would be aware of the fact the giant priest knew of his existence.

Bobbe stared incredulously, shock at the statement the chaplain had just made filling her eyes with a horror of familiarity. Somehow she seemed cognizant of the information but at the same time vaguely ignorant. Shaking her head, she stammered, trying to speak in her defense. "I—I—"

With sympathy etched deeply into his ruddy complexion, the Capuchin nodded his head in a contradictory gesture. "Yes, I'm afraid you did, Roberta. Has anything been bothering you since you've entered the convent? Anything at all?"

With shards of knowledge parted by gaps of ignorance flitting through her mind, Bobbe stared at the huge man. He was serious. Had she actually done what he said? For some reason, it seemed she had. But the idea was more like an unfulfilled thought, as nebulous as a forgotten memory. Hadn't she received the Host and returned to her seat to offer thanksgiving to God? Her throat felt dry and constricted but she forced herself to speak. "Did—did I really do that, Father?"

He nodded gravely. "Tell me, Roberta, has everything been all right since your arrival at the convent?"

She waited before answering while reflections of her tenure at the convent flashed through her mind. Everything had been as she had expected only—only—

"I have had some strange thoughts lately, Father." The words were barely audible as she whispered, "Weird ones. And—and—"

Wasn't there something else about which she wanted to talk with him? Something that at the time seemed as important as anything in her life. But what was it? Why couldn't she recall anything? Her mind began to slowly freeze in paralysis when she sensed it slipping deeper into the abyss she had come to know so well over the past months. Struggling to maintain contact with the priest, she watched detachedly while he leaned over the desk in anticipation of her words. But what was she trying to say? She must speak. She had to tell this man about the voices.

"Yes?" Father Becker, unaware of the conflict raging within the girl, leaned back in the chair, trying to dispel any misgivings she might feel and offer his support and comfort at the same time. He had to back off. Make her feel comfortable. Shouldn't act eager. Maintain serenity and she would feel secure.

"I hear—" Bobbe was amazed at the sound of her voice. She had actually spoken even though she felt herself sinking. Striving to continue, she pressed further in her attempts.

"Yes?" Becker suddenly felt helpless, realizing a maelstrom of confused emotions was bombarding her mind. How could he help her speak?

Bobbe stared at him fixedly. What if he thought she were crazy when and if she managed to tell him about the voices she heard? The thought instantly solidified, blanketing the surface of her mind. Maybe she was crazy! "I—I hear voices, Father. Voices," she blurted out in exasperation.

Finished, she slumped back in her chair, exhausted by the struggle to speak the few words that had the Capuchin hunched over the desk once more.

Becker leaned back slightly as he spoke, knowing he was making some progress that would help him when he spoke to Bishop King. Fighting to maintain a controlled voice, he said evenly, "What kind of voices, Roberta? What do the voices say?"

Bobbe sensed herself reeling and spiraling downward into the familiar blackness more rapidly than she had ever experienced before.

"That's none of your fucking business, sexless man!"

Balthasar Becker fell back in the chair as the deep bass voice roared from Bobbe's mouth.

PART FOUR

DRA-WOH

December 26, 1951
to
December 27, 1951

CHAPTER TWENTY

Stunned by the sudden intrusion of the demon's voice, Becker stared at the postulant who sat as though transfixed to the chair, the whites of her upturned eyes blankly riveted on the Capuchin. The temperature of the room dropped sharply but the priest ignored the puffs of vapor jetting from his nostrils. When he opened his mouth to speak, larger clouds vented forth.

"Who are you?" Becker's voice was firm but he had struggled to utter the few words. His surprise slowly began dissipating.

Now the question rang in his ears like an ominous warning that an answer could be forthcoming. Silence closed in on the priest while he waited for the demon to answer. The only sound in the room was the humming of the electric clock on the wall. Bobbe sat rigidly upright in her chair, completely oblivious to her surroundings or the giant Capuchin sitting opposite her. Slowly, the second hand circumvented the face of the clock twelve times while Balthasar Becker waited.

Impatient with the demon's refusal to answer, the priest stood, drawing himself up to his full height. He clutched the crucifix in the cincture about his waist but did not remove it. "In the name of Jesus Christ, who is the Saviour of all mankind, I demand you to tell me!"

Instantly, the voice roared forth once more. "*I am Dra-woh.*"

Father Becker mulled the name over in his mind, positive it was completely unknown to him. "Dra-woh? I have never heard of you. Are you not, in reality, Satan himself?"

A deep malevolent chuckle rumbled from Bobbe's throat. *"Not Satan but one of his chief lieutenants."*

"Then you are one of the fallen angels? You were not a human being who lost his soul to Lucifer?"

The beastly voice remained silent forcing the priest to focus his attention on the cold and quiet of the room. The minute hand of the clock slowly inched along its circular path passing one number after the other. Suddenly, the braying of an ass rang through the office. Becker's gaze intensified as he waited for the voice to answer his question.

When it came, the words were a high-pitched scream. *"I was human! I was not an angel! I lead those miserable humans who now pay homage to our prince, Lucifer, the Bearer of Light."*

Becker mulled the words over in his mind for several minutes before choosing his next question. Realizing he would have to be exceedingly careful since the bishop's permission still had to be gained to perform the holy rite of exorcism, he was keenly aware that any information he could attain in this manner would be invaluable in convincing the prelate and, possibly, in ridding the postulant of the brazen spirit within her.

"Why do you torment this child of God?"

"I do what I must do. My master has directed me."

"Why? For what reason? What is it you do to her?"

A deep gurgling growl began building within Bobbe, increasing in volume until the windows in the office rattled. When the voice spoke again it was coy and mocking. *"My master has rewarded me by letting me fuck the sow-bitch's cunt."*

Becker blanched at the demon's vulgarity but didn't hesitate in asking the next question when he realized the nature of the thing with which he was conversing. "You are an incubus?"

The deep gurgle, which continued while the words were spoken, changed until it became a hoarse chuckle. As though punctuating the unvoiced admission, the sudden oinking of a pig intermingled with chickens clucking and a hissing snake sound emitted from the mouth of the white-eyed postulant. When the sounds stopped precisely, as though on an unseen cue, the silence of deathly quietude swallowed the room, which was again accentuated by the quiet hum of the electric clock.

Unflinchingly fixing his eyes on the contorted face of the unseeing postulant, Becker persisted in his questioning. "What were you that you rank so high in the devil's black army?"

Screams and moans, accompanied by the gabble of many voices, filled the room but no intelligible answer was forthcoming. More seconds crawled by to form interminable minutes. At length, the priest repeated his question. "What were you that you rank so high in the devil's black army? Answer me, demon of the damned!"

Canine growls and barks spilled from Bobbe's mouth before they slowly became words the priest could understand. *"I was a businessman who had no scruples in dealing with my fellow man. Manipulations on my part ruined many people's lives and caused some to commit suicide. Others were killed because of me. I profited enormously from this and I have never repented. When I died, I was cursed to spend eternity with my master in hell."*

"Was Dra-woh your earthly name?"

"My name is Dra-woh and that is that. Enough of this bullshit, priest!" More animal sounds began bombarding the Capuchin as they marked the statements' end.

Becker waited patiently until the din subsided. When he felt his voice would be heard over the diminishing clamor, he spoke in demanding tones. "How long have you inflicted your unholy will on this girl?"

"None of your fucking business!" The words were clipped in a snarling growl.

Withdrawing the crucifix and holding it up, Becker stood facing the statuelike postulant. "I command you to tell me."

The results were instantaneous, the voice changing into a whimpering moan. *"Aghhhh! Take it away! I'll tell you, you bastard! Take it away!"*

Becker returned the cross to his girdle and waited. The only sound he could detect was the continued humming of the clock. Slowly moving his hand toward the symbol of Christ's death again, he stopped when the voice spoke.

"We were asked to take her into our possession."

"By whom?"

"I cannot say! I cannot say!" Barking and laughing began to accompany the voice when it continued. *"We know all about you, Balthasar Becker."*

"You will answer *me!*" Becker roared and brought forth the crucifix, choosing to ignore the demon's curious implication.

Moans and screams rent the room while Bobbe, still sitting erect as though held by invisible bonds, began foaming at the mouth, jerking convulsively. Her chair danced across the room away from the proximity of the small wooden cross with the figure of Christ pinioned to it.

"Tell me!" Becker's voice rose in volume.

When the chair bumped into the wall and could go no farther, the voice whimpered. *"Take it away! Take it away! I'll tell you!"*

Once more the priest returned the cross to his waist and waited for the answer to his question.

Animal sounds, intermixed with the babble of many voices, slowly changed into the voice of Dra-woh. *"It was an old man whom the girl made a fool of when she was a young sow. He tried to get her into his house to fuck the young cunt but she broke away from him. She threw something at him and he asked us to take her when she escaped. So—we did."*

"Didn't she tell anyone of this incident?" The Capuchin's words were filled with edged excitement as he spoke. If he could believe this demon, he was actually being told the reason for the possession.

A self-satisfied chuckle grated on the priest's ears. *"We blocked it from her mind as though it had not happened."* Then the laugh grew into a high-pitched, screaming giggle.

Roberta Moore had been cursed and no one apparently knew—until now. Concluding the curse had been nothing more than an idle threat which had been taken seriously in at least one place, Becker decided on a calculated gamble. Withdrawing his crucifix in a sweeping motion and holding it before him, he approached the grimacing postulant, roaring in a voice almost matching the demon's in volume.

"Depart, you fiend of hell! Leave this girl, who belongs to the Lion of Judah! Begone with—"

Without warning, the clock on the wall crashed to the floor. File drawers flew from their cabinets, spilling carefully arranged contents about the room in a blizzard of paper. Leaping from their places on shelves, books began floating about the room to form a cryptic mobile around the priest. Bobbe's mouth opened wide to vomit a steady stream of thick yellow paste. Dislodged pictures sailed across the room, smashing into the opposite walls.

Running to the door, Becker threw it open and was engulfed in a rush of warm air. For the first time since the voice of the demon had been heard he was consciously aware of the bitter coldness. As quickly as the destructive force had begun, it ceased.

Her face drained of color, Mother Job stood trembling in the hall. "Father, what on earth happened in there?"

"I have met our enemy, Mother. I believe Roberta is safe for the time being. Have her taken to her room and see she stays there. Have the nuns who are to help in the rite, stand watch. I'm sorry about your office. It'll need a thorough cleaning. I'm afraid it's a shambles."

Peering hesitantly into her office, the Reverend Mother gasped. Papers and books, some open, some torn into shreds, covered the desk and floor while file drawers lay askew about the room. The clock, which had been a gift from her brother, was shattered into hundreds of pieces as though it had been hurled to the floor with great strength. Chairs lay on their backs and sides, and the stench of the obnoxious vomitus hung like an ethereal vestige in the still freezing air. In the far corner, Bobbe sat slumped forward in her chair.

"Good Lord!" Mother Job managed under her breath.

"Have someone clean the mess up, Mother. We'll use one of the visiting rooms to talk." The Capuchin urged the nun into action with the commanding look he shot her.

When they were seated in one of the small visiting rooms, Becker said, "We will have to tell all the women the nature of the problem facing us, Mother. My immediate task is to inform the bishop of the results of my trip to Springfield and the recent manifestations occurring here yesterday and today."

"Father, please don't think I'm having misgivings now, but are you absolutely certain? I mean, couldn't the levitation and glossalalia Roberta spoke at Midnight Mass be the works of Christ and not—not of the devil?" Her voice pleading for a change of opinion but echoed the underlying fear that none would be forthcoming.

Becker shook an admonishing forefinger at the pale nun. "We've spoken of this before, Mother Job. This is exactly what the demon would have us believe. Those are the only two incidents that could be interpreted as holy while the overwhelming majority indicates there's an unholy spirit at work here. No. There's absolutely no doubt in my mind. We must proceed on the assumption Roberta is possessed if we are to save her. In addition to everything that's happened in the past weeks, how could the incident in your office be deduced as something holy?"

With a repentant shake of her head, Mother Job accepted the impending ordeal of exorcism. When she spoke, her voice rang with contriteness. "Mr. Tyler is waiting for you, Father. Are you still going to see the bishop?"

Looking at his watch, the Capuchin sucked in his breath. "Look at the time. It's going on two o'clock. I spent better than five hours with that unholy thing. I guess it's best if I telephone His Excellency, Mother. Since he knows of the situation here, he should be able to give me permission over the phone."

Becker recalled his last telephone conversation with the prelate. Permission could not be refused now. Time was running out for all of them and he would have to begin soon or they'd have to pay the consequences when the demon achieved such a strong hold in the convent, it would approach the impossible to rid themselves of him.

"Don't tell Mr. Tyler to leave until I call Bishop King, Mother. I don't think I'll have to plead my case in person but just in the event he would want to see me, I'll have to get there as soon as possible."

He nimbly extricated his huge frame from the overstuffed chair, and left the room. Deciding it would be best to check on Roberta before calling the bishop, he hurriedly climbed the two flights of stairs and found her sitting in her room, staring

251

out the window. He knew he'd have to pick and choose his words carefully, hoping the postulant would not question or even be aware of the four nuns standing guard outside her door. If the exorcism was to be a total success, the girl would have to be kept from knowing the reason why she was possessed in addition to the fact she was infested by a demon. In either instance, she could look upon the rite as a form of therapy to help expel her of this particular anxiety. And definitely, an anxiety it was not.

"Roberta? Are you feeling better?" His voice was soft and he moved cautiously when he entered her room.

Turning, she registered surprise to find the chaplain calling on her. Since being brought to her room from Mother Job's office by Sister John and Sister Timothy, her mind had reeled under the impact of tiny bits of memory—none of which seemed related to anything with which she was familiar. The only concrete conclusion she had drawn was that she had been sick again. Every time she had suffered a recurrence of—whatever she had—her thoughts always seemed to be totally disconnected. Now she sought affirmation of the fact from Father Becker.

"I—I've been sick again, haven't I, Father? I seem to remember and yet I find it impossible to pull my thoughts together."

"Tell me what you mean, Roberta."

Becker sat on the edge of the iron bed, waiting for her to continue. It was fortunate to have her coherent. Perhaps he would gain some additional insight.

"Little snatches keep flashing before me but none of them make sense. I see things I don't understand but feel I've already done them or have been responsible for them."

Her voice had a plaintive quality to it the Capuchin found impossible to ignore. "Can you describe any of them for me, Roberta?"

Her eyes seemed to search the space in front of her for an example but as they panicked in desperation, her mouth began pouting, tears flowing freely down her smooth cheeks. "What's wrong with me, Father?" she asked breaking into deep sobs.

Feeling totally helpless, Becker shrugged his broad shoulders. "The only thing all of us can do right now is pray for you. You're positive you can remember nothing that makes sense? Only bits and pieces of thoughts?"

Nodding, her voice cracked when she spoke. "Am I going insane, Father?"

Becker managed a rueful smile as he stood, placing his hands on the girl's shoulders. "No, child. Rest assured you are not mentally ill. However, we do want you to be certain of your real purpose here, don't we?"

Bobbe wiped her eyes with the back of one hand. "What do you mean, Father?"

The priest knew he was on shaky ground and might inadvertently reveal her problem, which could mean a dangerous and more difficult exorcism for everyone involved. "Pray to God Almighty for the strength you need if you are to stay here in the convent and do His work. You see, Roberta, if a ship goes astray on the ocean, adjustments must be made to correct the course. This is what we must pray for now. Do I make myself clear?"

Unable to comprehend the priest's analogy, Bobbe nodded in resigned agreement. What he said made no sense whatsoever to her. What did her illness or whatever was wrong with her, have to do with adjusting a ship's course? All she wanted from him—from someone—anyone—was the answer to her dilemma of not being able to recall certain periods of time. Nothing more. Electing to remain silent, she suddenly felt ill at ease in the Capuchin's presence, wishing he would leave her alone.

"Pray now, Roberta and I'll come back to you shortly."

Without waiting for any further comment, he left, hurrying to his own quarters. Uncertain if the girl had any suspicions of her problem's nature, he was thankful Roberta appeared normal and healthy and had no indications of physical deterioration that so often accompanied demon infestation. His immediate concern was that the bishop would understand her state.

Within minutes of entering his apartment, he was waiting for Father Hasker to summon the bishop to the telephone.

A loud click preceded the bishop's voice. "This is Bishop King."

253

"Balthasar Becker here, Your Excellency. I went to Springfield as you suggested and found nothing that would indicate mental disorder or abnormality of any type in the postulant's background." He explained the suddenness of her vocation and entry into the convent. For several minutes, he dwelt on Jay Livingston and her refusal of his marriage proposal. When he finished his report, he purposely waited to bring a question from the prelate.

"Have there been any other occurrences at the convent?"

Resisting the urge to smile triumphantly, Becker was confident the new evidence would sound more convincing if it came in answer to one of the bishop's questions instead of being offered. He quickly recounted the events of Christmas Eve and Day, emphasizing each detail in its proper perspective.

"In addition to those things, Your Excellency, I spoke with the demon just a short time ago." Now Becker would wait until the full impact of his last statement took effect. Nothing but dead silence drained from the receiver for several long minutes.

Then the bishop spoke. "How was that, Father? You spoke with the demon? Have you begun the rite without my permission?" His voice carried an edge that would have frightened the giant priest if such were the case.

"No, no! This morning at Mass, the girl made a horrible face at me and refused the Host during communion. I decided I should question her about it. I felt, although it was more than likely inspired by the demon, she might recall it and be able to give me some additional understanding of the problem at hand. Peculiarly enough, she recalled nothing of the incident and was under the impression she had received the Body of Christ and even gave thanksgiving when she returned to her pew."

"I see," the bishop said with just a hint of apology in his voice. "About the demon speaking to you—?"

"Yes. While I was questioning her, I found she has been having weird thoughts. She also claims to recall voices speaking to her. When I asked what the voices said, the demon told me it was none of my business. Rather emphatically, I might add. That was how the conversation began. The

254

whole time we spoke, the girl sat very rigid as though she were hypnotized. I learned that as a child, she was cursed by an old man when she broke away from him after he made sexual advances toward her. *There* is the reason for the infestation."

"Do you believe this, Balthasar?"

"It's all we have to go on but it does make sense. Yes, I guess I do believe it."

After a short pause, the bishop spoke again. "That seems to settle any doubts that may have existed."

Becker felt the last piece of evidence should be presented. "There is one other aspect I haven't told you yet. The demon informed me he is an incubus."

"An incubus?" the bishop whispered.

"Yes. The demon may have assumed at times the physical appearance of an animal or man and indulged in intercourse with the postulant."

"If this is the case, the demon has made much headway, hasn't he?"

"Indeed he has. If the demon I spoke with has actually done the physical act of copulating with the girl, we will have our hands full. He gave a demonstration of his power and really made a shambles of Mother Job's office. I sincerely believe this to be a genuine case, Your Excellency, and humbly ask your permission to exorcise the demon from the girl."

"Permission is granted, Father. Proceed as you see fit and I'll pray for you and the girl. Will you want another priest to assist you?"

Becker quickly told him of his plan to use the nuns Mother Job had selected and complied with the bishop's request to speak with the head of the convent. After signaling the switchboard, the Capuchin said good-bye and left his rooms to summon the nuns, novices, and postulants to the chapel.

"This is Mother Job, Your Excellency."

"Yes, Mother. I know full well you were the first to suspect the nature of the infestation at your convent but I want to make certain you're willing to allow the exorcism to take place there."

"I am, Your Excellency. I feel to do it anywhere else would permit outsiders to discover the truth. The fewer who know, the better. Do you agree?"

"Absolutely, Mother."

"I've no desire to partake in anything unusual or out of the ordinary but I really don't see any other course of action open to us." She was amazed by the cool, almost detached manner in which she spoke to the bishop. What had made her so self-confident? Was it the presence of the giant Capuchin?

"As your bishop, I must warn you about the possibility of being subjected to some very serious consequences personally. Has Father Becker warned you of the danger you might be in?"

She swallowed, trying to ease the lump she felt forming in her throat. "In a vague way, Your Excellency."

"Satan will undoubtedly seek revenge on you for permitting the rite to take place in the convent. He will show no restraint where you're concerned personally and you must be spiritually prepared to cope with anything he might try."

Closing her eyes, she fought back a tear and coughed to clear her throat. "God's protecting hand will not fail me or the community—or Roberta. The devil can do only what God permits him to do. If the Almighty sees fit to allow the devil certain privileges and freedoms here, I also know He will give us the strength to combat him. If we must suffer, we will suffer. We'll be only too happy to bear it, knowing Roberta's immortal soul will be freed from his clutches."

"God bless you, Mother, for that show of faith. I'll pray for a speedy and successful conclusion to this affair."

They said good-bye and Mother Job blessed herself as she left to go to the chapel where Father Becker was telling the others of the demon's presence.

Becker stood solemnly at the front of the chapel as the last women filed in. All of the convent's members were present except Mother Job and the sisters selected to help him who were guarding Bobbe in her cell. Knowing it was unusual to have an unscheduled service in midafternoon, the women looked at their chaplain expectantly.

He cleared his throat and began. "Dear Sisters, we have had thrust upon us a most trying situation—a despicable situation. One of your number is, I'm afraid, in the possession of a most unholy spirit."

Although the women reacted silently, horror and panic were quickly etched onto each face. The devil? Here? In their convent? Unthinkable! Still what about the strange things that had been going on the last while? Was this the explanation?

Becker waited until the statement was accepted. Accepted? How could the devil be accepted here?

"Do not fear for the soul of your sister. In cases like hers, the soul of the infested person is completely free of any stain of sin. The possessed person has no will when he, or as in this situation, she is controlled by Satan. All of you know a sin must be committed willfully. Our job is to drive from the body and soul of Roberta—"

The identification of the possessed girl brought a buzz flitting through the congregation.

"—the unclean and unholy spirit who possesses her. You have been most faithful in maintaining the vigil of prayer I requested and now I must ask you to intensify your efforts. It is seldom anyone can fight the devil and his pomps and works so directly. You as a community have the chance now.

"I was called by Bishop King to come here to observe the situation after you people had experienced several unnatural happenings. I have had much experience with Satan and I will need your prayers as much as Roberta. I have, in the course of my life, spent three days shy of two years in open confrontation with the devil and his hordes."

Another restless buzz of concerned whispers swept over the women.

"Now I must do battle with him again. I will need all the prayers you can offer. Kneel and pray with me now." He humbly turned to face the altar and began.

"Saint Michael, the archangel, defend us in battle. Be our safeguard against the wickedness and destruction of the devil. Restrain him, O God, we humbly beseech Thee and cast him into hell—"

CHAPTER TWENTY-ONE

Unaware of the nuns guarding her cell door, Bobbe lay on her bed staring at the dark ceiling through tear filled eyes. She had decided shortly after the chaplain left her room to telephone her parents and have them come to Cedar Falls and get her. However, the fit of lethargy she found herself in both puzzled and frightened her. If she knew her intent, why didn't she simply go to the telephone and call them? It was all so easy but she couldn't seem to muster the strength to walk.

She didn't belong here. She knew that now. There were too many strange things occurring she couldn't explain. Once she returned to Springfield, she would get her old job back and call Jay to apologize for her stupid actions.

Jay!

The tears that had been welling in her eyes suddenly took on a life of their own, streaming down the sides of her face toward her ears.

Jay was lost to her. Today was his wedding day. He was being married. And to Crystal Brauerman. Crystal didn't deserve Jay. Jay was rightfully hers. No—not anymore. Still, she found she wanted him just the same. Gone. He was gone—forever. No more Jay. Turning, she hid her face in the pillow, sobbing softly.

When the tortuous thoughts passed, she sat up, wiping her eyes. The cell seemed hot and stuffy. Standing, she crossed the room to the window and opened it. Fresh, winter air flowed in sending a welcome chill coursing through her body, awakening every cell—every nerve. After inhaling several deep breaths, she closed the window and turned the light on.

The pale yellow glow flooded the room and for the first time she was aware of another presence. Whirling about, she found Dra-woh sitting in the corner on the only chair in the room.

Bobbe gasped, her eyes glazing over when she spoke. "I didn't know you were here."

"Dumb cunt. I've been sitting here watching you for an hour. Tell me what you're crying about?"

Bobbe turned and walked to the window. "It's—it's nothing, really."

"I know what it is but I want you to tell me."

His voice compelled her to face him and she turned reluctantly while the force she felt tugging at her swept away any degree of self-control. "A—a friend of mine is getting married today and I was a little sad because I couldn't be there." Her voice rang dullishly through the small room when she recited the falsehood. Then with a seductive smile creasing her lips and a sense of compliance shutting out any remaining will power, she felt herself sinking into the pit of nothingness.

"Stupid slut! You wanted his cock in you all along, didn't you? Too dumb to give him anything, weren't you? Now, some other bitch is going to get fucked by him and you feel bad. Stupid! Stupid! Stupid!"

His mocking voice had little effect on Bobbe's numbed senses. Still she felt, deep within her, an overpowering urge to ask him a question. The realization of his words slowly registered and she felt her eyes widening.

Yes, it was true. She had rebuffed Jay's attempts at intimacy despite her craving hunger for him. For some reason she had never succumbed to her baser desires with him. Now, in addition to wondering about her sanity, she found herself struggling with the question of her own physical normalcy.

"How—how did you know about that?" She backed away as she whispered hoarsely.

"I've told you before. I've been with you a long time. I know everything that ever happened between you two. It was I, who made you resist his advances. You were meant for better things than his sour seed." An evil grin replaced

the mask of sarcasm, which had held his face rigid. *"I know what we'll do. Yes, that would be fun. Come on, you and I are going someplace."*

Obediently, Bobbe stepped forward and took his proffered hand. "Where are we going, Dra-woh?"

"Do you have to know everything? Come with me and you'll see."

After the Capuchin had dismissed the nuns in the chapel, he and Mother Job went to her office for a final consultation before initiating the rite of exorcism.

Once they were seated, the Reverend Mother looked at the exorcist in a troubled way. "Father, there is one thing that bothers me."

"What is that, Mother?"

"How can the devil remain in the presence of God, especially in a convent where the atmosphere is so holy? At least, that is our aim. How can he endure it? I would think he should flee back to hell as tainted by good as we are by evil."

A serene patience crowded the expression of anticipation from his face momentarily when he understood her question. "You must bear one thing in mind, Mother. While Jesus Himself fasted in the desert, Satan had the audacity to approach Him. He even dared to take our Saviour to the tallest pinnacle in Jerusalem and to the highest mountain top in all of Judea for the sole purpose of enticing Him, trying to make Him yield to human temptation. The devil asked Him to fall on His knees and adore his unholy presence. If he was powerful enough to tempt God Himself and remain in His presence, Satan will have no trouble existing in the same place here, with us mere mortals. There is no reason to believe his powers have diminished since that time."

The nun nodded in understanding and agreement. "I never thought of that particular incident. Of course, you're right. Will it be bad up there, Father?" Her face matched her voice's apprehensiveness when she asked the question.

The serene patience gave way to a pathetic smile that saddened his entire countenance. "You will never experience anything else like it in your lifetime. If devils, who were once numbered among the angels, present themselves, they will howl and curse and attack us when they find they are in the Sacred Presence of the Host. Demons, who have been men and women, will openly attack, boldly and fearlessly, as if they want to assault God Himself. But they are powerless to do anything to God. Instead, they attack Him through those faithful who are in attendance at the rite. I imagine that is the reason for having Roberta enter the convent. A way to wreak havoc from within."

Becker stood to leave, his eyes sweeping the restored office. "I'm glad you talked with Bishop King today. I would have told you the same as he did. However, I caution you to take his words of warning seriously, Mother Job. Be prepared for direct attack on yourself at anytime."

"Where are you going now, Father?"

"Right now, I'm going to get the items I need and pray for a few minutes. I'll meet you on the third floor at Roberta's cell in ten minutes. We must begin *now*."

After he left, the last word hung ominously in the air, echoing the urgency of the situation, sending a chill of anticipation down Mother Job's spine. For a moment, the Mother General pondered the warning of the Capuchin and the bishop. She knew she had made a general confession and should be in the necessary state of grace to assist at the rite. Confident Satan would make little if any headway within the confines of the convent, she glanced toward the clock on the wall and found the blank space jeeringly reminding her of the demon's power. Fumbling beneath her guimpe, she checked her own watch. Almost six-thirty. Her stomach heaved and gurgled, protesting the hasty meal she had eaten. Would their lives ever return to normal? Would she and the others who were to help the priest be up to facing the demon? Would the rest of the convent be able to cope with it?

Shaking her head, she stood and walked wearily toward the door. Even though Father Becker was experienced, he was no longer a young man. Did he have strength enough for another encounter with the unholy?

Crossing herself, she entered the hallway praying silently. *Please, dear God, give all of us the necessary strength to withstand the battle we face.* After mentally reciting the prayer to Saint Michael, the archangel, she shook her head and squared her shoulders. She was ready.

Once Bobbe's hand was locked within the grasp of Drawoh's she became engulfed in a swirling mass of dark clouds. Flashes of bright, spiraling colors seemed to draw her down the foggy corridor of time itself. Her body felt light, weightless as she gyrated in a lazy circle occasionally catching glimpses of a darkened countryside passing rapidly beneath her. The sensation of slowing pressed in on her when she felt herself being righted to a standing position. The black clouds scudded to either side and she sensed unfamiliar surroundings.

When her eyes adjusted to the gloom, she found herself alone in a hotel or motel room. Her attention was drawn to the far side by a noise from the bed which she could barely see in the shadows, standing between two windows. Squinting, she made out the forms of two people, a man and a woman, locked in sexual embrace.

Moving closer to see the faces of the couple, she gasped when the realization of her whereabouts struck her like a wet rag slapped across her face. It was Jay Livingston and Crystal, his wife, who were consummating their love and marriage. Jealousy clawed at Bobbe with the talons of memory.

"Fuck her, Jay!" Her voice was sharp and piercing as it hollowly echoed about the room.

The movement on the bed stopped and Jay craned his neck to see who had spoken. "Who's there?"

His voice was hoarse and breathless as he rolled off Crystal's heaving body. Groping for the bedside light, he shielded his eyes against the sudden brilliance flooding the room. When he recognized the naked girl standing at the foot of the bed smiling lasciviously, he gasped.

"Bobbe!"

Realizing there was someone else in the room, Crystal sat up, pulling a sheet around her nakedness and began crying and screaming. "Get out of here! What are you doing here?"

Bobbe threw her head back and laughed. "Is she good, Jay? She's nowhere near as good a lay as I am!" Chuckling, she ran her hands down her bare body before cupping her breasts. "Don't you want to stick your cock in me, Jay-Boy?"

Unable to speak or comprehend what was happening, Jay looked at Crystal.

Pointing accusingly at Bobbe, Crystal cried wildly, trying to understand. "She's supposed to be in the convent! What's she doing here?"

After regaining his composure, Jay swung his legs out of the bed and demanded, "Bobbe, get the hell out of here!"

"Make me, Jay! Yes, *make ME,* Jay. Fuck me instead of that bitch lying there alongside of you. She's had so many cocks stuck into her she's lost count. Come on, Jay, clean her slime off and I'll show you what fucking's all about." Pumping her hips back and forth, Bobbe enticingly motioned for him to embrace her.

"I don't believe this," Jay said covering his own nakedness as he got out of bed, now ashamed of his erect manhood, which was slowly withering.

Hysterically, Crystal threw a pillow at Bobbe but missed. "Get out of here, Bobbe. What are you doing here anyway?" Unable to comprehend the sudden appearance of her husband's former girl friend, she sobbed fitfully. None of this was real. Innocent Bobbe Moore who had gone to the convent was not acting very holy now. "How dare you just walk in on us like this!"

"For heaven's sake, Bobbe, put some clothes on," Jay ordered. "What are you doing running around naked? You have no business being here—you're supposed to be in the convent!"

Glaring at him, Bobbe snarled, "You hypocritical bastard! You always wanted to play with my snatch and fuck me. Now I offer it to you and you try to drive me away." Her voice changed from a growling rasp to a seductive whisper. "Don't you want to screw me, Jay?"

Livingston stared at her, disgust written on his face. "Of course, I don't. Have you gone crazy? How did you get in here?"

"I came through the wall, stupid!" Bobbe threw her head back and laughed again.

"I'll get her out of here!" Crystal stood in the middle of the bed and with a shriek, leaped toward the intruder who nimbly sidestepped the shocked girl's impulsive charge.

Avoiding Crystal, Bobbe lashed out with a well-aimed foot, catching the hysterical woman from behind. Kicking with all her strength, the naked postulant felt the soft wetness between Crystal's legs. With a scream of pain, the bride's head hit the wall and stunned, she fell to the floor.

Smiling in satisfaction, Bobbe turned her attention back to Jay. "Now we can fuck in peace, lover!"

When Jay tried to rush to his wife's side, Bobbe stepped between them and began grinding her pelvis against his groin.

"Let go of me, Bobbe!" Livingston struggled mightily to break the grip she maintained on his upper arms but found it impossible to wrest himself free. Wincing at her unnaturally superior strength, he screamed, *"Let go of me!"*

Laughing wickedly, she forced him back on the bed. "Now isn't this better than fucking that old sow there? I fixed her cunt good. She won't be able to fuck for a while so we may as well take advantage of the—"

Bobbe suddenly went rigid as if unseen hands grasped her.

"No! No!" she screamed. Without effort, she stood upright, her face reflecting the effort she was making to struggle free but failed to move in the least. "Not now! Let me go!"

To Jay, some force, not visible, seemed to be pulling the girl away from him. Slowly, Bobbe faded from sight and Jay, in a half sitting position on the bed, disbelievingly watched with fear-filled eyes. Then, he was alone with his unconscious wife.

Four of the nuns selected to assist Father Becker gripped Bobbe firmly by the shoulders and legs, her nightgown tearing at the hem in the struggle.

Writhing in anguish, Bobbe screamed as they forced her to the bed. "No! No! Not now! Let me go!"

The four women wrestling her to the mattress were too much for the postulant.

Stepping forward, the Capuchin positioned one woman at each shoulder and foot of the girl. "Remember, Sisters, the demon will probably attack us physically after we begin praying. If he does, make certain she is kept on the bed at all times."

They nodded in understanding.

"Let us begin."

He opened his Roman Ritual after placing a small purple stole on Bobbe's breasts. Her body stiffened rigidly.

"Please respond to the prayers, Sisters." He fumbled through the pages, trying to keep one eye on the postulant while finding the Litany of the Saints. When he found the lengthy prayer, he cleared his throat.

"Lord, have mercy on us."

As one, the four women holding Bobbe and Mother Job, who stood behind the priest ready to be of assistance, answered in unison. "Christ have mercy on us."

"Lord have mercy on us. Christ hear us."

"Christ graciously hear us," the nuns chorused.

Bobbe moved a little as the prayer continued and began writhing on the bed despite the firm grasp of the nuns.

"Holy Trinity, One God." Becker's voice was firm, precisely enunciating each word.

Bobbe relaxed.

"Have mercy on us." The nuns answered each phrase promptly, tending to relax in the solace they found in the prayer.

As the Saints of the Church were called on to help in exorcising the demon, Bobbe quieted down, her eyes clamped tightly shut. Not until the name of Saint Michael the Archangel was intoned did any further movement come from the captive held on the bed. Then she began foaming at the mouth, struggling mightily, trying to break loose. Without changing her facial expression she increased her efforts to be free of the restraining hold.

"Saint Agnes," Becker continued unabated in his effort.

"Pray for us."

As the other Saints' names were mentioned and each was asked to pray for the supplicants and their endeavor, Bobbe quieted down seemingly calmed by the chanting voices.

When they finished the prayer, Bobbe renewed her efforts to escape, thrashing about with renewed vigor.

"I—I don't think we can hold her, Father," Sister John cried.

Before the priest could step forward to assist, Bobbe freed

one arm and hit Sister Boniface flush across the face sending her tumbling to the floor. Striking out at the other three, she quickly sent them sprawling. Free of their restraining hold, the postulant flew through the air, hitting the wall above the door with a loud thump where she remained, pinioned by an unseen force.

"My God!" Sister John murmured, blessing herself.

"Lord God, help us!" Sister Boniface grunted, when she picked herself up from the floor, tenderly rubbing her face, a trickle of blood oozing from the corner of her mouth.

With her back to the wall, Bobbe's toes dangled five feet from the floor, her head brushing the ceiling. The only movement of her face, which remained impassive as it had on the bed, was her mouth opening, allowing torrents of black foam to bubble out.

"Pull her down! Get her down quickly!" Becker ordered. "She must be brought down and placed on the bed again. Hurry!" His voice, filled with urgency, brought the nuns into action instantly.

Despite their efforts, the four assistants and Mother Job were unable to budge Bobbe and remove her from the impossible position. Running from the room, Sister Gregory returned in seconds with another chair to place opposite the one on which Sister Michael stood. With two nuns standing on chairs and two pulling on her legs, Bobbe was dislodged with a great deal of exertion. What seemed to be invisible ropes still retained her after they brought the girl back to the bed. Just as they placed her in a reclining position once more, Bobbe began struggling again but this time the nuns were prepared and held fast.

Becker blessed the women and the infested girl. The prayers of exorcism were continued until a tiny, shrill sound began interrupting their flow of concentration. It began softly, like a far off siren until it quickly grew in intensity, rending the air with a deafening shriek.

The nuns looked fearfully at each other. Strength. They must pray for strength but they were frightened and their faces reflected the inner turmoil each was experiencing.

"Silence, you damned soul of hell!" Becker roared. Only the Capuchin seemed to be unshaken by the voice from the

266

bowels of eternity.

Ignoring the priest's order to be quiet, the demon continued howling and moaning as though it were being physically tortured. Reverberating through the halls, the unearthly cry filtered to the other floors of the convent bringing a shudder to the nuns, novices, and postulants who knelt in prayer two floors below, when they heard the demon's scream. Steadily, the volume increased until Sister Boniface and Sister Timothy released their grips, dashing from the room with hands covering their ears. Mother Job leaped forward to assist while Becker took the remaining shoulder and arm in command.

As suddenly as it had begun, the voice stopped, leaving only an echo in its place and when it had died away, silence crashed into the small room. Bobbe continued spewing out black foam and jerked convulsively causing the heavy iron bed to shake. Torrents of the yellow-white paste followed, splashing on the feet and habits of the attending women and priest. The stench of rot, sulphur, and mold filled the air, which was becoming colder with each passing second.

After several long minutes of remaining perfectly still, the women and priest noticed Bobbe visibly relax, appearing to be asleep. Gradually the room warmed.

Releasing his hold, Becker stepped away from the bed with a critical eye fixed on the reclining girl. "I believe we'll stop for now, sisters. It's been a trying evening. We'll resume in the morning. Have one or two of the sisters keep vigil here, Mother."

He blessed the women and postulant once more and then, crossing himself, left the room.

In the hall, Sisters Timothy and Boniface approached the Capuchin with downcast eyes. "Forgive us, Father. We were frightened and—"

"Please, Sisters, no apology is necessary." He placed his huge hand on Sister Timothy's shoulder gently. "Just pray to God and Saint Michael, the archangel, for the strength to continue." He blessed them and made his way to the chaplain quarters.

He knew now it would be a difficult exorcism. But, when had it ever been otherwise?

After she closed the door to her cell, Mother Job tiredly pulled her coif off and quickly undressed. When she was ready for bed, she ran a comb through her hair several times before turning the light out to bathe the room in blackness. Kneeling beside her bed, she breathed several prayers and fell onto the mattress, exhausted. Sleep soon erased the horror of the evening and she slipped into a deep slumber.

Wrestling aside the comfort of peaceful rest, her mother and father loomed in her mind, admonishingly shaking their forefingers at her. Their angry faces grew until they were gigantic and even though she was aware their mouths were moving in speech she couldn't hear a sound. Tears of frustration welled in her eyes when she realized what they were angrily scolding her about.

"I'm not too young." Her voice cut through the stillness of the cell as she muttered in her sleep. "I'm not! I love Tom. Please, let me marry him when he comes home. Please?"

Ignoring their daughter's pleading supplication, they continued their silent tirade while the nun sobbed quietly in her sleep.

Her parents slowly parted, floating out of sight to either side and she could see someone coming toward her, far off in the misty distance of her dream. The indistinct figure appeared to be wearing a uniform and lovespawned hope filled her breast. Could it be Tom? It must be Tom. It must be! As the apparition came closer she could make out leggings and the jodhpurs of a cavalry officer. It was Tom. But why was he riding a bicycle? Why was he going so slowly? Why didn't he hurry? She wanted to run to meet him but her legs refused to move.

Now the figure on the bicycle seemed to be going even slower until he finally stopped, resting his vehicle against a tree that had miraculously appeared in the fog. Then he began walking toward her. Why didn't he hurry? He was coming for her. Mentally, she begged him to run. Then, when he was only a few feet away, she could make out his face.

It *wasn't* Tom.

The man was a messenger of some sort and held an envelope out to her. Accepting the missive, she tried to tear it open but the paper refused to yield. A tiny rip appeared in one corner and widened when she pulled the flap away. A single piece of paper inside fluttered to the ground in front of her. Two words, in bold black letters, seared her mind again. *"TOM'S DEAD!"*

From either side of her peripheral vision, her parents floated into view, angrily confronting her to blot out the messenger and his sad communique. Turning his back, her father crossed the room to sit at a table where he began drumming his fingers on the bare wood.

Something was wrong. The sound she heard was all wrong for his actions. Instead of the steady tattoo of thumping, all she could hear was a rubbing, scratching sound. Slowly, the volume built, the noise increasing in tempo.

A loud crashing knock at the door of Mother Job's cell brought the exhausted nun bolt upright in bed.

"Who's there?" Her voice, although tired, was authoritative in her demand.

Then she became aware of the rubbing noise and its more pronounced nature then she had been in her dream. Again, the sound grew in volume and became scratching before another loud pounding bombarded the door unmercifully. Wiggling back toward the cold headboard of the iron bed, she clutched the blanket around her. Would the door hold or would she be inundated with demons from hell?

"Stop!" Her voice tore through the otherwise quiet of her room. "Stop it!"

CHAPTER TWENTY-TWO

Despite her fatigue, Mother Job quickly got out of bed to kneel in prayer. "Saint Michael, the archangel, defend us in this day of battle. Protect—" The pounding stopped abruptly and silence flooded the room, filling the void.

Hesitantly rising to her feet, she threw her robe around her shoulders, continuing to pray silently. The nun picked up a small crucifix from her bureau and slowly, reluctantly moved toward the ominous silence lurking behind the door. When she was three feet away, the door began creaking and groaning as it slowly began to bulge inward, taking the form of two hands reaching out for her.

"Saint Michael, help me!"

Her screaming prayer drowned out the moaning sound and the door instantly returned to its normal shape. Gingerly reaching out with a trembling hand, she turned the knob but it refused to budge. She gave it a tug. Then, a harder one. Clamping the crucifix in her mouth, she pulled with both hands. Still the latch would not yield. Understanding she was a prisoner in her own room, Mother Job backed warily to the center of the cell before kneeling again to pray aloud the supplicant petition to the devil's arch-enemy, over and over.

After several recitations she stopped and as the last sound of her voice died away, the crushing silence embraced the nun again. She waited.

There was nothing. Not a sound could be heard and she stood, relaxing slightly. Would the door open now? Tiptoeing silently toward it, she placed a gentle hand on the knob exerting a slight pressure. It turned. She eased the door open slowly and peered into the deserted hall, which was filled with swirling fog. Dense and gray, it began spilling into her room, roiling and surging about her feet before undulating upward to encase her trembling body. Praying feverishly, she backed away, retreating once more toward the center of her room.

When a small black spot appeared in the middle of the cloud and began growing in size, she stopped. Now she was able to recognize shadows of the familiar hallway through the opening as it became larger. Then a light appeared. At first it was a tiny pinpoint in the raven gloominess of the corridor but it began unfolding, expanding until the splotch of brightness reminded her of a spotlight and in the middle—

Mother Job blessed herself and tightly clasped her hands together in frenzied prayer. It couldn't be! Standing in the center of the clearing was Tom. His death-white face smiled sensually, beckoning her to come toward him.

Tightly clamping her eyes shut, the vision of her former love remained clearly in her mind. The uniform—the same uniform he had worn when he left that day years before—stood out vividly. But the dark stain covering his chest brought tears of sorrow to mingle with those of fright and confusion. A sob caught in her throat. It couldn't be! It could *not* be! It was not Tom! Not her Tom! The sob became a whimper and her shoulders convulsed when a flood of tears plummeted down her cheeks.

Tentatively opening her eyes, she saw the figure moving down the hall toward her. Closer. He was coming closer. When he held his arms out for her she shook her head vigorously.

Mother Job's voice cracked when she cried out. "No! No, Tom! Don't let them use you like this! Go away! Please go away! You don't belong with them! You were always good! Go back to where you belong! Oh, To-o-o-m." She fell to her knees sobbing the prayer she had recited so often before. "Saint Michael! Blessed Saint Michael, help me! Help Tom!"

Instantly, the hall was cleared of fog and the figure of the soldier evaporated. Looking up, the Mother General found the corridor was completely deserted but knew many things could be secreted in the dimly lighted recesses. Would the demon leave her in peace now? Had he vented his anger sufficiently or would there be more onslaughts like this until he was ultimately driven back to hell?

Exhausted, the nun stood and closed the door quietly. Unless she got to sleep now, she would be worthless to Father Becker in the morning. When she started for the bed, pounding began again more violently and much louder than before. Screams and moans accompanied the crashes and Mother Job ran to the far side of the cell. A picture of the Blessed Virgin, one her mother had given her when she repeated her final vows, fell to the floor, its glass covering splintering into countless needlelike shards. With her back to the wall, she stared at the door.

"Leave me alone, you devil! There's nothing here for you!" Despite her defiant shouts, evil laughter was her only answer. Laughter and the ceaseless pounding and screaming.

The window rattled in its casement and the bed began dancing across the floor toward her. A small bottle of holy water bouncing on the bureau caught her attention. Mustering courage to move from the wall, she ran the few steps to grasp the container. Making the sign of the cross definitively, she splashed the blessed liquid on the door.

A long scream, louder than anything the demon had unleashed before, pierced the quiet night. Then there wasn't a sound. A deathlike stillness filled her room.

Mother Job blessed herself and returned to the bed after repositioning it. Lying on her back, she stared at the dark ceiling mouthing a whispered prayer. "Father in heaven, do not forsake us in this hour of trial. Give us the strength to foil the works of Satan and his horde."

Her eyes fluttered and then closed as she mumbled half aloud, "How right you were, Bishop King. How right you were."

Following Mass the next morning, an exhausted Reverend Mother waited for the Capuchin outside the chapel. When he saw her haggard appearance an expression of shock crossed his ruddy face.

"Are you all right, Mother?" he asked, concern heavy in his voice.

"I waited for you, Father, to tell you of my night. I was

harassed and tormented for almost two hours after I had already gone to sleep. There was loud pounding at my door, moans and screams. At one time I couldn't turn the knob. I was locked in, even though there's no lock on the door."

Misinterpreting his look of concern for one of skepticism, she quickly added, "I was awake. Not dreaming."

"At this point in our relationship, Mother, I will believe most anything out of the ordinary."

She quickly recounted the appearance of the apparition of what had been Tom and her relationship with him in the past. As she finished a troubled look crossed her face. "Father, would that mean that Tom—is in—hell?"

"Most certainly not, Mother. If, as you told me, the young man and his death were on your mind lately, the demon probably used your own thoughts against you when he couldn't find anything else to his advantage. He's venting his rage, trying to punish you for allowing the rite to take place."

"Will there be more of this? I mean attacks on me, personally?" A touch of trepidation hung on the last word.

"There could be, Mother. But don't anticipate it or plan for it. Stay in the state of grace and there will be nothing he can do to you."

As they walked along the hall toward the dining room, she breathed a sigh of relief, knowing the bearded priest was correct in his thinking.

Without turning his head, Father Becker watched the nun walking next to him. She was a brave woman, trying to confront the demon alone like that. But then, she didn't have much of a choice. He reached out and patted her on the shoulder. "I trust the attack did not prevent you from getting some sleep, Mother?"

"Everything quieted down when I sprinkled some holy water on the door. My, I never heard such a scream before in my life. Did you hear it, Father?"

His beard trembled as he shook his head. "I'm certain the display the demon put on last night was for your benefit only, Mother."

"Such a sound. Much worse than the ones we heard in Roberta's room or in my office. But thank God, the holy water did the trick and I was left undisturbed the rest of the night."

273

"Have you looked in on Roberta, yet?"

"Not personally, Father. Sister Boniface watched the early morning shift and came off duty right before Mass. She told me Roberta slept peacefully all night."

"Good, good. She'll need the strength sleep will give her to withstand the physical abuse she'll have to endure." He left her at the refectory entrance and went to the chaplain's dining room across the hall.

When the morning meal was finished, the priest and the assisting nuns filed to the third floor, each one sensing the air of expectation surrounding them. Would the demon be driven out today? Sisters Michael, John, Timothy, and Gregory followed the Capuchin and their Mother General toward the infested postulant's cell. The rest of the community resumed the routine of praying in shifts.

Sister Raphael, who had received communion just before Mass had started, stood when the priest and his entourage approached.

"Is everything normal, Sister?" Becker asked as he stopped before her.

"Not a sound, Father."

He quietly opened the door and found Bobbe sound asleep. Gently awakening her, Becker studied her eyes as they opened. "Good morning, Roberta. How do you feel this morning?"

Rubbing her eyes, Bobbe looked about the room. "What happened? Did I fall asleep, Father?"

"Yes, my child." Glancing up at the others, he saw they understood that Bobbe was unaware of the previous evening's happenings. "You slept well, I presume?"

"Yes—yes, I guess I did. I did have some very mixed up dreams, though. The boy I dated for a while before I entered the convent was in one of them, too, Father. And—and—did I get sick again last night?" Her voice trembled, breaking as a paisley pattern of her subconscious activities forced their way into her waking mind. Why did she feel so alone? Would she ever feel normal again? Despite the presence of the large priest and his sincere empathy, she felt as though she had no friends any place on earth. Her sense of fear began mounting to a feeling of complete terror.

274

"Don't try to recall nightmares, child. Seek comfort in the Almighty and you'll be at ease with yourself. Are you hungry?"

"Not really, Father. I am thirsty, though." She tried to smile but found her face muscles stiff and sore.

Without a word of direction, one of the nuns left on his glance to get a pitcher of water and a glass. When she returned, Bobbe took two sips and lay back on the bed.

"Please remember, Roberta, we are here to pray for you. We want to help you pass this particular crisis. Now, just lie back and close your eyes and pray along with us if you want." Becker's attitude put her at ease and to his assistants, the gentle manner seemed foreign and unnatural to his performance of the previous evening.

Puzzled, Bobbe silently questioned the priest's peculiar statements. What was going on? Stay in bed? What for? What crisis? Pray along with "us"? Stealthily opening one eye, she saw Sister John standing near her left shoulder and Sister Gregory by her right. Sister Timothy stood by her left leg and Sister Michael was opposite her. The chaplain was at the foot of the bed and Mother Job was off to his right. *What was going on?*

Then she heard the voice calling her. It was far away but she could make out her name when it was cried out. Nothing else made sense. It sounded like gibberish. Closing her eyes, she concentrated on the voice. The sensation of sinking into the gelid abyss began in her feet and spread rapidly upward, toward her head. Desperately trying to call for help of some sort, she felt her throat constrict whenever she willed herself to cry out. When Becker nimbly stepped around the nuns and placed the purple stole on her breasts, her body grew rigid and she plunged into the freezing blackness.

"Pray with me, Sisters, to Saint Michael."

They began and were greeted immediately with a roar. *"Stop that heavenly bullshit, nun-fucker, and get those old sows out of here."* The obscenities erupted from Bobbe's mouth, now held impliably, unmoving as the words were born.

"I do not obey a demon and will continue praying until you are driven out of this poor child." Becker's voice was quiet and soft, ominously controlled.

The room grew colder as moans and screams began softly, increasing in volume. Joining the uproar was the sound of a pig grunting loudly.

Before continuing, the Capuchin looked at Bobbe who had assumed the same tight-eyed mask she had worn the previous night, her jaw hanging agape. "Why do you torment this girl, demon?"

"My name is Dra-woh, you dumb sonofabitch!" the demon roared, raving and cursing before lapsing into silence.

"Answer me. I command you." The priest's voice rose in volume now, demanding cooperation and losing all semblance of the gentleness he had demonstrated minutes before with the girl.

The answer came in a high-pitched falsetto, whining sarcastically. *"You have your harem of black sows. What's wrong with me having one of them to fuck? Besides, I'm better at that sort of thing than you are, you monkey!"* Insidious laughter followed, filling the room.

Becker winced at the reference to the primate who bore the same name as his beloved order. "Are you alone in your endeavors, demon?"

Dra-woh roared, causing the walls and window to shake. *"Call me by name!"*

"I'll call you whatever I wish. You insult me, don't you?"

"What applies to you doesn't apply to me. My name is Dra-woh! Call me that!"

The window and walls continued rattling and quaking but now the dresser bounced crazily in the corner. The demon's voice had grown until it was much louder than it had been during the two previous encounters the priest had experienced and the Capuchin reluctantly decided it would be better to humor him than for his screams and curses to be heard in the nearby town.

"Very well, then, *Dra-woh,* tell me, are you alone in your endeavors where this poor girl is concerned?"

"I am not alone."

"Who is with you?"

Only silence met the question. The five nuns stared wide eyed at the exchange taking place between the priest and the demon but Becker, undisturbed, spoke almost casually. Minutes crawled by as the priest and nuns waited for the demon's answer.

The lowing of a cow accompanied by a horse's neighing broke the stillness before the demon spoke.

"There are several of us here. They're under my direction and command. I am in control and will be where this young bitch is concerned. Does she not belong to me?"

"No!" Becker thundered in response. "She belongs to Christ and you have no right to be with her. Begone!"

"Non!" the demon countered. *"Il faut cultiver notre jardin!"*

The Capuchin, although recognizing the French language, did not understand what the demon had said. Turning, he looked questioningly at his helpers.

Sister Gregory stared at the priest with a knowing look but did not speak.

"Do you know what he said, Sister?"

"Yes, Father," she managed weakly. "He said, 'we must cultivate our garden.'"

"What?"

"It could also be translated as 'we must tend to our own affairs.'"

The priest nodded in understanding and returned his attention to the prostrate form of Bobbe Moore. "Is she aware of you and your horde of demons?"

The answer came back quickly. *"She knows me when she sees me and talks to me. Only then, though. I have clouded her mind so she doesn't remember what we do. I didn't want her to tip off my presence here to anyone. That wise-ass sow standing behind you is too damned smart. I'll send Tom around to give her a little cock. She'll get hers."* The demon cackled with laughter.

Mother Job, shocked at being mentioned in the conversation, conceded the propriety of the statement. It *had* been her suspicions that ultimately brought about the exorcism. She breathed a silent prayer for Tom, a tear rolling down her cheek nestled in the coif under her jaw.

"I hear you praying, you old sow-whore," Dra-woh

277

sneered. *"I want to fuck your twat, Job!"*

The nuns gasped and the Mother General's complexion became a sickly gray.

"Who gave you permission to look into her thoughts? Who gave you permission to enter this convent by possessing this girl's immortal soul?" Becker's voice rang angrily through the small room making the nuns wince at its hostile overtones.

"You're really stupid, asshole," Dra-woh whined. *"Don't I have to render obedience to Lucifer?"*

"Then you have done this and are here at the direction of Lucifer?"

"How could it be otherwise?"

Accepting the demon as the most brazen spirit he had ever encountered, Becker raised his crucifix and stepped closer to the bed. "I command you in the name of Jesus Christ, the Saviour of all mankind, to present the demons who assist you."

A soft moaning began, splitting into different crying voices that quickly became mumbling curses. One, different from that of Dra-woh, spoke above the din. *"What would you have of me, priest?"*

"Who are you?"

"No one you ever heard of. You may call me Bal." The voice spoke with a German accent and Father Becker knew if he were to speak German to this new demon, it would answer him in kind. But would it be genuine? Couldn't this new demon look into his mind and know the language from there?

"*I know what you think, priest.* Ich bin Deutsch!"

"When did you live?" Becker, as though asking an acquaintence the time of day, remained calm.

There was no answer forthcoming.

"I command you to answer me!" Holding his rough wooden cross before him, Becker's voice became more forceful.

Curses and screams were babbled in different languages before Bal spoke. *"I died in 1943. I was a guard at a concentration camp called Dachau and helped in the murders of thousands of Jews. A group of my friends and I* were returning from a drinking party one night. The driver was as drunk as the rest of us and drove off the road. We were all killed."

"You never regretted your actions on earth?"

"*I died relishing what I had done. Once you enter the realm of the Prince of Darkness, you have no chance to regret. Put that accursed cross away,* Arschloch!" The demon's voice moaned painfully.

Stepping forward, Mother Job tugged gently on the Capuchin's sleeve. "May I speak with you in the hall, Father?"

He nodded, turning to leave the room with the Mother General following him but saw the four women who held Bobbe on the bed, looking at him apprehensively. Feeling their concern, he stopped and returned to examine the girl who had not moved during the conversation with the demons and whose eyes remained clamped shut.

"I'll be right outside the door, Sisters, in case you need me." He managed a meager smile to reassure them and followed Mother Job into the hall.

The Mother Superior relaxed when she felt the warmer air in the hallway and for no reason other than the comfort it gave her, blessed herself. "Will this prove to be a problem, Father, having more than one demon to exorcise?" A tremulous note of fear hung on each word.

"In cases like this it's not uncommon to have all the attending demons leave at the same time. The power of Christ is stronger than all the combined forces in hell and we have His power on our side."

As though contradicting his confident words, a shriek pierced the hallway and both the Capuchin and the nun lunged for the door. Pushing it open, they saw Bobbe unattended, lying on the bed. After entering, Father Becker found the four women they had left in the room, huddled in one corner, pointing toward the bed. Becker turned just as Mothe Job screamed.

"My God! Father, do something. Look at her head!"

The Capuchin fixed his eyes on the girl's head which had changed shape to resemble the water pitcher resting on the night stand. Reaching inside his cassock, he brought forth a small golden pyx containing a consecrated Host which was held around his thick neck by a fragile chain. After slipping it over his head and beard, he began praying as he moved it the full length of Bobbe's body, the chain bouncing along after the container and the priest's huge hand.

"Look upon the Body of the Crucified Christ of Galilee, ye demons of the dark. Leave this girl at once. I command you."

His voice rasped the order over and over while Bobbe began writhing, struggling violently as though the pyx and his hand were white hot. The black foam preceded the yellow-white paste as both gushed from her mouth, the unearthly concoction running down her face. The nuns, who had returned to their posts, looked away as they held fast to her thrashing limbs. Rolling, tossing, Bobbe's body fought desperately to break their grip.

When Becker drew his crucifix again, he placed it near the pyx and armed with the consecrated Host and the symbol of Christ's death, commanded in a bellowing voice, "Look at the cross, you despicable slime! Begone, ye powers of hell! The Lion of Judah shall conquer you! Go back to the pits of hell and abandon your unholy enterprise!"

Where the vomit had poured from Bobbe's mouth, hundreds of hairy maggots now crawled. Making their way down the full length of the postulant's body, they wiggled over the hands of the attending nuns. Still, the women did not budge. The girl's body convulsed powerfully, before human excrement began gushing from her eyes, ears, and nose. Gagging at the awful stench now intermingling with the other putrid odors, the nuns strained until Sister Gregory ran to the door weeping and retching. Mother Job quickly took the fleeing nun's place.

Without warning, the temperature in the room plunged until hoarfrost began forming on the iron headboard of the bed. The hands holding down Bobbe began turning blue from the cold and the pressure they were exerting to keep the postulant on the bed. Unfazed by the bitter chill, the maggots continued their unholy journey over the girl's body.

"Stop! Stop it!" Dra-woh's voice bellowed over the screaming of the tormented demons as Bobbe's head slowly resumed its natural shape. *"We cannot stand such torture. Take them away. We cannot stand it."*

While the demon screamed in agony, Becker, watching the tortured body of the girl on the bed, decided for her physical well-being to stop the demon's punishment for now. It was apparent to him there would be more of this sort of thing and if Bobbe were to survive he would have to proceed carefully. At least the demons were cognizant of the fact he had in his possession the weapons that would eventually drive them from her soul's presence. When it happened, it should be final and complete.

Returning the crucifix to his girdle and the pyx containing the Host to his pocket, he retrieved his Roman Ritual from the bureau and continued with the prayers of exorcism. From a hidden pocket in his robe he withdrew a vial of holy water and sprinkled the blessed liquid in the form of a cross over the now quiet form of Roberta.

"Begone with it! Begone! Begone!" Dra-woh screamed harshly until the women's ears burned with pain. "*I cannot stand it! Such torture from a holy one? Stop! Stop it!"* A longer and louder piercing scream rent the convent when Becker returned the vial to his pocket.

Overpowering the noxious odors of bile, rot, and mildew, the stench of sulphur suddenly filled the air. The priest and nuns began choking.

A crackling sound seemed to surround them and before anyone could move, the room on the far side of the bed erupted in flames. With a single scream the four nuns released their holds, rushing for the door and into the hall. Only the giant Capuchin held his position, standing bearlike at the girl's bedside. Carefully drawing his crucifix out once more, he slowly backed away from the bed in the direction of the door.

The flames leaped, playing about the room, exploring it, claiming it, lapping out toward the priest but never touching him. Despite the crackling fire, the room seemed to get even colder than it had been. Father Becker focused his attention on a darker mass appearing in the center of the fire on the opposite side of the bed. Slowly the area solidified, taking the shape of a tall man.

The spectrelike figure stepped from the flames to stand facing the man of God. Holding up his left hand, which grasped a sceptre resembling a human thigh bone, his piercing yellow eyes bored out at the priest from beneath the flaming crown on his head. Pointing an accusing finger at the Capuchin the figure bellowed.

"Why do you torture my subjects with the abominable slime you carry?"

Balthasar Becker swallowed with difficulty, almost choking. "Who are you?"

The words hung heavily in the air when the demon answered. *"I am Lucifer!"*

CHAPTER TWENTY-THREE

Becker's heart fluttered rapidly, his breath coming in short, pumping gasps. How much torture would he have to endure before he would find solace in his chosen vocation? It was inconceivable one person should have to suffer the exposures to filth and degradation the way he had, simply to prove his worthiness and devotion to a yet unseen God. But here before him stood a figure claiming to be the epitome of evil, proving once more how absolutely real and tangible temptation could be along with its ultimately hollow reward. Every exorcism the Capuchin had ever been involved with, flashed before his mind's eye. Never, not once had he encountered the Prince of Evil.

The priest's shock gave way to disbelief and then finally acceptance that here before him stood the supreme test of his life. His intensity mounted, his eyes narrowed to mere slits to watch the fallen angel, Lucifer, step to the opposite side of Bobbe's bed.

"Answer me, priest! Why do you torture my subjects?" If the devil, with his unnatural powers, had detected Balthasar Becker's moment of hesitancy, he did not capitalize on it. Instead, his glowing eyes stared menacingly at the giant priest.

"It is my right to torture and drive them from this girl!" Becker's voice reflected no doubt or question about his authority or fearlessness as his adversary moved closer to the bed. In spite of his initial doubts, he now found himself filled with an inner strength of which he had never been aware, prior to this instant. Sliding his hand to the pocket of his cassock, he grasped the small vial of holy water and inched forward into position, directly opposite the fearful visage now bending over Bobbe.

"Why do you order your slaves to perpetrate evil deeds on weak mortals?" Becker's voice was calm, almost benign.

Raising his head until his face, marred with draining pustules, was only inches from the Capuchin's, the devil brayed like a jackass before laughing. *"I do not order them until someone asks us to take an individual soul. In most instances, we are welcomed into a person's life. It is not within my power to take a soul unless the person wants us to or has been cursed by someone else."*

Straightening up, Lucifer gazed down at the relaxed body on the bed and said philosophically, *"There is much about me man does not know. Many think I am an imaginary being cast into an imaginary hell by an imaginary God. Now you know differently, don't you, nun-fucking priest? And those who worship me are the ones I look after, giving them the means to enjoy the delights of the flesh and worldly pleasures. I have more followers than you think, God-seller. In the end, I will have more than my share of souls and I will have an army to lead against the forces opposing me!"*

"Braggart of hell!" Becker roared, causing the grim personage he confronted to flinch. "Despicable reprobate! Get back to the everlasting hell's fire from which you have dared to venture. This girl shall not become one of your tarts!"

"She will! She will!" Lucifer danced about the flames gleefully, laughing and pointing derisively at the priest. *"She already is mine! She's been given to me and no one knows anything of my plans for this whore!"*

"I know much about you, although we have never been face to face before. I know—"

"I know you used to jack off when you were a small boy, priest. You spilled your seed on the ground just like Onan, in direct opposition to the Bible you now support so strongly." Lucifer's words were snarled and growled in a cold, unrelenting voice.

"If I am guilty of no greater sins in my adult life than I was in my childhood, God will have me and love me. Therefore I am not afraid of what you or your demons know about me." Becker's confidence grew with each word.

"What you have confessed, I do not and cannot know," Lucifer said wistfully.

Becker studied the figure before him. Was he lying? Or was the statement merely a ruse to enforce the Capuchin's sense of security? Was this why Satan was unable to attack the Capuchin? For the first time since he had heard the crackling of flames, he began to feel at ease and more confident then he knew he had a right to. Slowly backing up, he turned the knob and opened the door without taking his eyes off Lucifer. "Sisters? Are you still there?"

The five nuns chorused weakly, "Yes, Father."

"Come in and meet the lowly piece of debauchery with whom we battle." His words were both kindly to them and contemptuous for the object of his derision. Throwing the door open, he stepped forward knowing the women would slip into the still flaming but freezing room. The nuns huddled behind the Capuchin peered from around his massive bulk to fix their eyes unbelievingly on the tall figure before them.

"Ah, priest, I'm so glad you brought me some of your harem to sample! These are rather old strumpets, though. Don't you have another, younger one like this pussy on the bed, I could fuck?" Satan's words whined through the room turning into a mocking laugh.

With horror etched on their faces, the nuns turned to glare at Father Becker accusingly. In the dancing shadows cast upon his face, they could see the calmness with which he stared at Lucifer and gained the needed confidence just from seeing their chaplain's expression.

"Good Sisters, remember we are dealing with the prince of lies. He is trying to embarrass me in front of you so you will lose your faith and trust in me. I assure you no such arrangement was made."

Sheepishly glancing at each other, the women dropped their eyes to the floor, ashamed of their gullibility.

Leaping about the flames, Lucifer soared high in the room before landing on both feet opposite Father Becker but with the iron bed still between them. Pointing his bone sceptre at the priest and nuns Lucifer growled, *"Stop bothering my subjects. Leave them alone. They haven't bothered you— yet. This young slut on the bed is mine. She was given to us and will serve us well."*

"How will she serve you, Satan?" Becker asked boldly.

"That is none of your business. Shut up!"

"It is my business! It is why I am here! I will—I must know the real reason for your presence here in this holy place."

"Non ad rem!" the devil barked crisply in Latin. *"That has nothing to do with this affair!"*

"It has everything to do with it, prince of lies!" As Becker spoke, he released the small vial of holy water he had grasped since beginning the dialogue with the demon and, in one swift movement, brought out the pyx with one hand and drew the crucifix from his girdle in the defiant manner of a knight drawing his sword. "By the Blood of the Divine Christ, who is this girl's personal Saviour, I command you to tell me what your intentions are where she is concerned."

Cringing before the presence of the consecrated Host, Lucifer fell back several steps screaming in pain. *"Hide them! Put them away! I cannot bear to be with them. They sear me! Put them away and I'll tell you what you wish to know."*

Knowing full well he could bring the powerful weapons into play again if needed, Becker accepted the bargain, returning the crucifix to his rope belt and the pyx to the folds of his cassock's pockets. "Speak then, or by the strength God Almighty gives me and with the help of Saint Michael, I shall return them to your view and destroy you."

At the mention of the archangel's name, Lucifer unleashed a piercing scream that made the nuns and priest cover their ears. *"She is—she is to—"* the devil struggled to speak but would not continue.

"Speak!"

"She is to go to the eastern part of—of—"

"Go on!"

"Africa!"

"What then?" Becker demanded. "When is she to go there?"

"The black sows will send her there as one of them."

"What then? What is she to do there when she arrives?"

"She is to—she will—oh, fuck you, Becker!" Lucifer snapped.

With a sweeping motion, the Capuchin brought the pyx out and his adversary, who had returned to the side of the bed, fell back, cursing. "Tell me, Satan, what I want to know or Saint Michael, the archangel, and I will make you and your demons suffer immeasurably because of this girl whom you have chosen to defile and torment."

Gnashing his teeth, and cowering before the presence of Christ under the appearance of bread, the fiend fell back again. *"There will be a baby born in the same country and the same year when she is sent. She is to care for him until his twentieth year."*

"What then?" Becker asked, fearful of what the answer might be.

"You'll find out! You'll find out, nun-fucker!" Lucifer threw his head back, laughing uncontrollably.

"Is he to be the Antichrist?" Becker's voice rang hollowly in the room while the nuns stared wide eyed at him.

"Non ad rem! Non ad rem!"

"You're a liar, Satan! The prince of all liars and you cannot ever be trusted. I command you to answer my question truthfully!"

"Non ad rem!" he screamed. *"Leave me alone so I can do my work."*

"What is your work?" Becker asked thinking it better to leave the question of the Antichrist alone for the time being.

"To train this whore lying between us!"

"I command you to leave her alone, Satan!"

"YOU LEAVE MY SUBJECTS A-L-O-O-O-N-E, BE-E-E-E-CK-K-E-E-E-R-R-R!"

"Force me to do that! I defy you to force me to do anything!"

Becker's words brought gasps of astonishment from the nuns. Was he insane to challenge the devil like that? What would happen to them if the devil reciprocated?

"You know I can't do that!"

"Then I will banish you and yours to the hell where you belong."

"How can you banish me to hell? I must be free to prepare the way for the Antichrist! We know a lot. We read the signs of the times. This is the last century. When people write the year 2000 the end will be at hand and the Antichrist will defeat your Christ's church and I WILL REIGN SUPREME!"

"You will have nothing to rule if the end of the world is then at hand," Becker retaliated.

"Enough! Leave me alone! Leave my subjects alone. Do not bother them or you will pay the consequences—you and the sow bitch of a whore standing behind you."

Mother Job's face reddened at the unwarranted attention and felt as though she should say something in her own defense but her throat was dry and—what *would* she say to Lucifer?

Becker slipped the cross from his girdle before returning the golden pyx to his pocket. "Depart this place at once, you cursed angel! Go to that place to which God the Almighty has banished you. Go there and never come back to this place again! *Lucifer! Go to hell!*" The priest's voice roared the directive, each word growled with hate and loathing. With a sweeping motion of his right hand that now held the small bottle of holy water, he splashed the blessed liquid on the grim personage before him.

When the droplets of water touched the figure of Lucifer, he and the flames disappeared instantly, but the priest and nuns could still hear his voice. *"Be-e-e-e-ck-k-e-e-e-r-r-r! We shall have her one way or another. You cannot rid yourself or her of me so easily. We shall win and I shall guide them."* Once more the braying of a jackass mixed with a dog's barking punctuated his statement. *"Your day is coming, Ba-a-a-lth-a-a-z-z-a-r- Be-e-e-eck-e-e-e-r-r-r! The torture you have just inflicted on me with that heavenly piss you carry has made us more deadly enemies than ever and will not go unpunished. You shall regret it, Be-e-e-e-ck-e-e-e-r-r-r!"*

"Ignore him, Sisters!" Becker snapped. "We have much to do." Retrieving his Roman Ritual from the bed, he felt more at ease, now that Lucifer no longer blighted the room. The cell, unharmed by the cold flames, began to warm after the prince

288

of hell disappeared.

Finishing the prayer that had been interrupted, the Capuchin brought forth the golden pyx once more with which to bless Bobbe. The demons in attendance moaned and cried out in agony only to increase their outburst when the crucifix was placed alongside the watchlike container.

"We cannot stand such pain and torture."

"Hell is not as bad as this!"

"Stop! Oh, please stop. The pain! The pain! The pain!"

As the cries of anguish continued, the bed began quivering and the entire building seemed to shake. Drawers from the bureau flew out, smashing against the opposite wall, barely missing Sister John's head. Pieces of plaster, shaken loose by the unseen assault were dislodged and sailed about like giant snowflakes.

Despite the havoc being wreaked upon them, Becker stood unmoving next to the iron bed praying aloud from the book he held. The nuns backed away from Bobbe, frightened for their very lives, ducking flying debris and chunks of plaster that were whipped about by an ever-increasing gale of foul air.

Slowly, the bed began rising. Individually, the women recalled Bobbe flying through the air the night before and feared the same thing might happen to all of them now. The power being unleashed was more than any of them had bargained for and they were willing to run for their own safety, abandoning Bobbe to whatever fate the demons may have had in store for her.

"Sit on it and hold her!" Becker shouted above the melee. The five nuns quickly added their weight to the iron bedstead but it persisted in bouncing and jumping across the room. One by one the nuns were thrown off and when the largest of the assistants, Sister Timothy, flew from the bed, it began gyrating in the middle of the room.

Stepping back to avoid being hit by the airborne piece of furniture, Becker raised his crucifix and pyx. "By the Blood of the Divine Saviour, I command you to release this girl. May the heel of his Blessed Mother crush your head again, Satan!"

A loud scream followed by a torrent of curses were flung back at the Capuchin but the bed settled gently to the floor and the quaking and wind subsided until the room was still and quiet. Picking themselves up, embarrassed by their unladylike positions on the floor, the nuns blessed themselves and mentally begged God's forgiveness for considering the abandonment of Bobbe's soul to the devil for their own safety.

For the first time in many hours, the only sound in the cell was their own labored breathing. Bobbe relaxed, appearing to be asleep.

"I believe they have gone for the time being, Sisters." Becker's taut face reflected the fatigue each word shouted as he spoke.

"It's not over, Father?" Sister Michael asked, shock and disbelief replacing the same sense of relief she had felt when the silence closed in on them.

"Dear me, no! They have to be worn down until the confines of hell seem like a bed of roses compared to the tortures we subject them to here."

The expressions on the nuns' faces displayed unasked questions—questions only time would answer. Would they be able to endure much more of this? The curses and vile language? The unnatural phenomena? And what of Roberta? Their concern for their little sister crowded out their selfish worry when they thought of her fragile body and the onslaughts the devil and his demons were perpetrating on her. Who would yield first? Roberta? The nuns themselves? God forbid it should be the Capuchin—their champion. It would have to be the devil and his horde who suffered the most. The devil must leave their presence forever.

"Don't worry, dear Sisters, we will pray to God for the strength to withstand the rigors of this exorcism and we mustn't forget to include Roberta in our petitions. She is the one who is suffering the most." The priest reached for the postulant's forehead when her eyelids fluttered and he touched her gently. "Are you awake, Roberta?"

Her eyes flew open at the mention of her name, searching frantically for some familiar sign or face. Locking with the steady gaze of Father Becker she began sobbing, tears cascading down the sides of her face. "Oh, Father, I've just had the most horrible nightmare."

Easing his bulk onto the edge of the bed, he tenderly put

his arm around her shoulder when she sat up. "There, there, Roberta. Trust in God Almighty and if you can, trust me and everything will be all right."

"Father, I want to go to confession. I feel—I feel—I may—" Her voice, barely a whisper, cracked and the priest dismissed the nuns with a glance.

"Would you like to talk first, Roberta? What do you feel?"

"I feel—I may—die soon and I—I want to go to confession."

"Now, Roberta, that kind of talk is not good to hear from one so young. You just confessed three or four days ago and I'm sure you haven't had occasion to commit any sin here in your bed. However—" He looked at the Mother General who was leading the assisting nuns from the room.

When they were alone, Becker refocused his attention on Bobbe. "Recall your sins, Roberta, and I will hear your confession."

"Father?"

"Yes, my child."

"Can we talk first?"

"Of course. Is there something you'd like to tell me?"

"I—I'm not sure. At times I feel there's so much I must tell someone that— Then at other times, I feel as though there's nothing of consequence and—"

"Could you tell me, perhaps, just one thing that's bothering you?"

Bobbe's eyes flitted over the bearded face, searching for some tangible sign that this man of God could be told some of her weird thoughts and memories that now seemed so fresh in her mind. Deciding he was a kindly person and would somehow be able to understand what she wanted to say, she stood and crossed the room to the window.

"I don't think I belong here, Father. I can't explain it but for some reason I feel I was forced to enter the convent." She spun about to fix her eyes unblinkingly on the huge man.

"Forced? By whom?"

Turning back to stare into the waning afternoon light, Bobbe said softly, "I don't know. I have dreams about a tall, handsome man who—who—does things to me and whenever I try to recall him, or my parents, I simply can't."

"Why do you mention your parents?"

"Because I should remember what they look like and—and," she began sobbing, "and I *can't!*"

"Do you want to tell me anymore about the voices, Roberta?"

For an instant, she turned to study him with a perplexed expression and then as though recalling the devastating episode in Mother Job's office, she nodded, shrugging her shoulders at the same time. "What is there I can say? They're with me all the time. I constantly hear them. Laughing. Cursing. Telling me what to do." She clasped her hands until the knuckles turned white. Sobs racked her body as she sank to the floor on her knees.

Standing, Becker hurried to her and with a comforting arm, helped her to her feet and then to the iron bed. The confusion the girl was experiencing concerned him. She was so near to being lucid about the infestation and still, unable to comprehendingly put together a single concrete memory. What would happen if suddenly the whole matter jelled in her mind? Would she merely accept the prayers of exorcism as therapy? Or would she accept the demon without reservation? The Capuchin shook his head. He didn't have the answers. Not now. Perhaps as the rite progressed the priorities would be served and each would fall into place. Understanding the girl's confusion better than he ever had enabled him to appreciate the mental agony she was suffering.

When Bobbe stopped crying, Becker asked, "Would you like to prepare for confession now, Roberta?"

For several minutes the girl maintained her rigid sitting position, staring into the far corner of the room unmindful of the plaster chips lying about the floor or the empty sockets of the bureau. With a shrug of her shoulders, she said, "There's nothing, Father. Absolutely nothing. I'm very tired now and would like to go to sleep."

Standing as she reclined on the bed, Becker blessed her and left the room.

Closing the door gently, Mother Job cut the conversation in the cell off and looked at her watch when she joined the other women. "Good heavens! It's almost five o'clock. Do you realize we've been at this since right after breakfast?"

Expressing their disbelief at the quick passage of time, the assistants were quickly assured much of the day had passed by the gnawing hunger pains in their stomachs, which they were suddenly aware of now with the tension gone.

"You Sisters go ahead and get ready for dinner and send Sister Raphael or Sister James up to sit outside Roberta's room. I'll wait for Father Becker."

Obediently, the four nuns left and several minutes later, Sister Raphael appeared at the top of the steps. Just as the Mother General was about to greet her friend, the door to the cell opened and the Capuchin emerged with a troubled look etched deeply into his craggy face.

"She didn't have a thing to say, Mother," he said softly, almost sadly as they walked toward the staircase.

Following the priest's lead, Mother Job nodded automatically to Sister Raphael as they passed, before staring at him. Was he violating the sanctity of the confessional?

Sensing her quizzical look without turning his head, he offered, "It's all right, Mother, we didn't have a confession in there. After we visited awhile, I asked her to prepare herself. She just sat and finally said, 'There's nothing, Father. Absolutely nothing.' She was very tired and wanted to go to sleep. I blessed her and left. I do think it's good she's resting since the next days will be exceedingly tiring for her. Perhaps you should tell Sister Raphael to be prepared to get something for Roberta to eat in the event she should ask for it. Normally, the infested person eats little if anything during the rite."

"Very well, Father," Mother Job said and turned to retrace her steps to the postulant's cell.

"I'll wait here for you, Mother."

In seconds, she returned to his side and they continued down the steps.

"It's been a trying day, hasn't it, Mother?"

"Trying is not the word for it, Father. I've never experienced such things before in my life." She fingered the beads of the long rosary at her side while they walked down the steps, recounting the day's abnormal activities.

Becker smiled ruefully after he left the nun, making his way to the chaplain's dining room. Recollections of his other exposures to the devil and his demons filled the priest. There was no such thing as an easy exorcism and this particular one appeared as though it could be the most difficult of his career.

Having eaten earlier, Sister Raphael sat at her lonely post outside Bobbe's room. She had straightened the cell without disturbing the sleeping postulant and now reflected, between decades of the rosary, on the strange events surrounding them. In many ways she found the situation facing the convent most intriguing. The devil—loose among them here at the convent. Most intriguing. She also found the presence of the giant Capuchin fascinating. His casual, almost indifferent attitude toward the problem seemed totally out of place. No. That wasn't being fair to the priest. He was strictly a professional and this sort of thing must seem almost commonplace to him by now. Lord. How could the sort of things that had been happening around the convent ever become accepted as prosaic?

When she looked at her watch, she couldn't believe her eyes. Seven o'clock. She had been sitting for almost two hours and nothing out of the ordinary had happened. It seemed a much longer time. At midnight, she would be relieved by Sister James and she would go to bed. Fatigue gnawed relentlessly at her mind and body. Her knees ached the most after having knelt in the chapel, praying most of the day and the thought of bed seemed more than appealing. The muscles of her legs, arms, and body felt like jelly, hurting every time she moved. The straight-backed chair was uncomfortable, and, despite having tried every possible position, she was unable to find comfort to relieve her pains.

Standing, Sister Raphael stretched and walked around the area outside the postulant's cell. She tiptoed softly toward the door and turned the knob quietly. The Reverend Mother had suggested looking in on Roberta from time to time to make certain everything was normal. In the half light of the room she could see the prostrate form of Bobbe locked in sound sleep, her breasts rising and falling in an even, steady cadence. That was good. No problem in her room. Restationing herself in the chair, the nun fidgeted for comfort again. At last, fatigue won out and her head nodded forward.

After dozing fitfully for several minutes a sound, foreign to the quiet of the hallway, rasped in her ears.

"Hmph? What's that?" Her sleepy voice drowned the other sound out but the nun, positive she had heard something, stood and listened intently. The scratching and rubbing came again and she turned in a slow circle trying to locate its source.

There. The noise seemed to come from within the room she was guarding. Stepping closer to the doorway, she reached for the knob and the sound stopped. Silence. Slowly, she turned the latch, opening the door.

CHAPTER TWENTY-FOUR

Her heart pounding like a triphammer, Sister Raphael pushed the door to Bobbe's cell wide open. She had shuddered when Sister Gregory had told her of the fiery experience earlier in the day and now she stared wide eyed at the dancing flames engulfing the freezing room. Lucifer, seated on a blazing throne, glared wickedly at her as shadowy figures knelt before him in worship. Searching the icy inferno for some sign of Roberta, she gasped when she saw the postulant draped over the bureau on her back, completely nude. A tall, handsome man dressed in white stood over her, cutting strips of flesh from her body, tattooing her breasts and abdomen with an inverted, bloody cross. Another demon, with a fat body and grotesquely shaped head, tottered on thin spindly legs to the throne where he offered the gory sacrifice to the prince of lies.

At the sound of Sister Raphael's gasp, the demons turned as one and snarled, gnashing their teeth and fangs. Catching her breath, she forced herself to turn and ran down the hall, screaming.

"Oh, my God! Oh, my good God! Help us, dear Jesus!"

The anguished cries echoed through the stillness, drifting to the first floor as she started down the steps. Catching her foot in the hem of her habit, she went sprawling head first, tumbling over and over until she came to an abrupt halt at the first landing, her head striking the wall with a sickening thud.

When the unholy congregation in Bobbe's cell heard her fall, they laughed gleefully until Lucifer stood and barked to his subjects. *"We must go! It serves that nosy sow right for*

butting into our business. Dra-woh, see the young slut does what she must do. Our plans for her are changed but we will win her to our side. Now, all of you make certain the priest and his whores show up to see what happens."
He spread his arms and the flames, along with the demons of hell, disappeared.

Immediately, Bobbe opened her eyes and sat up on the bureau. Staring blankly into the lonely darkness of her room, she slipped to the floor and stood rooted to the spot for several minutes. Although her breasts and stomach should have burned painfully where the strips of flesh had been removed, her face reflected no emotion. She didn't feel alone although no one was in the room with her. With a slow nodding of her head, she knew exactly what she was to do. Grabbing her robe, she threw it over her bare shoulders and left the confines of the small cubicle.

The hall, still empty as she ran toward the back staircase, would soon be filled with curious nuns. Now she could hear racing footsteps coming up the front stairwell. Without making a sound, she reached the main floor and hurried to the kitchen. Walking directly to the counter next to the stove, she fumbled through one of the drawer's contents and withdrew something she deposited in her robe pocket. Then quietly, she slipped out the side door. Undetected, Bobbe Moore hurried toward the garage to carry out the directive of Lucifer.

Father Becker stared into space without seeing the Reverend Mother who sat directly opposite him behind her desk. Laconically fingering his beard, he sighed deeply. "I'm worried, Reverend Mother."

Her spirit wilted. If he was worried, then they were surely lost. What could she and the others do without his strength to guide them? They had no other resource on which to rely. Could another priest conduct the exorcism? Shaking her head sadly, she prepared to hear him out.

"Worried, Father? About—"

"About this whole situation. Perhaps I should ask the bishop for help. Somehow I feel so very old and I don't know if I'll be able to fight off Lucifer's demons. The talk of the

Antichrist and the world's end doesn't bother me, since I have heard it before and know they're only boasting. Ah, me, it's a sad thing to admit. I know what has to be done and perhaps that is what's making me think I should quit. It takes so much out of me." Running the fat tips of his fingers over his fatigue-lined face he leaned forward, resting his head in his cupped hands.

Mother Job studied him for several moments and then offered lamely, "Perhaps you're looking at the whole problem and it would be better to take it one day—one step at a time, Father." How impertinent of her. What could she say to help comfort this man who had so much experience in fighting demons? Was she grasping for something that would help bolster his morale or was she afraid he would quit and abandon them to the devil?

Raising his head he managed a benign smile. "You may just be right, dear Sister. I think you may have found the solution to my mixed-up thoughts. At times I wonder why I've been selected as one of God's weapons against the devil. All priests are given the minor order of exorcism but most only use it when they bless their congregation or individuals with holy water. Why have I been selected to be exposed so often to the devil's hellmates? Will I win my heaven this way?"

Mother Job remained silent but nodded her understanding of the tired priest's dilemma.

With a shake of his bald head, he threw off the mental shackles of doubt. "Forgive me, Mother. I was wallowing in self-pity there. My duty is clear—I *know* what must be done. Every now and then I'll be filled with questions regarding my role in life when I'm involved with an exorcism. I'm glad I have someone as strong as yourself to talk with now."

Trying to conceal the smile generated by the pleasure she felt from Becker's compliment, the Reverend Mother covered her mouth, faked a cough, and said, "About today, Father?"

"Yes?"

"I have a question that might seem stupid but—"

"Any question you have, Mother, I'm sure will be valid."

"Well, if Lucifer has a plan calling for Roberta to—to care for the Antichrist, why did they tip their hand so readily? There's no rhyme or reason to the things they made her do

298

before you arrived. It seems so stupid."

Becker grinned at the irony of the nun's question. "No matter how hard we try, Mother, I don't think we'll ever understand fully. I might venture to guess that demons react to holiness and goodness as much as we do to sin, filth, and degradation. We want to stamp such things out. They, on the other hand, want to contaminate. It's probably deeply buried in their makeup. But you're right, it does seem stupid and fruitless."

"What languages were spoken besides French and Latin, Father?"

Before Becker could answer, Sister Raphael's screams for help filtered from the third floor onto the closed office. Both jumped instantly to their feet. What was wrong? Were the demons attacking Roberta again? Or had they attacked Sister Raphael?

Rushing up the steps, Becker shucked the weariness from his body like an unneeded garment. When they came to the last landing, they found the nun dazed, moaning as she tried to sit up.

"Look after her, Mother." Becker continued up the steps and hurried to the room Sister Raphael had been guarding. Throwing the door open he found it empty.

"She's gone!" he cried running back to the nuns on the landing where he found Mother Job kneeling by the side of her assistant. Others, who were not in the chapel, rushed up the steps. "What happened here, Sister?" Urgency hung on each of his words.

Sister Raphael slowly told them what she had seen, bursting into sobs at one point but managing to relate the awful scene she had witnessed.

With a shudder, Mother Job looked helplessly at the priest. Would he be capable of facing the challenge? When her eyes locked with his, she no longer saw the doubt-ridden man she had talked with minutes before in her office. Now, he was the same confident devil fighter she had known for the last twelve days. "What do we do now, Father?"

Standing, he helped the bewildered woman to her feet. "Are you all right, Sister Raphael?"

When she looked in his eyes to answer, she saw only

concern for her well-being—not for the problems she knew that had to be confronted. "I'll be all right, Father."

"We must quickly organize a search of the convent. If you can help Sister Raphael downstairs, Mother, I'll go on ahead and gather the nuns in the community room and have them begin looking everywhere until we find her."

Without waiting for an answer he wheeled about and raced down the steps to the first floor. When he found the bell used for summoning the women, he began ringing the bell in a staccato of quick echoing gongs that quickly grew into one panicky mass of sound. The clanging racket reverberated through the quiet halls as he persisted in sounding the alarm.

Within seconds, postulants and novices were running toward him, leading the more sedately moving nuns, to investigate the cause of the tocsin.

"Keep ringing the gong and tell the nuns to meet me in the community room." After a novice had picked up the signal, the Capuchin walked quickly to the appointed gathering place. In minutes the room was filled.

Stupefied, Bobbe searched the garage until she found what she felt was needed. Someone had ordered her to come here to the old building in back of the convent to find something. Pushing aside a canvas covered stepladder, her eyes locked on the gasoline cans used for the power mowers. A wicked smile stretched her full lips into a sinister leer. Her quest was over. One five-gallon can was half empty and the other two were full. Placing the half-used can outside, she slopped the contents of the other two about the garage walls and on the more flammable of the stored items. When she had removed the container outside to a safe distance from the building, Bobbe returned and fumbled in her robe pocket for a book of matches. After lighting one, she ignited the rest of the book, throwing it into the garage. With a muffled roar, the gasoline burst into flames. With a smirk dancing about the corners of her mouth and a strange light reflecting from her eyes, she turned to hurry back toward the convent building with the half-full can.

The gong was ringing now and she knew she would have to be careful of being discovered. Tiptoeing past the now deserted chapel, she found the little used door leading to the bell tower steps and ducked into the dark, dusty chamber after removing the key from the lock. Once she had quietly closed the entrance, she noiselessly locked it.

Standing by one of the library tables, Becker addressed the women. "Roberta has left her room. We believe she is in the power of demons again. If you find her, restrain her. It will be best if you search in parties of three or four. Now hurry. Find her!"

One of the postulants looked out the window and shrieked, "The garage is on fire!"

Rushing to the window, the women pushed to see the conflagration.

Becker clapped his hands for the women's attention. "Call the fire department quickly. But find Roberta before they get here—if possible."

The women dispersed in groups of three and four as the priest had directed. Sister Damien hurried to call the fire department.

Half walking, half running down the hall on the second floor with three other postulants, Connie desperately hunted for Bobbe. She still found it impossible to believe her friend—beautiful, effervescent Bobbe—could be possessed by a demon from hell. Mentally recounting some of the visits they had had while she searched, she dumbly shook her head in disbelief. Bobbe was always so bright and warm, how could something like this actually be? The time when a problem had formed in her friend's mind questioning her vocation surfaced in Connie's mind and she recalled how happy Bobbe was the next morning after she had resolved the nagging doubt, unaided, during the night. They simply had to find the girl and have Father Becker rid the convent of this demon. A questioning look crossed Connie's face. Had Bobbe brought the thing here, with her?

One by one, each classroom was explored, each closet thoroughly probed. No matter how small the area, it was gone over and scanned for some clue—some indication as to the infested postulant's whereabouts.

"What's that?" Kathy, one of the postulants with Connie, asked in a choking whisper. The sound was soft at first but gradually increased in volume as it rose and fell in a whining scream. Recalling the sound the demon had made earlier, the four girls paled at the thought of encountering the unholy thing alone, in the hall. Steadily, the wail grew louder.

"Fire engines!" Connie breathed the two words, forcing a giggle at their unspoken suspicions. Stopping at a window on their way to the first floor they could see the red lights of the Cedar Falls County fire trucks squirting crimson splashes on the whitened countryside as they raced up the winding road toward the convent.

Bobbe tiptoed up the creaking steps to the bell tower. She knew she must be quiet or someone would hear her. Who? Her mother? The thought of the night before her reception surfaced in her befuddled mind and she redoubled her efforts to be silent. The half-full can of gas was heavy but she stared straight ahead giving no indication the load was too much for her. When she reached the top floor, a short ladder remained to be climbed to reach the bell loft. Making her way to the ladder, she set the can down.

With both hands grabbing the sides of the ladder, she peered into the dark corner behind it and saw a yard through a bridal bouquet bush. An old man motioned for her to come closer. For an instant a tear formed but dissolved into nothingness.

Lifting her head, she waited until her eyes adjusted to the black gloom above her and could just make out the trapdoor.

"Look at all the cars!" Laurie said reaching over Connie's shoulder to point out the window. Cars were strung out behind the Cedar Falls Fire Department vehicles as far as the girls could see.

"That's not good. I don't think Father Becker or Mother Job will be happy when they see all the gawkers." Connie turned and motioned for her three companions to follow her. They had to find Bobbe. Perhaps Father Becker would allow her to talk with the possessed girl. She could talk some sense into her troubled friend. After all, the priest hardly knew

302

Bobbe and Mother Job wasn't that closely connected with the postulants. But, what would she say?

When they reached the first floor, they were directed toward the chapel by Sister Raphael who was standing at an intersection of hallways. Wearing a frightened expression, the still dazed nun dispersed the searching women as efficiently as possible. The four postulants obeyed, hurrying off in the direction of the church and bell tower in the back of the building. Reaching the ornately carved doors, they went in to find twelve others searching each pew while more were in the sanctuary peering behind the altar and its nooks and crannies.

Bobbe took the robe from about her shoulders and stood naked in the gloom of the bell tower. Holding her arms up, she allowed the mental image of her mother to dry her body as she had when Bobbe was a little girl. Slipping into her robe, she pulled the belt tightly about her waist, pressing the coarse material into the open wounds on her abdomen. After unscrewing the cap of the gasoline container, and setting another book of matches on one of the ladder's rungs, she lifted the can above her head, emptying the contents over her body, soaking the robe completely but avoiding her face and hair.

With the matches clamped firmly in her mouth, she carefully made her way to the trapdoor overhead. The throbbing, pink cross on her body shriveled as it reacted to the gasoline-soaked robe, but her face, a grim mask of determination, displayed no reaction to the pain.

Leaving the church, Connie and the girls in her search party turned toward the door which would lead them to the back of the convent, and where the firemen were congregating. "We should look outside, in the other buildings. Maybe, she's frightened silly and doesn't know what to do," Connie said, her voice breaking in a sob.

"What's this?" Kathy said, tugging at a door.

"Where's that lead?" Connie asked, elbowing the smaller girl aside to turn the knob. Facing the others, she found looks of apprehension replacing the ones of excitement that had been on their faces since the search had begun.

303

"I think it leads to the belfry," Laurie offered. "I asked Sister Damien once where it led."

Connie gave it one final tug. "Well, it's locked and we aren't going to get in. Come on. We'll probably find her outside anyway. The fire will more than likely attract her attention."

The four girls left the locked door, hurrying toward the back of the building.

Pushing the wooden trapdoor open, Bobbe climbed into the belfry. Four arches, each five feet across, opened on all sides of the giant bell. Keeping in the shadows, she peered into the flickering light of the fire. Below, firemen were still battling the blaze and she watched with a satisfied smirk as more cars pulled into the back courtyard spewing sightseers into the melee. The far off wail of sirens could be heard and in seconds, several police cars screeched to a halt.

Fingering the book of matches, she stepped back into the shadows and waited.

The four girls continued searching outside as dozens of firemen, some shouting orders and others dutifully carrying them out, hurried about, scattering hoses into a hopeless maze of canvas spaghetti. Curious onlookers from Cedar Falls milled about, disrupting the firefighters' work.

Each outbuilding was searched diligently by the different groups of nuns and girls all of whom appeared to be oblivious of the fire and throngs of people gathering in the yard behind the convent. When each possible hiding place had been looked into several times by the different search parties, the women were finally drawn like moths to the fire and its hypnotizing excitement.

Reluctantly, Connie followed her companions to join the ever-increasing crowd. Bobbe was nowhere to be found. She had simply disappeared.

"Stay back, lady," one of the Cedar Falls policemen, who had just arrived to help the sheriff's deputies, shouted at Connie. "Stay behind this rope."

Robotlike, Connie obeyed. Where was Bobbe? Tears gratefully accepted their release and crashed down her cheeks. Where was Bobbe?

In time, the blaze was brought under control and the search had been all but forgotten by most of the nuns and girls. Then a man's voice rang over the buzzing crowd and crackling flames. "Look! Look up in the tower!"

Bobbe precariously leaned out to look again at the scene below watching as Connie was pushed back by a policeman. For some reason the girl could not understand, she felt a pang of regret from within her when she saw the flames reflecting from the copper-colored hair of her friend. How had she failed Connie? Or had she failed herself the night she went to Connie's room and fondled the redhead's body?

Suddenly Jay's face appeared in the dark, opposite the arch she stood in. "Jay?" she said breathlessly. "Come for me, Jay. I don't want to be here anymore." She sobbed as his handsome countenance slowly shook a negative reply.

His cheeks began heaving and changing shape and her father's face replaced Jay's. Dan's eyes were tear filled, his mouth forming the words, *I'll come get you.*

"Daddy?" she whispered. "Daddy, come get me. Please."

Over Dan's shoulder, another blob of light appeared and slowly took the shape of her mother's face. Clare seemed serene and beautiful but her face appeared troubled, her eyes searching for something or someone.

"Mommy? I'm here. Over here. Come get me. Daddy promised you would come for me." Her voice was tiny and hoarse as she spoke.

Then she froze and didn't move when she heard another voice invading her mind.

"Now. Do it now. Do it for the master!"

The blaze in the garage was almost under control when she stepped forward in the dwindling firelight. Below her, she could hear a man shout, "Look! Look up in the bell tower!"

All eyes turned upward, following the anonymous order, to fix on the spire. Forgetting the dying embers which had been the garage, the firemen stared along with everyone else at the figure of a young woman standing in the arches. When she raised her arms, palms outstretched for quiet, the people fell silent one by one.

A contemptuous smile distorted her face before she

spoke. "May Lucifer take all of you into the folds of his wings! Forget your stupid God and follow the one leader who is a leader. Power to Satan! Hail, my lord and master. I am yours — forever!" Her voice cut through the still night like the peal of a bell.

The nuns and girls who lived at the convent, horrified, ignored the inquiring looks from those around them as the crowd gasped.

"Forget the teachings of Christ and enjoy yourselves. Prepare! Make the way clear for the coming of the Antichrist!" Bobbe stopped speaking and turned to watch the back door of the convent open. A snarling growl broke from her lips when she saw Balthasar Becker.

He held the door for Mother Job as they came out and both looked up when they heard the voice of the missing postulant. The Reverend Mother gasped and began weeping. Staring at the figure of the girl, the Capuchin breathed a silent prayer.

"I hate all of you. You who follow your Christ. Do what you want to do! Christ has been dead for thousands of years but my lord and master is alive and he shall win in the end!"

Mesmerized, no one in the throng moved. The only sound in the courtyard was that of crackling flames.

"Lucifer! I am yours! Take me!" Bobbe screamed the words as she lighted the book of matches. Instantly, her robe erupted into flames.

Shrieks of horror broke from the hypnotic silence below.

Slowly, she pitched forward, headfirst to the pavement below. Her body thudded, bounced, and hit again.

Weirdly curious because of the macabre scene they had just witnessed, people ran forward to watch her body burn. A fireman with an extinguisher elbowed his way through the tightening circle of prurient onlookers. The throng finally backed off to avoid being splashed with the chemical spray the man was playing on the smoldering body of Bobbe Moore.

Bowling aside anyone who stood in his way, Father Becker reached the charred body and knelt next to her. He lifted her head, cradling it in his arm, and leaned closer, placing his ear next to her mouth. Her lips moved.

"I saw my mother and father. They're coming for me. I'm going home." Her eyelids fluttered before her lips went slack.

Slowly he stood, towering over those next to him. "She's dead," he said simply and walked toward the convent to get the things he would need to perform the last rites.

Before he reached the door where Mother Job stood weeping, another gasp went up from the crowd and he spun about. Following the people's tilted heads and looking up, he saw the figure of a handsome man standing in the same arch from which Bobbe had jumped to her death.

Smiling evilly, Dra-woh glared at the crowd below him, his amber eyes glowing more brightly then the fire had. The night was suddenly cold as the temperature plummeted and an icy wind whined through the courtyard. Standing motionless, the crowd was unable to utter a sound.

Then, before their unbelieving eyes, the demon faded away.

EPILOGUE

DECEMBER 27, 1951

Sergeant Bertram Plossic of the Cedar Falls police department smoothed his thinning brown hair over his round head
and coughed, hoping the woman sitting in front of him would
explain in a way he could understand, everything that had
happened in the courtyard. His eyes constantly shifted about
the room unable to find a target on which to rest. Never in his
life had he been in a Catholic Church, much less a convent,
and now found himself to be disappointed at the Spartan-like
and mundane appearance of the few rooms he had seen.
Deciding the conversation would never get started if he kept
furtively inspecting his surroundings, he fixed his eyes on the
Reverend Mother.

Mother Job felt the officer's presence standing opposite
her desk like she would an unpleasant task that had to be
performed, but procrastinated about looking at him in the
hope he would somehow disappear. Clasping her hands on
the desk top, she tightened the grip, forcing the blood from
her knuckles. How could she answer his questions? Where
was Father Becker? He had agreed to help the firemen and
other policeman move Roberta's body into the convent and
then had told her he would call a mortician. Dontisch's, she
had insisted, because they had always taken care of those
nuns who had passed away at the convent.

Now it seemed as though hours had passed and, out of
habit, she glanced at the blank wall where the clock had hung
when the awful scene which had taken place in her office just
the day before, rushed back to her. She fumbled for her small
silver pocket watch. It was only eight-fifteen. Where was the

Capuchin?

"Er—ah—Ma'm? Are you all right?" Plossic asked noticing the expressions of changing emotions running rampant across her face.

With a jerk of her head, she snapped to attention and looked up, locking eyes with the policeman's intent, concerned gaze. "I'm sorry, young man. Did you say something?"

"Yes, I did. I asked what was going on out there tonight?" He had asked the question when they first entered her office and she had gone into her catalepticlike state. Now he hoped she would get on with it and he and his partner would be able to leave.

"I—I think you—should talk with Father Becker, our chaplain, Officer. He could tell you much better than I." Her words were barely audible while she fumbled for her watch again. Where was he? She needed him here to tell the policeman something—anything. She certainly had no idea what to say. How could anyone explain what had happened without sounding like a complete fool? If only—

The door opened and Becker walked in. His face still carried the shocked expression he had assumed when he watched Roberta crash to the pavement of the courtyard like a falling star. When he spoke, his voice carried only concern for the Mother General's well-being. "Mother? Are you all right? Is there something I can do for you or get for you?"

"Yes, Father. Please answer this officer's questions. I don't believe I'm able."

Turning, the priest peered down at the policeman who was patiently waiting for some type of explanation. "What would you like to know, young man?" He hoped the questions would not be too pertinent and embarrassing for the nun in the room or her religious order.

"I'd like to know just what in the world was going on here tonight? Why did that girl jump from the bell tower and what did she mean by all those crazy things she yelled before she jumped?" Plossic wished he could be more forceful but realized he should respect them because of their positions as religious people and would be polite under the circumstances. He waited, craning his neck to fix his stare on the huge man towering over him.

"The—ah, young lady—when you saw her jump, was— ah—" He hesitated and breathed a silent prayer asking forgiveness for the lies he was about to tell. The truth would do no one any good. "—mentally ill. She was to be treated, if you know what I mean, and unfortunately happened to break away at a very inopportune time during the fire." He could feel Mother Job's gaze on his back but preferred to believe she was approving his statement.

"What about all those things she yelled from the tower before she jumped, Father?" Plossic asked in a determined manner.

The priest, who now seemed old beyond his years, fingered his beard. "I can assure you, young man, she did not mean those things, nor was she responsible for saying them. She definitely was not in possession of her faculties and probably was not aware of anything going on about her, right up to the very end of her life."

Plossic jotted notes in a small book and said, "I see, Father. In other words, she was craz—I'm sorry, Ma'm. She was without a doubt then, mentally ill?" The policeman decided he could concentrate better if he directed his attention to the Capuchin.

Becker sighed deeply. "If not being cognizant of your surroundings or being responsible for what you say or do is looked upon as being mentally ill, then I must say in all humility, that she was ill."

"Okay then, Father." Plossic's voice had a slight ring of hope knowing he had brought the priest to the moment of truth and would not be able to explain his next query so easily. "What about the guy who stood up there and smiled after she jumped? Who in the hell was he? Oops! Forgive me, Ma'm!" His face turned a bright red.

Forcing a weak smile, Mother Job nodded toward the young man. If he only knew how close he was to the truth—

Becker had blanched at the expression and took advantage of the uncomfortable pause the officer had instigated to formulate his answer. He didn't know what his name was in real life and assumed the figure was that of the demon, Drawoh with whom he had spoken here in the Reverend Mother's office and in Roberta's room. How they managed to turn up in possession of someone's soul or how they traveled about was completely beyond him, too. This answer would not be much of a lie. "I assure you, Officer, I have no idea how he got up there or what his name was or anything about him. Is that all?"

"Just one or two more things and my report will be complete," he said jotting more notes. If they weren't concerned about the guy in the tower, he wouldn't be either. After all he and his partner had answered the call as a courtesy to the sheriff's department. "I need her name, Father."

"Roberta Moore," Mother Job offered softly.

Directing his attention to her, Plossic asked, "Next of kin?"

"Her parents. We'll notify them. Will this have to be made public, Officer?"

"I think we can keep it under wraps pretty much. We'll have to report the fact of her death, naturally. But we shouldn't have to elaborate on the circumstances leading up to it. There'll be a lot of talk and speculation around town about this thing here tonight. We can't keep the people who were here from talking. Maybe, we could list the death as accidental. No, too many people saw it to believe she lit herself on fire and jumped accidentally. Maybe, we could just list it as a suicide since no one in their right mind would kill themselves. Do you people feel that would be the best solution?" Plossic stared at Mother Job and then Father Becker, hoping they would agree.

"List it that way, but keep it confidential. If it must be reported in the paper or on the radio, just have them say she died. All right?" Becker sounded intimidating and hoped the officer would be satisfied and leave.

"I guess we could do that. Otherwise, I believe I have everything I need. Thank you both. You've been most cooperative and I'm sorry about the girl's death." He turned without waiting for any response and left the office.

When he was gone, Becker slumped onto a straight-back chair.

"Will you notify her parents, Father? Or would you rather have me do it?"

"I suggest I should do it, Mother. I would happily pass this particular cup to someone else if I could. However, since I was the one who visited with them about the infestation of their daughter, I suppose I should do it. Besides, I wouldn't want you to put yourself through an ordeal like that. The news will destroy them. She was an only child, was she not?"

Mother Job nodded.

"Very sad. Very, very sad." His voice broke in a sob as he stood to leave her office.

DECEMBER 30, 1951

After much pleading, the Moores' family physician reluctantly agreed to allow Clare to attend Bobbe's funeral Mass with Dan. Suffering from hysteria, she had been heavily sedated for the two days following Father Becker's telephone call wherein he told them of their daughter's sudden death. Now she sat zombielike, next to her husband as they drove toward Cedar Falls.

Dan had just managed to accept the fact his daughter was "away" as Bobbe had told them to think of her absence and that she was not gone for good. Now, she *was* gone for good. He would never see her beautiful face smiling again or hear that bubbly laughter, which was uniquely her own. Wiping a tear from his eyes, he concentrated on the road passing beneath the car. Possessed by a devil? His daughter? It was still difficult for him to accept—impossible to believe. Yet, she was dead.

Glancing at his wife, he wondered what their lives would be like in the future. He knew he shouldn't be driving. He was finding it difficult to concentrate. Too many things were going through his mind. Clare was his chief concern now. Taking his eyes from the road, he looked quickly at her again. She stared straight ahead, not seeing anything they passed.

Although mildly sedated, Clare could talk and rationalize if she chose, but her thoughts were jumbled memories of Bobbe and she preferred their silent balm to conversation. Dropping her attention to the dress bordering her coat from beneath, a tear formed again when she thought of the great care she had taken in choosing it. The dress had been Bobbe's favorite and Clare had planned to wear it for the first visiting Sunday in February.

Dan cleared his throat. "Clare? Are you feeling all right?"

Turning her head slightly toward him, she nodded. "Oh, Dan, she's dead. Our little girl is dead. What will we do without her?" Clare sobbed softly as she spoke.

"Now, Clare," he said soothingly. "You know she had chosen a life close to God. There's no reason to believe she's lost. We were getting used to not having her around anyway—"

The sobs became a racking, choking cry as Clare stifled a scream at the seemingly unfeeling statement.

Dan bit his tongue. "Darling, I'm sorry. I'm sorry. That wasn't what I meant at all." Knowing he had upset his wife, Dan clamped his mouth shut and vowed not to speak until they reached their destination.

After a while, Clare quieted down and turned to her husband. An aura of regret surrounded Dan and she slid across the seat closer to him, slipping an arm through his.

Although they didn't talk anymore, each was lost in his own sadness knowing they were drawing silent strength from the other. Twenty minutes later, they curved through the horse-shoe drive in front of the convent and Dan stopped the car. Stretching after they were out of the automobile, neither could shut out the recollection of the last time they had been here. Bobbe had said good-bye at the same spot and they both felt the burning of new tears forming as they walked to the front door.

Mother Job met them, offering her condolences before walking silently with them to the chapel. Neither Dan nor Clare noticed the covered statues when they entered. Bobbe's casket was in the center aisle, close to the communion rail, the lid open to enable the Moores to get one final glimpse of their daughter. Slowly, they walked up to it, afraid to look inside.

Miraculously, Bobbe's face had not been touched by the scarring flames and she was as beautiful in death as she had been in life. Dressed in her simple postulant attire with the small white collar, a black veil rested on her head. A square white cloth covered her charred hands.

Dan swallowed hard, tears flowing freely down his ruddy cheeks while a soft moan escaped Clare's lips when they gazed on the lifeless form. With a protective, comforting arm around his wife's shoulders, he guided her to the front pew, after several minutes, to be close to their daughter for this last precious time.

Quietly, the nuns, novices, and postulants filed in, taking seats several rows behind the bereaved parents. At Father Becker's suggestion, the Mass was to be open to no one other than her parents and the women of the convent. When everyone was in their place, the huge priest entered the sanctuary to begin the service.

In place of the still absent acolyte, the nuns answered the prayers and without the boy's assistance, the Mass seemed endless. After what seemed an intolerably long time, he finished and turned to address the congregation.

"Dear parents. Humble Sisters." He paused, knowing he would have to select his words carefully. "Your daughter and your sister has gone to her heavenly home with God. It is not possible for her immortal soul to have gone elsewhere. She was innocent of any sinful wrongdoing and in losing her mortal soul has gained eternal salvation with God in heaven for her immortal soul.

"*Our* souls are what we must be concerned with now. It would be so easy to become embittered because of Roberta's death. 'God is a mean God to allow one so young and beautiful to die such a horrible death' could be one way of rationalizing such a tragic event. But God allows us to be tempted only to that degree, which we can tolerate. Poor Roberta had no chance to fight the demon who held her in control. Given that chance, she would have been able to resist him. But for a reason we will never know, God did allow the demon certain freedoms with her body and soul and allowed him to commit the atrocious deeds he performed here. However, the devil has lost her soul because of his manipulation of her. He gained a hollow victory in commanding her to kill herself, for he defeated his own end by doing so."

Becker looked directly at Clare and Dan recalling Bobbe's last words. "If your daughter had any lucid thoughts prior to her death, I'm sure they were of you, her parents, whom she loved very much."

Raising his eyes back to the congregation, he continued. At one time it was, and I suppose it still is, to a certain degree, quite fashionable for educated people to scoff at things such as possession of a soul by the devil and his demons. I reply to that particular absurdity by saying we must learn anew in this day and age that no one is safe from the wickedness and snares of Lucifer.

"When Christ was on earth, He cast out devils at various times. We, who are priests, have received from Christ, through the succession of His Vicar here on Earth, the same powers He used to perform this deed. Knowing then, that priests have the same ability, we must take a more sober view on such things as possession. I—" He was getting off the idea of consoling and mentally chastised himself.

"Forgive me," he said humbly. "I am preaching to you about the devil when all of you here have had your lives touched by him. If this unholy thing could infiltrate the holy confines of a convent, certainly then, no one is really safe from his traps. But the temptations we all face are the handiworks of those damned souls, forever cursed to the darkness of hell.

"Now, we must commit Roberta's body to the earth from which it came and her immortal soul to God Almighty in heaven, for eternity. Perhaps you may be able to find solace in the words of the poet Longfellow, who said, 'The grave is but a covered bridge leading from light to light, through a brief darkness.' Roberta has passed through the darkness of the grave's covered bridge and now basks in the most glorious light of all—God Almighty Himself. If, by her death, we here are all the more staunch enemies of Lucifer, then Roberta has not died in vain.

"Let us pray now for that end and beg God to let her soul rest forever, in peace."

Father Becker turned and knelt to pray one more Our Father and Hail Mary for the peaceful repose of Bobbe's soul. Then without bothering to take the vestments of Mass off, he walked to the side of Bobbe's parents who were looking at their daughter for the last time. Studying their tortured faces, he decided the best thing he could do was close the casket.

Gently lowering the lid, he shut her face from her parents' eyes for the rest of their lives. With his arm around their shoulders, he escorted them from the chapel.

DECEMBER 31, 1951

Setting his light valise down outside Mother Job's office, Father Becker entered. Mr. Tyler would pick him up soon and take him to the bus depot. He wanted to say the right thing to Mother Job before he left and be able to count her among his few friends. Qualities of faith and strength of character were the points that had drawn him to her. Perhaps some day they would be able to sit down and have a normal conversation. He knew he'd enjoy that. He wondered if she would.

Thrusting his big hand out, he peered down at her and smiled. "Well, Mother, it's over. I hope someday we can have a good visit about anything we choose."

"I would enjoy that immensely, Father. Where are you going now?"

"Now, I must go to another church and conduct a mission for the people there. I'm sure it will be a good one because of my experience here."

A shocked expression quickly spread across her face.

"No, no, Mother. I don't intend to tell anyone, ever, of the particulars that took place here. I would advise you to do the same. I know it's impossible to forget but the less mentioned about it here, especially by those few who were so directly involved, the better. The memory will linger but won't persist if it's not discussed." A blissful, serene glow seemed to emanate from him and his manner was almost paternal to the woman. "Do you understand, Mother?"

"Yes, Father. I'm sorry things didn't turn out well and I hope you haven't suffered any ill effects because of this encounter. You *are* feeling all right?" Despite her concern, she managed a reassuring smile.

He threw his head back and laughed for the first time since she met him. "God saw fit to give me a large carcass to withstand the tribulations that have been heaped on me during my lifetime. I'm sure it fares well, even now, Mother. Thank you for your concern and for the hospitality you've shown me here."

"I only wish the circumstances could have been different, Father."

A knock sounded at the door and Sister Raphael entered without waiting to be asked. "Mr. Tyler is here, Father."

Father Becker and Mother Job left her office, walking silently with the other nun to the front of the building where Sam Tyler waited. The sun was masked with a heavy bank of clouds on the western horizon but the air was warm and balmy.

"Good-bye, Father," Sister Raphael said, extending her hand.

The Capuchin swallowed it in his own and took Mother Job's hand in his other after he set his suitcase down. "You are both fine women of God and I'll pray for you every day for the rest of my life. Please, if you have a minute, offer up a prayer for me, too."

He picked up his suitcase and got in the car. "Good evening, Mr. Tyler. Good-bye, Sisters. God bless you!"

The car slid around the driveway and down the hill until it was finally gone from sight. The two nuns waited until the automobile's sound could no longer be heard. Turning they started for the front door but Mother Job hesitated.

When she realized her superior had stopped, Sister Raphael turned to find the Mother General staring at the building in a curious manner. "Are you all right, Mother?"

"Yes, I'm fine. You go on inside."

Mother Job's voice sounded peculiar to Sister Raphael— as though her friend were speaking into an empty rain barrel. An unusual smile played at the corners of her thin lips while a strange light gleamed in her gray eyes.

"I'll be in shortly. Right now, I think I'll take a quiet walk in the garden before I come in."

ADDENDUM

Garden of the Incubus is a true story, but the names, places, and dates have been altered to protect those still living, who were involved.

At the behest of Father Becker, who felt it necessary to speak about Roberta Moore's possession when the minor order of exorcism was done away with, Mother Job related her experiences as well. Backtracking from there, the rest of the story was compiled. With Father Becker's assistance, Roberta Moore's confused state of mind was pieced together in a conjectural manner.

Although no further abnormal occurrences took place at the Bearer of the Divine Word Convent, Mother Job could offer no explanation concerning her thoughts when she made the peculiar statement to Sister Raphael.

Edgar Dudley died of exposure in February of 1952 when he fell in his backyard during a blizzard and broke his hip. He wasn't found for two days.

Clare Moore, Bobbe's mother, became a chronic alcoholic and was institutionalized in 1960. Hopelessly insane, she died June 20, 1969.

Dan Moore, Bobbe's father, was killed in a traffic accident shortly after his wife was hospitalized while on his way to visit her, September 5, 1960.

Mother Job died of natural causes August 13, 1977.

Father Balthasar Becker died of natural causes December 25, 1978.

Sisters Raphael, Timothy, John, James, Michael, and Gregory are still living and are retired at the Mother House of the convent.

Sisters Damien and Boniface died of natural causes in 1968 and 1971 respectively.

Connie Devler spoke her final vows in 1955 and taught grade school until 1965 when she elected to leave the convent. She is married and has one child.

Jay and Crystal Livingston live in the Southwestern United States and have three children. When interviewed, they had no explanation for the sudden appearance of Bobbe Moore in their motel room the night of their wedding.

Dra-woh is—?